Shadows Across The Sun

By
Josephine Chia

PublishBritannica
London   Baltimore

First printing

ISBN: 1-4137-6395-2
PUBLISHED BY PUBLISHBRITANNICA
www.publishbritannica.com
London   Baltimore

Dedication

This book is dedicated to my two wonderful sons, Roddy & Jon, who make me proud to be a mother.

"Old sins cast long shadows,"

Early 20th Century English proverb

What might have been and what has been
Point to one end, which is always present,
Footfalls echo in the memory
Down the passage which we did not take
Towards the door we never opened

—"Burnt Norton," T.S. Eliot

2

Someone switches on the bedroom light abruptly and I'm startled out of sleep. In reflex, I shield my eyes with my arm and mutter in English, "The bright is light." In my confusion and half-sleep, I've reverted to the structure of my first language, long disused, now surfacing like Judas to kiss me in betrayal. No matter how much and how long I had shaped myself to be something else—somebody else—the truth will out. The bones of my own culture and past are interred within me, no matter how I might cloth those bones, and no matter what accent I adopt. And when I'm consumed by fire and become ash, I am all that I began with. Nothing more, nothing less. Ultimately, there is no escaping one's roots.

The illumined twenty-four-hour clock on my bedside table tells me it's ten o'clock in the morning, yet the sky outside the windows is grey with the pall of a winter's hue. The trees thrash about as if moaning a loss, flailing their skeletal arms as though in despair. Sadness is in the air, as palpable as the goose bumps on the flesh of my bare arms. It's too much. I dive under the duvet and pull it over my head. Entomb myself in warmth, seeking comfort even when it is meager. I pull the other two pillows to me, extraneous now. They used to support the head of the man I love. I arrange the pillows so that they seem like a warm body embracing me. I need to falsify to continue with the pretense, putting emotions, thoughts and the world momentarily at bay. If only it were so easy in reality to escape, to find that space where I would

7

be beyond hurt. When I was a child back in Singapore, I remember seeing fenced-up areas, a row of barbed wire at the top. On the fence itself there were angry red boards that said *Kawasan Larangan* in Malay, *Protected Place* in English, followed by a line of Mandarin characters and Tamil script, the national language and the official languages of the country. I could only read the first two. The native Malays, who were part of my ancestors, pride themselves on being the indigenous people of the island when it was just a fishing settlement before the island was taken over by overlords from Britain and populated by immigrants from China and India. *Temasik,* it was once called. Then the Prince from Indonesia changed it to *Singa-Pura* (Lion City), when he saw the *singa*/lion on the island. And when Sir Stamford Raffles purchased the island from the Temenggong of Johore, he anglicised the name and called it Singapore. When I read that signboard, I had wondered how two languages can say such different things. How much do we lose in translation? Can one language capture the essence of another in totality? *Larangan* means "forbidden." Was the compound beyond the fence a forbidden place or was it a protected place? Is that the sort of place I can run to when I need strong arms to protect me, bouy me up and save me from drowning? Or am I forbidden to seek solace?

Veronica's sensible shoes clacked across the floorboards to the bed. Her steps used to be firm and strong; now they are slightly unsure.

"Kim Hiok. Come on," she coaxes, touching me on my shoulder underneath the duvet, a touch that persuades without sanction, reassuring. "I'm afraid it's time for you to get up. You have to get dressed. They'll be here soon."

It is good that Veronica hadn't heard my muttering. The arrival of my old friend shores up my crumbling edifice. So much over the years has slowly but surely undercut the earth of my being. I am *kosong* inside. Empty. And if I'm not careful, I might crumble under the weight of it all. But I know that Veronica will not let it happen. Veronica had arrived at my doorstep, summoned by one telephone call, yet she is not the type of woman one thinks of being receptive to a summon. But she has always been available for me, always there for me. I admire the way my English friend can put feelings into her voice, kneads it into the shape she wants, whereas my own flutters on the tongue, too tinny for the deep vowels of the English language, too easily escalating into a fish-wife's shrieks. How I would have liked to be able to enunciate like Veronica, swim around English words with the ease of an Olympic medalist. My friend had lived the life of someone who waded through the right waters yet has always kept an alert eye on all those about her without being sanctimonious. She had *adopted* me when I arrived in England twenty-five years ago. But these days, as she is approaching her eighty-fifth year, Veronica's voice wavers like heat rising from a hot asphalt road. Thin, trembling; precursors to eventual stillness.

"Nonsense!" Robert disagreed when I had apologised for my lack in speaking properly. "You speak English like a native. People would think that you're brought up here."

Ah, Robert. Robert with his eyes, so blue I could drown in them. To promise so much, to give so much hope—and then to leave me in this manner, without preparation or warning. For a middle-aged woman, this is a catastrophe. Of all the men in my life, it was him whom I loved most. He held up the right mirror to me, showed me I had beauty when I thought there was none, showed me my worth, helped me to laugh again. But now, he, too, has left. Like the others. But, there is no point in dwelling upon my loss; he would not return. Like the others. His was an irrevocable act.

"I'm sorry. But you have to get up."

She pulls the duvet away from me and cold air rushes in.

"It's cold. I don't feel like going," I say.

"But you must. You have to show people you are strong."

"But I'm not strong. I don't want to be strong."

"Kim, I'm not letting you give in. You're made of stronger stuff than you think." Veronica, as usual, like people in this country, uses only the first part of my name. Her tone is firm, a no-nonsense voice that caused people in the Hampshire village to be wary of her. Her father had been a sergeant-major and they think she had inherited some of his ways. People let her pass when she strides purposefully down High Street, her tweed cape billowing behind her, her grey hair wild, her face scored with her own life's experiences. People have often thought her paintings moody, almost formidable, they say, like that local Victorian painter, George Frederic Watts, whose paintings now hang in a gallery near the disused crematorium near Guildford.

"Does it matter now, whether I give in or not?"

"Of course it matters. Life always matter. Otherwise we might as well all give up—before we get old, before we get decrepit. To live life properly and to the fullest is a decision; anything other than that is mere existence."

"But Robert is dead. Why would I want to live?"

"Because you have lots to give to life still. Fifty-something isn't old these days. And you're still attractive. You've always been positive. Draw on your resources now. Life is about moving on, a process of learning and change. It's when you stop that you are dead. You can be dead even when you are still alive. Entombed in your own past."

"I'm such a failure."

"You're not a failure, you're just sad right now. And everything seems more bleak when you're sad. You are entitled to grief; it's natural." And then she mumbles something which I do not comprehend. "'*Modrate lamentation is the right of the dead; Excessive grief the enemy oft the living*'."

"But what will I wear?"

Veronica is so sensitive she does not deem this a facile remark.

"Let me help you. I know that our two cultures differ on the appropriate attire for the same occasion. But you're in England. It might be suitable for you to wear what is expected of you here in this situation. Black, I'd say."

"Veronica, who am I really?"

Janus, the Roman God of doorways and bridges, has two faces so that he can face two directions at once, simultaneously seeing the north and the south or the east and the west. He is usually depicted with one face expressing joy, the other expressing sadness, this duality often used in theatre masks to symbolise drama. But can we mere mortals hold two such varied perspectives at the same time? Have we the propensity to halve ourselves, one half holding one emotion and the other, a different one? This is my test. Just as I thought that I was sinking under the weight of sadness, an unexpected arrival brings me the flip side of joy. Having only one physical face, unlike Janus, I'm unsure which to put on. The two emotions wrestle inside me to gain dominance, each striving to be displayed. I try to box one whilst freeing the other.

"I'm so happy for you," Veronica whispers in my ear, her voice thick with emotion. "He has come at the right time."

Of my friends, only Veronica understands what this visit means; she has been privy to what went on before, and only she can grasp the true import of this occasion. At another level, I'm aware of how significant this new arrival means, but I'm unsure how to react. In the face of grief, joy seems wrong, like laughter at a funeral, a betrayal to the dead. Yet how can I contain this unexpected happiness? A miracle for me. *He* is here! My young man! A thirty-year-old, nearly twenty years younger than myself. From pages of my life that had been torn from me. An old love, resurrected from the dark cave of the past, history colliding with my present. He towers over me, nearly six-foot tall, and so handsome I could cry. How could I have had the heart to leave him? His skin is still glowing from the tropical sun, like burnished bronze, mine pale in comparison, yellowed by years of long winters. He brings the smells of the island to me, the salt air in his hair, the aroma of spices on his clothes, coconut oil on his skin, lemon grass on his breath. He rips open the old can of memories I have kept sealed for fear that they might fall apart.

"Oh, you've come at last!"

"Ya."

Can the one I love be replaced by another with such swiftness? No, never. Not replaced. Another love can only help dress the wound that is caused by the loss of one, acts as a balm to pad the raw space that is left. After all, there isn't much point in continuing to grieve, nothing will make Robert return.

"Dese are for you."

He comes laden with gifts too. A box of carefully trimmed Vanda Joachim orchids, the national flowers of Singapore, the base of their stems swaddled in wet cotton wool. I'm taken back to the land I'd tried so hard to expunge from my memory but without real success. There is no escaping one's roots. My long lost son stands awkwardly at first, uncertain of how to make the first move. Years of unspoken words and pain had piled up like bricks to stand between us. He acts by shifting his weight and runs his broad hand through his deep blue-black hair. I considered hugging him, but I, too, am awkward, unsure of how I would be received, still mixed with grief over Robert. Then the moment passes. A precious opportunity lost.

"I've come to take you home," he says, as if the years had not been.

Home. It's a single word that is inflated with promises. Succulent. Full of ripeness, fruits glimmering with sunshine. Home is about family, anchors you to hugs. Love. How far away I have been, tempted to a foreign land, an Odysseus, wandering for years. Searching. Searching. Would that I know where Ithaca is for me. So! He has held a place for me after all. Despite what I had done. Has he forgiven me? But I daren't ask. It's enough that he had set aside unresolved issues to come to me when my need is great. The eight thousand miles between us have been bridged at long last. The pain I must have caused him. What debts one incur from the infliction of pain. Even if he did forgive me, I'm not sure I could forgive myself. All this time apart, and yet, he had not let loose of me in his heart. The thought passes through me like a tremor. If I were not so sad, I would have whooped with joy. As it is, conflicting emotions rage through my being. What should I feel? I am already fraying at the edges.

"How did you know?"

"I made it my business to know-*wat*."

He sounds curt but I know it's his brand of English, which used to be mine too. I say nothing, too grateful for words. Besides, our relationship is not yet forged enough for criticisms. There is so much to catch up, so many years to knit back into shape, work over the gaps. I must be patient and not rush things. I've waited much of my life; I can wait a bit longer. To anticipate is to be filled with hope, to be filled with hope means that you are still living. It's when you lose hope that you die an inner death. His arrival lifts the slab of stone from my chest, plumps my breath back into fullness. His is a voice grown to maturity. Resonant. Familiar, yet unfamiliar.

"Thanks. Thanks for coming. You've never been far from my mind. And heart. I *have* written. Many times. I've tried to call too. Been there to look for you."

"I know now. I found out recently. Dad finally told me before he died."

I try to picture Victor as I last saw him.

"He was my first love. I was only seventeen. He was nineteen. You look so much like him when he had his physique: tall, broad-shouldered, small waist. I'm sorry to hear about it. So many deaths. It's such a finality. You can't put things right with people who die on you. What did he die of?"

"Cancer. His anger ate up his insides."

12

"It must be hard on you."

"I have my own family now."

"What's your wife's name?"

"Margaret."

"Am I a grandmother?"

"Twice over. A girl, Diana. She's nine. My boy's Harry. He's five." I savour the news.

"Five? The same as…"

"Let's not talk about dat."

"I've missed out on so much. Do you have photos? Tell me more about them. Who is the one who is interested in the royal family?"

"Margaret's mum. She doesn't use her own Chinese name now…calls herself Elizabeth."

He whips out his wallet. Givenchy. From underneath the clear plastic, he draws out the pictures. His family is held next to his body. We're on safe territory talking about *his* family. His face is less guarded, infused with a quiet contentment. I love the nearness of him, revel in the fact that we are breathing the same air at long last. I drink in his grown-up voice as he describes his wife and children, watch the expressions play on a face I have often coveted. Slowly, we begin to learn each other. The work on the torn tapestry has begun.

"Before we go home, I got to get things on my shopping list."

"Yes, of course. I'm still not hundred percent. If you don't mind, we won't disturb Veronica. She needs to get back to her own home. I'll get a taxi to take us into town. I know just what to get for your children—*my grandchildren.*" I say the last with pride. A new ownership for me. "Franklin Mint has made a beautiful figurine of Princess Diana. I don't think there is any of Prince Harry but since *Harry Potter* is the 'in' thing, I'll get Harry a figurine of Harry Potter on his broomstick in his outfit and cloak that he wore when he played Quidditch."

"Oh, Harry is very much into *Harry Potter*. We queued for hours to get him de *Order Of De Phoenix*. He can't read properly yet; Margaret reads it to him. Better den queueing hours to get a McDonald's toy!"

"Queueing for a McDonald's toy?"

"Yes, you know de giveaways dey put in de bag when you buy a *Kids*

Meal Deal. It was a huge marketing campaign. Singaporeans queued for hours to get de toy for deir kids. Every child must have one. In one queue, a fight broke out between de parents because one tort de udder was going to cut queue. One ended up in hospital, even."

"This world has gone mad."

"Was it not mad before?"

I'm not sure what he is inferring. I don't know him yet, not enough to raise questions like that anyway. The thought of shopping for my own grandchildren whom I had not known existed thrills my heart. Yet I am not totally free from Robert's death. I must rouse myself from my own private pain, and discard the cloak of melancholy. The old adage that when one door shuts, another opens has come true for me and I must make the most of it. I must not make a mistake the second time 'round. I go to the wardrobe to select something suitable to wear. The moment I open its doors, Robert confronts me in his personal belongings, the energy of which reaches out like his touch, grazing my face and arms.

"Sayang!" he calls out the endearment in Malay. Or so I imagined I heard. I think I feel a whoosh of air at the back of my neck. He had a habit of blowing on my nape when he came behind me. This renewal of memory disarms me, brings me to my knees as I bury my face in his clothes. I want him so much. I close my eyes and draw him in with my breath, the scent of his aftershave, *Aramis*, lingering on his shirts even after they had been laundered—a scent that spells comfort and protection. I remember the rich moistness of his armpits, the smell of his come. His and mine, body secretions that mingled and became one. Now even my smell is orphaned, single, unadulterated. There is a terrible ache in your chest when your smell is only your own. I reflect on people who are on their own, by choice and by fate. Do they feel this emptiness that comes from living alone only with their own smells? I force my wobbly knees to straighten. Standing there in front of the wardrobe, in front of the clothes that Robert used to wear, I imagine they are still holding the shape of him. Or perhaps I can see it only because I know intimately the way they fold themselves around his torso, his thighs, his buttocks. The shirts and trousers hang there, side-by-side with my clothes, like our limbs which used to entwine in bed, the difference in our complexion showing, mine a dull brown compared to his pale, English. Here, a jacket he wore to our weekend in London when we had seen *Blood Brothers* and stayed at *The Connaught;* and this was the shirt that had red wine spilled on it when we went to Portofino in Italy; and this was the silk shirt he wore when we made love on Cannon Beach in Oregon. Our shared life is caught in the fabric of his trousers, his socks, his handkerchiefs, and in other things we chose together…used together. Our laughter and our words seemed to be sewed into them. In the parapsychology of psychometry, it is believed that the energy molecules of a person is imbedded in the things they used so that facts about the person can be deduced from them even when the owner is not present. Is it psychometry or merely an intimate knowledge of Robert that makes me feel Robert's presence when I touch his things? How will I find the strength to divorce him from me when so much of what we had is so intrinsically linked? A wife picks up her husband's needs and desires so easily, strives to fulfill them because she loves him, and in so doing, makes them her own. It is hard to extricate oneself from all that, stand alone again in my own needs and desires. Single, unadulterated. I have to do something about his personal effects, of course, probably box them and send them to a charity or burn them like he had been cremated. But whatever I do is of no consequence to him; his was a final act, already registered onto a sheet of paper. Irrevocable. It is myself I have to consider. Later, when the raw ache has diminished, will I regret not having anything of his to remember? Like the fact that there has been no child, no oak tree to attest to the fact that his seed had ever been sowed in me? Is this why some people have children—to make public their private acts of intimacy to prove that they had loved…had *been* loved? Or are they simply trying to prove their youthful virility, or to ensure that some part of themselves passes into immortality? Ah, what is the use of raking up old leaves that have rotted with time? I'm past it now, already menopausal, and Robert is out of my life. Should I just tissue-wrap his things and store them in the attic of my mind?

For now, I need to set Robert aside, give room to my son who had crossed oceans of time to reach me. He is the present and Robert the past. I *have* to think like this; it's the only way to survive. To live in the past is to die a living death where no new stepping stones to the future can be created. I must not allow myself the indulgence of sorrow or defeat—*will* not allow. Turning my mind from thoughts that will drag my spirit down, I observe how the winter wind whips Peter's face red as we walk up the cobbled high street towards the eighteenth century town clock. Except for some traditionalists, very few people in Singapore use Chinese names now, preferring the lightweight Christian ones which can be delivered with panache, with its suggestion of modernity and progress. Peter the Rock, guardian to the celestial gates. Is he here to unlock Heaven for me? I capture every little detail about him—the tiny dimple that plays on the left corner of his mouth giving him a perpetual smile; the wide width of his forehead; the whorl of his ears— lapping everything up hungrily and searing it hotly into my mind. For years, I had to imagine what he might have looked like, how he would carry himself, what new mannerisms he would have. At last, I can stop imagining. He is visible before me. Occasionally, I think I am hallucinating, a result of my extreme sorrow over Robert. But the wind brushes Peter's coat across my arm and convinces me of his tangible presence. Unfelt by him, perhaps, but received so wholeheartedly by me. He looks dashing in the full-length Barbour coat, his way of letting me know his success, and perhaps in an oblique way, his connection to me. Have I a right to a sense of pride when I have been absent from his life for so long? I'm tempted to link my arm through his, but I suspect that he would find the familiarity awkward. It would be a gesture too soon. So I resist the inclination. It will take a while for us to get used to each other again, to live moments together so that experiences can be stitched into the memory pattern of our lives. Without these, we have no shared history. History is not birthed in the past; it is the present folded away. We have to set new markers, forage for food to feed our hearts and minds. Every single thing we do together counts. You cannot realise the value of this when your loved one is continually by your side. It is after you have lost someone that you regret not chalking up every angle of your loved one's face, the slightest movement he makes, the exquisite joy you feel in his very presence. We go into *Marks & Spencers* and the *House of Fraser* to buy clothes and items that are considered fashionable and smart to own in Singapore. Apparently, despite independence, there is still an affinity toward things English.

"Peter, what would you like for yourself? I'd like to buy you something."

I'm so elated that I would give him anything he asked. At this moment, I understand why lovers gilded their loved ones with gold. It is an expression of their deep joy. Perhaps in some subtle way, it is also to establish ownership, the possessor claiming the possessed. In this instance, my intent to give comes straight from my joy, I'm only thinking of pleasing him as he has pleased me by reconnecting. It's such a thrill to say his name, to taste its vowels and consonants, to let its shape touch the roof of my mouth, feel its sound reverberate in my throat. I could strike a Julie Andrews pose at the top of the Surrey hills and sing out, *Peter, Peter*, a name which I had kept shuttered behind my lips for years for fear of exposing my heart.

"I'm not here for dat kind of ting."

I feel the sting of his reproof. But I try not to let it show. Then I console myself that it might be his way of stating that his motive in contacting me was pure. Perhaps my desire to buy him something is a slip back into the mother role I had played all those years ago. Though it may be natural, to act too soon would be wrong. Too much has happened to make my natural role obsolete. I have forfeited my authority and rights when I left; I cannot presume to reinstate myself. Besides, he is different now; he's a grown man, able to make his own decisions. It is *he* who now plays the role of guardian and protector. He is deciding for me that it is time to go back to the land of my birth. Our birth.

His manner of assuming control could be interpreted as highhanded, but right now, I'm glad for his decisiveness and authority. He's rescuing me from a bleak emotional landscape. When Robert went, he took the sparkle out of my life. To be in England at the moment will make my loss greater and difficult to bear, too many familiar places to evoke warm scenes when we had been happy. I can probably cope with it all when I am back on my feet, grounded. But not right now. There had been others before Robert. If only it had been different. How the painting of my life would be so much brighter if he had entered the picture sooner. But it wasn't, and now it isn't. He was borrowed for a time. And now I am blue.

"At least, let me treat you to cream tea. You can't come to England without having a cream tea. It would be like going to Singapore without tasting *satay*." I colour my voice with gaiety to paint away the threatening gloom. We are all artists, free to choose the hues from the palette of life. It's up to me to make the right choice; only I can be responsible for my happiness. This is a lesson that adversity has taught me. They are all there in our lives—

the colours: red, orange, yellow, green, blue, indigo, violet. The spectrum of the rainbow. Someone taught me a mnemonic once to remember the colours: *R*ichard *Of* *Y*ork *G*ain *B*attle *In* *V*ain. Is there a mnemonic to remind me of happier moments? If only we can ignore the tug and pull of our baser emotions and always choose the brighter hues.

"Okay-*lah*."

The tag word he uses drags the old language back to me, reminds me of my roots. My tongue has gone rusty with disuse. *Pelat*. A stumbling over words. Perhaps he is aware of my discomfiture because since his arrival, he has not spoken in our patois combination of Chinese and Malay, but only in *Singlish*, a variant English peculiar to Singaporeans, laced with local idioms, English words awry in non-English construction. Language is a currency and I've forgotten its exchange.

The strong fragrance of freshly roasted coffee teases our taste buds and guides us to our choice of tearooms. It is one of those where the waitresses are in black uniforms and white aprons, white-frilled caps on their heads as though time has not passed for England. Tourists, particularly Americans, ride from Waterloo Station to the county-town of Surrey for an experience of countryside and English ways. What is a normal living habitat becomes quaint to them. The English tearoom is a citadel of tradition. Many years ago when I entered such an establishment, I would have been conscious of my own colour, a brown egg amongst a nest of white, acutely aware of the looks I received. Was my petticoat showing or a bra strap visible?

"People look at you because you're so beautiful," Hugh would assure me on his generous days. But I was not convinced. Ah, Hugh. He is a story unto himself. What was it in me that drew that kind of man?

Now, in the tearoom, I realise that I've come a long way in emotional miles. I'm now scrubbed clean of old anxieties, think myself a rightful resident, see myself undistinguished from the others. I order the cream teas with easy authority, smiling. The one thing I have learnt well is that a smile will help to whitewash an unintended wrong, smooth a rough path.

"Do you know that when I first arrived in this country I dropped clangers by the dozen, committed *faus pax* by the mouthful?"

"Clangers? Wat are dey?"

"Mistakes. I used the wrong expressions or turned them wrong-side up so they become funny to other people."

"Ya? Like wat?"

"Oh, I'd say something like, 'Might as well be hung for a lamb as a sheep,' when it should be the other way 'round. Or I might say, 'Let's go for a walk, you *potato couch*'!"

He laughs. Slightly hesitant, but it's still a laugh. It's a magical experience for me to know his laughter, to share in it. How clever he is to understands my mistakes. I was not so clever at his age.

I want to tell him that I had been afraid that Hugh would be ashamed of me if I did not race around with speed to collect English expressions—clothed myself with English manners—but I thought Peter might not like the reference to the man who had ruined his life. Hugh Bloodworth, so very English, so charming, was the proverbial knight in shining armour. He swept me off my feet. He spun me yarns that glittered with adventure and romance; made me see England like a fairyland. It was I who had to adopt his country and his culture. But it was a need, not a desire; otherwise I would have remained friendless—always the outsider. There are so many skeletons in my cupboard. I ought to take them out for an airing, dispose of those I had dealt with. But not now. Right now, I've too much to handle.

There is a comforting buzz of conversation in the tearoom which fills the awkward gap between Peter and I, a gap born from untested closeness. But I delight in his presence as proof of the validity of our connection. Then the middle-aged, portly waitress brings our coffee, warm scones, home-made jam and fresh Loseley cream from a local farm. My love for the afternoon ritual is my major claim to Englishness, if Englishness were a nationality, not just traits of a particular race.

"They're all cholesterol-free, right?" I say to the waitress with a wink, knowing full well it isn't. It's my stab at English humour—not easy to get right. "Have to watch my weight, you know."

"Sure," the woman says with a conspiring smile and I'm pleased that she had read the situation correctly. "Fat-free, sugar-free, as well."

After we've been served, I'm rudely awaken to the fact that the young man sitting in front of me is a stranger to me now as he eats with his mouth open, bringing body down toward his plate instead of sitting upright bringing food to his mouth. He's a total stranger today, yet he had long ago slept as one with me. I'm pained by my own traitorous thought, a result of *my* slavery to western manners and western mores. Why should I expect that he has to bend to rules made for others in an alien culture? He is only passing through, he doesn't have to change his ways as I had to do. There is so much to unlearn if I'm to get on in the country of my birth.

2

It is far easier to cross oceans than it is to cross emotional space. Peter is inches away on the seat next to me on the Singapore Airlines flight but he is chasms away in expression of feeling. Physical closeness is not akin to emotional intimacy. Look at some of the people about you, in an aeroplane, a train, restaurants and homes. See the emptiness in their faces and you will witness this tragic separateness. They are unable to make the link across the emotional synapse. People in crowded places, towns and cities protect their soft inner centers by bubble-wrapping their humanity so that all you see are bodies moving, like Disneyesque animatronics—mobility without life. We carry our social faces with us wherever we go, like mobile phones, simply as tools of communication—talking, chatting, but not really interacting. *How are you? Fine, thank you. What a lovely day.* Actually, we're not fine, but we don't say so. We put on our own game show, and smile for the audience. Beneath the skin of our faces are our real faces, invisible to mirrors, and sometimes, even to ourselves. I wish that I can peel off the layer of placid expression on Peter's face to peer underneath, so that I can understand what he feels…what he thinks of our situation. But his face is severely stitched in place, his heart and mind no longer mine to probe and explore—he's a book shut to me. I must read him by more subtle tweaks of nerves in his face—the way he holds his body, the manner in which he talks with his hands, hoping that one day he'll be comfortable enough to feed me some lines.

I would like the companionship of conversation so that my thoughts cannot be pulled back to Robert. But Peter recedes into himself by turning on his personal video on the back of the seat in front of him and watches a film. People indulge in action or armchair activity to still the tumultuous thoughts which rage the sea of their minds. It is stillness which calms the inner storm and brings peace. To understand this is not the same as achieving it. I've tried it all—transcendental meditation, yoga, tai-chi—and yet peace eludes me like the wisp of a fading dream. I need some technique now to pull my frayed self together. Why is it possible to master techniques in classrooms but impossible to apply in real situations? Having spent my energy in being ecstatic over Peter's arrival, I now find that I'm exhausted. I'm too weary to apply myself, to make the bridging moves, too weary even to watch a film. So, I gaze listlessly about me, suddenly aching for a glimpse of Robert in the Caucasian faces around me. When you are really starved, any morsel will do. A few seats along in front of me, a head catches my eyes, hair ash-greying in an irregular band around the ears and nape. The sight makes my breath catch. I almost raise myself from my seat to go for a better look. Of course I'm being ridiculous. It won't be possible. Then the man happens to turn to look down the aisle, right through me with eyes that have never looked into mine before, a head that has never nuzzled into my shoulder before. Except for the colour of his hair and the way it curls into a duck-tail at the back, the man has no likeness to Robert, yet seconds before, I could have sworn it was Robert sitting there before me. The loss of someone dear can create illusions. I must pull myself together. I'll have to get used to missing him.

It is when he is asleep that Peter abandons his guard. His face softens, his continually pursed lips relaxing, a little spittle escaping as his head lolls sideways onto my shoulders. His deep breathing, so close to my ears, makes me believe that we are one once again. My heart beats with exhilaration at this delicious surrendering, this feel of his body touching mine. It has been so long. Too long. He was mine first and this unconscious yielding is a tender moment for me, exquisitely precious because I know I'm stealing. I haven't the right anymore. But, I sit still and dare not move lest he awakens and in consciousness, pulls away from me; better to hold my bladder and to suffer the pins-and-needles from this contact than to be denied the opportunity. Surreptitiously, I run my hand lightly up his arm, taking the measure of him through my fingertips: the texture of his skin, the tone of his muscles so changed from the last time I had caressed him. Years ago, his fingers had laced mine, had sought for my touch; now I seek his—a role reversal. He is, indeed, a solid presence, not a phantom conception of my mind. So many images and dreams jumble through my mind that I'm sometimes unsure which of them is real. Sometimes my senses collide—I think I see Robert, hear him, feel him. But here is something really to touch or am I confused still? My son. The simple act of touching him is something I've dreamed of doing for such a long time. We've been apart for such a lifetime that he almost ceased to exist. Can there be love without the object of love? What have I *loved* all these years—an image of my own making? But he is here now and this contact is like a renewal of vows, a confirmation of his existence. I try to stay awake to savour this unexpected intimacy so that it can be weaved into my consciousness for subsequent retrieval, but am betrayed by my own weariness and the rocking of the plane which sends me into the same deep sleep as Peter's. Much later, whilst still sleeping, I'm half-aware that he has awaken to find himself perched on my shoulder. With a start, he straightens up and when my shoulder loses its weight and sags toward his arm, he pushes me away from him as if in recoil. I have to curb my reaction…tell myself it doesn't hurt. After all, I can't expect too much too quickly. So I continue to pretend to be still asleep. After a suitable time has lapsed, I yawn and stretch as though emerging from a real slumber. The dimness in the cabin conceals my true face and aids me in the charade.

"Gosh! I didn't realise how tired I was."

"Dey going to serve breakfast soon. Not far from landing."

There it is again—that distinct Singaporean speech. His voice is matter-of-fact, scraped of emotion. Have I set myself back with those few stolen moments? How often do we run too quickly to find ourselves stumbling, losing more ground than if we had walked? I must strive to pace myself. I cannot afford to lose him now that *I've* been found.

"So soon? When I first came to England, the flight took about twenty-three hours or so. We had to stop at Bombay and Dubai. It's not even called Bombay now. Mumbai now, isn't it?"

"Dose were de days wen policemen wear shorts-*lah*," he quips.

From the tone of his voice, I hear the shift in gravity, gather that he's trying to be amusing so I chuckle accordingly. The humour of each culture can be easily displaced in the wrong environment. Robert and myself were in Vail, Colorado, for a skiing holiday once and an American couple we met had invited us to a stand-up comedy event. I remember that everyone in the theatre was laughing till tears rolled down their faces at every single delivery of the comedian, and yet, Robert and I could not understand either the allusions or jokes. That was when it really struck home that some humour is not universal. I must wrest my mind away from Robert; thoughts of him will ink my mind with the darkness of our separation. My body and mind are sagging with the exhaustion of having to cope with such diverse emotions. I realise that I must be particularly vigilant in my interaction with Peter, dance with him to the music of our race. I cannot afford to miss a step, to let him guess that I've become an alien to *our culture*. He would expect that I think of myself as a Peranakan, not as some foreign hybrid who *looks* Peranakan. The pejorative term for such a person in our language is *chelop*, someone dunked into another culture. But who am I now? Surely I *am* already chelop, a toffee-apple, a brown veneer on the outside but white in the heart. But Peter must never find out. He had come to claim what he had lost; he would not want to take home an imitation. For his sake, I must core my center of whiteness and fill it with brown again.

"I must go to the toilet."

I need the interval, a private space to adjust my emotions. I wash my face to clear off the negative energy. Our people are like this, believing in all sorts of folklore.

"If you can't bathe, at least wash face, wash feet before sleep," my mother's voice enters my head."If you take bad day into dreams, you have bad dreams."

I have too many voices in my head. What do I have to do to exorcise them?

"Other people's energies stick like dust to you. Must wash off every day."

Yes. Water also cleanses things of the spirit. Have I really let slip so much of my culture or have these things just been pressed neatly down between the folds of my brain to resurface when triggered by a word or its association? Dare I bring things out of hiding? The thought of my mother threatens to pry open an old cupboard. Dare I look at its contents? No, I cannot. Not yet.

So I leave Mak in the lavatory, unable to cross that emotional boundary. I return a little refreshed to my young man, all smiles and facile gaiety. He seemed a little different too, eager to make attempts to smash the wall that had risen between us.

"Singapore so modern now, you know. We got expressways, MRT and recently, we even have a tunnel which goes right under Orchard Road."

"MRT?"

"Mass Rapid Transport. You know, an underground railway system. Like de Tube, only more technologically advanced."

"How can they build a tunnel? I thought that the island was waterlogged. Expressways on such a small island? Doesn't seem possible."

"Singapore is like *chilli padi*, small, but powerful-*wat!*"

Chilli padi. Ah, what a delightful expression. How could I have forgotten it? A chilli so small that it receives its name from an uncooked grain of rice. Supermarkets in England liken it to the bead of an eye: *bird's eye chilli*. The same thing, really. Though tiny, the chilli has a reputation of being the hottest. The expression is used in numerous ways, usually vested onto small-sized people with power, or a person with a hot temper or someone with a huge sexual appetite. Small but powerful. It is interesting that though I have painted over the canvas of my own customs and culture, a little reference such as that made by Peter readily transports me back to the earth from which I had sprung. *Bumiputra. Bumi*—Earth. *Putra*—Prince. The old language is resurfacing. Prince of the Earth, one half of my ancestors are called in Malaysia. Peter is my prince, the earth of my being. His laughter is loosening. I like his gurgle of pleasure with his own analogy. When his lips pronounce the name, *Singapore*, he seems to grow in stature as though swollen with pride. It gives me joy to be learning him, yet I'm suddenly afraid for him. What did he have to take on board without me, what ideas and opinions had he innocently allowed to settle into his mind without me there to sift them for him? Oh, how I have failed him in so many ways. The thought nearly make me maudlin, wash wet behind my eyes. Foolish woman. Regret can never change what has been. I must not open the floodgates. I might drown.

"I presume you did National Service?"

"Of course-*wat*. It's our duty."

"I met your father six months after he began National Service. He was the first batch of graduates to be drafted you know. He had a fabulous figure—broad-shouldered, slim waist, beautifully tanned. He reminded me of Johnny Weissmuller."

"Who?"

"American film star. Johnny Weissmuller. He was an Olympic swimmer and he played the part of *Tarzan* in a Hollywood film in the sixties."

"I've never seen Dad udder den de way I know him—very over-weight."

"People change," I say softly.

"I tink all youngsters should go into NS. It will make dem bow to discipline. Even in de short time dat I was in England, I saw how rude young people were. Dey lacked manners. On TV and in de papers, people were always wanting dis and dat, as if dey were owed a living. In Singapore, if we don't work for it, we don't get it. De government does not hand things to us free-of-charge. During NS, we learn to work with people of different races and from all walks of life."

The words flow out too smoothly, like learned platitudes.

"Do you not object to people teaching you how to kill?"

His face is suddenly pulled close like the bamboo chicks we used to have over our windows in the *attap* hut in which I was brought up. Ah! Mistake. It's so easy to gain his disapproval that for a moment, I'm unsure that I can cope with such fluctuation of emotion when I'm not quite so stable myself. Behind his worldly exterior, there is a suggestion of a fragility that requires pandering.

"We are not taught to kill; we are taught to protect our country. Dere is a difference."

His tone does not invite either dissension or discussion.

To avoid the silence which has slid open between us, I allow my mind to drift. Indeed, I have known a Singapore when policemen wore shorts. How far I have come, both in physical and emotional miles. What is it going to be like to return to all that heat and dust, to the angry words, the ashes of dreams? Have they been blown by the wind or have they been etched into a memorial stone in someone's heart?

I leapfrog the turbulent years, so full of regret. I started fresh in England—a new brown egg, pretending that there had been no past. If I was forced to talk about my life back in Singapore by inquisitive acquaintances or friends,

I conjured one up. It was as much for Hugh's sake as my own. He would not have wanted our friends to know that I was a daughter of a servant. Or that I had deserted my own child. Even *I* could not believe that I had deserted my own child—for love with a man. Indeed, I have sinned. *Mea Culpa. Mea Culpa.* Once you lie, the rest comes easy. Too easy. Until sometimes, I, too, can't remember if some of the things I had said were my own invention or if they had really happened. Hoist with my own petard. But I know that the day of reckoning is coming. Surely, I'll have to confront my real past when I get back to Singapore. But not yet. I would prefer not to have to deal with my past until later. But earlier thoughts about my mother had primed other memories to flow, brought Mak back into my mind. I recalled the day when my future was laid open in front of me although I didn't see it like that then. I must have been about five or six when I first heard Nenek Bongkok's prediction. I was lying prone on the straw mat, my legs thrashing the air in fun.

"Stop that!" My mother said in our langauge. "Very bad luck to raise your legs that way."

If I think about Mak, I'll remember sayings and customs she had taught me. There's a kind of comfort that comes from believing in certain customs. It gives you a sense of belonging. Mak and Nenek was sitting cross-legged on the cement floor, joining my mother in her daily ritual of chewing *sireh.* They usually spoke in Malay. Nenek wasn't my real grandmother, of course. People in the *kampung* call her *Grandmother*, because it was good manners and because she was old. And she was called *Bongkok*, because she was so bent. Nobody ever called her by her given name, whatever that was. I remember thinking that the two adults looked so incongruous, sitting side-by-side, one tall and slim and beautiful, the other so bent and wrinkled. My mother, Ang Huay (*Red Flower*), was strikingly attractive like the *Flame-of-the-Forest* she was named after. Her hair was straight and black, pulled tight into a bun which made her heart-shaped face more pronounced. At the left-hand corner of her lip is a tiny beauty spot which quivered when she smiled. Why she never married again, I didn't know. Surely there could not have been a shortage of suitors? But the cameo of the two women had stayed stuck in my mind all these years.

After a day of washing and ironing other people's clothes, Ang Huay allowed herself a little indulgence. We were sitting by the open front door so that we could catch the afternoon breeze that cooled the sweat on our nape. In the sandy compound, the children were quiet, lazing languidly like the dogs and chickens, cowering in the shade under the sprawling angsana tree. On days like this, the corrugated zinc roof turned our tiny kitchen into a blazing oven. Nenek Bongkok lived a couple of doors away from us. Mak was cooking *bubur kachang*—green mung beans—over the clay stove and the beans were bubbling away in coconut milk, filling our little hut with a delicious fragrance. My memory of Mak is always connected with food—either there was none or there was the smell of something nice. Nenek Bongkok, besides being bent, was also very thin, her cheeks like hollow cups. She stretched forward for the wooden box which held the betel-nut and lime. It was obviously a ritual she enjoyed. You could tell that from the way she held her body and the way her fingers picked up the betel-nut leaf, spreading lime onto it. There was something about those fingers that disturbed me, as if they belonged to a witch, bony and crooked, scaled like the claws of a chicken. Like all the village children, I was afraid of our neighbour, rumoured to be a descendant of the *orang battak*, the aborigines. Wrapped in my thoughts, I shrieked with fright when the old lady suddenly seized my leg.

"Oi! What have we here? A traveler. Your daughter will travel far, Nonya. She has a mole right here on the inside of her knee."

All the villagers called Ang Huay Nonya, the term for a Peranakan female—never ever her name.

"Travel? We can't even afford bus fare into town; how can we travel anywhere else? Oh, you are one for raising hopes, Nenek."

"I tell you…your girl will travel far far."

"I'd like to visit Penang-*lah*," I said, thinking it would be nice to see my father's big bungalow from the other side of the fence; maybe even meet him and persuade him to take me back. For years, I had secretly dreamed that my father would come looking for me. Every stranger that came into the kampong had the possibility of being him, until it was proved not to be so, shattering my illusions.

"Oh, my child. Not just to Malaya-*lah*. You will cross oceans!"

Nenek Bongkok cackled. But her words didn't mean anything to me then; weightless, like soap bubbles, ballooning around empty space to float for a while, then bursting into droplets of nothing. How could I ever hope to travel anywhere when my mother was already taking in all the neighbours' washings, and yet we haven't even got enough to eat nor have our own bathroom or toilet? The old lady must have been crazy. Though the day had not seemed significant at the time, it had settled into my consciousness. Every now and again, something would stir the seabed of my memory and the day would float free to surface in my mind's eye. Then I'd see it all again. In retrospect, the day took on greater significance. After all, Nenek Bongkok's prediction had, indeed, come true. True enough, I did travel, first and foremost, to faraway England, eight thousand miles away, then to the cities of America and Canada, then afterward to their remotest places, *Tok* and *Chicken* in Alaska, and *Dawson City* and *Innuvik* in Canada. One day whilst lying on our sheepskin rug in front of the open fire in an aftermath of love, the movement of the flames making shadow play across Hugh's bare flesh, white even in the reddish glow of the fire, I remembered Nenek Bongkok and the prediction. I had wondered how the old lady had seen what she had seen. Is a prophecy a kind of distance-reading into what has already been written?

My mother had fled from my father, left him somewhere in Penang and sought emotional asylum with her friends in Singapore. Ang Huay had left with nothing but a small money belt, a few treasures wrapped in a bundle, myself snug in the sarong sling strapped across her chest. She had to work, of course, but unskilled, could find no work except as a washer woman. My mother always talked about the beautiful house she lived in, the servants, the luxury. But she had walked away from it all and chosen a life of independent deprivation. How foolish, I thought. There were terrible days when all we had to eat was salt-fish with our boiled rice. As a child, I was envious of my imaginary half-brothers and sisters (were there any?) who, if they existed, would have a pick from the best food around. When I went to bed hungry, I would not be able to sleep. Then I would hear the scratching above in the dry attap roof and I knew with a terrible feeling in the pit of my stomach that cockroaches, lizards and centipedes lived amongst the folds of the attap leaves. Every now and again, a centipede or lizard would miss a footing and plunge headlong down from the old attap onto my blanket, or worse, onto my head, the hundred crawly legs of the centipede that made my flesh creep, or the chilling cold of the lizard, sucking my scalp, making me scream. When it rained and the roof leaked, I had to listen to the drumming it made into the kerosene tins that were placed to catch the leaks. Ang Huay would hurry and scurry, searching for pails or tins before the hut got flooded. Of all the things I hated about the village, the worst was when I had to make use of the village *jamban*, shared by all the neighbours. I was always afraid that I might fall down the hole into the metal bucket below which was overflowing with everybody's feces. I had to squat there over that disgusting heap, buzzing with flies, with a handkerchief over my mouth. You don't find your own smell offensive when you open your bowels, but it's not quite the same when you have to smell the droppings of others. There was no light in the toilet so in the evenings I had to carry a carbide lamp which hissed and spluttered, gingerly placing my feet over the hole to squat down. The cockroaches ran around me and my heart would squeeze in fear in case one of them decided to crawl up my leg and into other secret parts of me—so exposed there, squatting. And worse still were the rats that scuttled underneath the wooden platform, squeaking, squeaking, squeaking. For me, going to the toilet was a traumatic affair. At nights, my mother would allow me to use a chamber-pot placed in the kitchen in our hut but I didn't like using that because the smell would linger throughout the night. And worse, the rats would already be out and they would scuttle around the base of our platform bed, scratching and scratching, squeaking, squeaking, squeaking, and if I was using the chamber pot, they would traipse across my feet nonchalantly. The thought of the tiny nails of the rat scuttling over the body of my feet forced me to hold my bladder till morning. The memory of the rats' squeaking stayed lodged in my ears. Once I woke up to find one rat perching on my shoulders, its eyes like shiny marbles staring at me with such insolence. The horror of that incident was imprinted in my brain. I longed to run away somewhere where there were no rats or cockroaches. Those high-pitched squeaks stayed embedded in my brain and years later, I would still remember them. They entered my dreams and the horror of it would wake me up in a sweat, make me shake. One night, when we were in an old *pensione* by Lake Garda in Italy, I screamed and screamed in my sleep until Robert shook me awake.

"Sayang! Sayang!" He called me out from my cave of sleep.

"The rats! The rats are everywhere!"

"You're dreaming. You're safe here with me."

His voice was deep and low, different from Hugh's which fluttered lightly, sometimes shrill as glass. Over and over again, he used the Peranakan endearment to call me out, my saviour at the mouth of the cave. And finally, when I was free of my demon, he would sooth my damp hair away from my forehead, holding me tight, then caressing my arm continually to prove his presence. His warm breath breezed across my brow and his body threw out friendly heat that comforted me and sent me back into confident slumber. Yet, for years before him, I had suffered alone, unable to divulge to Hugh the cause of my nightmares. I couldn't make him a gift of my fear. You need to trust someone enough before you could expose your fear like that. It's like allowing them to retract the flesh of your psyche to peer inside

It was this, my visit to the outhouse, that brought the worst out in me and made me say things I otherwise would not have. How awfully I behaved. I was a little older, nearly ten when the experience made me react the way I did. Perhaps it was the many years of revulsion that had built up and suddenly heightened. It had been a public holiday and the night soil man hadn't come to replace the bucket with a fresh one. The night soil man drove a big truck which had many small compartments, each holding a bucket, and therefore it had as many doors.

"Here comes the limousine," the villagers joked.

I often wondered what the night soil man must smell like when he got home to his wife. Surely the nature of one's occupation must cling to your hair and clothes, like the smell of fish on a fishmonger, fresh blood on a butcher, the smell of bread on a baker. What must the night soil man himself feel when he had to sit down to a meal after having smelled and handled everybody's feces all day? If it was terrible for me, how much more terrible it must be for the night soil man, who had to earn a living in this way. But on that particular day, it was a day off for the man and so no truck with its many compartments arrived. It was an extremely hot day which made the stench in the *jamban* much more worse. If I hadn't been so urgent, I would not have gone, the smell making me want to retch. Squatting over the hole, I made the mistake of looking down. It was daylight and what I could see sickened me, rats running around the overflowing, filthy bucket below. Brown shit lay against black shit, pale shit against dark; some watery, some soft, others hard. Squares of newspapers crumpled and soggy lay amongst their midst. Fat, filthy flies hovered around the dribbling, disgusting mound of mess. It was smelly and horrible. The flies zipped about and some of them flew up the hole to land on the skin of my bare arms and legs, tainting me with their pollution. I was filled with despair, imagining that I had to live like this for the rest of my life. *I got to get out of this kampung*, I swore. Perhaps that was why I said what I did to my mother a little later, a child's unthinking words. Unforgivable. Regrettable.

When I finally escaped the *jamban*, I stumbled out blindly, gulping for air, my mouth working like a fish yanked out of water. A distance away, the air was sweet with the scent of the frangipani, its clusters brilliant white against the dark-green foliage of the tree. I plucked one to put near my nose so that I could forget the smell I had to endure when in the *jamban*. Never mind if frangipanis were meant to be funeral flowers, twisted into wreaths for the dead. Its scent lifted the feeling of sickness. But the experience in the *jamban* had unsettled me and I walked into the attap hut still manacled by the feeling. When I saw my mother sitting on her haunches on the floor ironing a giant pile of clothes that belonged to the rich people living at the top of the hill on *Atas Bukit*, something loosened in me. I was about to erupt. Yet, my mother seemed rather placid, uncomplaining about her lot. Her face was serene when she worked, running the coal-filled iron over a square of freshly plucked banana leaf to make the iron glide more easily over the stiffly starched clothes. Her forelocks were damp with sweat.

"Hiok, keep coals burn-burn, will you? I got more ironing to do."

Grudgingly, still caught in the mood that the filthy *jamban* had created, I went to the clay stove to stoke the coals. It was our one tiny stove that was also for cooking all our meals. Our meagerness was all around me, a yawning chasm of want. A huge earthen *tempayan* housed our drinking water which we had to bring in from a communal stand-pipe a quarter of a mile away; our washing-up water going into a small pit outside our kitchen, which my mother had to empty each day. Like our toilet, our bathroom was also communal, a roofless wooden cubicle around a well. Mak worked nonstop so that *I* could go to school, so I should be grateful. But I was thinking that up-country, my stepmother (was there one?) lived in luxury and had servants to wait on her, my half-brothers and sisters enjoying a wonderful life in a grand house with lots to eat.

"Mak, why don't you make life easier and just go back to Ah Tio? Did you leave him because there was another woman? It's all right-*wat*. You'll still be Big Wife; he would still have to take care of you. Of us."

My mother sighed, put down her iron, and wiped her brow. She turned her slender neck to look at me, her eyes looking huge in her thin face.

"You're still young-young. You don't understand."

"What don't I understand? He's living in big-big bungalow, right? Upstairs, downstairs. With big garden. With proper toilet and bathroom in the house? They have electricity? A car. Servants. His wife dripping in gold? His children have lots of food to eat, right? Pretty clothes to wear."

"Ya." It was the closest she had admitted to knowing that my father had a wife and children. "But those not only important things in life-*wat*."

"Not important? How come not important? I've just come from the *jamban*. Have you smelt it today? It nearly made me vomit. We have to share it with the rest of the village! I like to have my own toilet. Especially one that flushed, like the ones on *Atas Bukit*. How can you say these things are not important-huh? And what about food? I'm always hungry. I don't want to be hungry-*lah!* If you wanted to leave Ah Tio, why didn't you just go? Why didn't you just leave me behind?"

3

For all of my sins, I deserve to be boiled in oil.

Now that I have raked up my past, I burn with shame. I'll never forget that day. How could I have been so callous? Surely I had said those words without an intent to hurt? Today, I'm pained by the image of my mother's eyes which were shot with sorrow. Ang Huay was squatting but she still sank to the floor as though her legs had given way under the weight of her emotions.

"Oh, Kim Hiok," she said with a tattered voice. "You have something of your father in you."

The remark whipped my face in a painful lash. Even today, my mother's words ring in my ears like recurring tinnitus. *You have something of your father in you. You have something of your father in you.* There are so many things about my youth which I would like to undo, unpick the old threads sullied by mistakes and sew new ones into place. But unlike a piece of embroidery, life is not static. Designs do not stay in place; they move and change, sometimes even disappearing altogether out of the picture so that an attempt to right some wrong is no longer possible. That was how it was with my mother. But I'll not allow myself to dwell on that thought. Regret is an empty exercise of the ego. The only way *has* to be forward.

I lie back in my seat, grateful for the soothing darkness of the cabin, but my mother's words continue to censor me in the repetitive drone of the

34

aeroplane's engines. *You have something of your father in you. You have something of your father in you.* I feel as if I'm being flayed, my wounds open and raw. Why is everything coming back to accuse now? Especially now, when I finally have a chance to be happy with my son? Perhaps this trip back to Singapore is also a journey to my past, where old ghosts must be laid to rest, shadows that concealed the sun from me cleared. When something passed between the sun and our eyes, my mother used to call it a *bayang shadow.* You can pretend that the past is gone and the future is yet to come; but in reality, past, present and future exist all at once, except that they exist on different planes. Occasionally, the various planes intersect, and like the shifting and meeting of tectonic plates, will cause upheaval and eruption. For now, there is an uncomfortable calm like that before a thunderstorm. It's that feeling that grips your chest and makes breathing difficult and you know the clouds have to break soon.

Peter must have dozed off again because he is wrapped in silence. Too quickly the cabin lights come on, hurting my eyes. Other sleeping passengers are roused and start to shift in their seats. For the first time, I see Peter's morning face, unshaven and natural, not yet shaped into a social mask. This sighting is an unexpected gift. His chin is on his chest, making the flesh underneath his neck fold like linen, his hair falling over his forehead, his eyeballs moving rapidly under the lids. But it is momentary because the lights must have disturbed him too and he blinks and sits up, opening his dark brown eyes which makes him look young and unprotected, sleep glistening his lashes. This exposure of his vulnerability makes my heart catch. Why had I not stayed to care for him, shield him from harm? Why had I thought that the love of one man was worth the sacrifice, especially when I know now that Hugh had not even deemed it a sacrifice? He had taken me for granted, had taken my giving up my son for him as an expected move. My guilt returns full-force, bearing down on me like a huge boulder. I have so much to beg for forgiveness.

"Good morning, ladies and gentlemen. We trust dat you had a good rest. We will soon be serving breakfast before our descent into Singapore."

People around us stretch and yawn, some getting up to relieve their muscular cramps or their bladders. Before long, the cabin attendants are handing out warm wet towels. Some people wipe their faces, others wipe their face and neck, and some others wipe their face, neck and hands. Others wipe their face, neck, hands and arms. Still others wipe their face, neck, hands, arms and armpits. The cabin attendants put on a tabard over their still crisp *sarong kebaya* uniforms and they start to push trolleys up the narrow aisle. People who work in such a capacity must have a talent at painting on a fresh face and keeping sleep out of their voice. The cabin attendants are mostly very young, the men bursting with the vigour of youth, the women with twenty-inch waists and wrinkle-free skin. When you go on a Western airline, you notice straightaway how much older many of the cabin staff are, as if constant changes through different time zones age them in the same way that the sun affects their pale skin. An airline crew is generally representative of the broad base population of your nation. And you can tell that the majority of the Singaporeans are young, products of the people who had been colonised, merged with Malaysia and then separated. These youngsters have been born into a country brimming with wide-eyed wealth, the slums all bulldozed away, the past rewritten into history books. Although I feel youthful whilst in England, this exposure to such slim, young bodies and clear eyes knocks me back a bit, making me conscious of my years, broadening waistline and lackluster skin.

There is an anticipatory air in the cabin, people thirsting for a glass of cool water or juice, longing for that cup of steaming hot coffee or that first taste of food. People start to talk in their morning voices, without haste and without that adrenaline rush that characterises daytime speech. The indifferent passengers are those still hidden under blankets with airline pirate patches over their eyes. The unlucky ones with another leg of the journey left to Australia groan, fearing deep-vein thrombosis and claustrophobia; yet, compared to their forebears whose journey used to take weeks and months, their own would have been considered a miracle.

"Wat will you have Madam?" the Singapore girl asks with a smile, not quite as delightful as the one in the famous ad. Her fair complexion is a contrast against the dark blue Pierre Balmain batik. Unless you are Malay or Indian, the fairer you are, the more you are considered a beauty in Asia. I had long ago accepted that as far as my native countrymen were concerned; I fell short of their measure. Inheriting my Chinese genes, I was expected to be fair of face to denote my refinement. To be dark as I was when exposed to the hot sun relegated me to the status of a peasant working in the fields. I know that this is one of the things I'm returning to. Yet, it was my very tanned complexion that made Hugh fall in love with me. It would seem that what constitutes beauty in one culture may not be in the same in another. If beauty is relative and fashion can change, it seems foolish and vain to put yourself under the surgeon's knife to achieve a particular look, to take away real and healthy breasts to substitute them for false, or to starve yourself. I look at the young stewardess and wonder why one so young would want to cake her unlined face with liquid foundation and tattoo her eyebrows. Why reach for artificiality when nature is still so generous?

"Omelette or bacon and eggs?"

The Singaporean has a distinct manner of speaking that is easily recognizable around the world. Sometimes, it has to do with the use of expressions unique only to Singapore and Malaysia. But mostly, it has to do with the way the words are flung out, like the quick flicks of the *chichak's* tongue. Most of the time, the harder thrust of a *d* takes the place of the softer *th*. There is no lengthening or lingering over the ends of words, no roundness given to vowels, unlike the rich enunciation of good-spoken Mandarin. Colloquial speech is chopped-up and relaxed, throwing grammar to the winds. When put into English words, sometimes their speech sounds abrupt. And yet, it has a sense of fun, too, and is casual, a kind of teen-speak for adults. National traits draw people into a closely knit society and provide them with an identity. I realise with a jolt that it would be nice to belong once again to the world I had left behind. I must remember to retrieve the manner of speech of my ancestors when I arrive in Singapore. People used to denounce those who were educated in the West as *chiak kantang*, i.e. Eat Potatoes in Hokkien; or *Mat Salleh*, the euphemism for European, in Malay. For Peter's sake as well as my own, I must be neither. The smell of coffee brewing and food being heated up have got my digestive juices flowing and I'm aware that I'm really hungry. Besides, we did not eat when we boarded the plane because we went to the Indian in Godalming before catching our flight. The taste of bacon is already in my mouth; I'm imagining a couple of rashers nicely grilled, served with plum tomatoes and a fried egg with its center soft, becoming runny when I bite into it. It was Hugh who introduced me to bacon and plum tomatoes; I never had them before we met. He loved the way the soft tomatoes squished and squashed in his mouth. And he was very particular about the way his bacon was fried or grilled and could not bear the crispy and hard version so favoured by the Americans. He had a way of wiping his mouth delicately with the tip of his napkin, which, in the beginning I saw as refined, and later, as his fastidious manner. He was such a mess of contradictions that I suspected he himself did not know who he was or what he wanted to be.

"You know, darling, I wish you wouldn't eat with your fingers. It looks so gross," he used to say. "I know you're not gross but other people might think so; that's just as bad, isn't it?"

I wanted to say that food tasted so much better with my fingers, giving off no metallic aftertaste as forks and knives did. I wanted to say that my fingers touching my lips in the act of eating was as sensuous as a lover's kiss, but I did not. I desperately wanted him to think me fine. That was when I trained myself to see me as he saw me, picking up the grains of rice with my fingers, curry smudging them yellow, my body involved with my eating, moving toward the food like an eager child for its mother's milk, not rigid like his straight back, his distance from his plate. It was years later that Robert freed me from Hugh's tyranny. He was unafraid to be himself and just as unafraid to let me be who I was. Everything about Robert spoke of quiet confidence—the way he dressed, the way he spoke, easy in his body and his attitudes. Though his hair was greying, curling softly at the edges, he was unmindful of it, unmindful, too, of the strictures of his age, and behaved as if he was still young, moved with unbridled energy. He was so neat and so compact. Under six feet, he was just a head taller than myself which made us a perfect fit in bed.

"You're insatiable," he said many times. "My ever-ready battery."

It was true that I couldn't get enough of him. Never will, now. Perhaps that is what love is; it is a certain kind of hunger which cannot be totally assuaged. You want so much of the loved one, not just physically but mentally and emotionally. Every single move that your loved one makes—every look, every word he utters, every trait—is fodder for your hungry soul. I'm starving now, already missing the scrape of Robert's afternoon chin against my cheek, the texture of his broad hands as he clasped mine, the firmness of his upper arms, the rigid length of his thighs. These are the small tidbits that have made up my everyday life, but they're gone. But, of course, there's Peter now, but he's a different kind of cuisine.

"Madam?" The voice is less patient.

How far had my mind drifted? Isn't it amazing how a single word can be a boat to carry thoughts oceans away? No wonder the Buddhists talk about the Monkey Mind, always busy with chatter, no space between thoughts. It seems to me that I was gone a while. Thankfully, inner time is not the same as outer time for otherwise the woman standing there waiting for my order would be more exasperated.

"Bacon and eggs, please," I say.

The stewardess bends down toward the trolley to retrieve a tray which she then places on my table. When I lift the aluminum foil from my tray, the steam escapes with a puff from the hot food, letting out the smell of bacon.

"And what about you, sir?"

"De same," he says.

And I don't know why his choice should give me so much pleasure.

"Ladies and gentlemen, we are now about to make our descent into Changi International Airport."

"Did she say Changi Airport?"

"Yes," Peter says.

"Changi? The last time I was in Singapore, I came in and left from Paya lebar Airport."

"Dat was *definitely* de days wen policemen wore shorts."

"Oh, no. Singapore was no longer a colony then. We were already independent. Changi was where we used to picnic when we were children. We had not much money, you know, and Grandmother took in the neighbour's washings so that I could go to school. So when the neighbours have their picnic at Changi, they used to take me along."

"Nice neighbours."

"The *kampong* was like that. People were so friendly. Doors were never shut in the day. Our *kampong* was not on stilts, but the ones in Changi were with steps leading to the sea. The seawater used to rush under the attap huts. It fascinated me."

"It would be nice to see dose type of houses. I'm sure Diana and Harry would be thrilled. Must take them to de older parts of Malaysia or Indonesia sometime to see dem."

"Do they know that it was this stretch of beach that had attracted the Indonesian prince so many centuries ago?"

"Children in school don't do much of local history."

"That's a shame. The story is in the *Sejarah Melayu*, or Malay Annals. I'll tell them the white sand had sparkled like gold in the sunshine, enticing the prince to pay a visit, thus changing the destiny of the small fishing village of Temasik. When he and his courtiers landed, the Prince caught sight of a magnificent animal with a mane of red hair and asked what it was. "It's a *singa*, my Lord. A Lion." And so he was reputed to say, "I shall call this island *Singa Pura*. Lion City. It will be a great city one day." Do you think the kids will be interested?"

"Founders of countries forget dat de country dey were supposed to discover already had a name and its own residents. De likes of Columbus, Sir Stamford Raffles, claiming countries for their Queen or King ignore de true ownership of de land. How can countries be found wen dey had never been lost?"

There is a new edge to Peter's voice. I must say I never thought about it like that. He is quite clever, my son. But I can't claim any credit for it.

The picnics were one of the times I can clearly remember as being happy in my childhood. We children scuttled up and down the beach in total recklessness, not once pausing to regard the beach as an ancient historical site, for no plaque, bronze, wood or stone marked the landing. I loved the sound of the sea as it rolled into shore. I saw the waves like travelers fortunate enough to touch foreign soils. What would they say if they could speak? Were there hidden words in their roar as they rushed over rocks and sands? Were they trying to convey what they saw in faraway lands? At Changi, when they rushed into shore with full force, they reached the coconut palms, washing their feet and the coconut palms in turn leant toward the water margin as if welcoming home the errant travelers.

"Pakchik, Pakchik," I addressed the Malay neighbour. "Do trees feel thirst?"

"All living things have a spirit like you and I, child. So give thanks when they give you their fruits or when they have to die for you."

Pakchik Awang always talked funny. He was a small man and his head looked the size of a *sepak raga*, yet it was filled with such huge wisdom that people came from near and far to ask his advice. He lived on his own so whenever there was a picnic, the neighbours who organised the picnic would ask him along as he loved the sight of the sea. Then everybody would get onto the back of a small lorry, planks stretched across the width serving as seats for the multitude of village folks laden with their pots and pots of food and things for the picnic. We'd drive from our *kampung* to Changi, singing P. Ramlee or Saloma's songs and reciting *pantuns*, talking and laughing. I laughed with all the other village children and joined in their songs, the only non-Malay in the group. But being a Peranakan or Straits Chinese, I spoke their language well and they saw me as their kind.

"Mak, please. Come with us-*lah*? We can do the ironing later."

"No, So much-much to do. I won't be able to catch up."

"I'll help you, Mak. Just come out and enjoy yourself-*lah*."

"No, you go enjoy yourself. I'm too busy."

And I would be torn with guilt for wanting to go and leaving my mother behind with so much work to do. But if my mother had her way, there would be no pleasures at all in my life, just work and more work. My mother was beautiful, but she wouldn't do anything to attract any man that might give us a better home or more food. Once I said to her, "Why do you have to work and work?"

"What for work? For you-*lah!* So you can go to school, get proper job and don't end up like me."

You have a responsibility to succeed when someone had sacrificed so much to give you a head start. You are benefitting from someone's labour and sweat and you have to prove that it was not all for nothing.

I am a failure. In more ways than one. If I dwell upon this thought, the weight of it would crush my spirit...make it hard to go on. Your success and failure is not just your opinion; it is the image reflected by the mirror of those around you, especially those of your parents, your teachers and your spouse. You are stupid, someone might say, or you are worthless. And the words have a capacity to stick to your psyche like glue and you cannot detach them from yourself. You need to have an exceptional belief in yourself to smash reflections in the mirrors projected by others.

At Changi, the women spread out the straw mats and placed the heavy pots on their corners to prevent the seabreeze from lifting them away. I was always hungry but tried not to appear too greedy or curious; but I could smell the chicken curry in the pots, the peanut satay sauce for the hundreds and hundreds of sticks of satay, the *mee goreng* in the enamel basin. Such a wealth of food. Though I participated in the games on the beach, playing *teng-teng* or *chaptay*, one ear was always cocked to hear Mak Chik announce that it was time to eat.

"Have you ever played *chaptay*?" I ask Peter.

"No. What's dat?"

"I'll show you if they still sell them. We used to cut small, thin circles from rubber sheets or old tires and stick chicken feathers on top and kick them The person who manages to keep it aloft longest wins. I must teach the children. It was so much fun. Did you know that before we had Paya Lebar Airport, we had Kallang Airport."

"Oh, yes. I've hard about that." Peter looks really interested.

"Yes, the airport had a dusty apron and a wooden platform, which served as waving gallery."

"Wow! So advanced as dat?""

How kind the villagers were to me. They had taken pity on a fatherless girl and had taken me with them to watch the planes. I remember what a thrill it was to see the B.O.A.C. plane emerge from the clouds and skim over the tops of the coconut trees. Then, its wheels appearing from under its body like a giant bird about to land and as they touched the ground, it kicked up a flurry of dust which scattered onto clothes and into faces. The European women on the ground clutched their wide-brim hats and hold down their flowing skirts in the vortex of dust and wind created by the landing. When the stepladder had been wheeled to the plane, more women in beautiful clothes appeared with men in light-coloured suits. They looked like people fresh from the pages of fashion—idols and dreams of the masses. I watched with wonder as some of the men hugged their wives in public and even kissed them on the mouths.

"When I grow up," I had said, "I want someone who is unashamed to hug and kiss me in public."

And the other children mocked me. It was so utterly risqué.

Yes, I did find that someone. First Hugh, then Robert. But both have deserted me, leaving me to fend for myself. Am I ever worthy of love? *Robert, oh, Robert. Why did you have to go?*

With a start, I realise that I look somewhat old-fashioned in my tailored two-piece cream suit. People in the aeroplane do not dress like the passengers I remembered. There's a lack of elegance these days, people opting for comfort in elasticised trousers, track suits, kaftans and ugly trainers. Even those traveling in business and first-class slop about in easy wear and easy care; not the silks and satins of yesteryears, no string of long pearls, no wide-brimmed hats, no stockings and stilettos or well-polished brogues. The image of modern-day society is like products from a conveyor belt.

Like an eagle landing, the wheels of the aeroplane claw at the tarmac before coming to a gentle cruising speed. In days of yore, passengers applauded upon landing in appreciation of the pilot's skill and the acknowledgment of potential human error. There is no applause for automation now; modern folks are so blasé about the advances of technology. In my youth, I, like other village children, ran outdoors in excitement if a motor car came down the dirt road. We stood behind fences to look through the windows of the rich when the first black-and-white television program was screened; jumped with joy when electric lights were installed. In a way, when you have less, every small thing is a gift that is treasured; when you have everything, you don't appreciate your largess.

"Welcome to Changi International Airport," the female cabin attendant announces. "Please be aware dat de possession of narcotic drugs is illegal in Singapore and is punishable by hanging."

I wonder how many of the passengers actually take note of this warning. The stewardess who made the announcement kept her voice even and had not put any particular emphasis on the mandate just as if she was giving information about the outside temperature or something equally unshattering. The fact that there is no sudden surge of exclamations or excitable comments indicate that the announcement must have passed over the heads of many of the passengers. As soon as the plane pulls in to the gate, people unsnap the buckles of their seatbelts. Like the teeth that Jason had strewn on the ground, people spring up from their seats to open the overhead lockers. It is evident that the fourteen-hour flight has been a strain for most people and they are now eager to disembark. September 11 and the Gulf War have caused another hour to be added to flight time as the pilot has to avoid the airspace above the war zone. Peter collects my things and hands them down to me. Up until now, I had been quite relaxed. But now I worry if his family is going to accept me, be comfortable with me in their home. Perhaps I should stay in a hotel until they got used to me. How am I going to cope with their questions about my past, about Hugh and Robert and about leaving Peter behind?

Leaving the plane, I'm surprised how bright and spacious the airport terminal is, with an abundance of orchid sprays in all its variety—mauve, purple, white, pink and even yellow. 'Round every corner, there are beautifully appointed shops lining the concourse, walls of flowing water in simulated waterfalls, showers and beds for those in transit, free-city tours.

"My goodness me, this is a beautiful airport."

"Cleanest in de world," Peter says proudly. "Just like de whole country."

Coming down the escalator to Immigration, Peter walks ahead to the channel for citizens whilst I take the foreign visitors' channel. It gives me an odd feeling of alienation from him, as though our belonging to each other was not real. The immigration officer stamps "three months" on my passport. No matter what takes place here in Singapore, the issues that will be resolved, the stamp tells me that Singapore is not home now, has not been for a long while now. This fact pains me now, when I'm so in need of one. But, of course, I have to return to England to sort out unfinished business, lay the matter of Robert to eventual rest, decide what to do about the house and whether or not to move. Has Peter thought about all this when he came to collect me? There is an urgency in his steps now as he moves towards his own world, a world that had been closed to me. All due to my own stupid fault. I had given up my son, my country and all that I know for love. Had Hugh ever considered the enormity of my sacrifice? Was I so blinded that I could not see that no man could be worth that much? If I were able to visit the young woman who was myself, I would give her sacks of patience and jewels of perception. No one teaches more than living does. But the problem is you get pushed on to the next grade even if you've not passed any exams. Wisdom is not the prerogative of the old. In fact, the longer I live, the more I learn just how unwise I am. All I ask right now is that I should have the clarity to know how to behave correctly.

The baggage collection area is impressive. It is the only international airport I know that gives such an open feeling, with the glass walls affording a view of the people waiting outside, people anxious for the return of their loved ones, scanning faces as they come down the stairs to collect the trolleys and going to the designated carousel. Some of the children are waving frantically, some are hopping up and down excitedly, and others press their noses into the glass walls. Peter waves to someone, but there are so many who waved back that I cannot ascertain who he is waving to. I suffer a quick pang of jealously for I'm suddenly reminded that beyond the glass walls lies his life which has been separate from mine. I dare not speak in case my voice betrays my emotion. And he does not speak either, perhaps suddenly aware of the enormity of what he has done, bringing his past to face his present. We focus on the conveyer belt moving round and round piled up with bags and suitcases, testaments of people running away from each other or to each other. Lonely people are the ones who have no one to go to or to come home to. As my cases come 'round, I grab at the handles and Peter helps me to load them onto the trolley. After all our luggage has been rescued, Peter pushes the trolley and walks ahead. I follow behind tentatively, nervous now of the response I might receive. After all, I was the one who had left. How will I be viewed? Moments later, we glide past Customs and out through the automatic doors of the glass walls. I'm on uncharted territory now. Whatever has to be, has to be. There is no evading my past anymore. It's all up to my daughter-in-law now. Some mothers do not realise how instrumental daughters-in-law can be to make or break their relationship with their sons. In my case, it is doubly so. Everything depends on Margaret. Peter stops just beyond the crowd standing by the railings who are still waiting for their expected visitors. Peter approaches a young woman who is trying to persuade a little boy to come out from behind her ankle-length skirt.

"Hi," Peter says to the young woman, as though they have just been parted for the day. He resumes possession of her with his eyes but not through his action.

"Good flight or not?" She asks with a certain coyness in her voice that suggests their relationship. Her body leans toward his in familiarity, but they do not hug.

At Asian airports, you don't see as many an effusive public display of affection as you might do at Western airports. I remind myself that in this country, people regard a certain manner of behaviour as suitable only for the bedroom. The way Robert and I had gone on in public would be frowned on here, especially at our age, kissing mouth-to-mouth every time we meet whether in public or private, whether alone or surrounded by people. He couldn't walk by my side without taking my hand in his or brushing his arm against me, as if he must let me know how much I was desired and loved. In his presence, I had felt like fertile, moist ground, poised to yield a rich crop; without him, I suffer a famine, my body abandoned, parched and cracked, incapable of seeding.

"Okay-*lah*," says Peter in response to the young woman's query. He seems a little brusque only because he is keen to get over the awkwardness of the introduction. Turning to me, he presents his family with a show of his hand. "Dis is Margaret and Harry. Diana is at morning school."

The little boy emerges from behind his mother's skirt and asks, "Daddy, did you bring home any chewing gum?"

"Yes, make sure no one sees it." Peter hands him a pack, then turning to me, he says, "Chewing gum is banned here. Someone stuck it in the doors of the MRT and they jammed. So the whole country has to go without."

I smile as warmly a manner as I hope Margaret would perceive it and consider giving her a kiss but instead extend my hand. Margaret, who, I understand, is the same age as Peter, has a pleasant moon-shaped face and wears a huge smile. Since most Asian girls her age are slim, it comes as quite a surprise that she is on the heavy side; her arms extending out from her sleeveless blouse are rather podgy and her hips wide. But she has a very pleasant demeanour. She takes my hand.

"It's nice to meet you at last. I've heard so much about you from Peter."

"Girlie," Peter says to her. "Dis is my mudder."

As I have not heard him refer to me as his mother for so many years, his acknowledgment of me acts like a current of air to lift me off my feet.

4

As I reenter the atmosphere of Singapore, I shudder. At the point of entry, every single pore of my being flares with friction and I feel myself hurtling toward the ocean of my past which is waiting to engulf me. There is no escaping it now. Nowhere to hide. It is ironic that I should do this alone and not with Robert, when he had been the one to encourage me to make the contact and reestablish old ties. But then our love was newly found and I thought to revel in its security and peace rather than expose it to pressures which could break it. How foolish I have been and how selfish. I must make amends—it's the only way to unburden myself of the past and build a new present.

"Dis is the ECP. East Coast Parkway," Margaret says brightly, turning 'round briefly from her driver's seat to indicate that she's addressing me. "It takes you all de way into town, you know. During peak hours-*huh*, de ECP nearer town operates on EPS, an Electronic Pricing System. You see-*huh*, you got dis device that's fitted in your car courtesy of de government. When you pass a gantry, it automatically deducts de appropriate amount of money from de card dat is slot into de device. Of course, your card must be updated so dat it has to have enough credit-*lah*. Dis way, de government can control de volume of traffic going into de CBD, de Central Business District. By de way, can you see dose pots of bougainvillea dere at de central reservation or not? Dey are movable so dat if a plane needs to make an emergency landing, dis part of de expressway can be turned into a runway. Clever-*huh?*"

"The EPS is similar to your Congestion charge in London," Peter clarifies. "But it's done electronically."

ECP, EPS, CBD. Initials and jargons unify a group. They make little sense to the outsider, unless enlightened. Margaret speaks her words like the rat-tat-tat of a gun. She seems eager to inform, anxious to promote the efficiency and success of Singapore, eager to cement the gaping silence that tends to yawn between strangers. Is she just naturally talkative or is she nervous? After all, it is not every day that a mother-in-law descends from out of the blue, and particularly one with such a checkered past. Give her her due. Margaret is behaving impeccably. No awkward questions asked at the moment.

"Margaret is a conference organiser at *Temasik Hotel*," Peter says with pride.

"That sounds like a very responsible position."

"Oh, yes. She's very highly paid."

"No-*lah*," Margaret demurs. "I love working in a hotel. It's so exciting. It's like a small city dat never sleeps. And we executives get to eat in de Coffee House and restaurants for free."

I guess that probably accounts for her figure. At my polite entreaty, Margaret gives a blow-by-blow account of her work, sometimes gesticulating and lifting one hand off the steering wheel. Next to me, Harry sits in his car-seat and eyes me shyly. To see that little boy looking so much like the little boy I had lost causes my heart to contract. He sits in the front passenger seat, a man now, but it is the little boy he was that I have to address so that I can remove the shards caused by my betrayal.

"Does Harry speak English?"

"Oh, yes. All kids do in Singapore, nowadays. Harry, tell Grandma about your plane collection. He loves engines and aeroplanes. He's only five but he's able to tell you lots about de aeroplane's specifications."

Grandma. A simple word. An everyday word. Yet it is like rain on parched land. When you've deprived yourself of a family, every single recognition which returns you to the flock counts. Bless her. Marageret *is* generous. I want to hug the child to me and smother him in kisses, but I'm aware that he looks upon me as a stranger and I do not want to frighten him.

"Oh, that reminds me. Peter told me about Harry's hobby."

I rummage in my hand-carry and bring out a small model.

"A Concorde! Tank you."

"Tank you, Grandma." Margaret corrects him.

"Tank you, Grandma."

"You're welcome, *sayang*. I've got another present for you when we get home. A *Harry Potter* present."

Peter's head turned around when I said the Malay endearment. It was what I used to call him. The door to the past has slid open.

"There's a wonderful airshow near my place every year. It's in a place called Farnborough. I'll take you there someday."

"Did you hear dat, Mummy? Grandma will take me to an air show!"

Harry returns his attention to the plane. Harry is exactly the same age as Peter had been when I left. I close my eyes, remembering, and the pain of that parting makes me bleed afresh. How many hundreds of times had that one image of Peter's face been flashed on my mind screen over the years? The sight of his stricken face was like a Malay *kris* that cock-screwed itself into my heart—not a straight clean blade but one that twists and turns, making the wound irreparable. If I had foreseen that look, would it have given me the strength to remain with Victor for my son's sake? If human beings can snatch the future to see the possible consequences of a particular action, can we swerve to change direction? Or are our paths mapped out for us before we are born?

It happened on a day that has become both history and living nightmare for me, forever indelible, written in the ink of my son's suffering. I can still hear his little-boy voice, crying out in anguish, his eyes opened in horror. Victor had pinned him back with his arms. Peter was kicking and flailing his arms, trying to free himself from his father as I lunged for my little boy outside Mui Yoke's house.

"Mummy! Mummy!" he cried.

"Please, let me see him."

"Get out of here, you bitch! And take dat English bastard with you." Victor spat. "Don't ever bring him here again. I'll kill him. I told you before, if you leave me, you shall never have my son. He's mine. I'll make sure dat the courts will find you an unsuitable mother."

Even in his aggression, Victor possessed a womanish pout which seemed to somehow emasculate him. The well-washed T-shirt that he liked to wear at home was stretched short of his belly to expose an overripe melon of flesh. He was wearing a pair of Bermudas that displayed his meaty calves which sprouted with short dark hair. Everything about him was familiar...overfamiliar. The memory of him, the look of him, repulsed me. I had to escape him. For years, I had allowed him to own my body, but I couldn't anymore. How could I have lain so passively under all that flab, his belly pressing into mine, an acreage of loose flesh enveloping my body like some ectoplasmic creature? And then, that careless penetration that took no heed of my readiness nor need, a few spasmodic jerks as if he was relieving himself - and I, merely a receptacle. But it was not just his body that suffocated me. There was something else. He was never mine nor his own. His mother's shadow darkened his spirit and the love-hate relationship between mother and son created a roller coaster of moods in Victor. Do mothers know how much their nurturing or lack of determines how their children relate with their future partners? What about me? What about what I have done to Peter? Would his treatment of Margaret be my fault?

Mui Yoke's mothering love was a coiled snake that strangled his manhood. He was her first-born and she could never let him go. Wife to an aging Chinese businessman twenty years older than herself, who reclined on the settee in the evenings, plucking at the sparse hairs on his chin whilst watching TV, Mui Yoke put all her energies into raising her child. As long as he needed her, she was content. She was mother-perfect, a slave to his daily comforts. She made sure he did not have to exert himself to get a drink, his food was placed in front of him, his clothes washed and laundered, his aching muscles massaged. If he was hot, she'd put on the fan. If he was cold, she'd get a blanket to cover him. This was even after he was married and her own husband was long buried.

"At your home, your wife makes you wash your own plates. See how your mother loves you-*huh*? She does everything for you-*wat*."

And so he stood that day, letting Mui Yoke defend him against his adulterous wife. He stood there looking like a whipped dog as though he was guiltless and blameless. This public denial was what he needed to tip the scales so that from then on, he convinced himself that I was entirely to blame. For God-fearing Catholics like his family, I had committed a sin of the highest order. A mortal sin. It gave him justification for all his future actions against me to press the suit in court to deny me access to our son.

"Look! Look at this cheap little whore," Mui Yoke called out in Cantonese to her neighbours along the street of the smart housing estate. People cocked their heads in surprise at the venom in her voice. After all, Mui Yoke was known for her self-effacing manner and her piety. Every morning, after she had hung the washings outdoors in the back garden, she would trudge heavily up the hill to *St. Augustine's*, dip her fingers in the holy water to cross herself, find herself a pew and bow her head in abject obeisance. During Lent, her clothes would hang from her as she starved herself for Her Lord. Every Friday during Lent, she wouldn't cook meat nor eat meat. Just because the Church said so. She never questioned why it was all right at other times of the week or year. If the Church said so, it must be correct and therefore adhered to it. On Maundy Thursdays, she would join a busload of devout worshipers as they trudged through every single church on the island to show Christ that there were those who would stay awake in prayer and not sleep whilst he was in the Garden of Gethsemane. On Good Fridays, she would reflect the *Stations of The Cross* on her knees, dragging herself forward across *St. Augustine's* mosaic floor to move from one station to the other, ignoring her bruised and bleeding knees, ignoring Father Joachim's reminder that going around the *Stations of The Cross* was meant to be a symbolic sharing of Christ's journey to Golgotha, not an act of self-flagellation. She was a member of the *Legion Of Mary, St. Vincent de Paul, etc. etc.* When her hands are not busy with housework or mending the altar cloth or the priests' robes for Mass, they would be clutching the rosary, her fingers kneading each beads in nervous twitch, her eyes roaming the street, watching the goings-on of the neighbours, whilst her mouth moves in ceaseless prayer. That day, she called attention to herself by deriding me. Curious heads poked out over gates and fences. "A slut! She opened her legs for an *ang moh*. For some cheap White Trash!"

"Enough, Mother!"

"Mummy! Mummy!"

"Peter, Peter!"

Perhaps it was wrong to have come with Hugh who must fuel Victor's anger all the more. Yet, I knew Victor, knew that in his weakness, he was not opposed to exercising his muscular strength. Hugh looked out of place in the environment, tall and pale, in a street that only saw Europeans during the years when the British troops had been housed in the area. He was flushed with love then, and wanted to rise to my defense, and he made to go toward Victor, but I stopped him. What was the point? I never asked to be right for falling in love, just the right to see my little boy. In all that darkness, there was just one glimmer of light, I knew that Victor was a dedicated father and that Mui Yoke would be an indulgent grandmother. My son would have a stable home and would not be ill-treated. I was grateful that in each in his own way, neither Peter not Hugh understood Mui Yoke's vulgarity. Let it be *my* own shame, a hot brand on my heart.

The wrought-iron gates slammed in our faces, then the door. There was a finality to that sound. A guillotine that axed my son from me. The drapes were pulled across the windows and still I stood there, my arms through the railings of the gate, beckoning for my son, calling for him, hungering for a glimpse of my little boy. How could I have known that would be the last time I would hear him call me, *Mummy*. A simple word. An everyday word. Yet, from that day on, the word was not mine to own. And every time I heard it uttered by some other child, it drew blood in my heart. The neighbours clucked and clicked their tongues with disdain, shook their heads and eventually returned to their own affairs. And still, I stood there, hoping against hope that either Victor or Mui Yoke would relent. Until Hugh gently pried my fingers off their tight hold and said, "Come on, Darling. Let's go. We'll get the lawyers to sort it out."

"Linda." I called my best friend.

Linda Quek and I were in the same 1968 batch of newly recruited nurses at nursing school at Outram Road General Hospital. We became close and when we graduated and were sent to different hospitals, we still met up regularly. She got married before me and had a little girl. When Peter was born, her husband, Alfred Goh, became godfather.

"Will you talk to Alfred for me? Ask him to make Victor see reason."

"Victor has already called me," she said coldly. "Do you tink dis is a way for you to behave? Victor is a successful man and has provided for you. Why are you doing dis to him?"

"Linda! You know why."

"You should forgive and forget. Tink of your son."

"Of all people, Linda, I had expected you to understand."

"Why sully yourself with a white man. All dese Ang-mos tink dat Oriental girls are for de taking, like bar girls dat dey can pay. Dey come to de east and pick girls who dey tink will be complaint and submissive, not like deir own kind. Why do you tink dier own women don't want dem? Soon as he is tired of you, he will find himself another new toy. If he can't find one in Singapore, he can find a dozen in Bangkok. Is dat wat you want? Is it worth giving up your son for a man like dat?"

"We're in love," I said defensively.

But Linda was right, wasn't she?

"Dat's the Singapore Expo," Margaret says, pointing to a huge parking lot and series of buildings. "It has taken over from de World Trade Center as an exhibition and conference center. Did you know dat Singapore is now an international convention destination? I'm thinking of working for Singapore Expo so that I get a chance to organise bigger exhibitions and conferences."

I try to be polite and remain awake to listen to Margaret. But the resurgence of the memory of that day I lost Peter makes me feel heavy and weary. Margaret's voice is slowly disappearing amongst a cacophony of sounds that are rising in my ears—distant bells, sharp whistles, cymbals, the chirping of cicadas. Despite the air-conditioning in the car, I feel the humid heat wrapping around me like a tight blanket and I'm struggling to get my breath. Something verging on despair fills my spirit and my body sags with its weight and I sink back into the seat, letting the rhythm of the car take me.

I am waiting for Robert to come home. I feel as if he has been gone for some time and should have been back a long time ago. I walk about the house in a restive state picking up things and putting them down, unable to concentrate. Eventually I rush out of the house to look for him. But there's something amiss here. I am not in England. This is not our front garden in England. I am in the sandy backyard in the kampung where I grew up, a shanty attap village at the foot of the hill where Victor used to park his car when he came to pick me up.

Please, please. Don't let me be still married to Victor. Or Hugh. I am married to Robert. It's Robert I am waiting for. Robert, Robert! Where are you?

A firm hand is shaking my shoulder gently trying to rouse me. A man's hand.

"Robert?" Did I whisper his name?

"We're here," Peter says. "You can rest in your room-*lah*."

Your room. He has kept a space for me in his heart and in his home. I'm humbled by his and Margaret's gift. I don't deserve it.

"I'm so tired. I wish I was not so tired."

"You're not used to de flight. Or it could be de after-effects of de drugs. Veronica said dey had sedated you heavily. I'll email her to tell her we've arrived. Wen you wake up, you can call her. Dere's nothing you need to do here-*wat*, so you can just sleep."

"Ya-*lah*, sleep all you want," Margaret chips in.

She has a girlish cheeriness in her voice. I'm glad that Peter has found himself a sweet girl. I feel indebted to this girl who has loved and cared for Peter, probably repairing the damage I have done. I had difficulty shaking off the feeling of exhaustion. I had applied myself to take Peter shopping in Guildford, though now it feels as if all my energy has been spent. Peter is right; it must be the long flight or the drugs. I've not recovered the self I was; too much has happened to make me doubt myself. The thought that I will no longer see Robert nor be in his arms again makes me feel weak and shaky, and a little bit teary. Middle-aged women should not act like besotted teenagers. I allow myself to be led from the car, up in a lift and into the apartment which is a duplex on two floors; *maisonette* it's called here. I'm half-aware of it being spacious and airy, of an Indonesian maid greeting us. Everything is so strange, so grand from when I was last in Singapore. The en suite room they have allocated me is gracious and cool, the hum of the air-conditioning unit shutting out outside noise. Margaret buzzes around, pulling curtains across the windows to shield me from the harsh sunlight, showing me how the shower works, arranging my toiletries along the vanity unit by the bathroom sink. She instructs Siti, the maid, to unpack the case, is self-assured, yet proprietorial, clearly stating that this is her patch and that she's in charge. After they leave, I shower in a stupor that comes from a lack of sleep. Nothing seems real, not even myself; I am just a body moving in a space outside myself. With deep weariness, I lay myself on the bed, pulling the thin cover over me. Without Robert there beside me, the King-size bed seems huge and empty, as if I'm marooned on a desert island. Shipwrecked. Life-wrecked.

In sleep, one can cross borders, wade through the past as if it is the present, try to make right some wrongs. But in sleep, fear clutches you as much as it does in your waking moments. And just as in wakefulness, the fear is an unknown, nebulous shape and yet it has the potency to grip your innards, send you hither and thither in a frenzy of searching. I turn and toss as my mind's eye opens to the images that are projected across its inner screen. But before the sense of fear, there is that moment of exquisite joy. The continual humming of the air-conditioner translates itself into another sound in my mind, a sound that repeats itself over and over again.

Even though the sea is hidden from us by the sand dunes, I can hear the tide rushing into the shore and then the sucking sound of the fine sand as the waves draw back. There is comfort in the regularity and constancy of nature; it's like the town-crier announcing that all is well. Beyond us is Cardigan Bay, washing the coast of Northwestern Wales, and we, like nesting birds, have found a place, hidden from view, where our bodies have shaped themselves around the soft, white sand. The light sea-breeze, passing through the long marram grass, whispers its perennial ode of freedom, and I, too, have learnt to celebrate as Robert shows me how we can bare our bodies to the sun and to ourselves without fear of sanction or egocentric criticism of aging flesh and imperfect contours. Our sweat, resulting from tangled limbs propelled by lust and love, acts like glue so that the fine grains of sand stick to various bits of our bodies which have met the ground during our rolling around and grinding into each other.

"God, how I love you!" Robert says, as if his love-making is not proof enough.

I am humbled that a man can love me so. The desire in his eyes, even after his lust has been assuaged, is naked and raw. There is such power in that look, which has the effect of breathing new life into my care-worn body and afflicted spirit. Sated and content, confident of no intrusion, we sink into the cupped palms of the sand dunes and drift off into sleep.

A shadow passes over my eyes, and even though they are closed, I become aware that the thing that has come between the sun and myself, is huge. Spread-out, fluttering wings that suddenly fill me with an unnamed terror. My eyes shoot wide open, my hand instinctively reaching out for Robert's. But he is not beside me.

"Robert?" Then, "Robert!"

Under the umbrella of the giant wings, my body is suddenly robbed of heat, my nipples puckering. I sit up abruptly and fold my arms in front of my naked breasts. I am filled with dread that something has happened to Robert.

"Robert!" I cry more urgently now.

The shadow is huge and I cannot see…cannot make out what it is. It hovers between the sun and I, a shadow across the sun. I feel its menace and my skin starts to crawl. I know with a certainty that somehow it is connected with Robert's disappearance. It is then that I scream.

When I return to wakefulness, the screams are left behind in that other world. Only the terror remains, reverberating in my body like a struck gong. My heart is palpating furiously and my mouth is dry. Everything had seemed so real, so tangible, how could it have just been a dream? The anxiety about Robert still clings to me like sticky cobwebs, difficult to shake off. Instinctively, I turn toward Robert's body to seek his warmth and solidity. But he is not here. It is so much like the sensation in the dream that I feel a sense of foreboding. But I tell myself that perhaps he has only gone to the bathroom or has gone downstairs to read. Sometimes he would awake early and bring me a cup of coffee with my Sunday papers. On days when he was energetic, he even fried me some noodles. Once it was winter, he brought me breakfast, waking me up by saying, "Room service, madam." He was wearing a pinny and had a twinkle in his eye as he placed the breakfast tray on the bed, extending its legs to keep it firm and steady. As he turned from me in exaggerated posturing to show me his naked behind, I laughed aloud for he wasn't wearing anything besides the pinny. "Now for my payment," he said. "Quick. Move aside. It's cold." And he scrambled under the duvet with me, pressing his cold body to me, stealing my heat. It's amazing how much warmth another body in the bed emits, so welcoming in a cold room. It's when you're without that you begin to grasp the meaning of being alone. Yes, that's what he must be doing—preparing a surprise breakfast for me. I try to convince myself. I raise myself on my elbow to look toward the door expectantly. It will be all right in a minute. But slowly my befuddled mind clears. The door is unfamiliar and shut tight. My eyes scan the room. Nothing is familiar. No wonder. The touch of the sheet feels so sterile. It does not hold the energy of Robert's molecules—never has. That is when I realise that I'm not at home, that I'm in a bed that has not met his body nor felt the weight and fervour of our passion.

"You sleep well or not?" Margaret asks as I descend the polished wooden stairs onto the gleaming marble floor.

"Yes, thank you," I have to say. You can't wear your emotions like a garment for everyone to see; deep feelings are like lingerie—worn underneath, to be seen only by someone intimate. "The room is lovely. You really make a beautiful home. And that touch with the photograph on the bedside table is so kind. Where did you find it? I thought Victor had destroyed all the photo albums."

"Really-*huh*? Tank you-*lah*. I enjoy interior designing. Ya, sorry about de photograph, it's a bit crinkled. I couldn't iron it straight. Peter kept it all dese years. He told me about de Christmas pageant at kindergarten and how you had sewn him dat sheep's costume. Apparently, Dad, that's what I call Peter's father as my own had died. Well, he and his mother, Granny Mui Yoke, took out all the photos dat had you in dem and tore all of dem. Dis one of you and Peter was caught under a loose rattan at de bottom of de wastepaper basket and Peter found it. Come, let me show you de view. Peter says you love *chye tow kway*, so I've sent de maid out for some-*lah*. She'll buy it after picking Diana up from school. Dey should be back soon. Peter called to say he'll take us out for seafood at Ponggol. He said you liked *Chilli Crabs*."

"Peter remembers that?"

"Oh, he remembers a lot of things."

I detect a hint of something in Margaret's voice. Still groggy, I can't decipher it. Margaret leads the way to the balcony, jutting out from the apartment. A semicircular balcony, with a small bistro-type table and two chairs arranged in one corner. On a wooden staircase stand several flower pots, bright with orchids, hibiscus, roses and kumquat oranges for good luck, probably the remains of a Chinese New Year display. The view from the penthouse is, indeed, splendid. Now that the sun is going down, the atmosphere seems less harsh, the traffic noise less strident. Or perhaps it's because I'm now more rested. It is possible that we sometimes impose our feelings and moods upon a passive landscape. There are other plush condominium blocks along their same stretch of road, with their swimming pools and outdoor tennis courts, places so transformed from when I had last been here that it is almost like being in a foreign country. Beyond the ECP and the palm trees, I can see the sea though it is not an uninterrupted sea as you would find in Cornwall or Devon. Neither is it the brilliant blue of the carefully manipulated photographs of travel brochures, like the myth about an idyllic tropical isle in a tropical sea with friendly smiling faces and cheerful greetings. On my arrival at Immigration, when I had handed my passport, the immigration officer was short of being surly, not even responding to my "Good morning." Somewhere between the two probably lies reality. There is something unfortunate that even such a small stretch of water is being claimed by hulks of steel; for here, the freighters ply the international waters, which are only a mile out from shore. And beyond that, attempting to keep its own political distance is Indonesia, who receives the largess of affluent Singaporeans who go there regularly to shop or to beach resorts like Batam Island. That is, until the troubles over East Timor started and the bomb that went off in Bali.

"I don't remember Indonesia being so close before."

"Where we are now used to be de sea-*wat*. All of wat you see is built on reclaimed land. Lee Kuan Yew was marvelous-*hor*? He could even exercise a claim on land dat was from de sea."

"He was a good leader. Our generation admired him."

"Ya-*lah*. He did well for de nation. But we're not tird-world status anymore. He's not de prime minister—his son is—but he still pulls de strings. He should quit trying to control us-*lah*! We're not still kids learning to walk."

"His son is prime minister?"

"Ya. Lee Hsien Loong has just taken over from Goh Chok Tong. Everyone knew that Goh Chok Tong was only holding the reins until Hsien Loong was groomed. You know, a continuation of the Lee Dynasty."

Margaret laughs at her own political comment. When she speaks, she drops the essential 'hs' and speaks with so many end-of-sentence tag words that I'm wondering if I'm missing out on some kind of sub-text. I wonder if all young Singaporeans speak this way, like teenagers who make up their own lingo.

"So much has changed."

"Ya-*wat*," Margaret says. "Nothing stands still-*wat*. Not even de past."

Not unless you are tethered to it as I am, I thought.

5

Victor didn't destroy all the photographs. No, he did not. He had sent one back to me whilst I was still in Singapore, waiting for the decree nisi to become absolute. He had selected it with care. The photograph was one that was taken on a day of rejoicing. It had been a proud moment for me when Victor went on stage to receive his Doctorate in Engineering, an accolade for such a young man. Dr. Victor Liew. I had been so proud of him. Peter, still a toddler, was in my arms when we posed for that picture, with Victor in his graduation gown, a broad smile on his face, one hand holding the degree scroll, the other possessively around me. He was still trim then, his midriff not yet splurging from the waist-band of his trousers. In fact, Peter looked so like his father had looked as a young man that when I first set eyes on him, I was startled, thinking it was Victor come for me. Victor knew how much that photograph meant to me and that was why his deed seemed all the more treacherous. The photo encapsulated my joy—a woman with a successful husband, a lovely son. That was why he sent it back to me, altered for a purpose. If he behaved like a jilted man in the hot heat of discovery and came to thump my lover, I would understand it better. But he did not, choosing, instead, to send me the photograph. Or what was left of it. Years later when the Catholic priest in the local West Sussex village had contacted me about Victor seeking an annulment, I was reminded of that photograph and the purpose of his act.

"What's the big deal over a word? Why doesn't the Catholic Church just admit that it recognises *divorce* instead of using the word, *annulled*? How can a marriage be annulled? How can a Pope in Vatican, thousands of miles away from Singapore, have such authority to decide whose marriage was valid or invalid?" Hugh asked, when I told him about Victor wanting to marry again and needing the annulment so that he could marry his new wife in church. "How can a marriage be invalidated when there has been a child? Has Victor considered what this would mean to Peter? That his mother wasn't married in the eyes of the church? What does that make him, for crissakes? It's ridiculous—all this religious claptrap."

Hugh was still flushed in love with me then and rose to my defense quickly, the knight in shining armour. He willingly offered shoulder and handkerchief when I mourned my loss and regretted my move. But it irritated him in the end, the fact that I regretted leaving my son behind in Singapore. He saw it as an affront to himself, that I didn't value him enough to think the sacrifice worthwhile. He was an emotional person given to lightning changes of moods, but he was a kind person nonetheless.

Victor had carefully scissored his image, and even Peter's, away from the image of me in our family photograph. Vengeance required meticulous planning—a method. This was Victor's way of channeling his anger and his pain. He would not forgive me. In all probability, he would never even remember his part in driving me away; all he would focus on was my betrayal. Because I had been holding Peter in my arms, all that was left in my arms was Peter's bottom, chubby legs and part of his body. The mutilated photograph was twisted round and round Victor's wedding ring and sent back to me. It was like an act of a member of the mob, in Mario Puzo's *The Godfather*, who sent a severed head of an Arabian horse to someone who had double-crossed him.

"I'm cutting you out of my life—and my son's!" His short, terse message said.

Beware young wives of crossing your husband. There are no ends to which he would not go to make you grief in turn. But if you need to leave him, run away with your precious child. Don't do what I have done, believing that it is for the child's best. Learn from my guilt, my pain and my weakness. Most of all, learn from my mistakes.

I tread on knife's edge the day I left my son behind. No longer whole. I suffer his nightmares that must come from a mother leaving. I suffer his shame of not having a mother to belong to. I want to right the wrong, pull him into comfort in my arms. I hunger for the touch of him, his voice, the smell of him. I search his face in every child's face, watch with unbridled jealousy and agony when a young mother wipes ice cream off her child's face, ties his shoelaces, tucks in a shirt. These should be mine to do, too. But I have forfeited these things through my naivete.

"How did you meet Peter?" I ask Margaret.

A flock of *burung merpati* fly past the balcony, and a couple attempt to alight on the balcony, but Margaret shoos them away impatiently.

"Aiiyah, dese birds! Dey shit all over de place!"

I'm taken aback by Margaret's use of the word. After all, she's not an uncouth person. Then, just as quickly, I chide myself once again for being so westernized. It strikes me that the word is a direct translation from Chinese and in Chinese, it hasn't the same connotation as in English. How easy it is to misjudge a person by their language born from a different tongue.

"Oh, I met him in church. He used to go to *St. Augustine's-wat* and I belong to de choir dere."

"Oh, you sing, do you?"

"Only for fun-*lah*."

"How old were you?"

"Just before we were both twenty-one. How old were you wen you met Dad? I mean, Peter's father. Dat was wat I call Uncle Victor after Peter and I got married."

"Seventeen. He was nineteen." I pause, dragging back old memories that had long stayed buried. "Good girls weren't allowed to date in my time. We were chaperoned wherever we went."

"Do you tink dat part of de cause of your breakup was due to de fact dat you were both so young?"

"That was certainly a major factor. We were kids, really. We weren't compatible. But I think it was my fault mainly. I fell in love with a fairy tale. I wanted too much out of a marriage."

"It must have been hard to be a woman during your generation."

"Yes. We don't have the freedom you do. Certainly not for people like myself born and bred in the *kampung*. It might be different for women of wealthy families and those in the city."

What else is there to say? How do I explain to my daughter-in-law I didn't know the man I married? Also, I'm not ready to tell her about my father.

In the circumstances I grew up in, it was a relief to feed myself on torn books and comics that were thrown out by the people living in *Atas Bukit,* most of them English. I dreamed about the prince, who would come striding on his white steed to take me away from the *kampong* to live happily ever after. In the beginning, I had hoped that the prince would be my father, who would fight his dragon wife to come in search of me. My mother never did show me any photo of my father. When you have no face to picture, you invent one. I created my father from a collage of handsome men I had seen, eyes which I saw as kindly, a well-structured nose, a smile which melted my heart, a face that shone with love. There may have been other occasions, but I remembered that one incident when I thought the stranger who came into the *kampung* was, indeed, my father. The tall stranger had been asking the neighbours for Ang Huay. My heart leapt. At last he was here, my own father, a man whom I could love and who would love me and take care of me! I tracked the man's footsteps and followed the man to our little hut. He did not look as perfect as the image in my mind, but it was good enough, especially since he had come at long last to look for me. Of course that was what he was doing. I rushed up to him just as he approached Ang Huay, who was sitting on the threshold of our hut breaking off the tails from bean sprouts. I could not contain my excitement.

"Excuse me, Uncle," I cried out. "Are you my father?"

"Aiiyah!" Ang Huay scolded, raising herself in a rush and pulling me away from the man and smacking me. "*Siau* or what! How many times must I tell you that your father is dead?"

Ang Huay had told the neighbours that her husband had left her a widow with a young child. It was easy to start afresh when you were in a new country.

"So sad-*lah*," Nenek Bongkok, who was sitting just inside of the door, said. "Don't smack her-*lah*. The child just cannot accept that she has no father."

As it turned out, the man was actually a bill collector and Ang Huay owed him some money. I was miserable that day. I knew my mother was lying, that my father was not really dead, that he was somewhere up in Penang, living in luxury with his second wife and new children. I continued to harbour the hope that my father would come to look for me one day and I searched the faces of other strangers who came into our village. *Hmm, do I look like this one? Have I got his ears, his mouth? Do I walk like this one? Have I got his nose?* But as I grew older, my hope started to dim, my need to be wanted and loved by a man went unassuaged. Then when I was a teenager, I was introduced to the books of Denise Robbins and Barbara Cartland. I swapped the need for a father into romance with one of those brooding, bare-bodied, muscled heroes on the cover of their books, the kind of man who had the strength to sweep me up in his arms to carry me into the sunset. I was seventeen and wide-eyed with romance when Victor with his Johnny Weissmuller body walked into my life.

"Hi," Victor said, and my mouth went dry and my knees turned to jelly.

To be nineteen and sculpted like some Asian Adonis turned heads and won him admirers. That he should even address me was already a bonus in itself. What I didn't know was that his body was a compliment of the State, of the new Prime Minister Lee Kuan Yew's National Service training programme. You couldn't tell from looking at him then, deeply tanned and in great shape, that he wasn't really a physical person at all and that, in truth, he hated any form of exercise when not forced to do it. And it was the burgeoning economy which provided the opportunity for Victor to become successful. One of the American companies that had invested in the new nation was *Circuit Instruments*, who opened a huge manufacturing plant in Jurong. It gave Victor a job, after his NS stint, as Production Manager and sent him to California for training.

"I'm very proud of you," I said.

"When I come back, we'll get married. You'll wait for me, right? You won't go out with other boys, okay?"

It was Victor's big break for his career, but a downfall for his body. He got used to America food portions and to huge steaks. Once out of the discipline of National Service, Victor spent long hours working and when he got home, was so tired that he would eat, then go straight to bed. Weekends, he relaxed by eating out and flopping in front of the television. Each photograph he sent back showed a bigger Victor, taut body disappearing. If there was time-lapse photography taken of Victor's body, his rapid transformation could be likened to Lou Ferrigno in the transformation scene in *The Incredible Hulk*. Only in Victor's case, when his shirt started to split and the buttons went flying, it wasn't muscles that bulged, but girdles of fat growing and splurging from his once-impressive, taut frame. But even his soft yielding flesh wasn't the main cause of my disillusionment. There were other reasons.

I look at Margaret now to see if there are any tell-tale signs.

"What are you looking at?" Margaret asks, catching my scrutiny.

"You. You are very pretty," I say hastily though this was not itself untrue. "Peter made a wise choice. May I see your wedding album? I'm sad that I missed the event."

"I think Dad would not have attended if you did. Peter would have liked you dere; he was very sad dat you were not present at our wedding or at the children's births. We didn't know ware you were den. If Dad had not had his attack of conscience on his death bed, we probably still wouldn't know how to find you."

"So Peter had not forgotten me?"

"No, never. You were always close to his mind. He suffers so much on Mother's Day and dat sort of thing. He told me once dat wen he was in primary school and de teacher asked de kids to do a Mother's Day card, he was heartbroken."

"I have so much to be blamed." I could hardly say the words for the stones in my chest. What have I done?

"Don't be too hard on yourself. It was circumstances dat has caused de situation. I know wat Dad could be like; he was always so opinionated. And, of course, Granny Mui Yoke always over-*manja* him. She tried, too, with Peter, but I put my foot down. If women *manja* sons and grandsons too much, dey will be spoilt and dey will behave like dat wen dey get married and expect deir wives to serve dem hand-and-foot. I make sure dat Harry has de right attitude toward women."

"You're such an understanding person! Peter's guardian angel must have guided him to you."

"It has not always been easy," she says, her voice trembling for a few seconds, then she gets up abruptly. "I'll go and get the albums. We captured de kids on video too, so you have lots to watch."

My heart stumbles. Is she trying to tell me something? Yet, her body language is forbidding me to enquire. I feel a little sad. You never know if sons automatically inherit their father's genetic propensity to things. I used to think that a man with a compulsion of using their fists belonged to the category of drunks, labourers and the uneducated. Lots of people still believe this. But this is a fallacious belief. I, like many women with a similar experience, couldn't and didn't wash my dirty linen in public in such matters. It was my own private shame, and I blamed myself. It is worse when your husband is supposed to be a pillar of society, an educated man, a successful businessman, revered by many. But a woman who has been through such experiences can recognise another woman's attempts at camouflage, the strings of ingenious excuses invented for a limp—bruises on the face, a cut lip, a broken finger, a loose tooth, a burst ear-drum: *Oh, I ran into a door! I'm so careless. I knocked myself on a table. Would you believe it, I fell out of bed? I was cleaning out the cupboards and the tin of peas fell on my head; I slipped on a bar of wet soap.*

As a newly graduated nurse, I had been assigned to a rural government clinic in heavily forested Yio Chu Kang where the predominant residents were farmers and menial workers. There, I had been shocked to learn that lots of marriages were not bedrocks of romance or love but rather were necessary evils tolerated by women who were too old to live with their parents, but who had no means of self-support away from their husbands. I learnt of the darker side of marriage and saw daily evidence of this in many of the women who came to be treated. At a time, when it was legal for a man to have more than one wife, women dare not complain lest they be relegated to a minor position, stuck with a brood of children whom they could not afford to feed and school. The Woman's Charter was late in the coming and later still to be obeyed.

"Why didn't you leave?" I had asked the women in all naivete.

Like all youngsters, things were either black or white to me then—no space for grey. How could I have known the strictures and limitations of a woman's life? How could I have understood the humiliation? Years later, when I became victim to the same situation, I blushed with embarrassment for the facile question I had asked in my youth. How indulgent those women must have been not to rebuke me for my inexperience and callousness.

"You asked me once why I left your father," Ang Huay said in grave undertones when I returned home with testimonies of Victor's strength. "Now, you know."

I had not told Mak anything, but my mother knew. The only person I confided in was Linda. My mother knew how to read the signs on my face. Of course. After all, she, too, had to cover up and make up excuses. But the evidence was mapped out, at various times, in blue-black bruises over my cheekbones and my eyelids, in that raw split of a lip, a sudden limp. It would have been an opportunity to share a mutual grief with Ang Huay, but I was still holding my head high then, too, ashamed to admit to the degradation—and to failure. Years later, I regretted that I had let the moment pass without allowing my mother to spill out her own story and unburden her load. Perhaps I didn't want to hear it of my father and wanted to preserve the image I had of him. By the time *I* was ready to share with my mother, it was too late; Mak was already dead. Never leave to tomorrow what you can make right today. You don't always get a second chance.

"Oh, here's Diana. Diana, come and meet Grandma."

The nine-year-old has a round face like her mother's with lovely dimples that she inherited from her father. Though Peter's features are carved like his father's, his dimples, which mirrored mine, softened his face considerably. In his daughter, it made for a smile that is warm and delightful. Unlike the hesitancy of her brother, Diana ran toward me with a joyous welcome. When I knelt down to her height, my granddaughter threw her arms wide open to circle my neck. *My granddaughter.* What a lovely thing to say, what a precious being to own. The slim, tender arms around my neck, the softness of a child's skin and its own special scent, open a sluice of memory. Closing my eyes, I ride on its wave, hugging the child tightly to me, breathing her in, savouring her.

*   *   *

You don't know how much you've missed something until you've found it again. It is true what they say about the heart shutting down to keep out the wolves. The trouble with locking yourself away from danger is that you cannot walk freely through the wilderness to enjoy its beauty.

"I wanna sit next to Grandma. I really like the puzzle book, Grandma. I like words. And tank you for de figurine of Princess Diana. Tank you very much."

Grandma. A simple word. An everyday word. Yet it is like rain on parched land. When you've deprived yourself of a family, every single recognition which returns you to the flock counts. Diana's welcome tells me that my son and daughter-in-law have been exceedingly generous and have not tar-brushed my reputation. They have kept the myth intact. I am a grandmother returned, missed, not one who has forsaken her family.

"She's lovely, Margaret. Both of them are. I'm grateful to you."

"Come, come. Eat the *chye tow kway-lah*. Peter will be disappointed if you don't eat up. Siti, did you ask for a lot of chilli? Grandma loves to have everything with a lot of chilli."

How does Peter remember these things? And to pass them on to Margaret as well. They had obviously discussed me. Did he in the aftermath of love, snuggle up to her and speak to her of his pain? Or did small things along the way remind him of me so that he had freed himself by voicing his thoughts? When I had been so many miles away, hadn't I noticed when my ears burned or my scalp prickled? Are there not invisible wires that connect loved ones to another? Surely, love generates a kind of electricity that penetrates matter, flows through space? Is it the same kind of connection that ties me to Robert? We've been so profoundly interfaced with each other that it is nigh impossible to separate him from me. Ah, Robert. Did I have to lose one love to recover another?

6

Even when I don't turn to look, I'm aware that he has walked into the room. It is as if there is an unappeased part of him calling for my attention. And when he comes 'round to where I'm sitting, I notice for the first time that there is a slight stoop to his shoulders which seems to harbour a soul that is cowering inside. Would that I could run my hands down his spine to make it stretch and flower back into shape, to that freedom of state of an unburdened child. It is my punishment to see him like this and to know that I was the cause of his wounding.

Why do words fail when there is so much to be said? How we humans have prided ourselves that we have gone beyond gesticulations and grunts to make ourselves understood. We have moved from pictographs and hieroglyphs to learn the sophisticated use of morphemes and phonemes to form complicated words that describe so much. And yet, more than not, when faced with an emotional issue, we return to our primeval roots, unable to utter the sounds that will right some wrong, act as balm to the hurt we inflict. Are we capable of using words only as the window-dressing for our ego?

"Unkind words are those that emerge from the self to promote our own ego," Robert once said. "Words that rise from the spirit bring joy. I learnt that from Emas. It is she who taught me how I've wasted my words. In business, I spent my words, cajoling others, persuading them—all for my own ends.

I lived a life of work truly believing that this was the best I could do for my wife. And then when she died, I thought, what a wasted life I had led. Even with all the money I had, I couldn't buy more time with her. We had planned to go on a *Paris to Beijing* rally in an old car after my retirement. But fate decreed otherwise."

Every time Robert mentioned Emas, his voice was tender, yet so full of pride. It should have been a signal to me that I could never replace Emas. But you still try don't you? A divorced wife could be replaced if you strive to be better, give your new husband what the other wife had not. But a dead wife, especially one that was much-adored? Emas' death had left a gaping wound in Robert's heart. We each of us have a burden of the past to bear. We drag it like a ball-and-chain, sometimes not seeing how it influences the tone of our present life. What is it that prevents us from picking up a hacksaw to saw the past away? It should be so easy.

"Will you be too tired to go to Ponggol dis evening? Shall we leave it to anarder day or not?"

Peter's concern strikes a spark of joy in me. I'm moved that he can be so caring to one who had, in his knowledge, betrayed him. Where does his generosity of spirit come from? After all, he had been taught to hate me. Victor's and Mui Yoke's venom oozed over the telephone lines in the years when I had tried so hard to speak to Peter. Did Peter somehow sense that I didn't really desert him? Did he know of all the letters I sent? Is it he behaving so well because nature triumphs over nurture? It is possible, though, that he is being solicitous because of my recent bereavement. To be bereaved in the old-fashioned sense of the word is to lose someone of value to you. Can you be bereaved if you lost yourself?

"No, no. I'm looking forward to it. I haven't had *Chilli Crabs* for years."

"Okay-*lah*. Let's go. Margaret! Diana, Harry!"

He walks away to gather his family for their outing. He is the proud husband and father, the man about the house. Watching him do a task I had not seen him do before, I feel the gap between the boy I knew and the man he is today—lost years of knowing. The worst thing about it is that I've only myself to blame. As he walks away, the manner in which Peter is hunching his shoulders, the angle of its slope and that slight inward caving of his chest draws another memory to me. It reminds me of a similar sadness in Robert's posture when I first saw him.

I was night sister in Intensive Care when they brought the woman in from A&E. Despite the woman's condition, I could see straightaway that the woman was Malay. It was a surprise because I had worked so long at Weyfield General, an NHS hospital, and had not seen even one. I would loved to have had the opportunity to befriend a Malay so that we could have conversed in the same language. After all, I was descended from a marriage of Chinese and Malay ancestors. There's nothing like speaking in your own cultural tongue, unabashed in its usage, totally confident. The patient and her husband had been out jogging on that summer evening when a young man in a Morgan V8 came crashing through the country lane, rounded a sharp, blind corner and slammed right into her. Even with all the injuries to the face and limbs, I could tell that the fifty-five-year-old woman with her toned muscles, was someone who exercised regularly. The surgeons had sweated in the operating theatre and did their best, suturing what could be sutured back. Yet, the life-force was already seeping out of her. Robert Baker sat by the hospital bed holding his wife's hand, knowing the awful certainty of his wife's imminent demise, his anguish written all over his body. That was when I first saw him and thought how much in love with his wife, the man was. I thought how wonderful it would be to be loved like that. Perhaps it was fated that I shared a part of a name with the woman. *Mas* is short for *Emas*, which means gold or golden in Malay; and *Kim* also means gold or golden but in Chinese, a fact that I divulged to Robert when we became friends.

"We were having a little race," he told me, long after it was all over. "Mas was in a good humour because she was a little ahead. She was determined to prove that she could outrun me. I let her. Just where the lane twisted away out of sight, she turned to give me a playful wave, laughing as she did so. She didn't even see the car or had time to scream. But I saw it all."

The horror of that sight was in his voice and in his eyes. There were many occasions when I had come upon him and he would seem to be staring out into space but his inner eye must have been looking upon that terrible scene. It was not a haunting that I could exorcise for him. Ten years younger than Robert, who was the same age as his wife had been, I had nursed him back into living. Though he was not a defeatist, he never forgave himself for not having given Mas more of himself. It was a mistake he vowed never to repeat when our friendship heightened and became love. Can love and need be distinguished from each other? Which potent force drew our bodies together in the search to assuage our tortured minds, he because of Mas' death, and I, from Hugh's betrayal? Why did Robert marry me? Except for the two of us being Asian, Emas and myself were so different— Emas was taller, slimmer, more brown, more beautiful, sporty, intelligent. I was nothing like her. Why had Robert married me?

"Love is love," Robert said. "You don't go around with a list of the characteristics of what you want in a wife and when you meet someone, compare that person to the items on the list. Love is not data-oriented. It comes from the heart."

He sounded convincing. And I wanted to believe in him.

"Here we are," Peter announces.

We have arrived at Peter's country club by the sea, across the waters from Indonesia. The private country club is a symbol of status in Singapore, one of the five Cs that had become the average Singaporean's goal: Career, Cash, Car, Condominium and Country Club. There are many clubs such as this one, offering a swimming pool, gym, spa, tennis courts, squash courts, lounge and even boating facilities. The up-market ones began their life as tennis or golf clubs, once out of reach of the average Singapore citizen in the old days when the clubs were the bastions of the English. Obviously, the colonialists didn't think it odd that local people should be banned from clubs that existed in their own country. These days, there is no colour bar but money or your position on the corporate ladder provides your passport to the use of these amenities. The prolificacy of such places testify to the wealth of the country and the rising standard of living for the middle-class Singaporean. Beyond the restaurant is a wooden boardwalk with balustrades that separate it from the sea, wooden piers for people to access their boats.

"We are here, Grandma, we are here," Diana says excitedly.

"Sh, sh, calm down. Don't tire Grandma out."

When you have lived many years without young children around you, their boisterousness does tire you. Margaret is so perceptive. Perhaps it's also because I still feel jet-laggy. And yet, it is so wonderful to be with my son and daughter-in-law and my grandchildren after all this time. The joy of this unexpected reunion far outweighs the feeling of lethargy. Besides the smell of salt in the air, there is the delicious smell of food. There is something comforting about the smell of meat roasting, fish being fried. Perhaps that is why we tend to plug our stomach with food when our heart feels empty. Smells of places have their own distinctive character and they are the things that lodge in your memory which permit you a return visit in your mind. I love England and yet, because it doesn't have the smells of my native land, it always seems that something essential is missing to make it feel like *home*. In the restaurant overlooking the sea, Peter sits back and lets his wife take charge of the ordering. There is an ease between the two of them which I find pleasant. Though they are not effusive in their display of affection, the understanding that seems to exist between them has a measure of stability and comfort. Margaret is sure of her role, neither self-effacing nor too arrogant. She wears the status of the modern young woman rather well, a professional woman as well as a devoted mother. Obviously when it comes to food, she's in charge.

Like many restaurants in Singapore, the restaurant is noisy in a welcoming way, the waiters yelling their orders loudly, people talking to one another as if they are in their own living room, restless children weaving themselves in-and-out amongst the round tables, chasing one another. There isn't the stiffness and formality of smart restaurants in the West which also has a pronounced absence of young children. Although the restaurant is air-conditioned, the glass doors are left open so that the kids can run outdoors and parents can keep watch in case they should go too near the swimming pool. Several maids, Indonesian, Filipino, Thai and Sri Lankan, are looking after their young charges whilst their wealthy employers dined. Siti has been left at home today, but she comes along when Margaret decides she needs her to take Harry off her hands. Unlike the way some employers treat their maids, apparently Siti does get the occasional outing to a food center with the family or when Margaret's out food-shopping and needs help. On Sundays, she has the day off to meet fellow maids and countrymen at Lucky Plaza. It is accepted that there's nothing amiss about having a full-time maid who works from six or seven in the morning till nine or ten at night and sometimes later, when the household has visitors or a party. The light breeze shakes the fronds of the coconut palms and brings an occasional wave of warm air into the restaurant. It is the kind of balmy evening romatcised in novels about the East. Near the front entrance is a huge fish tank where lobsters crawl lazily at its bottom; in another, large specimen of fish fight each other for space to swim in.

"See dat?" Margaret says with a kind of pride. "I've selected the *Garoupa* to be steamed. Can't get fresher than dat right?"

It is the height of hospitality to provide a meal with such freshness. Yet I flinch at the thought of that live thing being fished out and cooked for my consumption. A long time ago, it would be something I would covet to. That's when I realise I *am* changed, as I immersed myself in English culture, I had loosened my own from me. But I respond with a smile so that Margaret is not hurt by my inner reaction. There is so much to unlearn if I'm to get on in the country of my birth.

"Dat's the *Stamford Raffles* dere," Margaret says, pointing to a motor-cruiser moored to the dock, its sides gently slapped by waves when other boats pass by. "Dey do dinner cruises on board. We'll take you one evening, want or not? Can see de coast of Malaysia and Indonesia."

For a moment, I'm horrified that Margaret might have lined up an ongoing series of outings and elaborate meals throughout my stay. Though I can appreciate Margaret's kind intentions, it will all be too much too soon. A waitress arrives with an oval platter and sets it in the middle of the table. The ill-fated fish that Margaret had selected arrives lying inert in a film of soya sauce, curls of fresh coriander scattered along the length of its body, its eyes seeming to plead sightlessly. Diana and Harry, sitting on either side of me, immediately raise themselves on their seats to dive their chopsticks into the dish. There was a time when youngsters were not permitted to begin a meal until they had done their round of calling out to the elders that they are going to eat and they couldn't proceed until the eldest present had invited them to *chiak, chiak,* or eat, eat.

"It is better to be poor than to be without manners," Ang Huay had taught me.

"Oi! You two. You haven't called Grandma yet!" Margaret reprimands the children. "And you haven't said Grace."

Following on from my earlier thought, I'm proud of Margaret's admonition. As my mother would say, she's definitely well brought up.

"Sorry! Grandma, *chiak,*" the two children chorus. "Mummy, *Chiak,* Daddy, *chiak.*"

Then they make the sign of the cross hastily and mumble something inaudible. It's nice to see that the children took the discipline as a matter of fact. Too many children in England have been permitted to do what they like, some mothers expressing the opinion that children should be free to express themselves. Also, school teachers are not allowed to discipline their pupils as we had been when we were young. Parents can be penalised for over-disciplining their children, losing them to public care. The latter would be unheard of here!

"*Chiak, chiak,*" I say feeling like a matriarch for the first time.

"Trouble is, they speak Mandarin now and dey forget deir own dialect."

"...and Teochew customs," Peter adds. "Including Peranakan."

"People are so modern today. It's hard to keep up with old customs. Luckily, I'm Peranakan. Peter is only half and Granny Mui Yoke never allowed him to talk like us; he speaks Cantonese at home. Anyway, most Peranakans nowadays just follow Chinese customs. I mean in school, we kids are forced to study Mandarin because we are classed as Chinese, so not allowed to take Malay anymore. So our kids too take Mandarin and can't speak a word of Malay or our Peranakan patois," Margaret says. "Pity, huh?"

"Yes, that's a shame. The Peranakan culture is unique. There are not many of us left. It's strange to feel like a historical relic."

"Actually, dere's a revival going on now-*wat.* Young people with Peranakan heritage are bonding and trying to keep de culture alive. Dere's an exhibition in town called *Peranakan Legacy* and this is a result of deir efforts and de efforts of de Peranakan Society-*lah.*"

"Fortunately, when de government were destroying old buildings, a group stopped them from destroying de Peranakan houses on Emerald Hill."

"Since you are here, wy don't you take de opportunity to tell de children about it? De exhibition is at de Asian Civilisation Museum on Armenian Street. Perhaps we'll all go dere one of dese days."

"Aiiyah! I can't reach," Harry cries out.

"Let me scoop it for you," Margaret says.

I was unprepared for the sudden stab of jealousy as I watch the mother helping the child. Such a simple act taken for granted by every mother. An everyday act. But for one who has been denied it and has searched for it like some Holy Grail, it is a treasure to die for. Denying oneself of something only creates a stronger desire for it. That's what the Tantric Yogis say. And my own unfulfilled desire is that of a young mother, pandering to her child's needs. Nursing fulfilled part of this yearning because every patient is, in some way, your child, to be attended to, to cajole, to pamper. Taking care of Hugh too fulfilled part of this need. But it is not quite the same. Especially when you've deliberately pulled yourself away from your own child.

Young mothers, this is my gift to you. On sleepness nights when your baby keeps you awake; when you are tired at the end of each day from all the cleaning and the caring, don't grumble. Pause and delight in your baby's smile, his gentle cooing, his baby-scent. Feel how precious it is that you can put him to your breast, bathe him, or tie his shoelaces for him. Remember your child's first words, his first stumbling steps, his complete trust in you. Hold fast the memory, for he won't need you forever. You may get exasperated from exhaustion, from his constant cries and clamouring, but just think how lucky you are to have him. I can't tell you enough what it is like to be without.

The dishes are laid out on the glass lazy Susan in the middle of the table which revolves on its own base. Besides the *Garrupa,* there is *steamed king prawns, crispy baby squids, stir-fried Tou Miao, special Ponggol Mee-Goreng, beef in black bean sauce,* and, of course, the *chilli crabs.* There is crusty French bread to sop up the spicy *chilli crab* sauce and boiled rice to go with the other dishes. They have slain the fatted calf for me. It's a feast for the prodigal mother returned.

"Mum, *chiak!*" Margaret invites.

I'm momentarily stunned, too shocked to respond at first. The word is so undeserving. She's not my daughter and yet Margaret has handed me an invaluable gift. It gives me a rush of anticipation. Has Peter healed enough to embrace me with the word too? Margaret looks at Peter, and he returns the look, then nodding his head in acknowledgement to me, he says, "*Chiak-hor?*" in a questioning manner to avoid his addressing me.

"*Chiak, chiak,*" I respond in the expected way, in as gracious a manner as I can manage though something akin to pain has sliced into me. Even in one's maturity it feels instinctive to want to lash out in reaction to one's pain. But in maturity, one has hopefully learnt to hold back words that should not be spoken.

An Indian guru once said, *"You have two rows of teeth that act as a fence to stop unnecessary and hurtful words from going out of your mouth. Breathe deeply before you speak and you will speak from the Higher Self."*

Is this Higher Self a wiser part of us or somebody who hovers above us like some guardian angel? But even if you don't believe in the world of spirits, the guru is still right. There is no need to hurl your words like spears; better to keep them fenced in until you can throw them out like rose petals. Once words are let loose, there is no reining them in, their hooves can trample hearts. I am glad that I've not said anything because Peter's next act is tender and loving. With his chopsticks, he picks up a crab shell full of roe and places it on Margaret's plate, then he picks up another and puts it on my plate.

"Why did you do that?" Hugh asked when I first did the same.

"It is our way to show our hospitality."

"I respect your custom in your country. But I really don't fancy having things put on my plate, if you don't mind. Besides, I might not like what you give me."

"We usually only give what we think are the choicest pieces."

"You're in England now. Perhaps you ought to have English table manners."

The thing about Hugh was that he exuded such charm that it was hard to be cross with him for long. He was also exceedingly good-looking, his hair a rich blond with a forelock always falling down over his forehead. When he smiled, he sent creases of pleasure in waves across his cheeks creating a delightful effect. He was tall and lanky and there was a sensuality about the way his legs moved under his trousers. Victor shattered my illusions about a Barbara Cartland type hero, Hugh affirmed it. He made love with a passion and tenderness I had not experienced before. But his moods epitomised

Wordsworth's words: *As high as we have mounted in delight/In our dejection do we sink as low.* Still, it was not this that destroyed me. His betrayal was unspeakable then, but he had not meant to ruin me. He was the Peter Pan of life, oblivious to his own good looks and charm which made him popular with both men and women. There was an innocence about him which made me mother him. He was my prince and yet, at the same time, was the little boy I lost. He spoke well and had a smart accent. Excellent manners. When we met in Singapore, amongst the local people, he looked like some fabled God, with his height and his looks. Disillusioned with Victor, in more ways than one, Hugh stole my affections because he had such a way with words which made me feel special and desired.

"You're the most beautiful woman I've ever seen," he said.

He flattered me despite being inebriated, the night we met. He was rescued from a street brawl, one that had involved him and his English friends from the embassy, a teasing of one of the *girls* on Bugis Street that had turned ugly. Local people went to Bugis Street for the hawker food; foreigners, mostly men, went there for the lovely ladies of the night with their smooth skin and gorgeous figures, so lovely that you could not tell they were not really female. One of Hughs' friends had tried to go for a free feel, to test if the *girl* was really a bloke in his tight hotpants. Drink had made him bold and foolish. The *girl* screamed in a husky voice. The bouncers came to teach the rude *ang-mo* a lesson. There is something about a fight that brings out people's suppressed aggression and a cohesion that never was there before. Soon, half the stall-holders on Bugis Street, the Western customers, and the bouncers, were at war. If people were not hurt, it would have been funny, the beautiful *ladies* clattering away on their high heels; scarves that hid their Adam's apple discarded, their long hair revealed to be wigs. It was mayhem until the sirens sounded and the police came. Some were taken to the lock-up, some to the hospital where I was working. Coward that Hugh was, he held my hand whilst the doctor sutured his lip. Was it my fate to meet my husband in a hospital? The kind who needed nurturing? In all the years I had known Victor, he had not even once said that I was beautiful. Not once had he sent me flowers. Yet, after his discharge, Hugh had sent giant bouquet after giant bouquet of flowers to the hospital. Expensive, imported-from-Holland fresh flowers—roses, stephanotis, tulips. Gorgeous, blooming flowers which scented the ward and brightened faces of patients and visitors. It was easy to be seduced. I can still see the Emercency Room looking and smelling like a funeral parlour with the bouquets that arrived for me. It had made me smile. In recollection, I smile once more.

"Wat are you smiling about?" Margaret asks.

"I'm glad to be here," I say. "Happy, actually."

"Dat's nice-*lah*. We hope you'll enjoy your stay. De children have been looking forward to it, you know. Dey're so excited to hear dat you live not far from London. At de moment with *Harry Porter* being popular, magic and things exciting is associated with anything or anyone English."

"Oh, yes!" Diana pipes up hearing the mention of Harry Potter. "I would like to go to Charring Cross Station to see where Platform 9 1/2 is!"

"It's only a story. Dere's no such station," Peter says.

"Dere is! Dere is! But you have to believe in it and concentrate hard before you try to go through the wall. Otherwise you'll hit your head."

"Well, you must come to England then and we can go to Charring Cross."

"And Diagon Alley!"

"Okay, okay, Diana, calm down."

Margaret, in a gesture of true Asian hospitality, gorges the eyes of the fish and places them on my plate. I try not to flinch. The round eyes stare at me, defying me to eat them.

"De cheeks and de eyes are de best part," she says.

"Did you know that they made the *Harry Potter* film in England?" I ask my grandchildren, wondering how I can divert attention from the two eyeballs resting on my plate. I would be so lucky to have a cat or dog underneath the table.

"Of course," Diana says. "Where else will they make the film? Harry Potter is from England."

"What a clever girl you are. You know the wizard's school? They used Lacock Abbey for some of the scenes. The abbey is in the county of Wiltshire, not far from where I live."

"Wow!" Harry says.

"Can we go dere, Grandma? Can we? Can we?"

"You'll have many places to see when you come and visit me, won't you?" I continue. "They also filmed in Gloucester Cathedral and Alnwick

Castle in Northumberland which is further north than London."

"Can we go to England, Mummy?" Diana asks.

"We'll see, we'll see. Diana is an excellent reader and Harry can read far above someone his age," Margaret says with pride. "But he can't read *Harry Porter* yet. I have to read it to him or Diana does. Look, we are talking too much, your fish eyes are getting cold."

"I can read it myself," Diana affirms proudly.

"I'm very proud of you, *sayang*," I say. Unable to stave off the deed anymore, I willed myself to pick up one fish eye with my chopsticks and put it in my mouth. I'm hoping that my face looks like a picture of enjoyment.

"Both de kids have your love for books," Peter says.

It's a while before I can answer. Despite my discomfiture, I'm wonderfully surprised that he should remember this sort of thing about me. It's as if he's handing small pieces of jewels to me. His words took me back to that time in my life which I had tried so hard to forget because of the frustration, worry and confusion associated with it. But it gives me pleasure to remember how I used to crawl into Peter's bed beside him to read him to sleep—Hans Christian Andersen, Mr. Noddy, and *Aesop Fables*. I'd wait till I heard the change in his breathing as it settled into a gentle rhythm, his lips purring softly, the facial muscles relaxing until that tranquil look shone from his face.

"Why you want to spoil him?" Victor said. "Let him sleep by himself. You come to bed now. I have to get up early tomorrow."

Usually it meant that he was ready for sex. It is true what they say about the difference between a woman and a man's attitude towards sex. For the woman, it's a time for love, for cuddles, for warmth. Since I had not known any man before Victor and had not gone beyond heavy petting before marriage, I assumed that all men were like Victor. He conducted his foreplay in probably the same way as he would conduct his engineering projects—everything subjected to a formula and to a set timing. Squeeze right breast two times, squeeze left breast same number of times. Run hands down body. Kiss. Use tongue to enter mouth. Put fingers in vagina to get the juices going, one probe, two probe. Ready for penetration. If he felt energetic, he went on top of me. If he was tired, he pulled me on top. If he was really, really tired, he pushed my head down for me to suck him off so that it would be quick and required least effort from him. Once I was penetrated, it was a matter of seconds before he ejaculated, let out one short groan and then it was over. Tupping, not love-making. Either he rolled off me or signaled that I was to disembark as though I was only a passenger on his train. In all the years of marriage, it never occurred to him that he had to speak to me whilst copulating, or that I might like things done in a certain way. And yet, he expected an affirmation. "*Shiok* or not?" he'd ask. Which wife dared to say otherwise? "*Siok! Shiok!*" I lied as convincing as I could. As many women do. Women are good at faking an orgasm and voicing satisfaction. It is far easier to practise and master these techniques than to deal with the bruised ego of a man. Satisfied on all counts, he'd turn on his side to sleep, snoring in just a few minutes. He would be oblivious to the motions of the bed as I loved myself afterwards, sometimes crying softly into my pillow.

"You loved books too. Maybe they take after you," I say to Peter. "What are you reading these days? Diana, have you read *The Goblet Of Fire* yet?"

"Not yet, Grandma."

"Why don't we go to the bookshop and buy one tomorrow. And you, what kind of stories do you like, Harry?"

"Adventure stories. And anything about aeroplanes, cars or rockets."

"Have you read the *Famous Five*? No? It used to be very popular. It's about five English schoolchildren always looking for adventure. Let's have a fun day out tomorrow after you come back from school. Is that all right Margaret?"

"Sure. I have to go to work anyway. I took *off* today to meet up with you. I'll show you where to go-*lah*. You can try de MRT, Diana knows how to travel on it. Maybe it's a good idea to take Siti with you."

"Oh, I'm sure I can manage."

After all these years away, it is fascinating to return to a typical Asian manner of talking and eating. Everyone use their fingers and it is nice for me to feel that I can blend in instead of looking like a peasant as I felt when I was in England. Robert helped me to return to that way of eating; Hugh had found it offensive. Eating crabs is not possible without fingers—one needs to break the crab shell, suck on the juice, and dig out the flesh. Most Westerners I know complain that eating unprepared crabs is a lot of work to get so little meat. They don't seem to understand the pleasure of the whole process, as if getting the meat out is the only purpose. Like the Buddhists say, the journey is just as interesting and important as the destination.

"Do you remember when we used to eat *chilli crabs* at Palm Beach?"

From his question and the direction of his gaze, I realise that Peter is addressing me. I've come to accept the fact that he is not going to call me *Mum*. Maybe it is early days yet or maybe, he finds it too awkward since he has not used the term for such a long time. Was it Shakespeare who said, *A rose by any name is still a rose*? So should it matter what he calls me? One part of me says, Yes, it does. His calling me *Mum* would remove my sentence of guilt, free me from continual pain. But it is not to be. At least not yet. I know I don't deserve to be handed that accolade yet; I hanker for it.

This is the problem with having expectations and desires. To desire is to want, to want is to need. When a need or desire is not fulfilled, one gets hurt. That's why the Buddha says, *All suffering arises from desires.* My biggest consolation is that it was he who made the first move, had crossed oceans and years to come for me. And it is quite obvious that he holds our past together quite dear and our life together is never far away from his mind. At the moment, he's talking about the stretch of beach which was on the east coast, nor far from Bedok Road, named for the *Traveler's Palms* and coconut palms that populated the area. I used to love it there because it reminded me of the place where I went with my neighbours to picnic when I was a child and Pak Awang had told me about the trees having a spirit. It was my favourite spot and Victor, on his good days, would take me there. Peter could be left to run around the sandy beach when he got bored sitting at the table with adults. Before the food arrived, I used to chase him 'round the palm trees or play *keledek* with him on the sand. I would always pretend to lose so that I had to piggyback him to the line drawn. And how he would laugh as he sat on my back, my arms around him to keep him safe, and he treating me like a workhorse and making me go faster and faster. Victor was a very responsible father but not childlike enough for some of the games. The one thing about Victor was that he was very indulgent about taking me to places to eat. Like me, he loved his food. When I was pregnant with Peter and had cravings for *laksa* and *chye tow kway*, he would drive miles to the hawker centers that were reputed to serve the best of whatever I craved. He even took me to Kukup in Johor because the restaurants there were renowned for their seafood. And we would go to Segamat because it had the choicest durians.

"Oh, yes. Whenever I think of that place, I always think about how you used to give me a run around amongst the trees. And the way, you ride on my back. I was fitter in those days. I don't think I can chase Diana or Harry around them now the way I used to do. Or play *keledek*."

"Palm Beach is gone. Land reclamation took place dere-*wat*. Condominiums on it now," Margaret informs in staccato fashion.

"I had to go dere for one last look before dey started reclaiming land in dat area," Peter says with a note of nostalgia in his voice. "Funny isn't it? A place can be changed, gone even, and yet it hasn't altered at all in your mind."

7

I go to my bedroom with a glow suffusing my entire being. I'm giddy with the treasures I've collected. Margaret called me *Mum* at least five times. Diana and Harry called me *Grandma* about twenty times. Ordinary everyday words. But to me, they are magical, like the special gifts a fairy godmother bestows. I know my heart would mend if Peter addressed me as well. But. Still. It's enough for now. The words acknowledged me as family, part of a bigger whole, no longer alone. A spiritual connection. Individualism is fine for some. But when you stand alone in your own needs and desires, you tend not to regard the needs and desires of others. Though this doesn't always necessitate selfishness, a preoccupation with the self, by its very nature, will mean that you don't share in the success and joys of others either. Invariably, you will transit from aloneness to loneliness. In some situations, this condition is self-inflicted, and in others, it is circumstantial. In Asia, where familial ties are considered of utmost importance to the survival, not only of the family but of society, an individual sometimes has to stifle his own individuality for the greater good. But he will never be alone. Having chosen my path in the years before, I became removed and alone. I had sentenced myself. Hugh had never realised how I felt, to have left country and home for him. When you are cut off from your child, you are doomed to be cut off from the generation that follows too. Hugh had never put himself in my place, never understood the enormity of my sacrifice. Funny how his newfound joy drags back that fateful time I had rung the changes.

"I can't see how you can bear to leave your son behind," chided Linda, when I told her I was going to marry Hugh and that Victor was not letting me take Peter to England. "No matter what happens between Alfred and me, I shall never ever leave Sophia."

"Ah, but you're a better person than I am."

Linda did not mince words. We had been good colleagues at work and remained friends for a long time. But as she grew older, as her dissatisfaction with her husband, Alfred, became more apparent, she became sharper with her tongue. She was very slim, had almost blue-black hair which she wore straight to the shoulders. The hair contrasts with her pale skin which she kept paler still by staying out of the sun or always carrying an umbrella when she was outdoors. The two of us were like the Yin-and Yang symbol, one white, the other dark. Perhaps we were very different in temperament too. But there was so much we had divulged to one another, so many sorrows halved. Yet, there were some things that were impossible to share even with the best of friends, unless you were prepared to expose the wriggling maggots inside the woodwork of your marriage. Pointing fingers would do no one any good. Besides, I had already damaged Victor's ego and self-esteem by falling in love; why hurt him more by taking his son away from him? Peter was my gift to him. Did Victor realise that? Did he appreciate that I gave great consideration to the fact that if there was anyone who should suffer a loss, it must be myself so that Peter wouldn't be caught in the middle, a pawn in our battle? Of course, my main concern had been Peter himself. What an irony that I who tried so hard to protect him from pain should be the one to cause him pain. Yet, his welfare was uppermost too in my mind. I was divided—woman and mother, ripped apart from different needs. Very few adults stand alone in a single role. If we are fortunate, each role has its place, its own timing on the stage, all the cogs oiled and moving in harmony. I had chosen, and my choice was the spanner that crunched the machinery of family to a stop.

"What kind of life you give your son if you take to England?" Ang Huay had asked me. "You really know this man or not? Okay, now both love-love and he'll do everything for you. He very handsome and very smile-smile. Look like child on merry-go-round, like fun-fun. Peter, not his son—what if later he not happy to have other people child around? What you do then so far away from mother help? Maybe, he bad-treat Peter? If Peter stay here, got father, got grandmothers to look after him. His father got money, give good school for Peter, good life. No problem you come to see him if you want. telephone him. Write to him. But take him to far-far place, his future not sure-sure, is too bad for him.

"I don't know if you remember or not. But long-long ago, you asked me why I didn't leave you behind with your father. Why I bring you to miserable life in *kampung* when your Ah Tio was rich and had big-big bungalow with a lot to eat. I was young-*wat*, like you now. Only think of running away from husband. Didn't think how I was going to bring you up with no money. You probably right, if you stayed with your Ah Tio, sure to live in big-big house, have many-many servants, a lot of food, beautiful clothes. Everything. I regret so much, give you bad childhood. I think mother-love not always enough if no comfort and security-*hor*?"

I squirm to think that I didn't even say to my mother that mother-love was enough. Why had I not said words which she craved? Had I been insensitive or had I been caught in my own confusion and dilemma and wasn't really aware of what my mother wanted to hear from me then? Or was I deaf to my mother's entreaties, filled only with my own misery? It was difficult enough trying to imagine one's mother as a twenty-something-year-old with the same problems as yourself, let alone be expected to reassure her. Do patterns repeat themselves if people share some similarities in their genetic make-up? What do we pick up from our parents, besides looks and mannerisms? Perhaps we are not as separate beings as we like to believe, perhaps somehow we are all weaved together in varying strands by what we share and what we have done.

At the time my mother was advising me, she was still living in the village. She lived there until they told her she had to get out because the bulldozers were coming to raze it to the ground to make way for new housing estates of concrete tower blocks. But at that stage, she still didn't have any piped water, but there had been progress—a generator had been installed that provided electricity for some hours of the day. Mak wanted to stay on until she was asked to move because she heard that the PAP government would pay her to move and would provide a flat with running water, electricity and its own bathroom and toilet. Progress plucked my mother from the shanty village to a block of flats where the wall between the neighbours was thick with concrete, not wooden planks with gaps that allowed conversations between households. Doors were shut tight all the time, a bid to retain the small bit of space there was. But Ang Huay was content, there was no more chamber pot to empty, no rats to avoid, no roof leaks to repair. If she thought that I had messed up my life, she did not say. After all, wasn't the daughter imitating the mother, running away from the man she married? Yet in the question of the child, her grandchild, Ang Huay, was steadfast.

"Don't do what I have done; take child away from good-good life."

Was my mother right? What security would I provide Peter if I took him away? Would I need to struggle as Mak had struggled to feed and clothe us? What if Hugh left me and I had to fend for myself and my child in a strange country and alien environment? Was this the kind of uncertainty I wanted for Peter? Shouldn't a boy be better off with his father who could teach him male things?

"Maybe I should just give Hugh up and live here with Peter."

"Ya, you can do that. But maybe you regret later for giving up chance for new life. And then what? You maybe start to angry-angry with Peter because he block your way to happiness. No easy answer-*lah*! Life is not like Arithmetic sum, either right or wrong. Life is mix-mix. *Rojak*. Let your spirit guide you."

Did Ang Huay have to give up some lover on account of me? Maybe because the lover didn't want someone's child? Was that why she never remarried? Surely, there was a note of regret in Mak's voice. But I also realised that in a backhanded way, my mother was giving me the freedom to seek a new love and life. *That* was mother-love. Why is it that even when I'm happy, the shadow of pain lingers? Perhaps Janus isn't two-faced at all. He is seen that way because the faces can only be depicted two-dimensionally. If he was depicted in a hologram, perhaps one face will lie upon the other, both existing at the same time, so when there is joy, sadness is lying underneath and the reverse is true too. Perhaps it is this very reason that causes Indian yogis to strive beyond the polarity of life. Only when you go beyond the two faces can you be truly free.

I had not closed my door so I can hear the family settling down. It's a comforting sound, like an old house creaking and muttering at nights before it finally goes into rest. Someone flushes the toilet, the children argue, a door shuts. Beyond the wall of my room lies *my* family. At last I can declare my ownership. When I had been with Hugh, I dare not stake such a claim, dare not disclose to anyone the life I had left behind and the treasures I could not own. I must concentrate on this thought, not on my loss of Robert. Now, I'm not alone; never will be again. How reassuring this is. The glow of the evening is still with me. I hug my gifts to me like precious gems. They will always be mine now and I can take them out to examine and admire whenever I choose. Then, suddenly, I've an idea. I hasten out of my room to go to the children's rooms, one on the other side of each other, the two rooms sharing a common bathroom and toilet suite.

"Harry. It's Grandma," I say as I knock on the door. A sense of joy leaps into my chest for addressing myself that way. My first. It gives me a wonderful feeling of belonging. I'm no longer a boat loosed of its mooring. Family is a sheltered harbour. Occasionally, there might be strong winds or tall waves that sweep inward to disturb the still waters, but the harbour will stand strong and proud. In England, before Robert, Hugh had been my entire family. I had given up my own and everything else for him. But he chose someone else in the end, shattering what little I owned. I let myself in and see that the nightlight is on, a plastic shell shaped like Pluto over a small bulb. It reminds me of something, but I don't know what. Harry is already in bed, a light cover over his legs. "Would you like to be tucked in?"

"Wat is 'tuck in', Grandma?"

"In England, parents usually tuck their children in. They put the covers right, like this, and say goodnight. Sometimes, they tell a story. Or read."

"Can you tell me a story about England?"

The adjoining bathroom door flies open and Diana sticks her head 'round, her mouth full of foamy toothpaste, a toothbrush in her hand. "I want to be tucked in too. After Harry, it's my turn. Okay, Grandma?"

"Okay, darling."

I struggle for a suitable story to tell. In these past years, there had been no need to know children's stories. Except for *Harry Potter* and *The Lord Of The Rings*, the ones I remember are those from long ago. Then I remember *Dick Whittington*. I couldn't remember if its eponymous hero traveled from Porstmouth to London or came from somewhere else on the coast, but I decide it did not matter too much. I'll make it Portsmouth so that I've a chance to mention my village in Hampshire and the treacherous Devil's Punchbowl, so named because in the old days, it used to claim the lives of cars still in their engineering infancy as they struggled to get up the hill.

"Shall I come on the bed with you?"

My grandson shifts to give me room on the bed, still a little shy. Even to see such a face is a gift in itself. I take his small hand in mine, savouring its touch and softness. It is so perfectly formed. The kind of thing a new mother examines when her baby is first handed to her. Two eyes, two ears, a nose, a mouth, ten fingers, ten toes. How can such perfection and beauty result from one body smashing hard into another? How can one small thing pull so strongly at your heart when it can come from so much hurt? When does a fetus pick up the thread of its own life and starts to assert its own volition? When I was pregnant with Peter, I used to stroke my distended belly and talked and sang to him. Instinctively, I knew I carried a boy confirmed by the kampung folks by the shape of my belly. *You are carrying boy-child if stomach small and sharp,* they said. *And girl-child if stomach is round-round.* I never doubted their prediction nor my own. I remember that when they brought Peter to me, he was a hazy hump of slippery flesh. I was still groggy from the fourteen-hour labour.

"Girl or boy? Girl or boy?" The nurse asked me, urgency in her voice, opening the baby's legs in a crude fashion. It seemed that it was essential for mothers to identify the sex of their baby because many mothers would prefer boys because of the pressures from their husband, mother-in-law and society, so some women insisted that they had given birth to boys when they actually had girls.

"Boy," I said feebly, exhaustion making me drowsy.

I gave birth to Peter at *Kandang Kerbau*, such an unfortunate name for a maternity hospital. The words in Malay means a corral or pen (*kandang*) for buffaloes, (*kerbau*). The hospital was probably named by a man with the sensitivity of a clothesbrush. I had fallen into an exhausted sleep after the birth. When I awoke, I thought I had lost my baby. Victor was sitting beside the bed, his head bowed as if in sorrow. It did not suit Victor to cut a figure of pathos; he looked like a caricature. Instead of sympathising with him, one had the opposite effect of wanting to laugh at his pouting mouth and sullen look. There was no baby in the cot beside me. Fear clutched at my heart and I scrambled out of bed in a seizure of panic before the stitches caught me unawares.

"It's okay, it's okay. De baby in Intensive Care-*lah*. Got tube in umbilical cord to feed it. His lungs did not inflate."

He was tender and kind that day. He had brought me my favourite foods from a hawker center, *chye tow kway*, fried crispy with lots of chilli. He supported my arm as he walked me to the Intensive Care Unit so that I could look upon the face of my new baby boy behind the wall of glass. My baby looked helpless in his nakedness, a tube attached to his umbilical cord which had not been cut nor knotted. So young and yet already alone. Perhaps it foreshadowed our imminent separation. I stood there and knew that there were things I could never protect him from. The thought brought the tears and made me maudlin. The birth was both a release and a tearing, my baby freeing itself from his dependency; yet for me his tearing away also filled me with a kind of desolation—our first parting. Nature can sometimes be unkind in its predictability. With or without baby at my breast, the milk still came on the third day, making my mammary glands engorged and tight with pain. The nurse taught me how to express the milk so that they could bottle-feed Peter when he was taken off the drip. What must it be like for mothers who lost their baby in birth? How they must be shattered when their milk arrived and there was no baby to feed. It was already torture for me to be in the maternity ward with other new mothers who were basking in the gurgles and cries of their newborn, asking me where my baby was. What must it be like for a woman to have to be in the same position as mine except worse, when she had to voice the terrible acknowledgment that her baby had died?

"'*Once upon a time…*'"

As I tell the story, making up bits that I had forgotten, I kiss Harry's hand and caresses his arm. I had been so hungry for the touch of a child's skin, the smell of it, that I feed on it now. It is not the child I had missed but it is enough that it is a child of his. Harry starts to relax and his body edges slowly towards mine. How easily trusting children are. It is right that children should be able to trust adults. It is a sorry state when we have to warn our children not to talk to strangers or accept sweets and chocolates proffered. It points to a degenerative disease that corrodes the soul of society. These days, from an early age, we teach our children the wrong side of an adult. We teach them to scorn and rebuff strangers who dare to come close. In doing so, we take away their delight in innocent familiarity and unconscious taking. Strangers who may be mothers and fathers themselves, who love to see the upturned face of a child, who relish in the sparkle of a child's eyes and that glorious smile when a gift is handed, are made to feel like societal pariahs—potential pedophiles. For both the child and the adult, we stamp out spontaneous delight.

"Oh, I didn't see you standing there. Aren't you asleep yet?" I say as I notice that Peter is standing by the door which has been left slightly ajar.

"I've been calling de States. Time difference and all dat."

"Daddy, Grandma is tucking me in!"

"Yes, I'd forgotten all about that. She used to do that when I was your age. Do you remember reading to me?" His voice trembles at the memory.

"How can I forget?"

"You made a cut-out of Pluto from a polystyrene sheet and painted it for me and put it on the wall of my room. Do you remember?"

"Ah, that's why I found Harry's nightlight familiar."

"Yes, when I saw it in KL, I had to buy it for him."

"Daddy, come and sit down and listen to the story."

Peter walks in to sit on the side of his son's bed. He sits hunched, as though he is folding over to protect his soft belly. I feel his confusion, his pain at the recovery of old memories, and I begin to feel confused too, unsure whether I was telling the story to my grandson or to my son of long ago. Harry's eyelids flutter as he slowly drifts off into sleep. I start stroking his forehead. Peter gets up abruptly to leave the room without saying anything, which jolts me a bit. Eventually when I hear Harry's steady breathing, I extricate myself gently so as not to wake him. I look in on Diana and she's already asleep, a book in her hands. I remove the book and tuck the covers around her as the air-conditioning is quite blowy. I'm returning to my room when I notice that one of the small lamps in the living room is still on. Perhaps Siti had forgotten to switch it off or Peter when he came out of his study. I was about to switch off the light when I see a shadowy Peter hunched over the balcony.

"Can't you sleep?"

"You frightened me."

"Oh, sorry."

His voice is not the same. He looks away, facing the dark landscaped gardens.

"I remember your stroking my forehead."

"Yes."

"Sometimes in those years, I used to wake up tinking you'd come back and was stroking my forehead."

"I'm sorry."

We stare into the landscaped garden, its paved paths gently lit so that they are no longer harsh, but still show the way. I wish someone can show me the way now, my son by my side, his pain stitched to his insides.

''I used to be so afraid of the dark," he laughs that humourless laugh. "I used to wait till you could come to my room to recite the *pantuns* and nursery rhymes to me."

"How your father used to get mad when I get into bed late. I always had to make sure you were asleep."

"I don't know what to remember…"

I know what he had been told about me. I learnt it from Linda. The picture that his father and grandmother painted of me. To clear myself in his eyes is to call them liars. They were his family too, have been his for all these years. It would not do to tarnish their reputation even though they are gone. When Linda told me what Mui Yoke used to shout at Peter, my heart bled: '*Your mother left you because she doesn't love you! Don't you understand? She doesn't love you!*'Sometimes I wonder if Linda was punishing me through her news. But then I was desperate for news of Peter and any morsel would do. But eventually, even Linda cut me off.

"I've never stopped loving you. Never stopped thinking of you."

I want so much to take him in my arms. But his demeanour prevents me.

"I'm a man now. I should be able to take things in my stride."

"I've still got your baby clothes."

8

"You can't walk into the past with the shoes you're wearing today. You're no longer what you were. Every second, every minute is a movement of time, a movement toward experience and to new learning. So you cannot judge yourself yesterday with today's knowledge," Veronica said all those years ago.

Veronica was friend, sister, mother. Even when she was painting, she didn't tie her dark hair back, and it would halo around her face, streaks of grey giving her a distinctive, bohemian look.

"Oh, how I wish I can undo my wrongs!"

"Kim! Listen to me! Right or wrong doesn't come into this. You made a decision which took your son's welfare into account. Maintain your perspective!"

But it was easier said than done. It was one of those days when I was weepy with regret for what might have been. Even watching a nature programme could bring on the guilt and the tears. If I saw the little lion cubs gambol joyfully beside their mother, I hated myself for not being there for Peter. If I watched the mother bird or animal forage for food to sustain their chicks or cubs; the way they fight off preys, giving up their own lives to protect their young, I felt not only selfish but like a lowdown, rotten freak. All around me, nature was reminding me that it was natural for a child to grow up with its mother. If you are a mother, your role is to protect and nurture. Mothers die for their young. They don't run away. Nature does not intend for mothers to run away leaving their young to fend for themselves. But I had. I had gone against the laws of nature. Unforgivable. *Mea Culpa. Mea Culpa.* For my sins, I had to live in a hell of my own making. No matter how many years have passed, each time Peter's birthday approached, my body would remind me of my loss. His birthday is my *birth day* too, the day I gave birth to him. I remembered every detail of that birth, every detail of my pregnancy, rejoicing in the life that was beating as one with me. How could I have done all that and yet leave him to fend for himself? How could he celebrate with no mother next to him, to help him cut the cake or blow out the candles? What would he feel with no mother to mother him and make him feel special? Headaches would seize my skull, shadows overwhelm my mood and my energy would dip to an unhealthy low. My guilt drained me in so many ways.

"Come on, darling. We're not going through all the drama again," Hugh said during such times when we were still together. "It's not as if he's been left in the woods for the wolves. He's well looked after by his father and grandmother. You can't let your past keep on interfering with our present. Snap out of it, darling. Put your glad rags on and I'll take you somewhere nice. How about going to the theatre? Let's go and see a comedy. It will take your mind off things."

Hugh wanted all of me. He hated the thought of my division of love. He did not understand what it was like to have a child, since he was so much a child himself. He could not see that once you've become a mother, you could never be undivided or stand alone again with your own needs and feelings. Unadulterated. Your child's need and welfare is indelibly written in your mind. Having fed on your body for nine months, he will feed on your spirit forever. The umbilical cord is not the only thing that binds. No amount of therapy could take away my guilt. The wisdom uttered in a therapy session sound acceptable in a room away from my emotions. Soon as the net fell over my head and I relived again Peter's large, frightened eyes on the day I left, I was drawn once again into the tentacles of pain. I would do anything now to reverse the chain of events that led me to be so negligent. And, of course, when Hugh eventually betrayed me I was stunned.

"I left my son for you," I groaned. "Is this how you repay me?"

Besides Veronica, it was Robert, dear Robert, who helped me deal with my guilt. He was different from Hugh. Older than I was, he had a tolerance and care that Hugh did not possess. Life can teach you a great deal in a decade. It is not that older people are necessarily wiser, but they certainly have seen enough to make their perspective truer. But perhaps it was easier for Robert to advise; he himself did not know what it was like to be committed to your child, having had none himself. Apparently, Emas had an early hysterectomy, so he wouldn't have known how a child could tug at your heartstrings or change your life.

"There's good and bad guilt. Bad guilt staples you to the past…makes you ineffectual. Good guilt helps you to move on. You recognise what you've committed, do something about it, then move on," he said.

"But I haven't done anything about it, have I? How could I have thought it was for Peter's good?" I cried.

"In the situation you were in, you did. And that's enough. You can't look at yesterday with today's knowledge or circumstance. It's not fair to yourself. Don't crucify yourself, *sayang*. You're neither a selfish nor cruel person so whatever decision you took at that time was with his interest at heart."

"I can't have been a good mother."

"There's a story in the bible about two women who quarreled over the ownership of a baby boy. King Solomon was known for his wisdom so the women took the child to him so that he could settle the dispute. To the mother's horror, the king decreed that the child should be cut in half so that each woman could take one part. Immediately, one woman, though grieving, chose to give up her half so that her baby would not be harmed. It was from this act of sacrifice that King Solomon knew who the real mother was."

Dear mothers everywhere, credit yourself for your love, tolerance and labour in bringing up a child. You are the best thing that can happen to humanity. Without you, no future loving mothers can be created. Without you, men in their childhood would not have known tenderness and security. You nurture the adults that are to come. You shape the future world with the way you bring your child up—your attitudes become their attitudes. This is no small task. Be proud of yourself for putting the welfare of your children first, before all else. Be proud of yourself if you have to struggle between finding time for your own creativity and your children's. Through the tedium of nappy changing, school runs, through bouts of ill temper or illness, you continued to stay. You were there to nurse a wounded knee, there to frighten the ghouls away. Mothers are the ones who give most of themselves. You are a special gift to mankind. Be proud of yourself. Be glad you are not me.

"Come on, Grandma," Diana says, pulling my hand and guiding me through the MRT procedures; Harry trying to keep pace beside us.

I feel a warmth of pleasure to have the children's trust. I suddenly feel less of the ogre I had made myself out to be. I'm smiling happily, wondering if people notice that I'm a privileged woman with two youngsters who are treating me as if I'm a normal grandmother. I stride with them up to the overhead platform. Even at this height, the moisture in the air clings to me, sucks my breath. The sleek silver bullet of a train arrives and I'm surprised how bright and clean the interior is; its plastic seats are gleaming and the air inside is fresh and cool. I had expected the dark and soiled look of the London Tube—the compressed atmosphere. There is something to be said to be a follower and not the leader. When you scout for new tracks, you know both the dangers and the excitement. You are crowned with success. But it is those who follow behind who are safe to feed on your sweat and labour, making new what you have etched in history. The children find their favourite seats and pull me down beside them. I marvel at the ease in which the children are so comfortable in touching and handling me like a prized possession. This was such an unexpected gift that I'm still riding high on the cloud of joy. The MRT train squiggles down the tracks, a long tube with compartments that open into each other, with rubbery joints that flex and move. We pass coconut palms and beautiful housing estates, not the shanty *attap* huts which I had grown up in, but luxurious brick or concrete houses with gardens. Everywhere, there are signs of a country that has grown into wealth. Further along, we pass by apartment blocks and then the river, Diana and Harry pointing and naming places for me, echo the names of the stations that are announced in a heavy Singaporean accent, *Lavender* becoming *La-*

Ven-Der.

"Do you know what lavender is?" I ask the children.

"De name of a MRT station!" Both of them say.

"It's a type of flower. I have a hedge in my garden totally made from lavender. It's a tall plant and the flowers are like rice grains but purple in colour, some are white, some pink. It smells lovely. People take out the flowers to put in cushions and pillows so that they can keep the scent."

"I would like a la-**ven**-der pillow, Grandma," Diana says.

"Try to say *lavender*," I coax, dropping my voice so that the other passengers could not hear.

"Why? Is la-**ven**-der wrong?"

"That's not the way it would be pronounced in England."

"Oh, I want to pronounce words as dey are pronounced in England, Grandma. Wat is the point of speaking English if you can't be understood by the English?"

"You are an intelligent child. I'm sure you will soon learn. You just needed to hear it pronounced correctly."

"Lavender, lavender, lavender."

"Look out, Grandma, we will be going underground soon," Harry says excitedly.

True enough. The train starts to dive down into the deep bowels of the earth. I hate this. Even in London, I hated it when the Tube travels underground. It was the same when I visited a cave. The sense of claustrophobia tightens my chest and I imagine that moles and rats live in these places, creatures with pointy ears, bristly whiskers and beady eyes. Thank goodness before I start to panic, the train stops and disengages its passengers, the children holding my hands one on each side. Modern, shiny escalators, not groaning wooden ones, pull the three of us up from the burrows dug by mechanical moles into the cloying heat and sunshine of City Hall Station.

At the exit, I turn into a pillar, not quite of salt but just as immovable. After the trauma of the underground, I now have to face the crowd all around me. I feel as if hundreds of people are pushing past me and the children to get out and hundreds more are elbowing us aside to get down. The rapid transition from a relatively peaceful condominium to bustling city is a shock. Tower blocks of concrete push the breath out of me. Bodies brush past me, pressing themselves into my own. Noise assaults my ears, people talk loudly, traffic snarl and grumble, cars hoot, pop music blare out from somewhere. The noise jangles my nerves, and all the different sounds seem suddenly high-pitched, the people pushing all about me, moving in restless speed like rats. Brown rats, black rats, grey rats, white rats. They are scuttling here and there and everywhere. Rats with their bristly whiskers and their beady, glassy eyes stare at me with a kind of insolence. Images of my *kampung* childhood flash across my mind's eye and I see the rats from those days again, under the platform bed, in the outhouse. They are all about me—squeaking, squeaking, squeaking.

"Grandma! Grandma!"

As if from a distance, I hear the children calling me out from the cave, their voices in distress. But the breaking of ice flows is in my ears, my head still spinning and the ground beneath me shifting. A flash-flood of sweat pours down my back. If only Robert was here, he would know what to do… how to help me. I feel my knees softening. Then, someone is supporting my elbow, guiding me as I stumble to a seat on the sidewalk café.

"Aunty, you all right or not?" A young female voice asks kindly.

"Grandma, you okay?"

My breathing is hard. I make an effort not to succumb. The noises in my ears start to recede. Slowly, the terrifying faces of the rats begin to dissolve, returning to the deep seat of my unconscious, and more human ones swim into focus. A young woman is peering at me, together with Diana, concern in their eyes.

"Yes, yes. Thank you. Must be the heat. I'm not used to the heat."

Little Harry starts to cry.

"I'm all right, darlings. I really am. Come here, Harry." I squeeze Diana's hand to assure her and fold Harry into my arms.

"Aunty, drink some water," the young woman urges, offering a glass.

I comply. Now that there isn't going to be any further drama, the people who have been standing by as if waiting for an installment of a soap opera start to disperse. But the noise is still around, though less threatening now. I hate noise. That's why I hadn't been to shop at Oxford Street for years. When I first went to England, I loved going to London, especially at Christmas when the lights were out and Santa Clauses stood at street corners, ringing their bells, department stores dressed in festive regalia. There was really a sense of good cheer. Either I have changed or things have changed. Oxford Street was not the same to me anymore. Big department stores seemed to have lost their individuality and their own brand names, bringing in so many designer labels that the store looked as if they had franchised bits of the store to different operators. Every day, on the streets of London, buses and cars bumped along at walking pace. There were so many people on the street that the local authorities threatened to create walking lanes like traffic flow where people could only walk in a stipulated direction to prevent them from crashing into one another. This is what we called civilisation. It is 1984 at its worst.

"Aunty, you want me to call anyone for you?"

"No, really. I'm okay. I'll sit here for a while. Maybe the children can order ice cream or something and I shall sit and get my breath back."

I'm not used to being fussed. Until Robert, I had always been the care-giver, both Victor and Hugh needing me so much. When you've given all your life, serviced others before self, you learn to force yourself up in the morning even when your mind is willing to let go, to float into oblivion. You learn not to notice that twinge in the knee or the pain in your heart. Perhaps living is a trial to test your courage, to see how much you can take; after all, without tests, you cannot know your own strength. There is a kind of responsibility when there are others who truly worry about you. You cannot simply give in; you have to learn to rise beyond your own feelings. I try to pay attention to the young woman who is talking to the children to restore their equilibrium. Then when she finds that I'm wholly revived, she says, "You don't live here, right, Aunty? You speak like an English school teacher."

"Oh, dear."

"Aunty, I mean it as a compliment-*lah*. So nice to hear. Not just like someone *chiak kantang* who sounds fake, but like very good English. Don't sound so *Singlish*. I'm studying English Literature at NUS. My dream is to hear Shakespeare being spoken with an English accent. Are you from England? Do you live near Shakespeare country?"

"I live in Hampshire—"

"Is dat near London?"

"*Hampshire* is in the south, outside London. In a village called Laurel

Downs." Then, thinking that this young woman with her interest in literature may be interested, I rattle on. "Our village is quite well-known for its literary heritage. George Bernard Shaw and Arthur Conan Doyle both lived nearby. Jane Austen lived a few miles away and Charles Dickens was born in Portsmouth. I loved going to the tearoom in Chawton, right in front of Jane Austen's house. The village is so attractive, with thatched cottages. But the author's house is a townhouse, very old, but made of bricks."

"Wah! Sounds like my dream place! We study Jane Austen's books at university. Aunty, are you on holiday here?"

Harry wriggles free of my arms and skips along to the taxi stand.

"Harry, darling, don't go too near the road. Diana, get him back here, please. I'm visiting my son and his family. These are my grandchildren," I say with real pride in my voice. I have a family now. I am not alone.

"Aunty, my name is Clarice. You mind or not if I sit here and ask you about England while de children have deir ice cream? I'll help dem with deir orders."

Even in my slightly woozy state, I'm surprised that an undergraduate studying English literature did not pronounce the 'th' properly, so that *the* comes out like a hard *de*. I had become used to Peter's and Margaret's speech and other English-speaking Singaporeans I met, but it is a greater disappointment when it's coming from a student of English. Perhaps the locals are not aware of how their English sound to others. They don't seem to realise that you don't drop your 'hs' in *that*, *they*, *there*, *this*, *them*, *than*, *why*, *what*, *when* and *who*. It suddenly occurs to me that it is the 'th' that causes the problem, not just the 'h' because words with 'hs' in them like *here*, *hair*, *hurry* and *home* do not cause any problem. But it appears as if their tongues would not shape the sound of 'th' properly—*other* becomes *arder*, *mother* becomes *marder*, *father* becomes *farder*. It is probably this that gives the Singaporean speech its distinct characteristic, plus the way words are shot out so quickly, like the flicks of a lizard's tongue. Both Diana and Harry have great intelligence for their age and they read widely and eclectically, yet their English pronunciation is poor. Perhaps I ought to do something about it.

"Would you like some ice cream, children?"

"Yeah!" Both enthused at the same time, their eyes sparkling.

The young lady has been so helpful that I assent to her request. Clarice takes Diana and Harry indoors so that they can look at the selection of flavours and light-box pictures of sundaes and floats. The children come out skipping, their smiles beaming as they describe to me what they've ordered. The incident of the last few minutes has already fled from their minds. How wonderful it is that children can let go so easily, can be bribed into merriment.

"I really appreciate dis, you know, Aunty. So nice to talk to someone who has lived in England."

Clarice is fine-boned and petite, her hair falling straight down to her shoulders, fitting the image of a typical Asian girl in her early twenties. When she tosses her head, the light catches the shine in her hair. It is so refreshing to discover such a well-mannered girl that I think that it would have been nice to have had such a daughter. The girl savours my description of life in Hampshire. Now that I'm feeling myself, I'm amused that I should be learning so much from this young girl who lives in Singapore but who knows more about places in England made famous by books, either birthplaces of authors or their characters.

"Wow, look at mine," Harry says as the waiter brings the sundaes out, "It's bigger dan yours."

"But mine is more colourful."

"Tanks for de coffee, Aunty. You know, one day, if I can afford it, I would like to visit literary Britain," Clarice announces. "I want to see Shakespeare country, de Lake District, Wordsworth's home, DH Lawrence in Nottingham, de Brontes' Yorkshire moors, Thomas Hardy's Wessex, James Joyce' Dublin."

The list is long. She pulls the words out as if from a magician's hat, excitement in her eyes and pleasure in her voice as if somehow these people and what they stood for is food to her. How interesting that this girl who lives ten thousand miles away should see the country like a kind of mecca. The mention of Lawrence brings Robert back to me. D.H. Lawrence. Robert has spoken of him that time we went on our first holiday. Perhaps Clarice will be interested to know what Robert had told me.

"D.H. Lawrence also lived in Cornwall for a time. During the Second World War. If I remember correctly, he was there with his German wife, which made the villagers suspicious of them. Their farm was not far from the village of Zennor. There's a book written about it by a young contemporary English author. Helen Dunmore. Have you heard of her?"

"How do you spell dat?" Clarice fishes out her notebook. "What's the name of her book?"

"*Zennor in Darkness*, I think it's called."

"How do you spell 'Zennor'? Wat make people suspicious of Lawrence and his wife?"

I look at Clarice and put it to her youth. I explain and then describe the village of Zennor. In that moment, Robert's face flashes across my mind's eye and returns me to our time together. We had found a cottage in Mousehole for our holiday week. It was a two-up-two-down, delightfully furnished, cozy and snug. We had packed a picnic, drove to St. Just and walked along the coastal path to Zennor. The wind was fresh and it was a delight to watch Robert walk in front of me, his back tall but relaxed, his gait sensuous. How could such a body, already sixty, still be so beguiling? Surely, it attested to the fact that sensuality does not merely lie in muscles and bones or taut skin—sensuality lies in movement and gestures. I loved the sound of the waves crashing into the foothills of rocks as we wend our way along the high path above the cliffs. My love for the sea was one of distance because I would hate the thought of the waves pulling me in, enveloping me; whereas Robert loved being in it, under it. Like Emas. Apparently, he and Mas had both been scuba divers. The two of them had shared so much in physical activity that I wondered if Robert still missed his wife. I was not much of an outdoor person; a little walk in fair weather was fine, but I could not imagine being like Mas, trekking through the wilderness with Robert, camping out for days, skiing in severe cold. Perhaps, I should try to be a better companion to Robert, learn to ski or scuba dive, even.

Robert had found an outcrop of rocks where the view was splendid, the sea foaming below the sharp cliffs, the gulls screeching, the sun shining brightly. There we stopped for lunch, pulling out things from our picnic rucksack, Robert enjoying a glass of wine with his cheese whilst I ate from the Tupperware that contained my *mee goreng*.

"You know, Mas never did like sandwiches, either. Like you, she used to pack noodles and Asian snacks on our hikes. You remind me so much of her." For a moment, his voice snagged. Then, as if he had made a mistake in his admission, he added quickly, "And yet . . . you are so different. You are so refreshingly straightforward. Let's toast to a new beginning. To us!"

That occasion was the first time Robert and I became an item. Two lives overlapping into one. It is not always that one can pinpoint a moment in time when a fateful decision is taken. This tends to reveal itself in hindsight usually, but when it does, it is well to stitch it tight to the fabric of your memory. The sunlight caught the wine glass, radiating rays of sunshine which lit up Robert's eyes, his eyes which were as blue as the summer sky. But there was a part of me that was jealous of the ghost of the capable, beautiful Emas, always hovering over us. Could Robert ever forget her?

Clarice saying something brings me back and suddenly, I wish to be elsewhere; I no longer want to sit and talk to a stranger. To be around anyone else when my thoughts are about Robert seems to violate something. If possible, I want to be alone when I think of him, so that I can totally give myself up to him.

"Can we keep in touch, Aunty? Maybe I can come and visit you when you return to England?"

"Maybe, maybe. Children, we must hurry; otherwise the bookshop will be closed."

"Shops don't close till ten o'clock," says Diana.

"Oh."

When the children finished their ice cream, I ask for the bill abruptly. "Thanks very much for your help but we have to go. I promise the children some books. And we want to get home before the rush hour."

Clarice, sensing a dismissal, looks hurt, and I'm flooded with shame.

"Why don't you give me your phone number. If I've time, maybe we can meet up again to have a chat."

The young girl breaks into a smile. She writes her name, address and telephone number on a loose leaf of paper.

"I'll include my email as well, in case you need it."

"That's not necessary. I'm a computer dyslexic."

But Clarice writes it down anyway.

"You know, Aunty, since you know so much about England, maybe you can give a talk about it. Dere are lots of students of English literature here and dey would love to hear about England. I can help by telling you de kind of places dey would be interested in and you can tell us about dem."

"Oh, I'm only here for a while. I want to spend all my time with my family."

"No harm tinking about it-*wat*."

"I'll think about it. Goodbye for now."

Clarice then swings her bag onto her shoulder and walks with a jaunty air into the shopping mall. Diana directs us to *Rumah Buku,* House (of) Books, a big bookstore on Stamford Road, just across the road from the café. I try to pull myself away from thoughts of Robert. It is not easy here, where it is bustling with tourists, Caucasians with his build or colour of hair and complexion standing out like speckled hens in a brood of brown. Would that a miracle should occur and that one of them truly turns out to be Robert. I am insane. Of course, there is no possibility of such a hope. There must come a time when I have to address the problems concerning him, but not now. Now is that sliver of sunshine in a sky of grey clouds and I must bask in its brightness.

"Here we are," Diana says, pulling the glass door open to let her brother and I through.

It is a two-storied building, one of the remaining few reminders of the colonial era. It has changed so much from when I was first here. I remember coming from the National Library up the road to browse through the shop when I was about thirteen, wondering at the beauty of the covers, the smell of new books, all of them beyond my reach. It was already a treat to afford the bus fare that took me into town. I had thought that Ang Huay might have objected to the use of her hard-earned cash but my mother had been as delighted as I was to learn of a place that let books out for free. So she encouraged me to go to the library. That was when I learnt how much my mother loved stories.

"Read to me," she said. "What does this say? And this? And this?"

My mother's face filled with pleasure and her eyes shone.

"In Grandmother's days, we tell-tell stories in evening. No TV or anything."

I took home large picture books so that I could point the pictures out to tell the story behind it. That was when I started reading the daily newspaper as well to Ang Huay. If circumstances were different, I knew that my mother would have loved to have gone to school to learn to read and write. Ahh, what a bitch life can be. There is no need to take books home for my mother now. Sometime or other, I'll have to pick up the courage to visit our old village and go up to Chua Chu Kang to visit my mother's grave.

"See here, Grandma. Dis is my favourite section," Diana says.

"You say *th*is, darling, not *dis*. Try it. You said you would you like to speak English properly. Shall I teach you?"

"I tort we already speak properly. How can we not know dat we were not speaking good English?"

"I think it's always good to listen to how native speakers speak their language. Next time you watch an imported TV programme from England, listen to how they pronounce words."

"Just now Aunty Clarice said you speak like an English school teacher. Dat means she is saying your English is very good. I want my English to be like yours, Garndma. Yes, I would like to improve. "*Th*is," Diana says, spittle escaping.

"I can say it too. *Th*is, *Th*is, *Th*is. Is it correct Grandma?" Harry's spit runs down his chin.

"Well done, children," I say encouragingly. "I'm not trying to turn you into English children. But it's important to pronounce your English properly so that people around the world can understand you. Shall we trade? You teach me Mandarin and I teach you English."

"Oh, it's like a game." Harry claps his hands.

"Yes, Grandma," Diana says. "Book is *Zhu* in Chinese. Say it Grandma."

"*Shooo*."

Both Diana and Harry giggled.

"No, Grandma, it's *Zhu*!"

I want to set the right tone for their learning, make it fun rather than tedious or overbearing. So I exaggerate and twist my mouth into a moue to make them laugh more at my efforts. Their laughter touches my heart—such a refreshing, undiluted laughter. We walk 'round the store laughing, the children muttering, *this, these, that, those, them* whilst I repeat the word *zhu* in variable tones to get the right one. We arrive at the children's section. Big books, little books, all dressed in beautiful covers like I remembered. Oh, the delicious smell of fresh books! Only now I can afford to buy them. Except that I am not very clever and could not read the kind of books that Clarice reads. Even today, I marvel at how I can walk into a bookshop to buy any book I like. Yes, these days, I can afford to buy most things I need. Buy any food I want. It is a liberating feeling.

"Grandma, wat's our budget?"

"*Wh, Wh*at, *Wh*at."

"*Whh*at," Diana says and more spittle escapes.

"*Whhh*at. *Whhh*at," Harry goes and wets the front of his tee-shirt.

"What do you mean by budget?" I ask.

"Mummy and daddy always tell us how much we are allowed to spend."

"Oh," I say, trying to figure out what's best. "How about ten pounds?"

"Thirty dollars?" Diana says without hesitation. "For de two of us?"

At her age, I could not multiply, let alone convert foreign currency.

"For each of you. Ten pounds. I mean thirty dollars each."

"Wow!" Harry says. "I can buy my aircraft book!"

"I can get de new *Harry Potter* and more."

"*Th*e. *Th*e new *Harry Potter*."

"*Th*e, *th*e, *th*e, *th*e, *th*e, *th*e, *th*e, *th*e," Harry starts to scale in a sing-song voice. "Grandma, am I like *th*e Prince or like Harry Potter?"

"You are special," I say.

Robert said that I was special. No one had told me that before. So I believe him. I want to believe him. My life before he came was a tattered cloak. He is mending me now, as I am mending him.

"You are my autumn gift," Robert says. "In complexion and in name."

We have just returned from Madeira, from an excursion into our new partnership, discovering and committing to memory each other's body, likes and dislikes. It was lovely by our seaside hotel, listening to the waves as they crashed over the rocks as we basked ourselves in the sun, like seals with nothing important to do. Thirsty for the sunshine, my skin drank and drank till my complexion glowed like burnished bronze.

"Brown girl in the ring, tra lalalala," he sang softly, as we strolled down the marina in the evening to see the boats and delight in the calls of the gulls. The full moon splashed the waves with its numerous facets

of light. Arms linked, we stopped every now and again to feast on each other in secluded enclosures of the sea-wall, and then later, on espada and calamari with frites. Robert was made more jolly by a bottle of a local red. His mood was infectious.

I recaptured some part of my youthful self when I'm with him, the part that has yet to know broken marriages or a wounded child. I hear my own voice, echoing the laughter from a self that sees a life of promise ahead not yet deadened by sorrow. When I'm with him, it's almost possible to forget that my waist has thickened or that my skin has thinned, that somehow the texture and shape of my face and lips have not changed. His hand on my body is the wand that wields this magic so that as long as he loves me, I feel beautiful.

We drive out from his home in Hampshire, now mine too, a huge place, a bit large for my comfort. We are wrapped warm in our newly declared love. He persuades the chuckling open-topped 1951 Jaquar XK120 through a tunnel of trees, the canopy of leaves above like a lacework of reds and gold, the sun shining through. The wind leaps across the fields alongside the hedgerow, making the trees shiver, nudging them to drop the golden coins from their branches. The leaves swirl and fall. We laugh as we are showered with a confetti of falling leaves befitting a bride and groom; his laughter coming from deep inside him. That is when I know that he is healed. Or so I thought. His face has lost that haunted look and for once, I pride myself for having done somebody some good. He picks up a leaf in his free hand and kisses it.

"Did I tell you that you're gorgeous? Autumn will always remind me of you," he says. "Kim Hiok. Golden Leaf. What a beautiful name."

9

Diana gushes out about my fainting spell as soon as her parents get home.

"I told you it wasn't a good idea for you to go out on your own-*wat*. It's too soon," Peter says, giving his briefcase to Siti.

"Aiiyah, it's not as if dey were in some remote place. If it was serious, dey'd go straight to hospital or catch a taxi back," Margaret says trying to calm him, handing her own briefcase to Siti. "Diana is quite capable. She would have called me on my handphone if she tort it was necessary. Dey're all back, safe and sound, right? Nothing more to worry-*lah*."

Her voice suggests the type of day she must have had. Or was it something else which had triggered off her mood?

"Yes, I'm okay. We're okay. It's just a short spell. Might be the heat," I say, not wanting a fuss. I wish I had anticipated that Diana was going to blurt the story, I could have persuaded her not to.

"Grandma bought us books! We had thirty dollars to spend each!" Harry announces.

"You mustn't spend too much money on dem," Margaret says.

"I haven't had the opportunity before, have I? It was my pleasure."

"Are you going to read for us before dinner, Grandma?"

"Is that all right, Margaret?"

"Sure, sure. Both of us need to shower anyway. By the way, I'm making *Asam pedas* with *ikan pari* for our dinner. Peter said it's one of your favourites. Good *ikan pari* is not so easy to get these days. If it's not fresh, you get a strong smell of ammonia. I like to cook it just as we're about to eat. If you cook it too long, de flesh will fall off. It's so tender. Siti! Siti! Ware are you?"

"Marm, I'm upstairs putting de aironed clothes away," Siti says in her Indonesian accent which has its own delightful lilt.

"Can you come down now and pound de onions and chillies for me?"

"Yes, Marm."

"I'm amazed by his memory. It's, indeed, one of my favourites. You can't get good tamarind in England. I used to substitute fresh lemon juice for it. And the skate wing from the Atlantic does not taste as sweet as the ones here. My mouth is already watering from the thought. You're so kind."

"Isn't she just wonderful? You are, you know, girlie!"

Margaret smiles at him, her slightly sour mood evaporating, and she chucks his chin in an intimate manner. They both go towards their room.

"It's my turn today, Grandma," Diana says. "Can you read *Goblet of Fire* to me? You didn't read to me last night."

"You were asleep when I came into your room."

"Oh."

"Wat about me? Wat about me?"

"Remember, children. Any word with a 'th' or 'wh' must be pronounced like this: I demonstrate with my tongue and lips—'*Th*at, *wh*at, *wh*y'. Try it."

"*Th*at, *wh*at, *wh*y." Both of them exaggerate the shape of their mouths and the position of their tongues to do it. They look quite comical so I try to keep a straight face.

"Excellent. Harry, you can come into Diana's room too. I'm sure your sister won't mind."

"So long as you don't mess my things up."

"And we'll sit on the bed, shall we?"

"Your turn now, Grandma," Harry commands. "Say the numbers in Chinese : *Yi, Er, San, Sze, Wu, Lui, Chi, Pa, Chui, Zi*."

So I go, "*Yi, Er, San…*"

It makes the children giggle hysterically, and they bend over, holding on to their sides from laughter.

"Grandma, it's *Zi*, not *Tzi*. It's *ten*, not *die!*"

"Did I say *die*? How extraordinary. Malay is definitely easier than Mandarin."

Looking through the eyes of the child I was, I'm amazed at the size of Diana's room which would have taken the entire space of our hut in the *kampung*. It is larger than Harry's, but with similarly fitted wardrobes, and is linked to his room by the interconnecting bathroom. Like Harry, she has a computer station with a *Game Boy* console beside which stands a holder full of CDs, VCDs and DVDs. Margaret has papered the room in a print crowded with pastel shade fairies—a population explosion of Tinker Bells. There are fairies everywhere—fairy dolls, fairy pictures and even a fairy mobile. Next to her favourite soft-clothed Tinker Bell, which they takes to bed each night, she has placed my gift to her, the figurine of Princess Diana. What seems more surprising for a girl her age is that Diana has books galore—hardbacks, paperbacks; books on fairy tales, classic children novels, adventure books, information books—all filling up the bookshelves, stacked up on tabletops, on the floor, bed, and in the bathroom; it is an Aladdin Cave of books.

This child obviously is very advanced in intellect and has never known want. I feel proud that it is *my* son, at least in part (since Margaret works too), who has given the children this privileged life. In some way, I suffer a kind of envy, perhaps, for not having these things as a child. It is amazing how unfulfilled needs stalk you to your adulthood, torment you for your lack. This, despite the fact that I live in luxury today. After all, Robert has provided well. With Hugh, everything had been a struggle—I worked whilst he played. But I needed him—needed to mother him—so I didn't mind his moving from job to job, in-between his parties and his trips whilst I worked. Perhaps if things were different, I could have gotten in touch with Peter earlier. But still. My life changed when I met Robert, in more ways than one. He took me from a terraced house in town to a big house in the country. How could a poor, *kampung* girl cope with all that luxury? Was this the sort of life my mother had before she ran away from a husband? I would have liked my mother to come to visit, to see the enormous house with its five bedrooms upstairs and just as many downstairs, with land enough for a whole HDB estate, but it was too late. My mother had died some years before. Duodenal cancer. Could it have been from the *sireh* she loved so much, though it usually caused buccal cancer of the cheeks? Perhaps it was from the terrible lack of nutrition she suffered in the days of the shanty-village. Had my father not thought to provide for his wife and daughter? Had he ever spared a thought about us, about me, or ever regret not making sure that his daughter had all she needed?

"What for you want to look for him?" Ang Huay had asked all those years ago.

It was a significant day, that, my turning sixteen. My mother had me when she was eighteen, so Ang Huay was thirty-four on my sixteenth birthday, but already aging from all the physical work—washing pails and pails of clothes on the scrubbing board, one item at a time. Huddled like that for hours, it was backbreaking work. Or, perhaps, the lack of love from a husband had parched her face and skin, stole the moistness from her lips. She had woken me up with my birthday ritual, a peeled hard-boiled egg in sweet noodle. The egg symbolised fertility, the noodle stood for long life and the sugared sauce for sweetness in my life. Had Ang Huay herself not been handed this gift? Was her life so sour because nobody brought her a bowl of sweetness when she woke on her birthday morning? I hated the stuff: the *mee sua*, too sweet and cloying for my liking, its taste quarreling with the taste of hard-boiled egg. It was hard to eat it, but I forced myself because it would please my mother, and secretly, I hoped that the ritual would really make a difference in my life. Since I was fourteen, I had taken over most of my mother's washing chores and still found time to give English tuition to the village children at $5 a child a month. I took in six children, all under eight, two one-hour sessions a week, fifty-two weeks a year. Compared to others in the village, my English was good, though I still had problems with tenses since the languages I spoke did not have similar ones to English. I taught the children how to spell and read, using Malay when the concept in English was too difficult or complex. It was fortunate that Ang Huay had decided to put me in a school that taught English. There was so much I was grateful to my mother for. Yet, I felt that there was still a yawning chasm in my life—I wanted a father. When my mother asked me why I wanted to meet him, I couldn't really explain. Perhaps I wanted to know what he looked like…*was* like. After all, he was one-half of what I had inherited. Nobody is born with a blank slate, surely. The genes we inherit predispose each of us to look a certain way, act a certain way—surely, our genes are the topography that shaped the weather of our life, mapped out on our slate.

"He's my father," I said, unsure of how I was to explain all that to my mother.

"Ah, yes. So true, so true. But, the type of man he is, he won't even remember he made you. Ah, but if you were boy, things might be different. Man like him so bothered about having son to carry his name into eternity, to make last rites at funeral. If you were boy, sure-sure, he wouldn't let me leave with you."

Ang Huay sighed as if the weight of her life was bearing down on her. I noticed that my mother sighed a great deal whenever she recollected her past life. Did she regret having given her youth to a man who had not loved her or did she regret running away from a husband who could have provided her all the comforts in life? Who could really know what goes on underneath the blanket of a marriage? But on my sixteenth birthday, I had not known a marriage, could not have guessed how tied a woman's hands could be in one. I was only thinking how I could have been born into my father's home, his wealth. Then, I cast a look around the small hut which was our home, at the sad wooden walls whitewashed with *kapor*/limestone, the used orange crates serving as table and chairs for those who found it uncomfortable to sit cross-legged on the floor or when the rats busied themselves scuttling around; the platform bed, hard and unrelenting; an old *almari* that someone had thrown out, the hinges of the door askew revealing the clothes inside. This, this was the reward of my mother's freedom and independence. Had she known what her life was going to be like after leaving her husband, would Ang Huay have deliberately chosen this type of existence?

"You're angry with him. That's why you don't want me to see him. And he's angry with you. But he may not be angry with me. How do you know he doesn't want to see me?"

"Has he come to look for you-*huh*?"

My mother's words were a rake that drew across my wound. I did not want to hear them. It was better for me to believe that my father really cared, that he was prevented from searching me out by his dragon-wife. Or that he had searched really hard but could not find me. Ang Huay's life must have been so unbearable that she went to great lengths to leave no trace of her whereabouts—so, it was impossible for my father to search the eleven states of Malaya, mountains and forests without clues. He probably did not guess that his errant wife had gone south nearly seven hundred miles away, to a different country, to an island with a safe harbour. Yet, I continued to live in hope. To anticipate is to be filled with hope, to be filled with hope means that you are still living. It's when you lose hope that you die an inner death. I must live to see my father—surely he loved me, his first-born, his own daughter. The starved mind has a great propensity for imagination, for turning hard facts into palatable placebos of truths.

"You keep saying that I'm like him. I have to see what he's like."

"I did not say you're totally like him-*lah*. It's natural to inherit some of him and some of me. I just don't want you to be hurt. He very hard businessman, no time for soft-soft things of heart. *Aiiyah*, if you must go look for him, go-*lah*. The only address I have is the one I know in Penang."

"I'll save up."

I sit on Diana's bed, each child on either side of me as I start to read. It's a joy to be given this task—a privilege, really. I can't get over how lucky I was to be pulled back into family life. I read slowly, pausing every now and again to explain something to Harry. Diana leans against me, one arm linked through mine, a contact I covet and welcome. I feel my granddaughter's body, its slight weight and warmth. I smell the freshness in the hair that sweeps my arm. Harry is leaning on my right shoulder, one thumb in his mouth, knees drawn up. There has been a yawning cavern in the place of my heart before and now it is slowly being in-filled by these children. I feel as if I'm in a beautiful dream, one from which I don't want to wake up from. Can it be that my trial has ended and that this is my sentence? What bliss. A deep sense of coming home enters my being, making me feel relaxed and my lids become heavy, the words in the book starting to blur and becoming jumbled. In that half-daze, I look at Harry and he seems to take on the shape and face of my own little boy.

" *'Once upon a time, there was a kind old woodcutter. He lived with his two children, Hansel and Gretel, and their stepmother in a little cottage. The pretty little cottage was set in a huge forest…'*"
As I read to him, Peter's joy is almost palpable. He snuggles close to me, claiming my body and my warmth. He is from me and always will own

part of me. This is the magic of procreation. You cannot have someone living in you, feeding on you, without your attachment to him. We are Siamese-twinned from the beginning, and when separated from my body, I will continue to experience his presence like a phantom limb that I have lost. But still, the magic goes deeper. Procreation is not just about posterity and lineage; it is about giving body to the spirit, to a soul that needs to be manifested to express itself. Motherhood is a woman's gift to the world.

"'...The next morning, Hansel and Gretel were taken to the woods again by their stepmother and father. This time, Hansel had no pebbles to mark his way so he broke off pieces of bread and threw the crumbs on the path so that they could find their way home. But later, after the stepmother and woodcutter had left them, Hansel could not find the path back. The birds must have eaten up the breadcrumbs. The brother and sister walked all over the forest. But they were lost and could not find their way home...'"

As the story advances, I feel my son's mood change, as if I have sensors on my skin. A mother, particularly a new mother, always has paranormal sensors that would make her spring awake when her baby cries, even if it's in the next room. So I know the exact moment when Peter stiffens his body.

"Mummy," he says, his voice plaintive as if he has just been given sight of his future. "Are you going to leave me?"

"No. Why, sayang? Why do you say that?"

"Hansel and Gretel's Mummy left them."

"My sayang," I say in a rush of emotion, putting aside the book and pulling him into my arms so that his chest is pressed against mine, his short legs wrapped around my waist. I shower him with a hundred kisses and with multiple words of assurance. "I love you. I love you. I shall never leave you."

How false one can be. How sure in one's falsehood.

"Mum, Mum."

"I'm coming, *sayang.* I'm coming." I mumble, still netted with sleep. I thought it was little Peter calling me.

"Dinner is ready."

The not-so-familiar voice startles me at first and I frown. Then, slowly, I open my eyes, expecting to see my small son but see instead a grown-up daughter gained through the law. I suffer a twinge of disappointment but tell myself not to belittle the worth of a relative gained through marriage. The girl is not from my body and yet, she is giving me the gift of being a mother again, has taken pains to cook food I like, behaving with such generosity of spirit like a true devoted daughter. I can't ask for more, especially since I have such a checkered past. Sometimes, you incur a debt not from your own spending but from the generous spending of others. I give a quick smile, then run my tongue over my teeth to scale the taste of sleep from my mouth.

"Oh, did I fall asleep reading to the children? I seem to tire so easily."

"Takes days to get rid of jet-lag-*lah*. Besides, you were given a heavy dose of drugs, difficult to get dem out of your system. Takes weeks."

"I never used to. Must be getting old."

In the open-concept dining area, the table is laid out with platters and tureens of steaming hot food, welcoming in their aroma. There is *bak kut* soup, chicken sauteed in fresh ginger strips and sesame oil, crispy onion omelettes, *pegedil*/potato cakes, *kangkong* and the *ikan pari*. Margaret has coordinated the dishes well. Ang Huay had always taught me that it was an art to make sure that each dish complemented the other, not just in flavours but also in its colour presentation, and more importantly, in the balance of the yin-and-yang of foods. Foods can be heaty or cooling to the body's *chi*; heaty ones energise a person's constitution, keeps him warm, makes him sexually able, appropriate when the libido and energy are low, when suffering from a cold. Cooling foods bring down a fever, cools a temper, dampens the fire of sexual arousal. Food is not just nourishment for the body, it is also medicine to the psyche. Obviously, Margaret is well taught. Siti is bustling in and out of the kitchen, bearing this-and-that. Diana acts the waitress and takes orders of drinks. There is a kind of wholesome unity about a family sitting down regularly together for a daily meal—a preservation of traditional values. So much is lost when members of a family eat at different times, especially when they eat sitting in front of the TV, watching the box instead of talking to each other or sharing each other's day.

"Grandma, you fell asleep!" Both children echo. "We've not heard the end of the story."

"You see, this is what old people are like. I promise, I'll continue the story another time." Then turning to Margaret, I ask, "Doesn't Siti mind cooking pork?"

"You know dey are so hard up in deir own country, dey have no choice. Compared to our neighbouring countries, Singapore is really wealthy. Dat's why the Indonesians, Thais, Filipinos, Sri Lankans all come to Singapore to look for jobs as maids. Their male counterparts come as labourers."

"De problem is dat if dey all left, Singapore's industry will come to a standstill," Peter interjects.

"Boy, you are so pessimistic."

"I'm realistic, girlie. Our own people won't get deir hands dirty. We produce hundreds of graduates each year and dey all want office jobs in management."

"It's the same in so-called civilized countries, isn't it? In England, we have to import foreign nurses, like myself, because English people don't want to work for so little money. But it's all relative, isn't it? What is little money to the English is a lot of money to foreign workers."

"Mummy, I'm hungry!" Harry says.

"Yes, let's eat."

"Wat drink would you like?"

"I miss fresh soya milk. Do you have any? Now what is it called in Teochew?"

"*Tao Huay Chwee*. Do you like it hot or cold?" Peter asks.

"Both. But for today, cold, please. I'm really thirsty and am still trying to reacclimatise myself to the heat here. *Tao Huay Chwee*. I remember it now. Amazing how words can disappear from one's memory."

"Only dose dat are painless." Then, turning to the children, he says, "Children, don't just sit dere. Go and help Siti bring de drinks in."

I'm startled by the acid in his tone. It corrodes his voice and tears his face into ribbons of displeasure. So, he is not immune to the past after all. Though he may not speak to me of it, he must still feel the residue of his abandonment. What worse fate could one have than that of being abandoned by one's own mother? How can I ever repay him or right the wrong I had done him? Sometimes I feel so terrible and evil that it would be easier if he were to pick up a sword to slay me. But I mustn't slip into melancholia, mustn't let my imagination run in a frenzy like a beheaded chicken. It is possible to read what is not there sometimes—our mind has been known to supply a script that is not in the play. The stage we see and the space our bodies move around in is not the only stage; there are plays within plays going on all the time in our lives. It is trying to sort out which is more real that becomes the difficult task. I'm glad that I hadn't responded because in the next moment, Peter is his usual amicable self, getting up to collect for me a glass of ice-cold *tao huay chwee*. He jokes about some Western people who think that you milk soya beans in the same way you milk cows and that the coconut contains milk in the hollow of its shell. I laugh loudly at his jokes, too loudly perhaps, keen to disperse the presage of gloom. Gathered in the cloud of potential pain, I suddenly remember Veronica, a friend whom I ran to when I had sought comfort.

"Oh, I've been so remiss," I cry. "I haven't told Veronica I got here."

"I've emailed her to tell her dat you've arrived safely. I've said dat you've been sleeping a lot and will call her wen you're ready."

"You did?"

"Yes," Peter says. "I hope you don't mind."

Exactly at that moment, both Diana and Harry arrive at the table with the appropriate drink for each person. They must have heard their father and both turn to him to say in unison, "It's *th*at, Daddy, not *dat*. It's *wh*en, not *wen*."

I smile.

"Wat's all dis about?"

"Oh, I'm trying to teach them to enunciate English properly and they're teaching me Mandarin."

"Good, good. *Th*at, *wh*en, *th*is. Satisfied? Now let's eat."

"*Chiak, chiak.*" Margaret invites as hostess. "Mum, *chiak*. I want you to taste de *ikan pari* first before you taste anything else. Tell me wat you tink."

"Mummy," both children say. "It's *th*e, not de, it's *th*ink, not tink."

"Aiiyah, I'm too old to learn-*lah.* Singaporean English good enough for around here-*lah.* No need to *chiak kantang*. It's okay for you kids to learn; maybe you want to go to university abroad."

After the rounds of calling and invitations to eat, I taste the sauce the skate wings are cooked in. The *asam pedas* has its own distinct aroma. The hot chilli strikes my palate with a cheerful zing and the freshly squeezed tamarind juice tickles my throat. An old familiar taste can call back years of long ago, remind you of where you've come from, what you have been. Each of our senses is linked to our history and it is this history that makes us respond in a particular way to what we eat, smell, see, hear or touch. *Gulia*, the scientists call this individual ownership of sensations. The *I* of today is a conglomerate of the *I*s of yesterdays—memories, feelings. *I* is never a blank card, never a Robinson Crusoe alone on a deserted island.

"This is delicious, just the way I remember my mother cooking it. We can't get fresh *asam* in England. And the fish, oh, see how it comes off the bone so easily. How fresh it is. And cooked just right. And the touch with the *kesum* is perfect. You really are clever."

"Tank you-*lah*. It's funny but I don't know what *kesum* is in English…"

"Mummy, it's *th*ank you, not tank you."

"Enough! Eat your food." Then her tone changes as she addresses me. "I don't know what *kesum* is in English."

"Sweet basil," I say. "The Thais use them for their curries too. Do you know that the *asam pedas* has inspired a Malay *pantun* that defines destiny or *jodoh*?"

"Really? Wat's dat?" Margaret asks.

"*Asam di-gunong*/Tamarind on the mountain
Garam di-laut/Salt in the sea
Kalau ada jodoh/If it is destined
Jumpa juga di-dalam periok./Will meet inside the (cooking) pot."

"Wah! Grandma, you can speak so many languages!" Diana says with admiration.

I'm surprised at myself, at how I had retrieved this bit of information that has traveled through time to inform me. No matter how much and how long I had shaped myself to be something else, somebody else, the truth will out. The bones of my own culture and past are interred within me, no matter how I might clothe those bones, no matter what accent I adopt. And when I'm consumed by fire and become ash, I'm that which I began with. Nothing more, nothing less. Ultimately, there is no escaping one's roots. Was it

Pakchik Awang who taught me the verse all those years ago or was it Nenek Bongkok? Perhaps I was wrong and Peter is right - words don't simply disappear, they just get lost in the wilderness of memory and we can find them again if we have the ability or dare to track through its tangled jungle. It is possible, then, that painful words heard and received are the predators that won't allow us to sleep easy; they continue to prey on our heart and mind.

10

"Veronica? Are you okay? You sound different."

"I'm getting better, had a touch of flu recently. I'm still on flucloxacillin."

"Listen, you mean a great deal to me, you know. Do take care. It's funny—just hearing your voice connects me back to England. Strange how England feels more like home to me now that I'm so far away. Aren't human beings tragic? We seem only to appreciate the worth of something when it's no longer there. Perhaps it's just me. You know what? Despite my new relationships, I still miss you terribly. What's the weather like? Is spring in sight yet? I love walking 'round the ponds at this time of year. I get such a thrill seeing those tiny leaves unfurling fresh from their buds. There is such promise in spring. I just realised how hard I'd find it to live in a place without seasons to break up the year."

"Me too. But, at the moment, it's miserable here. The cold makes these old bones ache. January and February have always been the worst times, haven't they? The festivities of Christmas and the New Year are gone, and winter seems to drag its feet. Besides, the flu bug is going 'round. Post me some of your warm sunshine. I miss you, too. Listen, I'm indestructible, the perpetual survivor. Don't you go fretting about me. It's time for you to enjoy yourself with the family. How are you getting on with them? Peter emailed me, you know; he's very considerate. You should be proud."

"I can't tell you how happy I am."

I go into details about my treasures, the gifts I've been given. Veronica listens patiently, letting me express my newfound joy. My friend and mentor has that knack of knowing when to speak, when to listen, when to encourage, when to come on strong—a really special person. She has been friend, sister, mother. Without her, I would probably not have survived. And yet, Veronica was not one to make friends easily; she hardly chats to neighbours, and definitely was not one to make small talk. That's probably why she gained the reputation of being formidable. Because she is always so engrossed in her thoughts, she tends not to notice people when she goes to the village; perhaps this is another reason why she is said to be unapproachable. But she is not even aware of what people think of her, nor does she care really. She lives in a renovated barn on a field that once was part of an enormous working farm, but what with BSE and Foot-and-Mouth destroying the livestock and the farmer's earnings, the farmer was now struggling to keep the farm going. The barn had been set apart from the farm years ago and sold separately. It was sufficiently far away from the main farmhouse and other outbuildings to accord Veronica the privacy she needs, yet without feeling vulnerable on her own. The barn is nearly four hundred years old and was cleverly converted with numerous rectangles of skylights and floor-to-ceiling windows that brought in the sun. It suited Veronica because she likes painting in natural light. Its vaulted beamed roof gives the hall and living room a feeling like in a cathedral. There is a definite feeling of peace in the barn, like the kind you find in churches. Perhaps it is not different, the search for a God or the search for truth in creative excellence. There is no conventionality about Veronica; she uses the whole downstairs area as a studio, canvases standing everywhere in different stages of completion, dust sheets over some of them, tubes of paints, easels. You would be lucky to find a stool to sit on when you visit. If not for her agent who marketed her paintings, Veronica would be an unknown, for she cared more about her work than the selling of it. I admire her dedication to her craft, her unshakable belief in her art. Life must be so meaningful when you can express your creativity. Unfortunately, I have no such talent. Even if I had any, I'd probably squander it, I'm so inapt. These days, Veronica paints for a different purpose—to keep her arthritic fingers moving, and her eyes from losing their sight. She hasn't sold any paintings for a while now. She paints so that she does not succumb.

"You deserve it, girl. Don't let anything spoil it, mind. Don't let the past shadow your present. The present is your sun—brilliant sunshine, happiness. Bask in it. There's no mileage in letting your guilt strangle you like a collar anymore. Make the most of your time with your son. Take it one step at a time. I know you've been through a lot lately…"

I feel a squeeze in the region of my heart. I'm aware of what Veronica is referring to and even that slight allusion makes my eyes wash wet. It's when you think you're in control that you are caught unawares. It makes me realise how I'm still hurting. I keep the threatening tears in check by maintaining a silence. How near sorrow tends to hover, quick to descend. Are humans the only species to be blighted with this constant polarity, the Janus syndrome, tugged here and there by our emotions? Something must be said for the efforts of those who try to transcend this: yogis, Zen masters, Buddhist monks. Every single effort they make is laying a brick to build a wall from which we can climb over and out of our human condition.

"… What has happened here has happened. Don't keep on going over and over it. You've done enough of that. You can't change it anymore than you can change the seasons. And stop blaming yourself. Nobody does. Not even the police. It is clear that Robert made his own fate. Unequivocally so. I know it's hard, but you've managed remarkably well so far. Courage is the resolution to move forward. And you have it, Kim. Tell yourself that. Leave your regrets behind. Someone once said, don't ask me who: '*Look towards the light/ And the shadows will fall behind you*'. If you think about it, it makes sense. What is the point of staying rooted in darkness which is causing you grief? You have to make the shift, move toward the light. Hello, Kim? Kim, are you still there? Are you all right, my dear?"

True friends are strands of a plait—individuals yet united. The way a successful marriage should be. Neither one should be pulled too tight or it will destroy the balance and harmony. Veronica is right; there is a lot in life to be thankful about, why rake through old issues? Like autumn leaves, it is best to let them die a natural death, decompose, *become* compost. In dying, they give back to the earth what they had received. As a Buddhist, I, like my mother before me, believe that when we die, we only give up our body to be turned over in the earth but our spirit lives on. No experience in life is a waste; everything has its place and purpose. They prepare you for the next life. Face to face, I probably would not have the courage to say it to Veronica but now I do.

"I love you," I say, and this time *she* is silent and I'm unsure if she felt I was stepping too close to her.

"Now, don't get all sentimental. Listen, I got to go."

She is definitely not comfortable. I say goodbye with a little sadness.

"Is everything okay or not? You look worried," Peter asks when he walks into the living room. I'm touched that he notices. With his exceptional height and the span of his shoulders, he is immediately arresting; I wonder if others find him so as well or am I just experiencing a mother's pride? It's a pity, though, that he should let his chest collapse forward that much. Has the burden of his loss in childhood been so great that he cannot stand up straight to face the world? I know his poor posture restricts his breath, imprison his spirit. Worse, I know, with an excruciating pain, that it was I who inflicted it on him.

"Veronica doesn't sound too good. A touch of flu, she says. But like all these English, you've got to read past their understatements."

"Wat opposites! In Singapore, most people describe their mishaps in superlatives. People tend to exaggerate deir symptoms to gain sympathy. So everyting dat happens becomes a kind of minor tragedy. So melodramatic-*one*!"

"That's rather observant of you. Usually someone living in his own culture has difficulty making an objective judgment."

"Ah, but I'm astute," he says in a self-mocking tone.

"I'm very proud of you, you know."

"What for-*lah*?"

"Well, your lovely family, this home, your obvious success as an IT specialist, the fact that you turned out so well despite…"

"Aiiyah, wat's in de past is in de past. Let's start from today-*ahh*?"

Does he really mean it? Is he saying it's time to let go of the past? Or is he just evading the issue? I want to throw out bouquets of love, beat my chest to confess my guilt and sorrow for their lost years, for the pain I have caused him, but I'm so overwhelmed, I cannot speak, cannot say the things I want to say. What clamps the tongue when millions of words are queuing to be spoken, have been waiting to be spoken? How can I have nothing to say when the Lego block of unused words have built up so high they hurt my thoughts? How can I have nothing to say when I ingest at least one hundred and twenty thousand words a week? That's six million, two hundred and forty thousand words a year. Where do they all go? Do the words topple off from its height, fall off the edge and into a black hole that exists inside me and are sucked into its swirling vortex, never to reappear? If words convey our inner world to the outer, the fact that we cannot articulate them means that our experiences remain prisoners, confined to the dungeons of our secret self.

"I think it's time to visit my mother's grave. If it's okay with you and Margaret, I'd like to go one of these days," I say instead, as though this would lighten the pressure pot of the moment. Isn't it amazing how we humans can skate away so readily from emotional thin ice?

"I'll take you," Peter volunteers quickly. "I can arrange for some time off from work. Chua Chu Kang is a long way from here."

"That's very kind. But you hardly knew her. Besides, you might not be comfortable in a Chinese cemetery. It doesn't look as neat and tidy as a Christian one. Anyway, I think I need to be on my own with her this time if it's all right with you. I want to connect with her spirit and it's more difficult if I'm distracted. Perhaps we can go together as a family at another time. It might be a good idea to talk to Margaret first though, to see if she'll be happy with the children visiting their great grandmother's grave. After all, the Chinese cemetery is a pagan place, and visiting it, you might be confronted with some pagan rituals, like the burning of joss sticks and the offering of food. Since you are all devout Catholics, she might object to it."

"Take a taxi den. Don't mess with bus or MRT."

Like father, like son. Like Peter, Victor had volunteered very quickly to take me to Penang when I told him about my father. Besides Victor's superb physique which I had fallen in love with, it was this attitude of taking things in hand and being able to wield a difference which impressed a naïve seventeen year-old. A man who has power is perfumed with a scent which a woman find irresistible; she becomes a rutting female waiting to be fulfilled. It is not just the money he acquires to buy her baubles which is important, it's the power behind it. That is why a man's looks are not as important as a woman's and he can pull a young girl even whatever age he is. Victor, at that time, dressed in his army uniform and his ambition to be somebody successful was an aphrodisiac. He was my prince personified, volunteering to go up to Penang, to fight my dragon. I was ready to swoon. In an age where dating wasn't encouraged and holding hands was tantamount to an engagement, even a bus ride together was an event. Our first bus ride was memorable. We were on our way to the pictures at *Capitol*, riding the STC (*Singapore Traction Company*) bus where we sat side-by-side. His shoulders were so broad that they touched mine and as the bus trundled along, passing other villages, then shop-houses with their five-foot way, his shoulders kept on tapping mine. I did not know if he purposely placed his shoulders in that position but I was thrilled, our first tentative physical contact. For a *kampung* girl in those days, that was daring! Nothing went unnoticed in a village where the attap huts were located in close proximity to each other. Nearly everyone knew everyone else. The villagers had a habit of sitting outdoors in the evening, on makeshift seats or on the doorsteps and threshold of their homes, gaily chatting, gossiping—and watching. If a young girl went out, heads would turn to observe who she went out with, how many different young men she went out with, and how she was dressed. If she was seen with more than one boyfriend, she was deemed *loose*. But I was not troubled, I knew that, though.

Victor was my first and only boyfriend; this was the man I wanted for a husband, for on that bus ride, an important feeling had emerged—I felt protected, felt as if I could depend on Victor for everything. That was why it was all the harder to bear when I discovered that my trust was actually misplaced. Trouble was that by the time I found out, we were far into the marriage, when I already had Peter.

"Let me come with you to Penang," he had said. "You don't want to go up-country by yourself-*lah*. Nowadays, so dangerous for a girl to travel alone. We can go by train or coach."

It wasn't so simple then. Traveling to Penang, more than seven hundred miles away from Singapore, and searching out my father's house, would mean at least a couple of days away, which meant nights away, too. By this time, I was eighteen and he was twenty. Still, it wasn't done for a young girl to consider being together all that time with a young man who was not yet her husband. My reputation would be tarnished. Unless of course, we were chaperoned or went in a group. But I desperately wanted to find my father, and having Victor with me would be an advantage.

"People will talk," I said.

"Not if they think we are married. You know I want to marry you, right? After I finish NS and have a job?"

"What will your mother say? She's such a devout Catholic."

"She's not going to know-*wat*. I'll tell her I'm going up-country with my NS friends-*lah*."

My heart leapt. We hadn't even kissed yet and he was as good as proposed. And he was even prepared to deceive his mother on account of me. But years of upbringing wasn't easy to shove aside. I wanted to be a good girl, for myself, for him, and for our social circle. Bad girl, good girl. There was no in-between. In the kampong, holding hands was tantamount to an engagement. Nobody would dream of kissing or hugging in public. There was *petting* and *heavy petting* and *going all the way.* Only bad girls go all the way. Yet, I wanted to look for my father. It was a dilemma. Then one day, he bought me a ring, a cheap gold ring with a small pearl cluster knotted at the top. To me, the ring seemed the most precious thing he could have given me. I'm sure I glowed.

"Dis is a Promise Ring. My promise to marry you wen I have a job and can support you. De day I saw you, I know dere will not be anybody for me anymore. Say you will give yourself only to me."

"I promise," I said.

Caught up in the pink of romance, I supplied my mind with all the words he didn't say exactly, all the feelings he did not utter. When I told my mother about his promise and particularly about his willingness to help me trace my father, she said, "He's an honorable man. You can trust him."

My need to locate my father helped me to overcome my prudishness. It was a comforting thought that I was not going to be alone when I confronted my father, just in case he was not pleased to see me. If he was, I would be proud to introduce Victor as my future husband and get my father's blessing. Also, he wouldn't have to feel that I had sought him for money or patronage; I had my own man now. Yes, finally, there was a man in my life, a man who wanted to take care of me, who loved me. The thought was intoxicating. In the end, I allowed myself to be persuaded to let Victor go up-country with me. He promised me a hotel room with twin beds, two rooms would be way beyond our financial capacity. I was in love so I trusted him entirely. Although I learnt a great deal about the body in nursing school and had lots of technical knowledge and that short-lived experience when that patient's penis came to life after coming out of the general anesthesia, I did not really have any experience about how married couples actually *do it*. The subject was one which my mother was very reticent about. Even when I was twelve and my period came and I thought I was bleeding to death, Ang Huay was not very enlightening.

"You are woman now. I make seven-flower-water and you bathe with it. When body is like this, keep away from male-people."

Ang Huay had many uses for the seven-flower ritual: when there was cause to celebrate, to remove bad luck or its prevention, to take away fear and illness. She would pluck the petals from seven different flowers like jasmine, rose, *bunga chempaka*, gardenia, lily, orchid and *bunga melor*. Why seven, I asked one day. *Seven good-good number for spirit*, my mother replied. She'd scatter the colourful petals into a basin of water, perfumed with her blessings. *Important to pour water from top of head down*, she reminded me each time. Was Ang Huay celebrating or clearing my aura of bad luck when I had my period? She took a square of cotton material and taught me how to fold it to make it into a pad and how to fasten it around my waist with a cloth tie and safety pins. Ang Huay had not known of such modern things like a sanitary pad nor a sanitary belt and, of course, she could not teach her daughter. Eventually when I discovered the sanitary pad, it was a small miracle for me. It was amazing for me to discover that you don't have to tackle the messy task of washing a used cloth-pad, nor did you have to fiddle with a home-made belt and pins. Under my clothes, the cloth-belt used to get tangled and the pad would move from where it should be. More than not, I ended up with bloody stains on my panties and skirt. In later years, when stick-on pads came into vogue where no belt was required, I thought how advanced things had become and how lucky young people were that they didn't have to cope with cloths and pins. And when tampons came into fashion, I was more amazed. Of course, they were not acceptable at first, people believed that the tampons caused a de-flowering of a virgin, broke her hymen, only married women were thought suitable to use them. Eventually, when I did try them after having had Peter, I could not believe the freedom tampons gave me. I really enjoyed swimming, and my periods, which were once an obstacle to my favourite pastime, weren't anymore.

This was the state of delicious innocence I was in when I went to meet Victor for our trip to Penang. I was full of expectancy of all that was nice and romantic. Such pleasure, such joy to be so pure in thought, not yet tainted by desires and expectations; not yet sated by Hollywood films of easy leaps into bed, or the raw sex of Internet sites. The train station was located at Keppel Road, not far from the harbour. It was the only train station on the island that was run by the Malaysian government. When I saw him there on the platform, anxiously looking out for me, my heart turned over. I knew I was embarking on a journey that was going to change my life in more ways than one.

When we got on the train, I was suddenly shy. Here I was alone with him, away from the prying eyes of the *kampung* folks, away from everyone who knew us. Although there were other passengers on the train, they would assume that the young couple was either engaged or married and therefore did not pay too much attention to us. Without saying a word, Victor took my hand clasped it in his own. His gesture seemed awkward, shy, rough even. It was the first time we had made such contact and my heart raced almost at the same speed as the train racing out of Singapore, onto the causeway and into Johor Bahru, the southernmost town of Peninsular Malaya. The green arms of the coconut palms in the plantations waved as the train swept past. Flat lands grew into mounds of hills and then spread out into valleys, changing and changing as the train went on its journey. Victor's shoulder was touching mine. It was reassuring then, not later. Later, the pressure of his body became the walls of a prison, his hands, an executioner's axe. Uncertain, not knowing how to behave or what to say, I pointed out the rubber tappers to him. They were mostly Indian, more women than men, their spines curved as they bend with the hollow drum on their backs. They go 'round systematically to each tree, cutting a deep-V into its trunk, then as the tree bleeds latex into the small cut hanging 'round its hip, the tappers tipped the contents of the cup into their drums. As the train sped northward, we left the state of Johor and went into Seremban and then into Selangor. I had fleeting views of low ground pineapple plantations, then buffalos raking the plough through the knee-high water of paddy fields. Women and children planted the seedlings into the water, their skin already brown by nature became darker still from their work in the hot sun. Whilst I was observing all this, Victor was quiet beside me. To fill the silence, I made up the words in my mind that he would have said if he was articulate. But I was content. When we disembarked from the train to board the ferry at Butterworth, he carried our bags as if we were, indeed, a couple. As the ferry crossed the Straits into Georgetown, capital of Penang, my joy evaporated and I was suddenly assailed with doubt and fear. Perhaps my mother was right; perhaps it was not a good idea to try to locate my father after all.

"What if my father disowns me?"

"Aiiyah, don't tink about bad tings-*one*," Victor said. "If he is still alive and he knows who you are, sure he will accept you-*lah*. Don't worry so much. Tomorrow, after breakfast, we will hire a car and drive to the address."

By the time we got to the hotel, it was late evening. I hung behind as Victor registered us as man-and-wife. And then, the enormity of what we were doing hit me and I was flushed with embarrassment, angry at myself for agreeing to it, confused over what to feel about Victor. He was so in charge. I was proud of him and at the same time, I resented his confidence. But we were here now, and his intent was good to help me find my father. He took me out to the hawker stalls lining the street outside the hotel where we sat on low stools right next to the satay man. The fragrance of the satay being roasted on the open fire made me salivate. I spoke to the satay-seller in Malay and the man beamed showing tobacco-stained teeth. He busied his hands whilst talking to us, cutting up the *ketupat*, laying out the pieces of cucumber and fresh onions, ladled the peanut sauce into two small bowls. Victor picked up a couple of satay sticks to put on my plate. It was the ultimate show of love. I was won over. The satay man nodded his approval, assuming that we were newlyweds. Later, as we were going up to our room, Victor said, "As soon as I get work, we get married-*hor*?" I had a vague sense that all this talk of marriage was leading up to something, but I wasn't sure what. But I was to find out.

We had turned the light off and the room was lit only by the blue haze coming from the hotel's neon sign outside. I was in my own bed when I heard him get out of his bed to move toward me. Suddenly afraid, I pulled the coverlet tightly around me. He stood beside my bed, then whipped off the coverlet and clambered in beside me without so much as a *May I please*? I was wearing a pair of cotton pajamas and he was wearing a singlet and shorts. Before I could react, he pulled me tight towards him.

"I love you. I love you. You love me too, right?" He asked, his voice changing into a tone I had not heard before, hoarse with urgency and hunger.

"Yes, of course."

In the half-light, he seemed like a beast descended on me as he swung a heavy leg over me. Without preamble, he planted a wet mouth on mine, capturing my lips, imprisoning my breath. Was this a kiss? Was I supposed to enjoy this? When his tongue snaked into my mouth, I nearly retched so violent was the intrusion. Surely, it was my inexperience which made me so unprepared and therefore made me feel revulsed. This was presumably what all adults do. I should be whipped for not knowing. I was, after all, a junior nurse. But knowing what the physical body looked like and what you do with different parts of the anatomy when you were with the opposite sex were two different things. I should try to relax and learn to submit to the strange sensations. He pushed hard against me and he slipped his hands under my pajama top to clutch at my breasts as if they were some kind of prize he had been yearning for. I wanted to fight him off, yet I wanted to be held. He squeezed and he kneaded, making little sounds in his throat which made me wonder if he was choking. But I daren't ask. This was all about Victor and what Victor wanted. I told myself it was all right. This was what people in love do. I knew I loved him, and I would give him what he needed, even if he took without asking. After all, hadn't he professed how much he loved me? His large hand traced the curves of my body and to my surprise, I discovered I liked the feel of it, liked the feeling of power that came from knowing that he found me desirable. Yet I did not respond, laying there like an inert lump of flesh for him to knead. His movements were sharp and short as though he was in a hurry. I was totally confused by my opposing emotions and felt incapable of knowing how to respond. I felt his hand move away from my body to that place between my legs. It was so unexpected and rough that I was taken aback. Yet the pressure that he put there awakened a new sensation and I felt ashamed to realise that I rather enjoyed it too. In the next instant, he withdrew his hand to shove it under his own shorts. In the next moment, he was jerking and jerking—and then a rough push toward me as his body and legs stiffened. When he groaned, I thought he was sick. I still wasn't clear what was happening. I lay there feeling confused and unhappy, my body out-of-sorts, desires awakened yet not fulfilled. And then I felt his body convulse again, but this time, the rhythm was different. With a shock, I realised that he was sobbing. I propped my elbow up in alarm, wondering what was happening now. I wasn't prepared for this, my hero, my knight in shining armour, nose running in an undignified fashion.

"What's…what's the matter?"

"You shouldn't tempt me like this-*one*," he sniveled. "You shouldn't let me into your bed. You shouldn't let me touch your breasts. We're not married-*wat*. It's a mortal sin. Because of you, I have to go to confession tomorrow."

22

One of the things I missed most about Singapore, besides its hawker food, is swimming under the canopy of natural sky, in the heat of the tropical sun. As long as my feet can touch a sandy seabed without me swallowing salt water, I can relax enough to relish in the push and pull of waves. But I prefer the swimming pool. When I was a teenager and the first public swimming pool was opened at Farrer Park, I learnt to completely give myself to the sensations of my body floating in water, no fear of the waves pulling me too far offshore. It is, indeed, a special gift when you're able to be at one with your action, totally absorbed and relaxed to the exclusion of all else, especially from the tyranny of thoughts. For me to enjoy that blissful abandonment, it boosted my confidence to know that the pool had a defined perimeter which meant that I was safe and unlikely to be swept by currents out into the open sea inadvertently. Some people, like Robert, break boundaries as a challenge, whereas I, coward that I was, was one of those who relished in the security of boundaries. It was not something that Robert could ever understand. In the end, I was sure I disappointed him. I was nowhere anything like Emas, the tall elgant woman who was so good in everything she did, so courageous, so adventurous. I must have been such a weak imitation to her. Being a second wife is not easy; you are always in the shadow of the first, either because the first was much hated, or worse, much loved. It's harder still if you are in competition to a much-adored ghost.

I felt a bit like the second Mrs. De Winter when she first arrived at Manderley, though in Robert's situation, he would never have killed his wife. It seems to be my lot that I disappoint and do not measure up to what people expect of me. It's an affliction that—being a misfit—works into your psyche and inevitably undermines your belief in yourself.

Not being a sporty person even as a teenager, swimming became my regular exercise routine, affordable because it cost only forty cents to get into the public pool. Though the pool was nothing near the luxury of the pool at the condominium where Peter and Margaret have their apartment, it had seemed magnificent then, a deep rectangle of bright blue water that beckoned in the open sunshine, although the water smelled strongly of chlorine. It would have been an impossible dream when I was a teenager to have conceived of a home with privileged access to a swimming pool as it was at my son's home.

Now that I'm more settled in, I have developed a daily routine. I wake up when the family wakes up at seven. I sit and have breakfast with them. Not just toasts and cereals—definitely *not* toasts or cereals—but a fascinating variety of Singaporean breakfasts: *pau* and *siew mai*, the dumplings steamed by Siti before the family awakes; or fried *roti prata* with fish curry, noodles, and *lontong,* whose gravy Siti had prepared the evening before, the rice cakes cut into squares; *nasi lemak*—coconut rice wrapped in banana leaves; and *chok*, a rice gruel. The list was endless. These were the sort of foods I missed most whilst in England. You can change a lot about the way you talk, the way you dress and everything else when you adopt a new culture but the most difficult thing to change is your diet and your way of eating. It is etched in your DNA. The thing is that the variety of food is so easily available here, in food centers from very early in the morning to late at night, all cooked fresh when you order, fast food with a difference. People here can afford to eat proper meals three or four times a day and yet not have to cook even if they don't have a full-time maid.

"Grandma, would you comb my hair for me?"

"Grandma, would you tie my shoes for me?"

Grandma. A simple word. An everyday word. Yet it is like rain on parched land. When you've deprived yourself of a family, every single recognition which returns you to the flock counts. I revel in it, filled with joy to be given the opportunities to do such things.

"Ware's my school bag? Siti! Ware did you put my school bag?" Then, as if he suddenly remembers, Harry says with spittle escaping, "*Wh*ere? Where is it?"

"I can't find my *Social Science* book!" Diana races around the apartment.

"Don't forget to give your teachers de notes I wrote."

"Dese socks don't match. Have you seen my club tie, girlie?"

This is the nature of mornings in the apartment. The close familiarity of family is both delightful and jarring since I've been without for so many years and had become used to a more gentle return to the world. As you get older, too, you cannot cope as well with the frenzy and the noise like you could when you were younger. It is nature's way that you have your children when you are young. Even if science and technology make it possible for a fifty-something-year-old woman to have a child, it would not really be a normal condition, mentally and emotionally; you wouldn't have the energy to give your young child what he or she needs. This should be the grandparent stage where you are privileged to enjoy your grandchildren for a while, but are glad when they go home too. I delight in kissing the children goodbye as they set off for school, the sensation of their arms around my neck lingering in a delicious way long after they have gone. Did Hugh know how much I had given up for him? That in giving up Peter, I had given up *his* children too because we would not have been in the same country? At least not, until Peter came for me. How is it that a man can take so much from a woman and not know or value the enormity of her sacrifice?

Peter takes one car and Margaret the other, and he drops the children off at their respective schools. In the afternoons, Siti takes the taxi to collect the children. After everyone has left, the apartment settles back into normality.

"Whew! Is it always as hectic in the mornings?" I speak to Siti in Malay which is a close enough relative of the Indonesian language. Though I stumble for the right word occasionally, I know I have primed its flow and the old language, buried within me for so long is reemerging.

"Sometimes it's worse. The children are so dependent on me to get their things ready. But it's okay. I keep thinking that if I do everything properly for them, someone will do the same for my children." Her voice breaks a little.

"You have children? You look like a teenager." I'm incredulous.

"Yes, Marm. I'm already thirty. And my children, they are nearly the same age as Diana and Harry."

"So why did you leave Indonesia?"

"To earn money, Marm. So that I can afford to send them to school. My husband left me for another woman. My mother is helping me look after my son, Abu, who is twelve and Salimah—she is nine, Marm."

Stupid, stupid question. How tactless can I be? My heart squeezes. Here is one truly loving mother, not like myself. This is a mother who leaves her children, not by choice, so that she suffers their loss so that *they* can benefit. I'm ashamed and humbled.

"Where is your home?"

"Outside Jarkarta, Marm."

"Can't you get work there?"

"No, Marm. There's no work in the villages except tending the fields. But the crops are poor so there isn't enough. There is work in Jakarta, but I get more pay here."

"Do you have photos of your children."

"Yes, Marm. Do you want to see them?"

"Oh, yes, please."

There had been days in England when I had wanted to talk about Peter, wanted someone to ask me about my son so that I, too, could whip out the one precious photograph I had of him that I carried in my wallet. But no one asked because no one knew of his existence. Hugh, so busy with his life, never thought to ask about him. Perhaps he thought he would be hurting me more by asking. Only Veronica knew. Only Veronica asked. Veronica who quietly invited me out to the theatre or a film when she knew it was Peter's birthday.

Peter's and Margaret's maisonette is luxurious and well-appointed, but when Siti leads me to her room, I'm mildly shocked. The small room is adjacent to the kitchen, next to the utility area, next to the rubbish chute, so small that the single bed had to be pushed against the wall. It has obviously been designed as a storeroom in the days when foreign maids were not so easily available. Siti also does the ironing here as is evident from the open ironing board standing in the little space there was left. Her few clothes are folded neatly and placed onto open shelves, her meager belongings in one plastic crate. On the window sill is a framed photo which she picks up to hand to me, proudly pointing out her son and daughter, telling me about their likes and dislikes. She is voluble. It must be so hard to live amongst other people's children, caring for other people's children and not to see your own nor to talk about them. I shared her pain, her longing. I could cry.

"They're lovely," I manage to say.

"I miss them," Siti says and her voice catches. "But I earn so much here."

"Oh, yes?"

"Yes, Marm. I earn two hundred and fifty a month, Marm. One Singapore dollar is thousands of rupiahs. And I can send nearly all of that home. But the first six months was hard; I didn't get any money at all. I had to pay off the agency who got me this job and the flight cost to Singapore from Jakarta."

I gulp. No wages for six months? And one Singapore dollar is only twenty-seven pence! She works from seven o'clock in the morning to nine or ten at night, six days a week, for less than a hundred pounds a month! Surely this is exploitation. But by whom? Yet, I'm cautious not to say too much in case I make waves. But I remind myself to ask Margaret about the situation, whether this is normal practice for the employment agency who brings the maids across, from the Philippines, Indonesia, Thailand, and Sri Lanka. Perhaps whilst I'm here, I can add to Siti's wages for the extra washing and work. But I'd better speak to Margaret first. She is, after all, the lady of the house.

"But I can send home all of my salary, Marm, because I have nothing to spend here. Marm Margaret and Sir Peter, they give me all the food I can eat. Sometimes too much! Look, I am already putting on weight. When I go back to Indonesia, my family will not recognise me. And they take me out too in their car so I see some places of Singapore. We have even been to Malaysia at golf resorts. Sir Peter and Marm Margret are keen golfers. And they buy me clothes too. For my birthday, Marm bought me a pair of golf earrings. Real gold, twenty-four carat. If I am desperate for money, I could always pawn them."

"Don't you take a day off?"

"Only sometimes, Marm, to meet my cousin who also works in this country. She gets to go to Canada and the U.S. with her employers because they have small children. They always go for skiing holidays and Wati dresses the children and takes them to the slopes whilst their parents ski off somewhere else. Wati is so lucky; she has seen snow. I've not seen snow. Is there snow in England, Marm? Wati and I usually meet at Lucky Plaza. But we don't lunch out; it's too expensive for us. Why waste money when we can eat at home? We catch up on our news, do a bit of shopping. I get a chance to buy presents for my children. But mostly, I work Sundays so Marm Margaret gives me another twenty dollars for each Sunday that I don't take off."

If my mother had not educated me, I thought, I would have been in Siti's position. What was that English saying? *There but for the grace of God go I?* Something like that anyway. The days in the *kampong* had been grim for me—the lack of food, the cockroaches and rats—but Siti's life must be worse, way out in the sticks outside Jakarta, children neglected by their father. How is it that men can buck and thrust without conscience? How can they not connect a child with the product of their act? How can they not realise that as their desire ends, a new life can begin? I know what Siti's children will feel; after all, my own father, too, never came for me, never acknowledged my existence. In my childhood, I had searched for my father in every man that came to the *kampong*, such a futile task. During those times too, there were not many consumer goods around, goods which tempted and beguiled, things that really showed you your lack if you had none. It must be terrible for people like Siti these days when there is so much wealth around yet you are situated at the other end of the scale. I must ask Margaret if I can contribute.

So it seems such an indulgence afterwards when Siti goes about her duties in the apartment and I make my way downstairs to swim. Maids are permitted by the poolside and other recreational facilities in the condominium only as appendages to their employers, to fetch and carry or to look after the children. They are not allowed to swim or play squash and tennis. It's a *us* and *them* culture. I feel some guilt, yet the very idea that here is a swimming pool just at the doorstep for me to swim in excites me to no end. What privilege! I'm learning quickly the convenience of living in a city where everything is close at hand. When you live in the country, you have to drive miles to the nearest swimming pool, supermarket or shopping center. I feel proud of my son as I take the lift down and walk into the well-landscaped park that sprawls in front of the crescent of towering blocks, a park that contains a gymnasium, three outdoor tennis courts and four indoor glass squash courts. This is one of the wonderful things about being a parent; you can lay claim to the achievements of your children so that even as your own life is ebbing, a small measure of your life, like an egg on a spoon, is carried forward by them to continue the relay. Around the Olympic-size swimming pool, palm trees have been planted nearby to provide shade from the relentless tropical sun. It makes the whole place look like some sleek brochure advertisement.

The Olympic-size pool is not busy at that time of the morning or on hot days. Most Asians, particularly the Chinese, prefer to stay out of the sun since they rate a fair complexion as an example of beauty. It's an interesting phenomenon to see Asians when they go swimming for the moment they emerge from the pool, many of them will lay on the deck chairs but will have towels thrown over their bodies to protect them from being tanned. So, except for some Asian children, the exposed bodies lying on the deck chairs when it's sunny are usually Caucasians. On a weekday such as it is today, there is no one at the pool. The orange orb of sun strikes the glazed tiles at the bottom and sides of the pool and makes the water seem very blue. It is one of those modern pools where the water overflows into the flood zone running all 'round its borders making the water, which is level to the ground, dance and skip in the breeze coming in from the sea. Earlier when I had put on my swimsuit, I was appalled at the looseness of my belly and worse, at how much of it there was! I scanned my hips disapprovingly and noticed how pear-shaped I had become as if an avalanche of flesh had taken place from chest and breasts sliding to a stop at my tummy and bottom. Because Robert had always told me what a great body I had, I had been lulled into a false image of myself. It is lethal to base your image on someone else's opinion of yourself, whether it's a body image or one that has to do with character. You tend to lose sight of your real self. Now that Robert was not around to sustain the fantasy, the mirror has cracked and I have to face my own uncomfortable reality. It is not just this thought that suddenly troubles me; there is something else lurking behind it which disturbs me more, though I can't figure it out yet. I stand there at the side of the pool in a state of confusion, trying to sort out my muddled thoughts. Then I remember something, something which in the beginning seemed innocuous enough, natural even. I see again the image of the Malay woman, deeply Coppertone brown and elegant, standing tall, poised on a ledge which separated the wading pool from the main pool. The water skimming over the ledge made her look as if her feet were resting on water. Robert's voice came over the video cam-recorder. "*Sayang*, How about doing the *Dancer*?" he suggested. Emas was in a white-thonged bikini which showed her toned posterior and long tanned legs to advantage. How could a woman in her fifties looked that good? She was a hard act to follow. Emas arched her slim body forward, stretching one leg out behind her, forming this and an outstretched arm into an upside down 'C' and held the yoga pose—a figure of perfect health and grace. "You're so beautiful!" Robert breathed into the microphone.

My heart had snagged when I heard the endearment. How foolish I had been to think that I taught it to Robert. Of course, he would have addressed his wife in her own language too. *You're so beautiful*, Robert had said, exactly as he had said to me. Since that day, hearing him utter those words to his wife, a worm of misgiving began to wriggle in my breast; when he said *I* was beautiful, did he mean me or was he thinking of Emas, superimposing her image onto me? When I saw that taped video of Robert's and Emas' Spanish holiday, their last together before Emas' death, I experienced that first stab of jealousy and doubt. The two had been very much in love. Was it possible that Robert could love me as he professed or was he projecting his love for Emas onto me? Was it possible that I was just a proxy for Emas? More than anything else, it was the tone he used which undid me, when I heard that raw lust in Robert's voice. Instinctively, I knew that he was getting an erection just from watching his wife's body. She was dead but not gone.

"Not yet," I say to myself. "I mustn't think about it yet. I have so much to be happy about right now. Like Veronica says, I must enjoy my newfound family."

I will the thoughts to go away, then sit on the edge of the pool to dunk my feet before plunging in. In the water, I am reincarnated, a river otter who loves water but is nonetheless happy that there are banks on either side to confine its depth and volume. My head bobs up and down the length of the pool like a delighted, carefree otter. The morning sun is still rising into the sky eating up shadows. Would that it eats up the shadows that blocks out my own sun. I know that I should be happy, that there is nothing to fear, yet the thoughts will not disperse, hovering around me like a miasma until it arrests my strokes and yank me out of sync. I swallow chlorinated water and splutter. My eyes tear and I start to cough.

"You're okay, you're okay," Robert said, supporting me under my armpits. "Don't panic."

But still my arms and legs threshed the water as I tried to gulp air, swallowing water instead and coughing. The weight of the aqua lungs on my back seemed intent on dragging me back down to the womb of the English sea where the incident had occurred. It would have been all right with Robert there swimming close by me, holding my hand if I had not lost my diving face mask. I felt safe behind the mask, the strong plastic a wall between my face, particularly my nose and the water, water that was not clear or blue even in summer. But when the mask loosened and fell from me, the seawater washed my face, threatened to go up my exposed nostrils and jolted me to the realisation that there was a lot of seawater surrounding me, waiting to enter me—through my nose, my mouth. The thought created a band of steel around my chest which continued to constrict. The wetsuit suddenly felt like a claustrophobic mummy-wrap. Robert noted my anxiety, grabbed my hand and with the other was gesturing upwards with his thumb, an international diving code, for us to surface. But I could not see clearly and my nostrils felt the cold salt water threatening to rush in. A moment of inattention and I would breathe in and all that water would go into my lungs! My body would swell like a puffer fish as I choked to death and then I'd end up belly side up. Robert must have seen the horror in my eyes and sensed my fear because he quickly put his hands under my armpits to pull me up toward the surface, his powerful legs with his feet in flippers churning the water like an outboard motor. I threshed wildly.

"Don't panic," he shouted over the waves when he was free from his own mask. "You're safe!"

Later when he had dragged me back to the Dorset shore and we had lain at the water margin tired out by the incident, I had begun to sob, first from the release of tension and second, from the anger that spilled over.

"It's all your fault. I told you it was too soon for me to go so deep underwater. You wouldn't listen!"

"You were doing all right. Losing the mask was an accident. It could happen to anyone. We weren't far from the surface. A good hold on the breath and we were back up. There was no need to be so frightened." His voice was testy.

"You are such a bully! You keep on forcing me to do things beyond my capability—skiing, climbing, even walking at an unmanageable pace. You're trying to make me into something I'm not. I know I'm much younger than Emas but I've never been involved in sports; I was too poor and too busy earning a living! You are trying to make me become like her! If you idolised her so much, why did you marry me? Do you really love me?"

"Don't beat yourself up, Kim. You have to learn to trust."

But I was in a mood for a quarrel and would not let go.

"So why don't you say you love me?"

"There are different kinds of love with different people. Would I marry you if I don't love you? Of course I love you."

"Huh? Now you're saying it to appease me."

"Oh, for crissakes!"

Much later, after he had soaped me in the hot bath in the hotel and we had ended up making love, he said, "You're right. I was remiss in pushing you to go underwater so quickly when you've just passed your exams. You're not really comfortable in deep water, are you? It can prove to be dangerous. I appreciate that you tried to scuba dive on account of me but there are other things we can do together. Besides, I'm getting too old to continue to dive. It's a young man's sport, really."

Then he took me out for a nice Indian meal. I was easy to bribe.

Now, I pull myself out of the water, glad that there is no one to witness my foolish spluttering. It is distancing my body from my mind that has done it, caused the mismatched coordination. That is what yoga is all about, to keep the union of body to mind. It's a way of discovering that you are beyond both. The trouble is that I am ensnared in both, unable to free myself enough to recognise my real self. The sad thing is that there is no Robert to help me now—I have to live life unaided. When you live life without a spouse or partner, you stand alone. No one to ask about your day, no one to wonder where you've been and what time you are coming home. Single.

Unadulterated. Even your smell is orphaned. There is a terrible ache in your chest when your smell is only your own. Nothing, not even a close-knit family, can take the place of that unique sharing between a man and a woman. They are different creatures. I sag into the deck chair and despite the increasing strength of the sun, shiver under the beach towel. When you are weary and defenseless, it is easy for negative thoughts to prey on your mind. Negative thoughts act like ocean waves that erode your confidence and dash at your self-esteem. I suffer an acute moment of despair. What have I done with my life for crissakes? I'm so useless, caused so much pain to so many. There is no doubt about it—the shadows are still splashed across my sun and I can't clear them, like I have difficulty shaking off this ennui that descends upon me so readily. Am I suffering from depression? I really have to snap out of this low mood. It's indulgent—and too dangerous.

"Siti, I'm going to visit my mother's grave," I say after I've showered and dressed. "Don't worry about lunch. I'll eat at a hawker center after visiting the cemetery. Is there anything you would like? How about *Soto Ayam* or *Nasi Padang*?"

"No, Marm, I 'm okay. Really. Marm Margaret always makes sure that I don't miss my own kind of food. Even if I stay in on Sunday, I don't cook. Sir will go to the hawker center and buy food home. Always something I like. Will you be all right going out on your own, Marm? Do you want me to come with you? Or shall I book a taxi for you?"

"I'll be all right. Yes, do book a taxi. Tell him *Chua Chu Kang Cemetery*."

When you are about to face something unpleasant or difficult, your heart pounds and your tummy gurgles uncomfortably. You have a sense of the darkness of the situation and you wish your task to be over as soon as possible. This is how I feel as I set out for my mother's grave. As the taxi takes me along roads and expressways that are now changed and unfamiliar, I wonder if it is at all possible for me to right my wrongs, begin life anew. The trouble seems to be that if you do one thing wrong, it sets off a domino effect and the repercussions of one single act become endless. I attended a yoga lecture once and the renowned Indian guru said, *"If you throw a stone into a lake, the ripples will spread out all the way to the other side. "* How careful we must be not to throw a stone we don't intend. How vigilant we must be to ensure that what we throw out is in the best interest of others, as well as oneself. Sitting in the taxi, this thought comes into my mind with a clarity that has eluded me even when I had heard the words of the guru. The enormity of the actions I've taken in life comes flooding in to accuse me, my relationship with my mother, with Victor, my flight from Peter, my life with Hugh, and my love for Robert.

"Don't let yourself become depressed," Veronica said every time I had run to my friend, spilling out hurt and tears. "Depression is a deep well that has no limits. Negative thoughts breed more negative thoughts, they multiply rapidly like mutant cells. And before you know it, the negativity has snuffed out all that is joyful, all that is bright and good in you."

With her deep insights, Veronica could be a yogi. She certainly exhibited the kind of calmness that one associated with enlightened souls. After all, wisdom of the spirit need not come from organised religions or new age fads. Perhaps the heightened awareness of creativity is a kind of spiritual enlightenment. How far I myself am from either. I wish my friend was here now. Still, the casting back to Veronica's words has pulled in a small measure of optimism and I straighten up in the taxi, breathing in deeply so that new air can freshen my lungs and refresh my mind. But I breathe in, instead, the manufactured fragrance of an air freshener that the turbaned Sikh taxi driver had placed near the air-conditioning vent. Next to this is his taxi licence with a picture of him, a smile through the grey-black beard. On the dashboard where some people might have a furry animal, the taxi driver has a plastic religious statue of *Guru Nanak*, a garland around his neck. The radio is on an English channel and a male deejay in a facile American accent comes on air with facile cheer to promote some chart-topping CD. It is interesting that in a country which was once a British colony, that there should be many people with this pseudo accent, on air, on television and in the streets. Perhaps McDonald's manifests only the tip of the iceberg of American influence. The deejay is followed by the song itself, a cacophony of strident instruments and voices. The taxi driver looks too old to enjoy that sort of music but perhaps he needs the noise to keep him alert or he might be waiting to hear the news in English.

Suddenly, I long for the peace of a countryside where you hear no mechanical sound except for the occasional lawnmower in summer, but only the sound of the wind or the birds chattering, the pheasant, like a squeaky gate, the fox like a child crying. I look out the window. Even your eyes get tired of seeing buildings upon buildings, people and more people, traffic bumper to bumper. It seems ironic that there should be so much land in some places like the Yukon and Alaska where there are huge forests, mountains ranges and glacial fields with hardly a soul in them, and yet in other places, humanity congregates tightly in cities, making more crowded what is already dense. Then something outside catches my attention, a name on a board at the entrance to a drive: *St. Joan of Arc Convent*. I hadn't noticed the route the taxi had taken but now I recognise the name of the road—*Thomson Road*. The convent was where Peter went to kindergarten all those years ago! It was Mui Yoke's idea that her grandson should have a Catholic upbringing and Catholic schooling. "*Especially*," she had said pointedly, "because his mother is a *pagan*!" She had spat the word out as if it was a dirty word. Now that I remember the convent, my heart thuds uncontrollably in my chest. The painful past is never dead; it crouches like a hurt animal, waiting to spring into your mind the moment a trigger occurs.

"Shall I come with you?" Hugh asked before I had left the hotel all those years ago.

"Thanks. But I think it might be better if I go on my own."

"Call me if you need me," he said, holding me for a moment and then kissing me fondly. I drew strength from his touch for I needed strength for what I was about to do. "I'll be by the pool. I have to try to give this sickly pale body some colour. I don't want to turn up like a slug soaked in formaldehyde at the British Club party tonight."

We kissed on the mouth, the sort of kiss I had longed for when I was a child watching the planes come in at Kallang Airport and watching the Caucasian men kiss their wives on the mouths openly. The taste of him was so delicious. Hugh was my dream come true, at least I thought so then. But still, we had loved each other to the very end. Except that his love for me was not what I thought it was. No one told me that when dreams come true, they can bring so much pain as well. Why couldn't he have arrived on the scene sooner before I married Victor, before I had Peter? Not that I regretted having Peter; I just regretted having to leave him. At first, I had battled for him in court. Victor would not let his son be brought up in a foreign culture and because Peter was so young, the court agreed that I could have custody if I continued to live in the country or I would have to give up his custody to Victor. Why was it that life always had to be out of sync? On the one hand, I was delirious with joy; on the other, I was sinking under the weight of sadness. Having only one physical face, unlike Janus, I was unsure which to put on. The two emotions wrestle inside me to gain dominance, each striving to be displayed. I tried to box one whilst freeing the other. Mother or lover? It was obvious which I should be right now but why was life so complicated?

I had taken a taxi out to the convent on the hill. I wanted to see Peter again before Hugh and I left Singapore. The taxi deposited me outside the gates and I made towards the two-storied building. Away from the main building was the kindergarten also run by the foreign nuns. I could hear the children laughing and shouting in the playground. That was good; I wouldn't have to interrupt a class. I would get a chance to say goodbye. A mixture of emotions was coursing through me, the promise of happiness with a man awaited and yet the indescribable pain of the loss of my own child. My mother's words came from inside my head. *"What kind of life you give your son if take to England? If Peter stay here, got father, got grandmothers to look after him. His father got money, give good school for Peter, good life. No problem you come to see him if you want. Telephone him. Write to him. But take him to far-far place, his future not sure-sure, is too bad for him. Don't do what I have done—take child away from good-good life."*

But my mother's advice was now academic; if I chose to live in England, I could not have my son. I truly, truly wanted him to be safe and happy. It is possible, isn't it, for him to live a new life with Victor and his mother? It is possible, isn't it, for him to know love and security when he did not have to live with the fear of constant shouts and quarrels that he had to put up with if I had remained with Victor? It is possible, isn't it, for him to be so content that he would not need me?

It is amazing how you can recognise a voice, the footsteps, the shape, the touch, of someone you love even from afar. From behind a pillar, I saw his head amongst a sea of other small heads and yet I picked his out immediately.

This was my son, the one I had denied; it was ironic that he should have been the one to be named Peter. His namesake was the one who denied, proven by the crowing of the cock. But it wasn't my son who was doing the denying; it was me. How stone-hearted people must think me.

Linda had said, *I can't see how you can bear to leave your son behind.* Should I have admitted that I didn't know either? Would I have won some sympathy from my friend if I said I could not bear it too, leaving my son behind? But then I couldn't bear staying either, the way Victor was treating me. What was right for Peter? An environment that must distress him too or run away with him and make him face the possibility of an uncertain future, with a man who wasn't his father? I knew what it was like to be without a father, knew that there was as much sorrow in being without him as it was to be with a mother who could not provide a reasonable life. Yet, there was no doubt that as a mother, I had failed my child; as a mother, I had betrayed him. I needed no cock to crow my treachery; my heart was there to remind me. I watched him as he hopped energetically with his classmates, his eyes bright with joy, his smile wide. Did he have the capacity at that age to play-act or was he genuinely settled and happy? I stood there a long time, taking the measure of him with my eyes, my soul, heard his little boy's voice echo in my ears. How long had we been apart? It seemed like years. Days and nights of excruciating torment shut out only by Hugh's intense love-making— his ferocious love. What aberration was there in my make-up as a mother that I could tumble and wrestle with Hugh in ecstasy, reaching new sexual heights when my son was down the road, suffering nightmares, sobbing his heart out for a lost mother? I should be hung and quartered. I should be mother first and put aside my woman's needs. But I had not. *Mea Culpa, Mea Culpa.* But there was still time to make amends. Just as I stepped from out of the shadows, a hand seized my arm.

"Mrs. Liew!" the voice said with enough sternness to arrest my steps.

"Mother Agnes," I said, acknowledging the Caucasian Mother Superior.

"The teacher told me you came. Would you come into my office please?"

I sensed that my opportunity to see my son was about to be lost and I surged forward in desperation. But the hand was strong, pulling me back firmly.

"If you truly love him, you will not upset him by letting him know you're here."

It was my big test. There was nothing else to do but follow the rustle of Mother Agnes' brown habit, my head downcast watching the large crucifix swing back and forth from the long rosary beads which dangled from the nun's waist. My eyes were fixed on the tortured face of Christ, his body writhed in pain, and in that moment, I shared his agony. All the time I could hear the shouts of the children, now receding, trying in my head to decipher which belonged to Peter. In the nun's office, another replica of a crucifix, this time almost life-sized, hung on the wall behind the desk. It seemed that Catholics were determined to project not the joy of life but the pain of living. Pictures of other saints on the wall had raptured looks, but the one of St. Joan depicted her roped to the stakes, the flames licking her body.

"We understand from Mr. Liew and his mother that you have chosen to leave the marriage and your son. You obviously have your reasons and we won't go into them here," Mother Agnes said without preamble in a very English voice. It was obvious from her tone whom she thought had been wronged. "It's not in our power to resolve domestic issues but we do take good care of all our young charges; their welfare is our concern. Peter has been very distressed since you left…"

As my son's name was spoken aloud, and his suffering confirmed, I broke down, the days and hours of anguish at being separated from Peter catching up with me in an eruption of pent-up grief. Mother Superior sat back in her chair, her features unmoving though she tapped her fingertips together with a show of impatience, waiting. When the sobbing and blowing of nose had subsided, the nun continued. "It's only natural. But he's coming 'round now. He's got used to the idea that you're not coming back. It's important that he is not torn asunder again. For his sake, you ought just to leave and not see him again."

The sentence was delivered and the nun rose from her chair to indicate that the interview was over. I felt as if my knees were soft and my legs were going to buckle under me when I stood up. My eyes were washed wet, but this time I didn't let the tears fall, already regretting the first outburst. It is terrible when you expose your emotions to someone who exhibits no iota of sympathy because it leaves you feeling gutted. I walked out of the office with deliberate steps and with as much dignity as I could muster. Then when I felt more sure of my legs, I ran as fast as I could to the playground to see my son. Just to see him. Oh, just to see him. I wouldn't call him, no, I wouldn't want to upset him, but just to see his dear face one last time. But it appeared that either Mother Superior or the teacher had anticipated my move for the children had been removed. They were no longer in the playground, nor were they in the classrooms. I raced around like a mad woman, going from room to room, seeing the little desks and little chairs, deserted, banging doors, trying to catch a glimpse of his precious face. Yet my lips were zipped tight. I had to swallow his name whole for fear of upsetting him. This non-release formed an uncomfortable lump in my chest. The place was silent and empty. Empty. I stumbled out into the garden where earlier the children were playing. Empty. Just then, something came between me and the sun, casting shadows across the sun, shadows that I could never erase forevermore. I sank to the ground on my knees, bowed my head, hugged my tummy with a pain which was not physical. It was in that moment that I knew that a part of me had been hacked off.

On my return to the hotel, Hugh rose like a God from the blue waters of the swimming pool to greet me, a male Venus, beautifully proportioned. He dripped water as he emerged from the pool in his swimming trunks, his torso, arms and legs burnt an antique gold by the tropical sun. In contrast, his hair was a bright yellow nimbus around his face. He would look stunning in his cream summer suit which I had helped picked out for the party that night. People would flock 'round him and he would charm them with his easy laugh and his wit. Usually, I basked in his glory; this in itself is a kind of love, when you ask nothing for yourself but that your loved one be fulfilled and happy. But tonight I would have to paint on a smile and regurgitate a remembered laugh. This is what most of life is—an emotional subterfuge. We wear our social faces for social effect, sometimes to camouflage our real opinions, other times to hide a breaking heart. Hugh smiled at me and his face glowed. To look at him who looked upon me with such pleasure and such longing was to know a different kind of love from that between mother and child, the kind that had eluded me for so long. And yet, oh, the price I had to pay! The fact that he was so boyish and so yielding was the thing that saved my sanity. I knew that in the complexity of his make-up, he needed me as much as I needed him; he would be there for me to care and to suckle, lover and child.

He was mine to mother as I could not mother my own—an ice pack for a hangover, soothing affirmations at bedtime, kind words for a bruised ego, kisses for a wounded pride. He was all I had now.

"How did it go?" he asked with genuine concern.

I simply shook my head. Words could not describe what I felt.

12

*Devoted mothers everywhere: take me to the market-cross. Stand
me there and strip me of my motherhood. Flay me with curses. Cast
every single stone so that my flesh should bleed as I am bleeding inside.
Pierce my eyes so that I cannot see the pain I caused. And when you are
done, gorge out my heart so that it can no longer beat the drum of my
treachery. Why should it matter? For I am dead already anyway.*

You may not see any pattern in your life till you move back from where
you're looking. All a pattern needs is a single thread that joins itself to another.
If we repeat an action again and again, respond in a certain way each time
to a particular stimulus, we are creating a pattern. Patterns, like habits, are
hard to break. To break a habit, we have to make a radical change. To break
a pattern, we have to cut off the thread. Occasionally, only occasionally, I
catch a glimpse of the pattern that I had created. But because the insight is
so brief—one single illuminated moment—I have no time to grasp its full
measure. It seems as if there is an opening between our mind and what lies
beyond, but the opening is hidden by the weeds of our tangled thoughts, our
undergrowth of emotions. Like the prince who battled his way through the
thicket to get to Sleeping Beauty, we, too, have to hack at the vegetation that
blocks our path so that we can walk through the opening to see the beauty

that lies beyond and to look back at our lives with a new perspective and see the patterns we have formed.

I notice the Sikh taxi driver peering surreptitiously into his mirror. But I don't care. Let him see me cry. Shall I tell him of my treachery? He must be a sensitive man because he reaches out to turn the radio off.

"*Boleh tolong tak*? Can help or not?" he asked in Malay.

I look up at the dark eyes in the mirror. What a kind man expressing a sentiment that the villagers in the *kampungs* would have expressed. It's not just attap houses that have gone, it's also the communal spirit, the friendliness, the concern for one's neighbour. These days, people live physically closer to each other than before, stacked on top of each other like Lego blocks, yet their hearts are miles apart. It is so lovely to find someone with such an archaic courtesy. It reminds me of my childhood days when the community spirit of *gotong royong* was strong, where people helped one another and behaved liked one big extended family, difference in race, status and age all forgotten. Although all the ethnic groups coexist well together these days, there isn't that true mingling as it had been then. Young people don't know a lot about the other's culture and custom, each race gluing itself to its own kind. Though I was touched by the taxi-driver's kindness, I didn't really want to tell him of my treachery.

"Oh, I was thinking of my mother. I'm going to *Chua Chu Kang* to visit her mother's grave. I've been abroad for years."

"Oh, very sad-sad when parent die. But this is pattern in life-*lah*, cannot escape. *Apa nak buat*? What to do-*ya*? Hope not too much suffering for her. My parents gone too. "

He gave me a dose of philosophy, of the Sikh way of looking at the cycle of birth and death.

"Where were you abroad?"

"England."

"My Chinese boss, owner of big company where I work before as *jaga*, he got son who studied in England. They say rice is very expensive there. Three dollars for one small bowl. We pay fifty cents here! They say that people saved leftover rice after a meal, to keep in fridge for eating another day. Is it true this is what people do?"

"Yes, I'm afraid so. Rice is more expensive there-*lah*."

"Wah! Very funny-*huh*!"

"It used to be difficult to get as well. You can only buy proper rice at Chinese supermarkets. Now that English people are eating a lot more rice, you can buy good rice at any supermarket."

I'm surprised how easily I slip back into the gear of my native language now that I'm in the environment. No matter how much and how long I had shaped myself to be something else, somebody else, the truth will out. The bones of my own culture and past are interred within me, no matter how I might clothe those bones and no matter what accent I adopt. And when I am consumed by fire and become ash, I am that which I began with. Nothing more, nothing less. Ultimately, there is no escaping one's roots.

"I used to be a *jaga*."

"Oh," I say. "I remember. There were many like you when I left Singapore all those years ago. How wonderful it was that you could sleep outdoor on your roped bed guarding a building…"

"*Chapoy.* The roped bed is called a *chapoy*."

"Yes, of course. Thanks for reminding me. Yes, I can't imagine a *jaga* guarding a building in London, New York or Chicago. He'd be murdered in his sleep!"

"It's that bad in those places, is it?"

"You can't begin to imagine."

"I used to have my chest bare, my hair hanging loose to my waist. Not quite the image that modern international corporations would like guarding their posh offices. So they have uniformed security guards now. I'm obsolete, like the old *kampungs*, all gone now, concrete buildings in their places, sometimes even concrete in hearts. Many youngsters today, they don't know what it was like to live amongst open sewers and derelict housing, they with their designer clothes, Nike shoes and mobile phones. I ferry lots of these youngsters about, picking them up from fancy restaurants, cinemas or clubs to other clubs and restaurants or to plush homes. In the old days, youngsters took the bus or the trishaws, bicycles or were on foot— hardly ever taxis. But things have changed. It's the MRT or taxis for them these days. It's usually the old now who are in buses and trishaws, not that there are many trishaws left; the ones that are left are used for tourists."

I'm grateful for his stream of chatter. It draws me away from my painful memory of the convent. When I arrive at my destination, I tip him extravagantly. He is about to protest but I don't give him a chance, say goodbye, then move away. Only after he has gone out of sight did it occur to me that he was talking so volubly because he did it intentionally to steer me away from my tears. What a perceptive man.

Chua Chu Kang in the Northeast of the island is quite a distance away from the East coast where Peter and Margaret live. In the days before expressways, MRT and satellite HDB towns, this place was considered *ulu*—the Malay term for being *way out in the sticks*. This was where the animal and vegetable farms used to be, where cows mooed, pigs grunted, ducks quacked and chickens clucked; the vegetables fresh and green in healthy manure which scented the countryside. Today the sounds that you hear are the screeching of tires, the grumbling of engines, the teeming hum of a city's white noise. The only animals you get here these days are the pale, dismembered corpses that lie inert on styrofoam trays sealed over with cellophane wrap. Sometimes, underneath the clear plastic, there are traces of moisture as though the flesh was still breathing when the cellophane was stretched over it. Meat and vegetables are now all imported—from Malaysia, Indonesia, Australia, New Zealand and countries still further afield where fruits and vegetables have to be picked even before they are naturally ripe so that they appear to be just right when they get here. Meat is slaughtered days or even weeks before so that they can be cleaned, frozen and packaged. "*Fresh* chicken! *Fresh* pork! *Fresh* Australian beef! *Fresh* air-flown New Zealand lamb!" Supermarket placards shout. The meaning of words is what you want them to be.

Unlike the neat rectangles of Christian graves with white statues of angels and cherubs, the Chinese cemetery has upright semi-circles of concrete at the foot of the graves to serve as tombstones. Mandarin script is etched on these memorials from top to bottom in the traditional way, like in old books and scrolls. The words might be the name of the deceased, a poem or epithet. Sadly, the characters are like hieroglyphics to me since I can't read the words, having studied Malay at school. In my time, Straits Chinese people were allowed to study Malay, the language of half their ancestors. These days, all Chinese, like Diana and Harry, had no choice but to take Mandarin as their second language if they were in an English school. So due to my inaptitude, I had to locate my mother's grave by the serial number of the plot, a worn-out photo, and rely on the fragment of memory that would guide me there. I climb the hillside and find myself puffing unhealthily so I pause for breath and take the opportunity to reassess where my mother's grave might be. Some of the memorials have a photo, some none. At the base of these memorials are altars on which visitors placed several incense holders with joss sticks and dishes for food. Taoists and Buddhists alike offer food and drink to the spirit of the deceased on home altars or at the cemetery, especially on *Sin Ming*, the Chinese All Souls Day. People take generous portions of roast duck, steamed chicken, rice, delicacies and fruits to the graves of their loved ones. It is fascinating that one considers feeding the spirit with food of this carnal world. I'm sad that because I've been abroad, Ang Huay's spirit has not been fed for years. Neglect, neglect, neglect. Is there nothing that I can do right? And worse, I realise that I am remissed even now because I haven't brought any food today either because I had been unsettled by the incident at the swimming pool earlier.

These days, there are no vases filled with fresh flowers amongst the graves. Water left in vases used to stagnate and became breeding grounds for mosquitoes resulting in epidemics of cholera, malaria and dysentery, so the government had disallowed their use. Instead people have to use plastic flowers in an attempt to bring a little cheer to the tombstone. But the hillside still looks grim as I struggle to locate my mother's grave. Strangely, now that I've been exposed to the churchyards of rural England where pitted, mildewed tombstones lie peacefully amongst immaculate lawns under sprawling yew trees, the atmosphere of a Chinese cemetery has been transformed for me and is no longer one that projects tranquillity. The surroundings now produce a sense of unrest and thrust me into the shadows of the past. I did come home to bury my mother. Because of my estrangement from Peter, my mother didn't have either a son or grandson to conduct the essential ceremonies, no male to walk 'round her coffin. Mui Yoke and Victor did not permit Peter to see his maternal grandmother. How Ang Huay must have missed her only grandchild. But she never complained. Was it six months or a year after I had left for England that my mother had died? What did she really die from? Loneliness? Heartbreak? The doctors said cancer of the duodenum but I knew better, knew that my mother had nothing to live for once I left the country.

"Why do you blame yourself for everything, darling?" Hugh had said. "You said so yourself, her diet wasn't good and she loved to chew betel leaves."

"*Sireh* causes cancer of the cheeks, not her duodenum," I had said woodenly.

"Maybe moving to the HDB flats didn't suit her. Maybe she missed the old way of life."

"Maybe I shouldn't have left her on her own."

"But we did invite her to come to live with us. She refused, remember?"

"Did we?"

But he had not come to the funeral.

"I'm sorry, darling. But I really have to make this appointment. Someone is considering funding the Kebab cart project."

Another one of many schemes. He was always full of moneymaking ideas, pizza delivery, mail-order wedding stationery, catalogue for gardening needs. He started them with excitement, talked about them with enough enthusiasm to convince the banks or someone gullible to back his schemes but halfway through the projects, when the slog began, he'd lose interest and start thinking of another thing to do. He was more interested in playing cricket and having a pint with the lads, a Bohemian. He was pulled too much by his emotions to be a businessman. That was why it was I who had to work. But he was still lovable, one praise from him and I was putty, one touch and I melted. Cliched but oh, so true. After all, aren't cliches born from common occurrences, like pop lyrics from heartfelt sentiments?

It was only later, after I came back, that I learnt he did not even have the decency to observe my day of mourning with quiet pursuits.

"You didn't even send a wreath," I said.

He had the grace to look sheepish.

"Oh, darling," he took me in his arms. "I didn't think. Forgive me?"

"I tried to call you on the day of the funeral. Where were you?"

"Where was I? Where was I? Oh, yes. Do you remember that chap who lives up at the top of that posh house on the hill, that businessman, Ian Blackman? Well, he's a business associate of Colin who was thinking of funding my project. Ian owned a fleet of vintage cars and he wanted to do the London to Brighton run and invited me. So I went. My god, you should have seen the cars! They were smashing. One group went in a Bentley and another in a Lagonda. Real McCoy, they were. We were on the road all day and I couldn't call you."

"You went on a vintage car run on the day of my mother's funeral?"

"You weren't here and I was on my own. There didn't seem any harm."

"On the day I buried my mother, you were out enjoying yourself?"

He was not there for me on the day I needed to lean on him, be enveloped by his arms. He had not even spared me or my mother any thought but was having the time of his life. Hugh thought that I stretched things too far. But, give him his due, he acted as if he was sorry, tried to make amends, bought me flowers afterwards, took me for a weekend away. But the hurt was an infested sore. Worse, it was much, much later that I learnt that not only was he out with Ian and Colin the day I buried my mother, he was out with Jeremy—Jeremy whom he went to live with eventually. The love of his life. His words for me once. What did that make me? The trouble is you can't stop someone from falling out of love with you and falling in love with another. It is a fait accompli, not something given to discussion or argument. The truth is that you can't be given something which is no longer there, or worse still, has never been there.

But I had been unsuspecting of all these when I was out in Singapore attending to the final rites for my mother. The difficulty I had of being in Singapore and coping with my mother's death was made worse by the fact that though I was here, I had no chance of seeing Peter. Every place that held memories for me with him speared my insides, drew blood; this was where I took him for walks, that was where I bought his clothes, here was his favourite playground, there was where I taught him to swim. Did Hugh ever think of what it must have been like for me to return to the country of my son's birth and yet, was unable to see my son? Did he think that I gave up my son for him only once? It was sheer punishment. One needn't be incarcerated to comprehend punishment. But I had only myself to blame; my crime befitted it.

Ang Huay's friends from the old village came, each whispering to me, "She missed you, you know," and, "She lived just for you." It was a responsibility to be the sole reason of another's life. I did all the right things, said all the right things to my mother's friends but my heart didn't feel right. I felt a failure, as if I hadn't done enough for my mother. As Hugh was not obtainable, it was Veronica I spoke to about my sorrow.

"We all feel that way about our parents," Veronica said to me. "When they go, we ask ourselves if we couldn't have done more."

"I wanted her to come to England so I can take care of her in her old age. She's only forty-three, Veronica. She never told me about the cancer."

To show my respects for my mother, I had to go the whole hog for the funeral, not that I begrudged any of the expenditure but because I would have preferred a quiet funeral. But I organised the four-day wake, making sure that I alternated with friends to maintain a twenty-four-hour vigil by the open coffin. As visitors come and go, some friends stayed to play mahjong and *jeki*, food and soft drinks on offer at all times as though it was a merry affair instead of a death. When the beloved wife of Chuang Tze, the great Chinese philosopher, died, friends found him beating a drum when they visited. *Why are you rejoicing when your wife has just died*, they asked. *Why should I grieve when her Soul is now free of its mortal bonds and has gone to its true home*, he responded. The good thing about reincarnation is that you will still have opportunities to make reparations. When I meet up with my mother again in the other world, I would throw myself at my mother's feet, wash them with my tears and my hair, beg for forgiveness. For the funeral, I engaged the services of an old neighbour to record the sum of money each visitor brought as a final gift to Ang Huay, a practical custom that also paid for the elaborate funeral; like *ang pows,* red packets of money for weddings instead of presents that paid for the ten-course dinner and expenses. I had to walk the visitor to the coffin, present each with a couple of joss-sticks which they waved over Ang Huay lying, clad in her beautiful sarong kebaya, her eyes shut tight totally oblivious to the activity around her. I remembered to give some boiled sweets and a small length of red cotton thread for each parting visitor so that they did not take the death energies with them back into their homes. The hearse was elaborate, filled with paper money, a paper house and paper servants. There was even a paper car, though in this lifetime my mother never drove. The paper products were to ensure that my mother would have their real equivalent in her afterlife. I even hired a team of mourners and brass band. I was not sure whether it was Hugh's influence or the fact that the English culture had truly rubbed off on me but I winced at the overt display of the mourners' facile emotions. And worse, when the band, walking behind the hearse, played with gusto: *Happy days are here again.* The Chinese ensemble probably didn't know the words to the tune.

I would have preferred to weep in private, hold back my tears, like people at an English funeral. But here in Singapore, it would be disrespectful if my eyes were not raw and red, so I let the tears flow unchecked and let my nose run. I paraded like a dutiful daughter wearing my sack-cloth but every fibre of my being protested at this charade. Shamed by the memory of words I had hurtled at my mother, I bowed my head. The Chinese coffin was unwieldy, almost gross in its size and form. My mother was really rather small and delicate to be entombed in such a monstrosity. I imagined her being thrown from side to side like an umoored boat in a storm as the coffin was being lowered. This then is the finality of our earthly life, earth to earth, dust to dust. But the spirit still lives on and in some other life, I will meet my mother again, in another form, in another shape, until I have learnt to repay my debt.

"If you wanted to leave Ah Tio, why didn't you just go? Why didn't you just leave me behind?"

I carried the words from childhood to adulthood like a necklace around my neck. Did my mother forget that I ever said them? It would take senile dementia or even Alzheimer to erase *my* memory of my mother's face when I uttered those words. The eight-by-ten-inch photo of Ang Huay at the front of the hearse looked back at me with such soulfulness. How could I, *dutiful daughter* that I was supposed to have been, have shot my mother's eyes with such sorrow? When I said those blasphemous words, Ang Huay had been squatting, but she still sank to the floor as though her legs had given way under the weight of her emotions.

"Oh, Kim Hiok," she said with a tattered voice. *"You have something of your father in you." You have something of your father in you. You have something of your father in you.*

The tinnitus in my ears has started again. The trouble with a sound inside your head is that you can't shut it out. It is a bee that has crept inside you, buzzing round and round inside your ears with no way of getting out. It's the same with a painful thought. There is no escape. Trapped. How we are thrown asunder by our thoughts. I suddenly come to the realisation that a fly is literally buzzing around my face and I slap it away. How long have I been sitting here by this stranger's tomb, dragging back old memories? It must have been a while because my skin feels overwarm, as if I have been burnt. I never used to get burnt before, the long winters must have weakened the strength of my melanocytes. I get up to skirt the tombstones and more tombstones looking for my mother's grave. The sun is now high in the sky and the sweat trickles down my back underneath my blouse. Amongst the altars in the cemetery are remainders of food offerings. Food left out in the hot, humid temperature attracts flies which grow fat on it. I wave my arms about to keep them away. It is easier than trying to wave away these big, fat guilts that have fed on my insecurities. I peer at faded tombstones, at worn-out photos, to see if I recognise the face on them. The rising heat shimmers in waves across my eyes. I realise with a shock that the skin of my arms are getting burnt. I would never have burnt in the old days. My skin and my blood must have changed to suit the English climate. Now I wish I had brought an umbrella to give me some shade.

This is impossible. I don't find this place familiar. Surely, this confluence of roads that are running in the vicinity didn't use to be here? I had remembered the cemetery as being larger than this or is my memory flawed? What is it about the human brain that we remember things we don't want to remember and forget things we want to remember?

"So, did you meet your father?" Ang Huay had asked when I had come home from my trip with Victor to Penang. Her voice had a strange hard edge to it, but was also tinged with curiosity. Yet she turned away quickly as if she couldn't bear to speak about the man who had changed the shape of her life so drastically.

"We looked everywhere. The address you gave me is now a block of flats."

"So, he never even bothered to let us know." She said this in a half-voice as though it was not meant to be spoken. "Not that it matters."

"I asked about town to see if anyone might know him or his whereabouts but no one seemed to know. It would have been nice to have a picture or something, just to see what he was like. I supposed he only cares about his new family. "

"Is it finished now—your hankering? Or will you still try to search for him?"

"Victor has asked me to marry him. I shall have a husband. I don't need a father anymore."

Had I been trying to convince myself?

When I buried my mother, I learned how important the ceremony of a funeral was. A funeral is not for the dead; it's for the living so that a closure can be made properly in their minds and hearts. Without a closure, the dead remains a ghost that hovers around your life. That is why it is so hard for those who cannot find the bodies of their loved ones to bury, as in an accident or disaster, a war, or a terrorist attack. You cannot stitch close a shroud when there's no corpse. You cannot box up a person when there's no body. How, then, can there be a closure for my father?

I am so tired. Thoughts can be quite heavy too. I sit down again, this time on a bank of grass to rest. I look around briefly in case there are grass snakes; there were lots of them in the old days. The grass here is tough and sturdy, not soft and pliant like English hillside grass. In the fields behind their *kampung*, there used to be clumps of wild grass, *lallang*, they were called, which grew to great heights, their edges like the edges of skis—sharp enough to slice into exposed flesh. The pythons used to hide amongst the *lallang* and at nights they came out to steal a chicken or a duck, sometimes even a goat, winding their body around their victims and crushing them to death. One night, the villagers, angry that a python had been preying on the chickens and ducks, decided to trap it. I can see this so clearly as if it was yesterday. Perhaps it was the sacrifice that had kept the memory glued to my mind. Didn't the scientists say something about painful or frightening incidents being stored more easily in the brain's memory bank? The villagers tied a goat to a stake in the sandy compound to lure the python and bring it out of its hiding place into the open. The billy-goat was dirty white and had a small beard and horns. Its hooves clawed at the sand and kicked up dust around the wooden stake. Even when I was a child, I remembered thinking how terrified the goat must be, tied to the stake, waiting for the python to pounce on him. Or did it not know? When night fell, the villagers moved stealthily into the darkness bearing lamps of many types, kerosene, carbide and hurricane. They sat amongst the bushes to watch the goat. True enough, the unsuspecting python turned up to kill the goat. It coiled its body around the goat, crushed the life out of it and broke every single vertebrae until it became like a soft, pulpy rag so that it was easy to swallow. The villagers waited as the python ate the goat. Finally when it was bulging with the goat and could hardly move with the weight of its victim, the villagers leapt out of the bushes and pinned the python down with forked sticks right along the length of its body. The headman of the village was given the privilege of using the *parang* to hack at its head. The next day, the whole village feasted on python steaks, each housewife preparing them in her own favourite way: barbecued, fried or curried. I was surprised at how delicious it tasted—gamey, like wild boar, but its texture was like chicken.

Strange, the mind, how it drags back scenes and tastes from so long ago. Instinctively, I look around cautiously for signs of snakes, a trial of slime, a pattern of leaves and debris on the ground, any slithering sound. I'm disappointed that I haven't found my mother's grave. Peter had offered to come. Perhaps I should have accepted his help; he would probably be better at tracing the whereabouts of my mother's grave. Perhaps I'll give up for now and come back another time. Just as I am getting up for one last search, I see a visitor, a middle-aged Chinese woman in a samfoo, her stocky body bent from the effort of climbing up the hillside. The woman was well-prepared and was carrying an umbrella and a carrier bag from *NTUC Fairprice*, probably with some food to place on a grave.

"*Ah Cheh*, big sister," I greet her. "Hot day, isn't it?"

"Yes, very hot, very hot." She is puffing.

"I am looking for my mother's grave."

"My Male Person. Today is ten years of his death. I brought food for him."

The mention of a husband stops my breath. All this time that I've been here in the cemetery, my mind focused only on finding my mother's grave, I had not given a single thought to Robert. Now this woman uttering her own loss triggers something in me and the scene before me shifts and changes. Once again, I'm there standing at the edge of the cliff, the sound of the waves roaring in my ears.

On a clear day, Beachy Head is lovely. If you don't go there on the weekend, when the city folks flock to this headland and many others along the East Sussex coast, you can enjoy the beautiful scenery in peace. I love the hills in this region the way they undulate, curves of green sloping into wide, open fields dotted with dandelions, newborn lamb gamboling about. When I first came to England and saw the flowers growing wild in the fields, I rushed out of our cottage and gathered them by the armfuls and placed them in vases all around the house. Hugh came home and said, "What are you doing?"

"Aren't they beautiful? Imagine all these from the fields. I didn't have to pay for any of these."

"You silly goose," he said with a laugh. "These things are weeds."

"If pretty things are weeds, does it mean we can't enjoy them and have them in the house then?"

There are many things to learn—and some to unlearn when you're in a culture that's different from yours. You may compare, but you may not judge because what may fit snugly into one culture may stick out grossly in another. I am eternally grateful to Robert, who understands this necessary balance, unlike Hugh, who wanted to cram me into a square hole when I'm a round peg. It is also Robert who brings me out here to show me the beauty of this coast and the sea crashing at the foot of the headlands. We eat at the restaurant with its panoramic view of open fields, sea and sky, talking and laughing. With Robert, there is nearly always laughter, his laugh sparkly, a sound that carries me across many hours of sadness. I love the way his face creases and the way the light seems to bounce off his pupils when he laughs. Cliched as it may be, I feel safe in his company as though I can depend on him if the wolves should attack or the elephant should charge. What's more, when I am with him, I feel as if I am good.

We are so full that we have to walk off our lunch. Though bright, the air is still cool, and Robert helps me with my anorak. He's the proverbial gentleman, always ready to assist, opening car doors, standing up when I come into the room, carrying my shopping, walking on the traffic side of the pavement. I feel treasured and special. He takes my hand in his, making me joyously happy. We leave the restaurant and climb the slope and we walk along the coastal path. The gulls screeched and cried, winging across the blue sky. The wind creeps under my anorak and billows out behind me. I feel as light as the wind, and just as carefree. At the wooden fencepost that was erected to deter people from stepping too close to the cliff edge, we stop to watch a kestrel, its face intent, its wings steady with just the merest of movement, as it hovers in one spot.

"That's how paragliders do it, you know," he said.

"Oh, really?" I say in a cheeky voice.

"The trouble with you is that you only have one thing on your mind. I don't mean that at all. I mean they hover like this kestrel on a thermal. They use the air beneath them to keep them buoyed up. I'm going to have a go at paragliding. Want to try it? We can start with a tandem, see if we like it."

"Surely, we're too old."

"Never!"

Even as we are standing there in the brilliant sunshine of an English spring, two paragliders swooped by, their legs dangling from their harnesses. Their rectangular parachutes are brightly coloured, spreading out like giant butterfly wings. The wind picks up and the parachutes flap, the sound of rich silk rustling. The pilots underneath the great wings tug and pull but the wind picks up stronger still, pushing them with force here and there. Looking at them, I feel their agitation and I am suddenly anxious, filled with a sense of foreboding.

"Do you think they are all right?" I asked.

There is no answer.

"Robert. Robert?"

I turn to look, but he is no longer beside me. The space where he was standing only a moment ago is bare. I feel that sour taste in my mouth, of panic rising from the pit of my stomach. Robert. What has happened to Robert? Below me, the foam spit and flies into the air breaking up into a million fragments. The waves continue in its ceaseless motion, crashing loudly into the huge, sharp rocks then receding, crashing loudly then receding.

"Aiyyoh! You okay or not? Maybe sun too hot for you; your face all red—red like cooked prawns. Sit down, sit down. Drink some water."

The woman's voice, speaking in Teochew, pulls me back to the present. I feel as if the ground underneath me has turned to sliding mud. In a half-daze, I sit down, unaware whether I have sat on a bank or a tombstone. The woman is taking a bottle of water to my lips. I reach out and notice that my hand is shaking.

"Ah, better now? Good, good, life come back to eyes."

"Thank you." I stammer, trying to select words from a muddled brain. I have other images flashing through my brain, but I won't think of them yet. "*Ya-lah*, too hot for me. I've been searching for my mother's grave for hours."

"Ahhh, so! Afternoon sun always too strong. Next time bring umbrella-*lah!*"

"*Ah Cheh*, maybe you know. I seemed to remember that there used to be graves around here," I say. "I thought my mother's grave was somewhere here-*lah*."

"Possible, possible. I come back every month to my male person's grave so I see change. A few years ago, government exhumed many, many graves. They did not contact you? Notice was in newspapers for family to come and collect remains-*wat*. If nobody come to collect, government take away bones and everything with earth for building flats. Here, government cleared land to make new-new expressway. You didn't know-*ahhh*?"

23

Mother of mine, when I am grown
And I can walk straight all on my own
I'll give to you what you gave to me,
Mother, sweet Mother of mine.

The lyrics of a sixties song seep through layers of memory to make me maudlin. Funny how words even when uttered by a stranger can affect you. That's the intention of such songs and advertisements, isn't it, to sway your emotions and press some buttons? Do words have a power of their own or do we give them power through our own mind association? Ah, how I wish that I could say the right words to my mother. After all, what have I given to Ang Huay but hard work? I recall how my mother scrubbed and scrubbed at the wooden washboard, washing clothes for other people so that *I* could go to school. Then what? What had I done with those opportunities that education has given me except to squander them? What good is education if it only stays in your head and does not improve your own or anyone else's life? It hasn't even helped me make any successful marriage, for goodness sakes! At least my mother could say that *her* marriage failed because it was an arranged marriage and not one of choice, but I…I can't even have that excuse. And yet Ang Huay, without a husband, and without an education, had managed to raise a daughter and educate a daughter. Where did she find the intelligence and the drive? If I am genetically linked to my mother, how is it that I lack the same characteristics? What can I say for myself? What can I say to my mother who is no longer present? And worse, when there isn't even have a grave to kneel at, no urn of ashes, no ancestral altar, to beg for forgiveness for words wrongly flung.

Mother, you gave me happiness
Much more than words can say.

Sentimental mush. Is it mush because it's a surfeit of sentiment or emotion? Yet, wouldn't it be nice to be able to express the sentiment to your mother? Better still, if your child can say them to you. What a reward that would be for one's mothering efforts. Surely Peter wouldn't say that to me! Ahh, how the words accuse me for my own lack. Success is not what you can buy for your child, it's what you can give of yourself. Perhaps it means depriving yourself, too. Had I been right to deprive myself and walk away from my child so that he could have a stable life? Who has the right to sanction, to make that judgement? But I still feel as if I had made a right mess of my life. This thought pounds at my head with such ferocity that I feel like being sick. Nothing is worse than knowing you've done wrong when there's no longer any way to correct it. Now, the bright sunshine hurts my eyes and I feel the heat burning my neck and face. Perhaps it's just a menopausal flush or I'm coming down with something. Suddenly, I feel I have to get away— the cemetery has become oppressive. Excusing myself from the woman, I rush out of the cemetery, putting out a hand to flag down a taxi. Unlike the yellow-topped taxi I came in, this one is sky-blue. Like Robert's eyes. Ahh, Robert, dear Robert with his eyes so blue I could drown in them. Have I failed him, too? I mustn't think about this yet; there is just so much for me to deal with right now. Otherwise there will be an emotional landslide. But the thought of him has snagged at something in me, a fishbone caught in my throat. I have to get back to the apartment. Earlier, I had planned to go to a food center for lunch, eat *nasi lemak* and rice boiled in coconut milk complete with trimmings like *sambal, ikan bilis, omellette,* washed down with freshly squeezed pineapple juice or *chendol.* But now all I want is to run as far away from everyone as possible—better still, as far away from myself as possible. But how can I unstitch this shadow that insists on following me?

"Marm, are you all right, Marm?" Siti asks anxiously when I arrive back at the maisonette.

"I think I need to lie down."

"Can I get you anything? Panadol? Call a doctor?"

"No, no. I'll be all right. I think I stayed too long in the sun, first at the swimming pool, then at the cemetery. I'm not used to the heat now. On second thought, maybe some iced water would be nice, thanks. Make it a jug. I'll cool down with a cold shower first."

I turn on the air-conditioning and shed my clothes. My skin is like hot asphalt. As the fine needles of cold water run down on me, I can feel the heat rising from my body. Maybe I've caught a fever. When I was little and had a fever, Ang Huay used to mix wheat and rice flour with herbs and oil. When the dough had been well kneaded, she made me lie down naked as she rolled a dollop onto my flesh, rolling it round and round till the fresh dough turned gray, then another was used in its place. She repeated the process with another lump of dough and another until the whole landscape of my body had been dusted with flour. Ang Huay believed that the dough helped to extract the fever from the body. My mother peppered her life with such folklore and superstitions. Perhaps it wasn't folk medicine at all but a need in a mother to do something practical when her child was ill, when she didn't have enough money to visit the doctor. But then, who had been there to extract the fever of sorrow and loneliness from Peter's and Ang Huay's life?

When I come out of the shower, I'm no different. I'm still hot. I dry my hair with the towel but was too weary to put a hair dryer to it. Normally, I don't like the sensation of damp hair sticking to my neck, but I will let it pass this time. There is an inner trembling in me that's suggesting that what I had kept on hold is threatening to burst its banks. Sleep should blank it out of my mind. In a distracted way, I notice that Siti had already brought up the jug of iced water which is on the bedside table, beads of sweat already forming on its surface. Next to it is a tall glass with a sliver of freshly sliced *limau nipis*, a local lime which is difficult to find in England. This is one of the pleasures of life in middle-class Singapore where you can afford a full-time maid to cater to your everyday comforts. Some people take maids for granted. For me, where full-time house help in England is costly, I still regard it as a luxury. I go to the window to draw the drapes, shut out the sun. My head is still pounding. Utterly out of sorts now, I climb into the big double bed and slip under the counterpane. No matter how hot I am, I cannot sleep without a light cover over my breasts, feeling exposed if my nipples stick out. Despite the fact that the temperature in the room has been lowered considerably by the blast of the air conditioner, my body continues to smoulder, I've become a live furnace. Perhaps it will burn out all the dross in me, make me pure. It is sheer weariness that makes my lids close, not a sense of relaxation.

Peter is only knee-high and he toddles about on the tiled floor like a penguin, his arms outstretched like wings to balance himself. It is an occasion when your baby takes his first unaided walk. You delight in this, but it is also the moment you know that he is a life unto himself and can walk away from you, not tied to you by his umbilical cord. The first separation is when he no longer depends on you to take breath, the second is when he walks on his own two feet.

"Clever boy, clever boy!" I clap my hands in encouragement.

He turns his head to look at me, his eyes round and bright and I feel a surge of tenderness, a feeling most mothers would know. He chuckles happily, throws up his hands and says, "Mum-my." At this moment, I am his sun; he still looks to me to brighten his life and cater to his needs. There are no shadows between us yet. He is in an active mood, exploring our apartment on the twenty-sixth floor of this residential block that overlooks the Kallang River, clutching at objects and turning them over, sometimes testing their shapes through his mouth.

I am sitting on the floor, my legs tucked underneath me, keeping watch, keeping him within easy reach so that he doesn't come to any real danger. I have to squash my instinct to always keep him safe and close to me—I know that he has to experience the world in his own way to find himself. He is approaching the dining table and I foresee the lethal combination of his height and the height of the table. My heart skips a beat, but I don't want to exhibit my panic in case he reacts to it. So I slowly raise myself from the floor to make towards him to steer him away. He sees me getting up and moving towards him and he thinks it's a game so he chuckles and runs away from me, blindly, so confident of a clear passage. And then, as I feared, it happens—he runs right bang into the underside of the table. I feel his pain reverberate in my being. He is shocked into silence momentarily and I scoop him up with swiftness. Then he bawls loudly. I rub his forehead vigorously, alternating my action with kisses.

"Bad table," I say, smacking the table. "Bad table!"

He smiles a wavering smile through his brimming eyes, then he, too, smacks the table. "Bad table, bad table," he articulates in his newfound speech. He snuggles into me, seeking comfort, and I hold him tightly as though I might somehow lose him. Perhaps I already sense our separation. Suddenly our front door slams open, startling us, and we both look up. Mui Yoke dressed in her Chinese trouser-suit walks in, her fingers pointing.

"You whore! Stay away from my grandson. Take him away from that woman!" she says.

Victor emerges from behind her in response to her command, as if he is a manservant following in his mother's wake. His mouth is pouting but his eyes are blank as he waddles in robot fashion towards us.

"Come to Daddy," he says as if a switch has been thrown.

"No!" I cry.

He yanks Peter forcibly from me.

"Bad dad-dy! Bad dad-dy!"

I try to hold on to Peter's feet as he's being pulled from me. Mui Yoke arrives at Victor's side and together, they pull Peter out of my arms. With the loss of the weight I had anchored myself to, I fall forward and hit my nose on the floor tiles. Victor has Peter in his arms and I call out, my nose bleeding, "Let me have my son. Please, let me have my son!" Peter is screaming, "Mum-my! Mum-my!" Mui Yoke turns to spit at me; the spray flies from her mouth onto my face. The look in her eyes is venomous. She turns away with disdain, then takes hold of Victor's elbow and steers him to the open window. Their heels come off the floor, then their toes and then there is space between their feet and the floor as they lift off, Victor holding tight to Peter. Together the threesome fly out of the window of our twenty-six floor apartment and over the other blocks of flats in the housing estate and over the Kallang River. I can hear Peter calling, "Mum-my! Mum-my!" But his voice soon trails off *into the sky, like the tail of a rare comet—never to be seen again for years.*

In the darkened room, the woman on the bed pleads for her son, arms outstretched to pull her son back to her. Her voice is ragged, full of loss. The counterpane ruffles up around her hips and tangles her legs. She fights it as if it is some kind of demon.

I am hot. So very hot. I feel as if a sluice of fire is being poured into my throat. How do fire-eaters eat fire without burning their throats? How did I come to eat fire? But I could not have learnt well. I feel the fire burning, burning in my throat. Please, somebody, help! Blow this body of molten glass so I may cool down. Shape me into something beautiful, kinder, wiser. Veronica, where is Robert? Where is Robert? No, I don't want an injection, I want to be here and conscious when he comes home. Please, I need to see him. Please donnnnnnn't.

"It's a sun-stroke," the doctor says.
"I told her I'd take her but she refused," the son says.
"I'll boil some cooling herbs," daughter-in-law offers.

The picture slides flip pass my mental screen in no specific order. Confusing, incoherent. Baby Peter, young Peter, adult Peter. Or is it Victor? The two of them are so alike in looks. Gargoyle faces are leering, taunting me—Victor's, Mui Yoke's, Linda's. Looming large, then receding, then looming large again. 'No matter what my husband does, I will never leave my child,' Linda says, her voice echoing across canyons of time. "Mum-my! Mum-my!" Peter's cries sewn like appliques into my memory. I am gasping for breath, drowning in a sea of spit. Or is it a sea of my mother's tears? "You have something of your father in you. You have something of your father in you." Soulful eyes,

171

accusing eyes. Whose eyes are these that look on me so? 'I'm sorry it has to be like this but I shall always love you", Hugh says. There is sweetness in his voice. Even now, when he's leaving, there is no hatred. "You can't leave me! I left Peter for you. Please, don't go, don't leave me like this!" But still he turns away from me, walks towards his lover who is waiting. He turns to give me one last look, lingering, regretful. "Sorry, darling. I have to be who I am". I have to be who I am. I have to be who I am. His words are like the persistent pecking of a woodpecker. But what about me? Fatherless, motherless, childless, now husbandless. Can I exist without being appended to someone? Who am I? What am I? I never noticed it before, but now I see a seam that runs from my forehead, down my chest and belly, to my pubis. As if a disturbance has occurred underfoot, the seam rises to a ridge then starts to split. I am splitting. Flesh ripped apart. But there is nothing to spill, no heart, no intestines, no organs. Nothing. Why, I am empty—made of nothing. Kosong.

Daughter-in-law applies wet flannel to hot forehead, arms and bare legs. Together with the maid, they change the woman's clothes which have become damp. Fresh clothes, more wet flannels.

I am very hot, Mak, so hot-lah! All right, turn over, my mother says. I'll remove this fever from you. She rolls the lump of dough onto my forehead and I feel its coolness. Ah, coolness. Then she runs it up and down my arms, my back, kneading the dough as though my body is a pastry board. She takes another lump of dough, then another lump. "Is it getting better?" she asks.
"Hmm," I say, not wanting to disappoint her, but my head is still burning.

"Is it always this hot?" I ask Robert.
"A hundred and forty in the shade today," he says.

"No wonder this place is called Death Valley, I say. Can any animal survive in this heat?"

"Yes." He laughs. "Scorpions."

"I feel as if I am in hell," I say. "Look at all this expanse of brown land, not a single blade of grass. See how the earth is cracking, gasping for water. Robert, my throat is so dry. Oh, that sun, it is too bright, it's hurting my eyes. Sayang, don't go near the sun, you'll get burned!"

"What's wrong with Grandma?" The children ask.

"She'll be okay. She stayed too long in de sun. Probably not used to it now. Try to make her drink de soup. De herbs should be cooling."

Whoosh! I feel the rush of air as the wings fly past me, almost touching me. They're the wings of a giant bird. No, it is Icarus, flying too near the sun, blocking out the sun. And then a cry. Wings singed. Then a desperate flapping. Soon after, falling, falling. Right before my very eyes, tumbling out of the autumn sky. Below me, the waves crash loudly into the huge, sharp rocks. He is falling fast. Wait! It is not Icarus; it is Robert, my Robert, falling from the sky. No! No! Noooooooooooooo..."

The woman on the bed won't keep still, tossing, turning. Her arms windmilling, her mouth open as if calling out but no words ensued, just a gurgling sound in her throat as if the words are fishes caught in a net, struggling, unable to be free. Son and daughter-in-law look on, brows knitted. The children stand outside the door, thumbs in mouths, waiting, listening, fearful for their newly-found grandmother. Doctor comes to give another shot. The days stretch. Then, when all seems lost, the woman emerges from her fever. Like a diver who has been holding her breath for too long, she bursts into consciousness gulping air, her upper body coming up in a violent jerk. The son who has been sitting by her bedside quickly gets up and holds her shoulders down.

"It's okay, it's okay," he says.

"Robert! Where is Robert?"

He presses her shoulders back to the pillows. Her eyes are darting here and there, unseeing, her arms and legs thrashing.

"Let me go, Victor, let me go! Please don't hit me anymore. Please!"

Peter wants to call out, *Mum, it's me, Peter, you don't have to be afraid*, but he cannot say the words. He sinks back into his chair. Her limbs slowly stop their agitated thrashing and she settles, becoming calm. He sits by her side patiently as she falls back into sleep. Soon he is half-asleep himself, dozing off on the lazy armchair. When she reawakens, he senses her return to the world like a vigilant mother watching over a sick child. He gets up to pour her something from out of a thermos.

"Here, drink this. Margaret boiled some ginger water for you. It will cool you down."

"Do you know that you look so much like your father?"

Her voice is ragged as if her spirit has been torn from it. He does not respond, simply raising her upper body from the bed and supports her as she takes the tumbler with both hands like a child. She sips slowly, then he realises that the tumbler is shaking, her hands are shaking, and so are her shoulders. He puts the tumbler away and he sees that the tears are streaming down her face

"I've made a mess of my life, haven't I? He's dead, isn't he? Robert is dead, isn't he? Tell me the truth!" Her voice rises an octave as if she has only just realised the fact. "He's dead, isn't he?"

"Yes." His voice is small.

Please, somebody, core out my heart! Plug my ears so I may not hear. Blind my eyes so that I may not see. Take me to the glue factory. Tan my hide. For this body is nothing without Robert. Kosong. Empty.

Peter cannot bear the sight. He gets up to leave her sobbing by herself.

"I can't deal with it," he says to Margaret. "You are better at dis sort of tink. De impact of Robert's death has finally hit her."

Daughter-in-law walks in to the room and takes the woman in her arms and lets her cry. How our roles can change so quickly—mother becoming daughter, daughter becoming mother. You can even mother those who are not your own. Kim Hiok's body heaves and shakes; every sob is wrenching. Knowledge can be a painful thing. Perhaps in some way, nature assists people in pain to forget, sometimes momentarily, sometimes permanently. Do people who suffer from senile dementia and Alzheimer's understand their loss of memory or are they better off because they can't remember?

"Robert is dead. He's really dead." I long to hear a denial but none comes.

"Let it all out now, it's better for you-*lah*."

I weep, not just for Robert, but for my other losses—my child Peter, Ang Huay and Hugh, my father whom I've never met. I have failed them. I'm no good. No wonder my father never came for me. I have failed myself. I allow the shadows to draw me into darkness. Is there any purpose in my life now?

"You have us, now-*wat*. We are your family. You are not alone-*lah*."

It takes a lot of tears and tissue papers before the words travel to my consciousness. Can the one I loved be replaced by another with such swiftness? No, never. Not replaced. Another love can only help dress the wound that is caused by the loss of one, acting as a balm to pad the raw space that is left. After all, there isn't much point in continuing to grieve; nothing will make Robert return. He has already been cremated, the fact registered onto a piece of paper. Life is about moving on, a process of learning and change. It's when you stop that you are dead. You can be dead even when you are still alive. Entombed in your own past.

"I'm no good to anyone."

"You can be good to yourself for a start-*wat*."

I look at my daughter-in-law with a new respect. Wisdom can come from young minds too; it's not the prerogative of the old. In fact, the longer I live, the more I learn just how unwise I was. All I ask right now is that I should have the clarity to know how to behave correctly. I've been so long in the West that Western philosophy has influenced my thinking. In the East, chronological age isn't always the same as the soul's age—a young body can be the home of an old soul and vice-versa. It is the soul that provides the wisdom, not the physical brain. Margaret has to be an old soul, just as Peter has to be, to take on board the challenges they have done by marrying each other with Peter's history. But I can't tell her that because being a Catholic means that Margaret, like all Catholics, has adopted a Western idea of religion and by its implication, some of their principles.

"You are so wise. What a lovely girl you are." I snivel to a stop, clearing my nose. "I'm so pleased that you are my daughter-in-law…"

"You don't have to go back to England-*wat*. Dis can be your home-*lah*."

The generosity of the offer makes me want to weep afresh.

"I don't deserve your kindness." I pause. "I'll remember that. But I feel as if I've some unfinished business there. Or is it here? I keep thinking that there is still something that I have not remembered."

"Aiiyah! Don't worry so much-*lah*. Listen, you rest now and I will cook sometink nice for you, okay? You haven't eaten properly for days. I will get Siti to go out and buy some fresh pig's liver. It has a lot of iron to get your strength back. De ginger and sesame oil will also be good for purifying your blood."

"Who taught you these things, Margaret? Modern youngsters don't know much about such things."

"My mother-*lah*. She's a really good Peranakan cook-*wat*."

"I must meet her someday."

"Yes, pity she's still in Perth."

It's only after Margaret has left that I allow myself to sag against the pillows once more. You have a responsibility to step out of your misery when people are being solicitous. A few tears is permissible, a lot is understandable in some circumstances, tolerable even. But too many becomes an indulgence. People can't cope with indulgence. Alone now, I can let myself indulge—let all that pain and sorrow erupt, the hot tears slipping over the edge of my eyes as I recollect the tragedy that ended yet another phase of my life.

Robert did persuade me to do a tandem flight. At first, I was unsure, apprehensive. But I was determined to prove that I could be as good a companion as Emas had been. I wanted to win Robert from her, wrest him away from memories of her beauty and her perfections. So I gritted my teeth and agreed to do it. Our introduction to paragliding was through an experimental flight that we took at a renowned school in Wales. Up until the moment, when my instructor and myself took off and flew into nothingness, my teeth were chattering, knees soft and wobbly. But oh, that moment of flight! To my surprise, I loved it. Though weighed down by the weight of the instructor's body, I felt like a bird soaring. It was marvelous—a miracle created by men. Robert, flying with his instructor, was alongside us. I experienced a newfound joy as we flew over the beautiful mountains of Snowdonia with their rounded bumps of green. From our height, we could see the puffs of smoke of the steam train as it took tourists up the mountain where trees stood up straight against a backdrop of blue sky. It was the kind of scene I used to draw as a child in school, the image prompted by the suggestions of colonist teachers who were teaching their conquered people, *Janet and John, Jack and Jill, Mother Hubbard, Pounds Shillings and Pence and God Save The Queen.* It was the sort of scene that was removed from any in my own country which was a small, flat island, a scene that had so far existed only in my imagination. At last, I could now view a real scene to collude with the one in my head. There's a kind of magic in this, like a fairytale coming true.

Delighted with our tandem flight experience, Robert and I treated ourselves to a holiday and stayed on for a basic course in paragliding. A few weeks later, we returned to Wales for another course to get our Elementary Pilot Certificate. There were schools closer to us in Hampshire, but we loved the Welsh scenery and people. Another six days of flying instructions and we graduate into club pilots. Robert thoroughly enjoyed the sport and was confident in the air as he was in so many of the things he did. But I was not as confident. In truth, I knew that I would always experience that stomach-twisting fear just before I got airborne, but I did find the sport exhilarating, and relished the wind in my face and the sense of flying through the air, the ground a few hundred feet below. *And* it was a sport that Robert and I had learnt together, not something I had inherited from Emas. At last we had something that was genuinely *ours.* He would be proud of me yet.

On that fateful day, we decided to fly out from Beachy Head which was a lot nearer to our home than Wales. We had a few flights on our own already so we knew exactly what to do. We organised our equipment and drove down to East Sussex. The wind was picking up and the visibility good, though flukey, typical autumn weather. But it was dry. The trees were shaking their heads vigorously and were dropping their leaves like golden coins. "*Kim Hiok!*" Robert yelled above the noise of our open car. "My beautiful *Golden Leaf!*" Autumn always makes him a bit sentimental. Whenever he got the chance, Robert would opt for his convertible with its hood down.

So, we dressed warm for the journey, our equipment battened down in the back seat. I delighted in seeing his face so joyful as the wind whipped his grey hair as the Jaguar wend its way through forested country lanes. He was in a playful mood and every now and then when there was no danger of crashing into anyone else, he swerved the car so that I fell into his lap. Then he laughed, a lighthearted laughter which rang in my ears like church bells on a Sunday morning in a quiet English hamlet. *I* am the one making *him* happy. Not Emas. It was me he loved. Finally, we burst into the open wonder of the South Downs, a huge vista of space—of rolling hills and meandering rivers, a sky unadulterated by towering buildings, a wild sea dotted only by a few wind-surfers and sailboats. The wind-surfers and sailboats looked right on the sea; they are in harmony with nature, unlike the peace-shattering jet-skis and motorboats.

I prepared for the ascent. Trussed up in a boiler-type suit, crash helmet, goggles and harness, my identity was hidden. I could be anybody. The yellow and blue canopy was limp and stretched out behind me on the ground as I waited on the hill near the lighthouse for the wave of air to come. The windsock we had erected filled indicating the direction of the wind. I waited until I felt the tendrils of air caressing my face.

"Okay, off you go," Robert said.

I summoned my courage and ran down the slope, my heart beating furiously from the feeling of apprehension and, to be really honest, my age. I was not as fit as I should be. But I mustn't show it. I must exhibit the kind of stoicism that Emas must have exhibited. There was that twist in my stomach as always just before my canopy began to fill up to pull me upwards. It was that first leap, away from the ground and into the air to surf that wave of air, which gave me a momentary feeling of uncertainty. But it soon passed when I was up in the air, trusting that the parachute would keep me up there and knowing that I was in control. Any time I felt unsure, I could pilot my way back down on the hillside. My breath settled so I leant back into the harness to enjoy the unique sensation of flying—a woman imitating a bird. I smiled. It was Robert's turn. I watched him, below me, as he ran down the hillside like a much younger person, his canopy of pink and mauve, looking like a giant butterfly wing, billowed and filled. Then he was airborne and flew close by me. We exchanged the *okay* signal with our fingers to indicate that all was well. Then we sat back and drank in the view of the fields and the sea, the waves crashing into the rocks below. The wind chased the clouds away in rapid spurts and the sun came out, strong and bright. I felt deliriously happy as if at long last my life was coming out right. Robert and myself have started a hobby together; surely Emas will be forgotten now. I could make Robert truly happy, be the companion he missed. Without Robert to persuade and encourage me, I would never have had the temerity to handle a sport like this. Especially at my time in life. For that and many things else, I was grateful to him.

Perspectives change when you are in the air. Earthbound things look different. You experience a sense of calm in your detachment. Except for the sound of the wind in my ears, there was a certain kind of silence. This was the closest I had come to being at one with nature. My eyes scanned the land and seascape. In the harness, I felt as if I was being cradled, rocked gently by the thermal of air. I sighed with contentment. That was when I saw the seals, three of them, a family perhaps, of two adults and a calf sunning themselves on the rocks below in a calmer part of the water where the waves could not reach them, fat commas of grey-brown bodies. You had to look closely to see that they were seals because they looked so much like part of the rocks. Robert must have seen them the same time I did because he was waving to me and pointing below. I thought I heard him call out. But the wind was in my ears and I could not hear him clearly. I tugged at the control handle so that I could edge closer to him to hear what he was saying. Then I caught the words. At first, I could not believe what I had heard. I must be wrong. The wind was rushing in my ears. Then he called out again and this time, it was unmistakable.

"Emas!" He yelled cheerfully. "Mas, *sayang*, look!"

The name was a lance that speared my heart. All that I had believed about Robert loving me was my own invention. All was revealed in that moment. He did not love me, could not love me with Emas so full in his mind and heart.

He was not mine, never had been mine. Need and lust can easily masquerade for love. And when you yourself are needy, you are vulnerable to another person's attention, you are quick to claim it as love. Of course, Robert could not give his heart because it was already taken. Perhaps I had suspected it all along but didn't want to know. But on that fateful day, when he called out Emas' name, he nullified me, scraped away the falsehood of our love. That was when I lost it.

Startled and confused, my hands took on minds of their own and I tugged too hard on the control handles. My action made my canopy swerve and turn too abruptly, swaying this way and that. Robert was caught off-guard, so intent was he on the sighting of the seals. He was unprepared for my violent moves and could not get out of the way in time and I slammed headlong into him. Shocked, he had no time to react. The impact made me stagger and lose my balance and I was tossed about in the wind. Momentarily, his canopy and body hid the sun from me—shadows across the sun—engulfing me in darkness. The wind pushed him aside and I could see again. With tremendous effort, I fought hard, tugging and pulling. Eventually, I managed to get back in control. But I saw that Robert was still struggling to right his parachute. I did not know what to do to help him. He could not get the wind to fill his canopy and it went limp, like a balloon whose air had escaped. His lines were getting tangled and the canopy wrapped around him like a shroud. And then it appeared to me that he stopped struggling, almost as if he had decided to give up. I watched in horror as he tumbled out of the sky to crash into the rocks below.

24

Lightning zigzags across the equatorial sky. It seems to miss the top of the tower blocks by inches. Of course, this is an optical illusion, a situation that arises from the curve of our earth and the angle of light as it strikes our eyes. Like this physical illusion sometimes, there is also an optical illusion of our inner eye, the way we see a situation is deflected by the way we perceive it. It is where we are coming from, what we tell ourselves. Not an easy one to resolve. And worse, sometimes, we are not even privy to our own self-deception. Whilst the storm rages on in my mind, in the sky, a series of lightning flashes tear the sky apart. Then the claps of thunder follow, their sound like a stampede of wild horses. Typical of the tropics, there is at first nothing, and in the next, like a flash-flood that begins from nowhere, huge curtains of rain fall, so dense that you cannot see beyond your nose. The torrent swells the monsoon drains, lakes and rivers, it slaps the faces of coconut palms; umbrellas mushroom upwards, people and stray animals scuttle for shelter. The people without umbrellas but are caught in the storm use their shopping bags, handbags, briefcases or any sheets that are available, holding them overhead to get some respite from the heavy rain as they ran for cover. Sometimes the ones holding an open broadsheet newspaper aloft get a shock as the paper tears apart in the middle and the deluge of rainwater gushes down on them. The wonder of an equatorial storm is that it can go as quickly as it comes. You can be standing on one side of the road, waiting for the traffic lights to change and the green man to appear, then the sky is split open and you will be drenched. By the time you cross the four-lane road, the rain has stopped and the sun has come out. You can be made to feel a bit silly standing there with your soaked clothes and your hair hanging like rat tails in the bright sunlight, with only the wash on the pavements and droplets on the leaves to testify to the storm that passed. The storm in my mind is harder to deal with, you can't get out of it or away from it.. In practise, we can put up an umbrella or run for shelter but how do you do that with a storm that is inside yourself? Wherever you go, it follows. I wish I had tried harder at yoga, learnt from the gurus how to weather a mental and emotional storm

One thing is certain—in an equatorial country, the sun does shine on most days. Residents hankering for coolness wish it otherwise but the sun is unfailing, diligent in its duty. Huge parcels of sunshine toast your skin in minutes during the day. The evenings borrow the sun's heat and though its light is completely gone, its heat lingers through so that you can walk outdoors in shorts and swim in sun-warmed water under the moon and stars. In the old days, the roofs of the *kampongs* were made of attap, leaves from the nipah palm. When the sun shone relentlessly on the attap, they dried and browned quickly, crackling when the mynah birds waded through them or when the centipedes wriggled amongst the sheaves of leaves. A careless cigarette thrown, a mirror placed accidentally at an angle which caught the sun rays or an open stove left unguarded could start a conflagration. There is no such danger these days; these villages have slipped into the pages of history like the colonial past. The only *kampong* which can be seen is a made-up one to impress tourists. There is independent ruling now and modernisation, houses and roofs of concrete, hard, firm—to withstand most assaults. Families walk, cycle and jog in the parks around reservoirs and along the sea. Parents who worked all day whilst their maids looked after their children still have time to spend with their young ones, taking them out to catch the sea breeze or a film or shopping and supper in a city that never sleeps. Shopping centers bustle with adults, children trailing, the music blaring from the sound system. Everywhere, you can see hoards of people, on the streets, at the cinemas and in food centers. Singapore is bulging at the seams with people. Some measure of escape is still possible on the outer fringes of the island—

to public parks or private country clubs.

"Isn't Grandma coming with us?" Diana asks when the family was getting ready to leave for East Coast Park.

"She needs to rest. Maybe next time."

Peter hires three bicycles for himself and the kids to cycle along the tarmac path that runs along the beach illuminated by globes of electric light. Margaret is less energetic and prefers to stay by the barbecue pit with Siti to prepare the barbecue. She is a proud homemaker using her own marinade for the meats: ground ginger, onions, garlic and a touch of ground coriander and cummin. She was the one who booked the use of the barbecue pit. The parks are well-organised, each activity has its own place, places where you can barbecue, places where you can walk or cycle, places where you can throw your rubbish. No one dreams of throwing their rubbish in a willy-nilly fashion. No, not in Singapore - the fine is too heavy. It's cheaper and less nasty to clear up your own mess. There are not many cities in the world that can boast of such pristine-clean streets, not a single cigarette packet in sight, no fast-food boxes scuttling about moved by the wind. If only noise was as well controlled. There are many youngsters on the beach, their ghetto-blasters turned up loud, some of them pirouetting and gyrating around the campfires. Occasionally, laughter bursts out like firecrackers. There is something about laughter—it can delight you even if it is not yours and put a smile on your face. The moon's wan light is eclipsed by the fierce light from freighters, street lamps, homes, factories, businesses, neon signs, traffic lights and headlamps. A city of light. If you are in space, you are sure to see its glow, like the pulsating egg yolk of Las Vegas with the dark desert spread around the city.

Peter's mind is elsewhere, dragged into places he had not allowed it to go before until his mother inadvertently voiced her fear. There are scenes which he would like to have stayed zipped in his memory files. But they are open now and he is compelled to look. Although he was in the apartment on the twenty-six floor of the residential block that overlooked the Kallang River for only the first five years of his life, he could remember so much of it, perhaps because his mother was a part of his life then. He can see his bedroom with the polysterene cut-outs of Pluto on one side of the wall next to the window, and a scene from Puss-In-Boots on the other—Puss-In-Boots standing by the drawbridge, the castle behind him. He could see her now at their dining table, bending over the sheets of polysterene foam drawing the pictures and painting them in watercolour before she cut around their shapes. He knelt on one of the chairs to play with the paints on the sheet of paper she gave him. Sometimes he propped his chin on his upturned palms to watch her bring his favourite cartoon characters to life. She was very slim and her hair was waist-long, straight and black, the fringe falling over her forehead as she worked. Every now and then, she would push her hair back and tucked it behind her ears. If she looked up and saw him looking at her, she'd smile at him, her dimple deepening, her eyes shining. That's the way he would like to remember her. Not the broken look that came afterwards, the corners of her mouth often quivering, her eyes brimming with unshed tears, her hair and emotions in disarray. When she was not herself, she caned him for little things—i.e., for wetting himself, for being afraid of the dark. But always, she would hug him afterwards, soothe away his pain, and sob into his shoulders. He tries to shut out the sounds that used to come from his parents' bedroom, of muffled cries, of flesh hitting flesh, of objects that crashed onto the tiled floor.

Once, he got out of his bed to push their bedroom door open and his mother was cowering on the floor, arms shielding her head whilst Victor stood over her, his arm arrested in midair by Peter's entrance. Peter rushed up to his father and, using his small fists, he pounded his father. "*Bad Daddy! Bad Daddy!*" he cried out. Was this something that had really happened or was it a nightmare that he pulled into reality? No, he'd rather not remember. He also didn't want to remember the images that his father and grandmother etched into his brain, of a woman who did not know how to mother; of someone who screamed like a banshee; of a slut who opened her legs for white trash.

Krrnnnnnngggg…A bicycle bell jars him back to the beach. Peter had been so engrossed that he nearly ran into another push-bike coming the other way, the cyclist expressing his annoyance with that long, irritated ring.

"Eh! You blind or wat-ah?"

"Oops, sorry-*lah*!"

"Daddy, you're not looking where you're going," Harry says.

"Ya, I must be careful-*lah*. I tink it's time for our barbecue."

"It's *th*ink, daddy, *th-th-th*!" both children say in unison.

*   *   *

My Dear Veronica,

I hope you've got over the flu bug. I really do miss you, you know. Isn't this new technology wonderful? I can email you while you are in your bed sleeping.

I want you to know that the impact of Robert's death had hit me. But I'm okay now. Isn't it strange how I knew and didn't know, as if one part of me is concealing the knowledge from another part of me? How could I have kept the truth zipped inside me? It's like one of those computer files, isn't it, where the information is compressed and sent to you zipped? And though you have the files there on your computer and know that something is in those files, you need the right programme to decompress and unzip the files before you can read the information inside? How much of our past pain and emotions is like this, zipped into unreadable files, but there lying in wait for the right trigger to open them and make us experience them anew?

The awful thing about remembering is knowing the truth. To know with certainty that I will never see Robert again or hear his voice is to suffer an inner death. My future, without Robert beside me, is a yawning chasm ahead of me.

Did I tell you what happened that day? I probably must have bored you with it a hundred times over. It still torments me. I remember now that the police came with the coast guards' rescue team. Of course, later, the ambulance. Apparently there had been witnesses to the incident and they called the emergency services. How I managed to land back on the hillside, I do not know. My mind is still a daze about that, and many other things. I remember, though, that when I was in the air and watched Robert plunging downward, I wanted very much to follow him, commit suttee. But you see, I still had hope then. I believed that he couldn't be snatched from me, that he would be all right. After all, I knew he knew how to break a fall. If he was just hurt, badly hurt even, he would need me to nurse him back to health.

I don't think I've remembered everything because there's something else niggling me though I don't know what. You know how cobwebs tend to stick to you? Well, it's like that. Something feels wrong and sticky, but I cannot

shake it off. But I ask myself, what can be important now that Robert is gone?
Kim Hiok

My Dear Kim,
Apologies for this late reply. It took me longer than I expected to sort out this damn computer! It shows up my age, doesn't it? How did we manage to cope without them before? Listen, don't distress yourself. I'm aware that it must be an awful realisation. I said that to Peter before you left. The doctor told me you were in a kind of denial and that at some point, the full impact of the realisation will hit you. I am so sorry. I know it's tough. I didn't know whether I should have let you go so that I'd be around when you remembered or for you to be with your family when you did. I think Peter coming for you just at this time was a miracle. So you know you're not alone. He is such a nice young man. If his wife is just as lovely, you're lucky to have them. This is not an easy time for you, but it must be nice to know you have a family again.
Try to look forward, put the past behind you. I know it's easier said than done, but it's what you must do to survive. Focus on the happiness you had with Robert, though it was brief. Remember that it was an accident. I repeat, it *was* an accident. That was the decision at the enquiry. So don't go distressing yourself further.
Veronica

My Dear Veronica,
You've been a great friend. What would I have done without you?
Kim Hiok

*　　*　　*

Yes, I must focus on the thought that I've a very good friend and a new family now. A close-knit family is like a harbour for individual boats to come into, to rest, to enjoy the camaraderie of others or simply to take refuge. I can partake of familial love, a different cuisine to Robert's but delicious nonetheless, with my son, daughter-in-law and two lovely grandchildren. What more can I ask for at my stage in life? There are many others who are worse off than myself.

Although I only had my mother when I was growing up, the people in the village were like a big, extended family, children playing together like siblings, grown-ups treating every child the same, like their own. I learned to use this to effect, running to a neighbour's house when it was mealtime so that I got fed and then to another household. If I was lucky to get the timing right, I got another meal before I went home to Ang Huay, who might have dug up some tapioca or yam for our meal. My greed made me rotund. My mother used to wonder how I could have gotten so fat with our lack of food. Thank goodness I shot up when I was a teenager. On bad days, the tubers were simply boiled, then served. On better days, Ang Huay boiled wedges of sweet potatoes with tapioca leaves in coconut milk for a delicious *lemak*. And if we were really lucky, we might have steamed rice and a fish to share between us.

It was this feeling of close relationships that I missed when I went to England. Hugh's family was scattered around the country, but since he was not in touch with them it didn't make any difference. I often asked about them, but he never volunteered any information. Perhaps they already know what I didn't know then and had disowned him. How wise we should be to heed telltale clues, let the scales built up by love drop from our eyes so that we open them to truth. We should examine the kind of friends that our partner or spouse have to give us an idea of the person behind the face. I felt too desolated to notice Hugh's type of friends when I first arrived. What was worse than not having a family was not having any memories of the place. I couldn't go to any place as Hugh could do and recalled a time when I had been there or had known of it. Everything in a new country was new, devoid of any emotional attachments for me and it was hard to build on nothing. And, of course, I had that unspoken pain at the loss of Peter, a hard-boiled egg of discomfort in my chest that made my breathing short. Once Hugh had brought me back to England, he expected to go about his life as he had done before me, and he did, busying himself with his various projects that didn't seem to bring home any money.

"You know that chap we met in that crafts shop when we were in

Singapore? Lawrence Britten? He's got a gift shop in London. I'll go and see him. Perhaps we can bring over some batik, jade pieces and wooden carvings and other things that he can sell. Why don't you come with me?"

"You know I'm on duty. Surely he has contacts in the Far East already?"

"Don't be a wet blanket, darling. This might be my big break."

Some days he was away for a day and other times he was away for longer. The days stretched for me in this land which I could not call my own, no one to speak my language, no one to run into at the shops or supermarkets who might recognise me. It is hard when you have to sacrifice your own culture to learn another to get on in the adopted country. Hugh was not unkind, just negligent, unthinking in the manner of a man. He probably didn't even realise that I might have special needs because I was an alien to his country and culture. But when he came home, he would be in high spirits, laden with gifts. He'd come in with a big smile, his face unlined as if his trip had taken away all his tensions. I didn't know why but was to find out later. His gifts were a kind of offering, if only I knew what type then. He stood with his gift behind his back, as if I was a child waiting to be surprised—or appeased perhaps.

"Darling, I've got something for you," he'd say.

Then he'd produced his gift with a flourish, a huge floral bouquet usually and some things he knew I'd like: a pair of earrings; a brooch; a perfumed soap; or sometimes just a packet of food from a Singaporean restaurant, and if he couldn't find one, a take-away from an Asian restaurant.

"I love you, I love you," he'd say, picking me up and twirling me around. "You're so lovely to come home to."

How could such adoration turn out to be so treacherous?

Our thatched cottage was tucked in the woods and our nearest neighbour was in a barn across the fields. I had heard that English people respected your privacy and would not make the first move, afraid to intrude. So I decided that if I was going to stop being lonely, I would have to make the first move. I put on my coat and wellies and strode across the fields to the barn, heart hammering in its cage with the fear that my advances might be met with disapproval.

"Hello, sorry to disturb you, you look like you're in the middle of work.

My name is Kim Hiok. I've just come from Singapore and I don't know anyone here."

Veronica arrived at the door ready to berate the person for the intrusion thinking it was a salesperson or a Jehovah Witness enthusiast. She was in her paint-spattered smock, brush still in hand, a growl ready to spring from her throat when she saw the Oriental girl, standing on her doorstep looking like a lost Gretel who had stumbled onto the gingerbread house.

"Come in, come in," she said instead, wiping her hands, then putting her brush down. She observed how the girl took off her wellies and set them aside on the porch outside before she walked into the hall in her socks. This was someone who respected another's space, revered the sanctity of home. And she was impressed.

"What a beautiful place! All this light coming from the lovely windows! Our cottage is too dark, with low ceilings and dark carpets. It feels like an animal that is going to swallow me up. But here, oh, here, under this vaulted ceiling, I can breathe freely. Wow, you're so talented," she said, admiring the paintings, finished and unfinished, propped up here and there, landscapes of the English countryside. "What a privilege to meet a real-life painter. I used to paint for a hobby."

"Oh, yes, what medium did you paint in?"

"Watercolour mostly. But I'm not good at controlling the wash-*lah*. I only do it for fun. But I can't do oils like you; they're too difficult for me."

"Still-life? Portraits? Landscapes?"

"Still-life. Flowers mostly. Sometimes I copy pictures from children's books. I'm actually a nurse. I work at the local hospital."

"That's commendable. At least you're doing something for society. Being an artist means I'm doing something for myself. Although my agent has to sell my pictures, I myself don't really care what people think of my paintings. I just do what I want. I just have to do it. It's like a disease. I just need to paint and paint. That's selfishness, don't you think?"

"I would like to be an artist, seeing the beauty in things instead of seeing sick people all the time. I think an artist gives a lot to society. You give more of yourself. You translate your vision into a work of art. You bare your soul."

"That doesn't sound like me." Veronica laughed. She was surprised how releasing it was, the sound of her own laughter, and she liked it. It was rare for her to laugh. Being on your own a lot didn't give you the opportunity.

"Nursing fulfills my need to be needed. That's self-oriented too, isn't it? Even when we are doing something for others, mostly it's because we have this yearning to satisfy ourselves. Perhaps it's only me. I'm not a good person."

Veronica frowned at the declaration, so full of self-deprecation but their relationship was too new for probing questions. Not usually one given to loneliness, she felt the girl's loneliness emanating like an odour.

"Why don't you come 'round next Sunday for tea. I'll invite some of the women in the village so that you'll get to meet them."

And to the astonishment of the village folks, an invitation was issued for tea at The Barn. Invited were the florist, the grocer, the lady who ran the teashop, the lady farmer, the hairdresser and the postmistress. And of course they went, mostly out of curiosity. Veronica covered her pictures with dust sheets and unearthed her mother's silver cutlery and good china. Her medley of visitors seemed a little unsure of her, but she didn't notice. They sat around the walnut table and ate dainty cucumber sandwiches and smoked salmon sandwiches; cakes, scones, jam, clotted cream and Earl Grey.

"This is Kim everyone, she has just moved here from Singapore."

"Singapore. Isn't that somewhere in China?"

"No, dear, it's in Southeast Asia, south of Malaya," the lady farmer said.

"One of our former colonies," a voice said in *sotto voce*.

"Er, did we kill anyone there? Massacre or something like that?"

"We actually made a fool of ourselves," Veronica said in her booming voice.

"We pointed the guns out to sea and allowed the Japs, literally, to walk into the country whilst our people scuttled away like frightened rabbits actually! If I were them, I wouldn't forgive us."

"The British has given us a very good infrastructure." Kim Hiok had interjected, trying to win friends. "Our legal system is still based on yours."

"Haven't you got a lovely skin," the postmistress said, changing subjects quickly. "I wish I could be so brown. I look like a dead slug next to you."

"This is delicious-*lah*. We never thought of a cucumber as a sandwich filling before. What a novel idea."

"That's quaint. What's *lah*?"

"Oops, sorry. It's a Singaporean expression. It's tagged on to end of words to soften. I must learn some English ones now."

"Have you heard of the Earl of Sandwich…?"

Recalling our early days, I smile. Veronica has been a wonderful friend, a stoic supporter. I should buy her a gift from here. A batik painting will be nice, something ethnic, cultural. When I'm better, I'll ask Margaret where I can get one by a renowned local artist; Veronica would appreciate that. I worry about Veronica now that she is getting older. But she wouldn't consider a retirement flat or a warden-assisted home. That woman is proud. Will I be able to survive on my own like Veronica? Have I that kind of courage and resilience? It is quiet in the apartment. I hadn't gone out with the family because I wanted some time to adjust to my knowledge about Robert, but now the silent maisonette pulls me too much into sadness, too much into thoughts well left alone. Now I can't wait for the family to get back. Robert is gone. Truly gone. It's a bitter fact to swallow. But, there is nothing I can do to bring him back. Besides, Veronica, I have friends at the hospital I worked but you can't burden colleagues with your loneliness. It's a family I need, a family who cares, a family who remembers that I'm on my own.

It is ten o'clock when the family leaves East Coast Park. The children sit behind in the car with Siti, subdued after all the activity. Peter is motoring back when Margaret says, "Let's buy some food for your mother-*lah*. She might be hungry-*hor*."

"Dat's a good idea. We're not far from Geylang. My father used to take us for de *Beef Hor Fan* dere. She used to love it."

"Aiiyah, Dad-dy!"

"*Th*e, *th*e, *th*e," says Harry, spittle escaping.

"Lots of chilli for Grandma," Diana reminds them.

Still too restless to read, I switch on the television. The television has a plasma screen so thin that it is hung on the wall in the living room. With its stereo and theatre gizmo with sound that reverberates around the room, it's like watching a film at the cinema. I skip channels distractedly using the remote control and settles on a nature programme. With cable TV, the world has become a technological village. David Attenborough's distinct voice brings England back to me and for a moment, I'm back in my own living room, watching TV with Robert, snuggling my back into his warm body, his arms snaking around me. However I regard him now, I have keepsakes of those times when I *believed* ourselves to be truly in love—*believed* that he did love me. I have to live on such morsels. It's a survival tactic. David Attenborough is explaining about the octopus and the intelligence tests that are being set, a maze the octopus has to go through in order to get at its food and three different doors marked with symbols. Then the scene switches to the sea, to an octopus living in the wild. He says, *"An octopus in the wild lives for a maximum of one year. A female octopus starves herself to keep her fertilised eggs alive and then she dies even before her babies are born. These baby octopuses never meet their mother."*

His commentary slaps me with guilt again. I am thinking, even in the lowest form of life, a mother sacrifices herself for her children—what sin I have committed! Something that can never be made right. Old sins do cast long shadows. Distressed, I switch channels and catches a local drama series *Growing Up* that depicts life in Singapore in the 1940s. Though I didn't live as far back as that, it amuses me to see the old Singapore that I remember, the clothes people wore, the chophouses with their five-foot-way buses, the hawkers. When you can identify with bygone days and nostalgia, you know you're old! The thought makes me smile, takes me to a different mood. Old age is inevitable; why make it a source of despair? I always think it's so amusing that people should have their face sliced, cut and pinned so that their wrinkles would be removed. What good is all that in promoting true happiness when all your fears still wrinkle the inside of your mind and heart?

My ears are now listening for the family's return. There is a kind of anticipatory pleasure when you can look forward to someone coming home. When I hear the key turning in the lock, my heart experiences a tremor of joy. I'm thinking how welcoming that sound is. It must be sad for people who live alone, people like Veronica, who will not have anyone coming home to her. And worse, if you live alone, you know that there is *no one* waiting for *you* to come home, no one to care, no one to know if you are early or late or if you came back at all. This will be my fate if I return to England now that Robert is gone forever. Of course there's Veronica, but my friendship with Veronica requires space and distance; Veronica is not one who can cope with a clinging relationship.

Diana skips into the room, with Harry at her heels, their parents walking behind.

"Grandma, we bought supper for you."

"And for us."

Siti goes straight into the kitchen to unpack the supper. Apparently, enough was bought for everyone's supper despite the fact that they had a barbecue not so long ago. But this way of eating is not unusual in Signapore. Afterwards, Siti will wash the dishes they had used for the barbecue and unpack all the gear. Then she will clear their supper things. She wouldn't go to bed until the family has gone to bed, although she gets up at six-thirty every morning to prepare breakfast.

"Did you enjoy your barbecue?"

"We went cycling too. Daddy was so dreamy he nearly ran into someone."

"Tort you might like some *beef hor fan*. Peter took us to Geylang to buy it. He said it used to be one of your favourite stalls-*wat*."

How does Peter remember these things? Is he like me? Has he squirreled our precious years together, holding tight to them and burying the treasures deep in his heart because they had to last a winter of want? I'm moved. I disguise my emotions with a lightness in my voice.

"Aiiyah! You feed me so much!" I call back a local expression to appear less formal. "What's going to happen when I want to go back? I'll be so fat, I won't be able to get into my seat on the aeroplane-*lah*!"

"Grandma! You're not leaving us, are you?" Diana exclaims, her eyes large.

There is a moment of silence as my newfound family awaits my answer. Are they really expecting me to stay forever? Can I let myself believe that this is what they really want? Really and truly? What does Peter think? Is this what he wants? What he expects? The last thing I wish to do is become a burden to my family. Harry detaches himself from the group, walks up to me, and takes my hand in both of his, putting it to his lips. For a shy boy, this is a huge gesture. He looks at me with soulful eyes, eyes which remind me of my own mother.

"I don't want you to go-*lah*, Grandma," he says.

25

Answers, like words, have to be measured carefully before being uttered. They are like medicine. The right dose can be healing; too little is ineffective, too much can be lethal. Sometimes it is better altogether not to say anything. There are all sorts of reasons why you cannot reply. You may not know how, or you may be moved to loose emotions. Perhaps it's because you don't want to tell a lie yet the truth will hurt someone. Generally, men seem to have a natural ability to fence off a question, especially their wife's, especially if their answer will get them into trouble. So you can be like a man, pretending that you didn't hear the question, or you can answer a question with a question. Or better still, evade it completely by changing the subject. Harry had tried to find out if I was leaving Singapore. I don't know what I wanted to do myself.

"Hmm, the *hor fan* smells good. I must eat it before it gets cold."

We go to the dining area where Siti has laid out the plates, chopsticks and china spoons, with the *hor fan* in a large tureen in the middle of the table. Margaret portions it out onto the various plates; her body, though an indulgent body, plump in places she shouldn't be plump, sings and moves with love for her children, husband, and now for me too. Love can be given in so many ways and this is one of them. A very Asian way—a very Singaporean way. Mui Yoke, too, was such a mother, mothering Victor in the only way she knew, feeding him till he became corpulent. Ang Huay, too, tried to feed *me* without whatever food she could get. I'm thinking that, at least they stayed to mother the children they brought forth. But I don't want to dwell on my failure; I draw, instead, the memory of my mother buying the leftover scraps of meat from the butcher, the wilted part of the vegetables that the vegetable-seller threw away. It was nice that when I began nursing, I could take my mother to Swee Kee Chicken Rice Restaurant reputed to have the best chicken rice in the country in the seventies. I smile at the recollection—I did give something back to my mother after all. How silly we are to pull in only painful memories or those that remind us of how inadequate we have been; better to pull in memories of our well-meaning deeds that can plump up our sense of self-worth.

"You know, this sort of thing—sitting down to supper after we've taken dinner is unlikely to take place in an English household. Especially *not* at eleven o'clock at night."

"Ya, dis is very Singaporean, right?"

"Enough chilli or not?" Margaret asks.

"I reminded Mummy and Daddy that you like lots of chilli, Grandma."

"What a good memory you have. Grandma is proud of you. And your memory, too, Peter, to remember that I like this. It is absolutely delicious. If this is not done properly the strands of *kway teow* stick together. I can never find this sort of food near where I live. I have to go to Chinatown in London for it. The Hong Kong chefs there are very good. Apparently, they produce the best *Roast Duck* outside of Asia. Hmm, the chilli is just right, thanks."

"Grandma, you didn't answer. Are you staying with us?" Harry persists.

"Oy! Don't disturb Grandma. Let her eat in peace," Peter says.

"I *am* staying with you. In England, to *stay* is for a visit and to *live* means being in a place longer, like in your own home."

"Okay. So…will you live with us then?"

"Let us discuss it another time. I want to enjoy this *hor fan*. How do you say *eat* in Chinese?"

"*Ze*," The children echo.

"*Che*." I try to emulate but fail miserably and the children giggle. I try again. "*Cher*."

"That's a car, Grandma!" Harry says, laughing out with great mirth.

"There are four tones in Mandarin: *Ze, Ze, Ze, Ze*," Diana shows off.

"To the unpractised ear, they all sound the same," Peter says.

"The problem is that each tone changes the same word into a different one," Margaret laughs, her eyes sparkling.

"In the old days, us Peranakans studied Malay at school. Also, it was the national language when Singapore was part of Malaysia. So I can't speak Mandarin. You kids are clever. Teach me again another time. I want to hear what you've been doing this evening."

The children tell me. I smile, nod and ask questions. Their chatter is a rescue from my evening of silence. Peter and Margaret join in. The buzz of family is reinvigorating, acting as balm to wounds. Yes, why should I not enjoy this forever? Why go back to England where there is no family, no Robert? The idea is becoming tempting. It lifts my spirit.

"It's my turn to be tucked in, Grandma," Diana says. "What story will it be today?"

"Grandma is just getting over her illness; she might be too tired."

He won't call me *Mum* but at least he has said, *grandma*, and he's caring. Perhaps this should be enough for me.

"No, I'm all right. It will do me good." And then I turn to Diana. "Have you heard of *Little Women*?"

"No…"

"Well, why don't I tell you about it? If you like the story and want to read it for yourself, we can go and buy the book."

"Are they tiny, tiny women from a different planet, Grandma?" Harry asks.

Children are such blessings. I really have missed out on so much. Perhaps if I accept my family's generous offer, it will give me an opportunity to gain back what I had lost and become a mother again, though this time to my own grandchildren. It might do Peter good, too, to see me relate to children, see me give what he didn't get from me. This is my regret, of course, that *he* had been deprived. It pains me to think that his deprivation may have shaped him in adverse ways, perhaps make him needy or lacking confidence in himself, untrusting of relationships. How can I ever undo all that, repay him, and reinstate the qualities that should have been his in the first place? Is it a kind of conceit to think that I would have been such a great influence in his life? Looking at him now, a successful executive in an international conglomerate with a lovely wife and children, he doesn't seem any different from those who had their mothers with them in the nurturing years. Whatever Mui Yoke had instilled in Peter's mind against me, at least she was there to bring him up. That, I have to be grateful for. Perhaps I'm overworrying, my guilt weighing like an anvil in my mind. Perhaps it *is* time to let it go. After we finished our supper, the children scraped their chairs back and helped Siti by carrying the plates into the kitchen.

"That's nice to see," I say. "You've raised the children right, Margaret."

"I don't want dem to behave badly just because we can afford a maid. You know, in some households, children are so spoilt dey never even have to lift a plate. When dey want anything, dey just scream the maid's name. De maid does everytink for dem, dress dem, even bathing and combing deir hair for dem sometimes. Most of dem don't even say *please* and *tank you*."

"You know, I feel like you're my own daughter. When you have some time, let's have a meal together, just you and I. Oh, I want to ask a favour. Can you take me to an art gallery that sells batik paintings by local artists? I'd like to get something for Veronica."

"No prob," she says.

The expression is so American. Since the colonialists had left and the American conglomerates had invested in the country, bringing with them their fast food chains, television programmes and films, Americanism has dug its roots in and sprouted prolifically. The worst thing is some people can't even tell the difference between an American and English spelling, word or expression. And it's not just in Singapore. But does it matter? Especially in this nation of immigrants which is a melting pot of Chinese, Malay, Indians, Eurasians and Caucasians?

When we are about to go to our rooms, Peter stops me briefly and says, "You know you don't have to go back, right? I can go to England and sort out your house and do all de necessary paperwork. We can go to Singapore Immigration and get you an extended stay or something."

I look at him, my heart too fluttery to speak. I cannot believe my good fortune and wonder where his generosity of spirit has come from. I simply nod.

There was hardly a gap between Hugh's betrayal and my friendship with Robert. Perhaps it would have been wiser for me to have experienced life on my own for a while, instead of plunging headlong into a relationship with

Robert. But then I didn't know how to be on my own. Never have been. I went from Victor to Hugh to Robert, exchanging one for the other, a Linus, dragging a security blanket through life, fearful to be without. Where is my backbone then? Can't I stand on my own? Had my mother slaved for nothing? What advice would Ang Huay give me now? Would she tell her daughter to choose to live with her family? I sigh. Why are decisions so hard to make? If I choose to remain in Singapore, am I being fair to my family? Am I replacing my loss of Robert with them?

"Marry me. Please say you will marry me," Hugh begged all those years ago. "I can't live without you."

"But what about Peter?"

"We'll take him with us."

"You mean it?" I was ecstatic.

"Of course, why not? So long as he doesn't take you too much away from me."

"No. You'll be first in my life."

But I had not bargained for Victor's wrath. Honesty and a confession do not always necessitate an acquiescence or understanding. Perhaps that is why people opt for subterfuge and indulge in long-term, illicit affairs.

"You fucking cunt! You whore! Get out!" He swung out a leg and I fell to the floor. "You'll never have my son. If you want that English bastard, you go!"

"Our marriage is finished before he came on the scene..."

"Don't open your mouth like you open your cunt! Get out of my sight."

In a fury, he took a suitcase and started to fling my things into it. I got up and rushed to Peter's room to pick him up. All I needed was my son and my handbag with a bit of money and I would leave. Victor came striding into the room, his face aflamed, his eyes wild. He yanked Peter from me. Peter cried and I screamed as Victor's fist connected with my jaw.

"I told you! You're not taking my son. Get out! Now!"

He placed Peter down on the floor to free his hands. Peter was confused and frightened, his voice hoarse from crying. I wished he hadn't seen what Victor did. Victor forcibly dragged me to the front door. With his other hand, he unlocked the door, then the steel gate that was a burglar-preventive feature of the high-rise flats. He shoved me out to the landing between the four apartments of what used to be termed a point-block. Swiftly, he locked the gate. Eyes blurred, I tripped over the shoes and sandals that were customarily left at the entrance. I stumbled, picked myself up, then returned to clutch at the railings.

"Please, let me have Peter, please!"

Victor came to the door with the suitcase. I thought he might open the door to hand it to me, it would give me the opportunity to rush at him, then get Peter out. Instead, he put the case down and picked up my clothes and fed them through the rails to fall outside. His movements were frenetic and pained. I saw that he was hurting too. For that I was sorry. Yet, he must have realised that our marriage had ended a long time ago. Still, that was different from learning that your wife had fallen in love with someone else.

Peter came rushing up to him. "*Bad Daddy! Bad Daddy!*" he cried.

Victor pushed him away and slammed the wooden door shut catching my fingers. From behind the closed wooden door, I heard him shout at Peter, "*Shut up! Shut up!*" Then the stereo came on, its volume turned to blasting proportions presumably so that Victor could not hear me banging at the door. I knocked at the door repeatedly till my knuckles were bruised. I stood there, my forehead pressed into the railings of the gate of the twenty-six storeys of what used to be my home in a gesture of despair, items of clothing strewn around my feet over the top of the shoes, sandals and slippers— a life scattered. *Mea culpa, mea culpa.* The terrible knowledge sunk into me— it was *I* who had broken up my family. My jaw began to swell.

I went back to live with my mother. When I returned to the apartment some days later, there was a thick chain holding the gate closed and the locks had been changed. There were no shoes, sandals and slippers at the front door. For an Asian home, this was unusual, an indication that its owners were away or that no one was living there. It was likely that Victor had taken Peter to Mui Yoke to be looked after. There was something despairing about an empty home, as if its spirit has been wrenched from it. I went to Mui Yoke, not once but again and again, to beg Victor and Mui Yoke to let me see my son. And on that one occasion when I had gone with Hugh, both Victor and Mui Yoke had stepped into the forecourt to swear at us, providing entertainment for their neighbours.

"Remember this," I said to Hugh tearfully in the hotel after the unsuccessful attempt to see Peter. "Remember this moment of heartbreak. Remember what I'm giving up for you."

"Darling," he said, gathering me into his arms and smothering me with kisses. "Would I ever!"

He was so sure. Or maybe he was already pretending. Those were the days when he could pluck me from despair with just his touch and caresses, took me to new heights of pleasure. He seemed to adore my body—adore me. It was a kind of magic to be loved like that, my sense of self like one of Jack's magical beans, taking seed, then sprouting and growing into a giant stalk. But it was not a cow that I had used to trade for the beans but something far more precious - my son, my only son. It was all the more reason why the marriage should not fail. I who had been deserted by a father am deserting my son for promise of love with a man. I must have been insane. I so wanted to believe in Hugh's love, loyalty and steadfastness. I needed the affirmation, hoping that when he said the words, he would live by them too.

"Promise you'll never leave me!"

"Would I ever!"

But he did, didn't he?

"Promise you'll never leave me!" I say to Robert.

But even as I utter the words, I know how futile it is to try to hold on to something or someone. It's like trying to hold on to the wind. After all, life is about change; you cannot clutch the present as if it will remain unchanged by time and circumstances. How many times have I said it, Don't leave me, to one or the other. I beg because I am poor in courage to stand on my own. But there is no certainty to words, no guarantee that because they are uttered, the meaning should hold true. Yet, I have to hear them.

"Sayang," he says. "My heart is taken. There's no other for me."

"I mean, don't leave me. Don't die before me."

"Sayang, sayang! You must have the courage to live your own life. I'm older than you. Chances are, I'll go before you. But who are we to decide? We are but 'flies to wanton boys'."

Foolish, foolish child! I am middle-aged but my mind harks back to the pain of childhood, the pain of betrayal by a father I have never seen. I allow my loss to shape my thoughts, keep me in darkness. Nothing will grow without sunlight. I must take this child out into the open, free her, and let her out into the green meadows.

They have come for Robert now. He did leave too, didn't he?

"I don't feel like going," I say.

"But you must. You have to show people you are strong," Veronica says

"But I'm not strong. I don't want to be strong."

"Kim, I'm not letting you give in. You're made of stronger stuff than you think."

The men in black. Not alien destroyers but destroyers of human hope. In their coming, they destroy the hope that the dead might have only been asleep. Walking in with backs straight like pillars. Sombre, immobile faces. Taking my Robert away from me forever. Can I bear it? Do they know what they are doing, carting away what is intrinsically part of me? Can they imagine that the inert flesh they are boxing once met mine in waves of pleasure, in moments of exquisite love? Can they imagine that the voice that is now silent used to sing of my womanhood, made me feel whole? Would it be any different if they were dressed in flowing white robes, massive wings sprouting from in between their shoulder blades? I think not. They will still be taking from me, depriving me. I don't want to be stoic at a funeral like the English. I want to express grief the way my people express grief. Never mind the stiff upper lip. Never mind dignity. What use is all that pretence when all I want to do is howl? My life is being ripped from me—my insides are coming apart. I want to gather my pain and give voice to it like a wolf howling when she has lost her mate.

But I cannot. I'm in England and I must behave as I'm expected to behave. People don't mind it when you are a bit different. They can tolerate your foreignness; be nice to you, especially when you make small mistakes; and are humble. But they become uncomfortable when you are too different or herd with your own kind, gathering strength from sameness like a team of buffalos, sharing agreement and snorting anger, ready to begin a stampede. When I was with Hugh and Robert,

I infused into their Englishness, shared their colour so that I was not just a brown egg in a nest of white but had borrowed their chameleon colours. But when they left, I became exposed as if the colours that were concealing me were stripped away and I became visible in my own complexion, alone, stark brown against the white all around me—not a true native of this land. I am branded by my colour.

In his will, Robert has spared me the agony of a burial, the embarrassment of him sharing a twin plot with Emas or worse, a shared single plot, him lying forever on top of her, coffin against coffin, his body and hers intimately housed in the same soil. If he had asked for the latter, I'm not sure if I would have been honorable enough to carry out his wish. But what he has inadvertently willed me is even more unbearable, his last words that scorched my heart, made me lose control of my senses. They came out so naturally out of his mouth that they proved to me that I wasn't the one who had taken his heart. I wasn't the one he loved when he called out Sayang or when he said, I love you so much. I was a shadow for her - the woman he truly loved and never stopped loving. I only took her place as proxy—similar Asian features, similar complexion, except that she was taller, more elegant, more beautiful, more lovable. We spoke the same language, probably used the same expressions, ate the same kind of food. But I never really replaced her. I suspected it before, but never so unmistakable as on the day he died just how he was intrinsically bound to her. Although dead, she was ever present - always in his heart, always on his mind. "Emas!" He had yelled cheerfully. "Mas, sayang, look!"

16

An inheritance is not always given intentionally. Some things can be passed on without thought, without our knowledge even, like our genes, mannerisms or propensity to diseases. Words can be gifted accidentally with their surprised pleasure or unintended pain, becoming inscribed indelibly in someone else's heart and mind. We influence more than we know so we have to be vigilant in what we give out. They say that no man is an island. Does this mean that each of us is bound to another in some way so that if we were able to stand back, we can see the whole pattern where we all share the same web, traced to a single beginning? We see shadows of a man or woman in a child, the child mirrored in a parent or grandparent, a relative. We feel feelings that bind us to other beings who do not share the same genes, nor the same name. We suffer the residues of unrequited feelings, suffer the silence of unspoken words. Yes, each of us is connected to the other in more ways than one. No, no man is truly an island.

"Our culture is our legacy to our children. Our heritage is their inheritance—without culture, we are components on an assembly belt."

"*Wah*, Mum, that's really *cheam-man!*"

I still thrill to the sound of that single word that is meant for me alone: *Mum*. Ordinary things are jewels in disguise. You need the right light to see their true beauty. If only the word, *mum*, were uttered by my own offspring. Will I live to hear him call me by that name again?

"What is *cheam*, Mummy?"

"Oh, it's Teochew for *deep*."

"In this case, darling, your mummy thinks I've said something profound."

"Er, what is *profound*, Grandma?"

"Let's change subjects, shall we? Otherwise we'll be going round and round in circles." I laugh. "Come, Diana, Harry. Look at this picture. That's how my mother, your great-grandmother use to dress. The outfit is called a *kebaya panjang*."

We are at *The Peranakan Legacy* exhibition on Armenian Street in a Victorian building that was formerly a school in the colonial days. It is a well thought-out exhibition attempting to trace our unique Peranakan culture, a small tribe of Chinese people who intermarried with the Malays, dressed like them, spoke their language and yet adopted the Chinese religion producing this new race of people. But some sociologists claim that there wasn't really any new breed of people, merely a cultural integration of the immigrant Chinese with the indigenous Malays. But the sociologists could not account for the distinctive features of the Peranakans who often have mixed features of the two races. I remember how I was alienated in school because I did not belong to either camp; I looked dark like a Malay and yet had a Chinese name and ate pork. It seems that I'm always destined to be alienated, first in my own country and later in England. Perhaps when you're different, you try harder at making friends, try harder to fit in, afraid to remain the outsider.

Singapore, as a nation, is coming to maturity now. When it was birthed after the expulsion from Malaysia, there was a dire need to concentrate on commerce to enrich the lives of its people. There was a need to establish its place in the wide world with its own identity so colonial traces were wiped away and old buildings were torn down.

"When Lee Kuan Yew came into power, I was a teenager living in Singapore where my father was in the RAF," my English friend, Susan, from Surrey, said. "He tried to do away with Western influence. He even had the jukebox chained up."

She was talking about the situation around 1959 when I must have been about eight. Even if jukeboxes were allowed to be operated, the likes of me would never have seen one. We were too poor. But I did not tell Susan that when she recounted her life in Singapore. Indeed. For a time in Lee Kuan Yew's early reign, the pursuit of the arts and culture was deemed an unnecessary indulgence. But now Singapore is a rich nation. The majority of people dress in Western clothes and pursue a Western style of individualism and success—expensive homes, model cars, designer clothes and mobile phones. The ease of travel, television and the Internet make it normal for Western culture to encroach on the world. Amongst the discerning, there is a growing suspicion that the Asian culture with its own customs and tradition had been neglected and could disappear like the dinosaurs. So a shift is taking place, with the government trying to instill Asian values, reminding the populace of Confucian teachings, and reminding the people of our cultural richness. There is now a revival of interest in the Peranakan culture, of a people who had truly integrated in their adopted country and who dared to be different. At this exhibition, there are exhibits of jewelry, beaded slippers, belts and bags, crochet doilies and lace runners, vases, crockery, everything that's uniquely Peranakan, the décor of houses and costumes, including a bridal bed and an ancestral altar with all its trimmings.

''Isn't it strange to have your culture exhibited in a museum. Don't you feel that we are like historical artifacts?" I ask.

"I guess we are kinda off historical artifcacts." Margaret laughs. "Dere are not many of us left. Peranakans are well-integrated with de Chinese dese days. If we don't have an exhibition like dis in time, no one will remember wat a Peranakan is or was. Do you know, I have a sepia photo of *my* grandmother wearing something like dat. We still have de *kerosang* from dat picture. Since it's not a chained *kerosang*, my mother has given one to me to use as a brooch. Wen I die, it will go to Diana."

"Mummy, you're not going to die, are you?"

"No, *sayang*."

If only we are like children—easily assured. Eventually Diana and Harry get bored. Too much information given in a formal way bore children; they cope better when it is interactive. Margaret takes them downstairs to the playroom where the museum staff teach them how to play games that used to be played in the kind of *kampong* where I grew up in. It is strange to think that what were your childhood games should now be taught in a museum. It says something about the shift in time, about the shift in living. Diana and Harry giggle as they learn how to play *chaptay*, *teng-teng*, marbles and *five-stones*. They also learn how to weave *ketupat* boxes from coconut palm leaves, filling each box with uncooked rice grains. Satay sellers still make them today, boiling the boxes of rice for hours. The rice grains swell and swell till they fill the space in the box. Still they continue to be boiled until each grain becomes mushy and merge with the other, compressed tightly together to form a cake of cooked rice or *ketupat*, the individualities of the rice grain becoming inseparable. How similar this culinary concept is to the goal the Singapore government has for its people, this bid towards unity and racial integration. "*All for one and one for all*," the Musketeers' call, could well be theirs. The coconut leaves flavoured and coloured the cakes. When ready, the rice cakes are cut into cubes. They are served as an accompaniment to the skewers of barbecued meat and are dipped in peanut satay sauce.

"Remind me to teach you how to play *congkak*," I tell the children before I leave them and wander into the museum shop.

A middle-aged Chinese woman is behind the cash till. She gives me a tight smile and a brief nod. When our eyes meet it is as if a chord of familiarity has been struck. I feel as if I have seen her before, but then her kind are plentiful around here, the middle-aged woman with her strong make-up on very fair skin that had been kept out of the sun deliberately. I detach myself from the gaze to walk 'round the small shop examining some of the crafts and batik paintings wondering if Veronica might be interested in any of them. I can tell that the shop lady was eyeing me too. She, too, must have felt that we have met each other before. Eventually, she decides to approach me.

"Hiok?" The voice says hesitantly.

I turn, surprised that anyone should still know me in this country. A place becomes almost like home when you're recognised on the street or in a supermarket or shop. How I had yearned to be recognised when I first went to England, thirsting for a familiar face like water in a desert. But England is home now and this call reminds me that my roots had once been here. I regard the thin woman, hair dyed too black, fair skin crumpled across the face like folded muslin, jowls already loose. Her prominent cheekbones which were once her attractive features now make her face look gaunt. But the eyes, though not youthful anymore, fan a flame in my memory. I've definitely seen them before, especially those thin lips, now with lines feathered around them. I rack my brain for clues. But my recent sunstroke and my recollection of Robert have taken a toll on me and my mind is feeble.

"I'm sorry," I say. "Do I know you?"

"You are…*were* Mrs. Victor Liew, aren't you? Nurse Tay Kim Hiok? You trained at Outram Road General Hospital? 1968 batch?"

"Yes…"

"It's Linda. I'm Linda Quek. We were in de same batch."

"Oh."

A name, a voice can pull yesterday into today. History is the past folded away but the linen can be unfolded. I'm once again the bright-eyed seventeen-year-old at the assembly of newly recruited nurses. We were in our whites: white cotton uniform, white canvas shoes newly blancoed, a starched nurse's cap on their heads, one blue stripe on each of our epaulets to indicate that we were First Years. One girl was so shy and nervous that she kept dropping her file and things and I went forward to help her pick her things up, introducing myself. That girl was Linda Quek. Very thin, very needy. But we're middle-aged now and I'm a great distance away from that young girl that I had been, both in body and in mind. I'm unsure of how to react. The last time Linda and I met, twenty-five years ago, just before I left Singapore, Linda had screwed up her mouth with disapproval when I told her about marrying Hugh and leaving Peter. She had said, "I can't see how you can bear to leave your son behind. No matter what happens between Alfred and I, I shall never ever leave Sophia."

"Don't you think that I am sparing Peter the tug-o'-love between divorced couples? That I'm giving him the chance to have a stable life? No matter what Victor is to me, he loves his son. So does his mother. What will I serve if I take Peter away from that security?" I had challenged.

"I don't know how you can tink like this," Linda said. "Falling in love with an *ang mo kui* is one ting, to leave your child is another. I mean wat has Victor done to deserve dis? He is a university graduate, a successful executive. He provides you with a lovely son, nice home, Mercedes. He is every girl's dream."

We had been close friends but we did not share the same values. Sometimes people appear to be close to you, but it is possible that one becomes close for all sorts of reasons and not always from compatibility. We were not that close that I should share with her what had really happened in my marriage. Linda's voice had been cutting, but I offered no further explanation, no excuse. How could she understand? She was a devoted wife, an epitome of a mother. She resigned from work when Sophia was born to take care of her. Whenever we met, Linda always brought Sophia's latest snapshot and filled our conversations with, *So-phia dis, So-phia dat*, the ever proud mother. And I? What was I? Always yearning for something else, I guess.

"When did you come back? Are you living here now?" Linda now asks.

"Peter came to collect me when my husband died."

It's the first time I've mentioned Robert's death in public and the statement snags like a fishhook in my throat.

"Oh, so sorry to hear about your husband."

I should have said my third husband, but I did not want to go into explanations let Linda assume it was Hugh. Why give Linda pleasure by telling her of my yet another failure in marriage? Once is an accident, two is unlucky…well, three? I did not feel inclined to chart my history nor bare my soul to this woman who had not been exactly supportive all those years ago. I remain aloof but polite. Perhaps I had assimilated more of the English culture than I realised.

"I tort you left Peter for good. You mean you were in touch with him-*ahh*?" Her voice is still cutting now with an edge of sarcasm in it. "He must be a grown man now."

"Yes, he's an executive at Globalcomp, you know, they deal in computers." I try to ignore her barb. If you can breathe deeply and hold yourself back when you're distressed by someone else's words, the moment will pass. I need not be pained. This will be a momentary encounter. I can paint a social face, adopt a congenial voice. "He has a lovely family. I'm so lucky. They want me to live with them. What about you? How are you? Why are you working here? How's your family? How is Albert? Is Sophia married? Has she any children?"

The questions must have roiled up deep-seated issues in Linda and she masticates silently for a few moments as if she is chewing difficult words. She looks like a woman trying not to cry. When a woman wants to stop herself from crying, she has to stop speaking in case her voice let loose her emotion. She may fidget with her hands or something, bang cooking pots around, throw plates, or cast her eyes at distant objects. Well, there are no plates to throw and no cooking pots to bang. But the unease has taken over Linda's body; there is agitation in her eyes and facial muscles.

"Dat *sinang kui*! Dat bloody devil, Albert. Not long after you went, he left too—found himself some young chicken-*wat*. Left me to raise So-phia by myself. *Aiiyah*! I am so *sway*, so bad luck. My daughter was really *chiak hwek*, eat blood! Always, always give me trouble-*one*. Dat ungrateful girl! I waste my life bringing her up and de moment she turned twenty-one, she migrated to Vancouver, Ca-na-da. She said I was too possessive—crammed her style or something stupid like dat. Never give one moment's tort to me being here alone in my old age. Can you believe dat or not?"

Fortunately, no one else is about. Linda is so incensed that her spittle escapes from her thin lips in her high-pitched ravings. Her shoulders droop and her chest is squeezed tight. Everything about her speaks of unhappiness and misfortune. This is a woman scorned.

"I'm really sorry to hear it," I say. "Give her time, she'll come 'round and she'll contact you. They all do, look at Peter."

"*Aiiyah*! I'm not as lucky as you-*lah*. How come you so lucky-*ahh*? You abandon Peter and he still go and look for you. You don't know wat my life has been like, first Albert, than So-phia. I had to get a job but I couldn't go back to nursing. I couldn't cope with night duties and having to look after Sophia. *Pai miah*! Bad Life! So hard to tell udder people about it, but I tink you'll understand." She starts to sob.

I feel awkward. A long time ago, I would have folded this woman into my arms to console her but now I'm kept back by the residue pain caused by this woman's bluntness so many years ago. I pat Linda's arm instead, fishing out a tissue paper from my handbag to give to Linda who blows loudly into it. There might be something tender, charming even to see a young girl in tears but quite another when it's a middle-aged wrinkled woman crying theatrically. There is certainly no beauty in sorrow.

"Can I get you anything? A cold drink? Coffee?"

"No need-*lah*." She blows her nose loudly to abruptly end her sobbing. "Wat for waste some more tears-*huh*? I gave up everything for my child and see ware it gets me? You know wat she said to me? Dat I was so bitter about Albert going, I take it all out on her. Imagine your flesh-and-blood talking to you like dat! She was my prime reason for living – and she has turned out to be so ungrateful. Den I hear dat she visits her father and his whore-of-a-wife. Is dat not being a traitor? My own daughter going out with her stepmother! No one cares about how I feel. Now I'm menopausal, I suffer hot flushes, migraines. Sometimes I feel like going to one of the tower blocks and just jump off."

"*Aiiyah!* Don't say things like that. Why not try to look for the silver lining? There's always one."

Linda dries her eyes and goes behind the counter to bring out her compact to powder her nose. Whilst filling me in with more details about how miserable she had been, left to cope with a child, she brushes on her mascara, reapplies her lipstick. The vibrant red of the lipstick with its suggestion of moistness and freshness clashes with the aging skin but Linda seems oblivious and slaps it on thickly. In applying her make-up, she seems to have repainted her composure and perhaps regretting her outburst, tries to stand up tall, look her severe self.

"But of course, it's all right for you, right?" A sour note floods into Linda's voice. "You found yourself a nice, handsome *ang mo* husband and you started a new life with him in a new country. You were free to enjoy yourself. No need to worry about bringing up your kid. Probably Victor did you a favour after all."

This is the real Linda. She has changed only in physical characteristics.

Just then, Diana and Harry run into the shop, Margaret close on their heels.

"Children, careful! Don't bump into anytink!"

"Grandma, look what we made," they say joyfully, holding up the bunch of *ketupat* for my inspection. "This is our present to you."

Never was I more grateful for that term, *grandma*, than that very moment, uttered in front of someone who regarded me in such low esteem. I swell with pride, grateful to the children, grateful to Margaret who taught them well, grateful to Peter who had not poisoned his children against me.

"Oh, thank you. How clever you both are. I've always wanted to learn how to weave a *ketupat*. You must teach me."

"Are they Peter's children?" The question has a bitter note.

"Yes, aren't they lovely? This is Diana, she's nine. Harry is five. And this is my daughter-in-law, Margaret. She's a Conference Organizer in *Temasik*

Hotel. Children, this is Aunty Linda, we were in nursing school at the same time."

"Doesn't he look like his dad? Didn't you leave Peter at that age?"

"I tink it's time to go, my parking coupon is up," Margaret says with great firmness, ever vigilant, rescuing me. "Come on kids."

Luckily, the children had not heard.

"Thanks," I mutter to Margaret when outside, walking towards the car.

"You're welcome. I mean dat woman has got a *kepala batu* or wat?"

"Do you know, I haven't heard that expression since the *kampong.*"

"What is *kelapa batu*, Mummy?"

Margaret and I laugh at Diana's misuse of the word, dissolving the tension that had arisen earlier.

"*Kelapa* is Malay for a coconut and it is spelled k-e-l-a-p-a, but *kepala* spelt k-e-p-a-l-a is your *head*. *Kepala batu* is someone whose head is like stone. It refers to a person who is not very clever or someone who's stubborn."

"So! *Kelapa* is a *coconut.* Change the letters about and you get *kepala* and it becomes a *head*," says Diana, amused by it all. "You know, Grandma, you are so clever to speak so many languages. Maybe you can teach me Malay too."

She starts to skip towards the car and sings the two words to a tune she has just made up, gesturing with her hands, the left for *kelapa*, the right for *kepala*: "Kelapa, kepala, kelapa, kepala, kelapa, kepala…"

17

Old sins do cast long shadows, indeed. Can I ever wipe mine out, start again with a clean slate? Linda has reminded me that even if you forget your misdeeds, there are others who won't. As long as there is someone who remembers your old deed, you hurtle back to the past as though through a time tunnel to relive it again. Imagine how much of the past is still hovering around us, with us. If each of us hold on to memories of past deeds, our own and other people's, all our misdeeds will be like a pall that hangs over our lives. If I expect that people like Linda should forget my misdeeds, perhaps I have to begin with myself. I have to learn to forgive and forget what other people have done to me. Victor for instance, and Hugh. Robert even. To be honest, I am still prey to the emotions created by Hugh's treachery.

"It might not make sense to you, darling, but I still love you," Hugh had said.

"Don't! Don't do this to me!"

Hugh had held my arms whilst I kicked and struggled and pounded on his chest. Eventually I lost all strength and sunk to my knees, weeping. He had finally come out with the truth—that he had a lover. What was worse was that he had different ones for a long time—all the time we had been married. You may be able to fight another woman since you have a chance to do better that what she does but you could not fight when your husband goes for something altogether different.

"I have to be true to myself," he said quietly, neither in triumph or arrogance.

"You've destroyed my belief in myself. I trusted you, loved you, and worst, I believed that you loved me. All these years have been a lie. And I have left Peter for nothing. I left Peter for you."

Did he understand that I wept not just for a loss of a husband but for what I had given up? But it was no use. You can't ask someone else to understand your grief. You also can't ask for love when it is not there for you. He had decided—he was going to live with Jeremy. It was clear at last: his trips away from home, the euphoria when he came back, the fact that he could spend so much when he wasn't earning any money, the way both men and women loved him. Though it was a revelation, I was not entirely shocked that he was bisexual. Perhaps I had already suspected it. But it was not this that caused my pain; it was knowing that I had left my son for nothing that crucified me.

"No, you didn't," he said, the lightning change came over him. This same man who could be so loving and so kind could switch moods in seconds. "You left because of what Victor did. You would have left Victor sooner or later whether I came along or not. And you know that you left Peter because Victor could provide him with a better home and more security."

I was staggered by this turn of thought. Was he doing this to ease his own burden—loosen his responsibility?

"But if I was in Singapore, I could have had him. I wouldn't have to sign over the custody to Victor, don't you see?"

"Darling, that's all water under the bridge now."

"It's so simple for you to utter clichés! It can never be water under the bridge for me. I have to suffer my son's loss forever. And don't, don't you dare call me darling anymore! You are a traitor."

He shrugged his shoulder in a way that infuriated me further, the shrug that said *Have it your* way. Only someone who does not care can exhibit such nonchalance. Wounded, it was easy for me to fall for Robert. *He* was wounded by Emas' death. I began as his nurse, his helpmate and companion. I walked into Emas' shoes only because they were there, vacated. How could I have known that all the time, Robert coped by pretending that *I* was Emas?

Margaret takes us to lunch at the food center in Geyland Serai. It is adjacent to the Malay market. I had told her that Ang Huay used to take me there too when we had money to buy our kind of ingredients. The area is predominantly Malay with hawkers selling Malay and Peranakan food, *nasi lemak, lontong, rendang*. The food center is packed, people talking loudly but with joy and merriment. It's a wonderful atmosphere.

"I brought you here so dat we can shop at De Malay Village afterwards. De Tourist Board had built *attap* houses and wooden-roofed houses in the style of the old *kampong*, like the kind you used to live in so that tourists and our own youngsters can see what Singapore was like. There are stall-holders selling local crafts and I thought you might like to look for something for Veronica here."

"You are really thoughtful. I might be able to find a *congkak* for the children."

"What is *congkak*, Grandma?"

"It's a game. The board is like a half-log with eight holes on each side and one on each end. It's played with cowrie shells. In the days of the Sultanate, the young princesses used to while away their hours with the game. They didn't have TV or computer games, you know. It's easier to show you how to play it than to explain. Now what are you all going to eat? Let me treat. Also, let me order, Margaret. I want to practise my Malay, I am already *pelat*."

"What's *pelat*, Grandma?"

"It's like being rusty in a language."

"I want satay," Harry says.

"Say, *I would like*, darling. *Want* is too demanding in this case."

"*I would like* satay, Grandma."

"*I would like nasi lemak* for me, Grandma," Diana says, learning quickly.

"I really should not be eating again. I had a huge bowl of Maggie Mee at breakfast. Well, maybe a small plate of *bryani*," Mariane says, easily persuaded.

I go to the different stalls to order the food in Malay. The children are in tow, enjoying my performance as I struggle to remember the old language. The Malay words have been lying in wait in my throat for years, kept in shadow and they now emerge hesitantly. Soon our table is filled with plates of *mee goreng, bryani, sup kambing, rojak, sotong*. On top of the requested orders, I buy *crispy chicken wings* and *otak* and I order *bandung* and *chendol* to drink. Food is a celebration of the senses, uniting people and plugging up an emotional hollow.

"Grandma! You ordered too much!" The children giggle.

"Now, it's your turn to eat. We can buy some to take home for your daddy and Siti later. After we get our *congkak*."

"*Chiak*, Grandma, *Chiak*, Mummy," the children say in unison.

As Margaret and the children tuck in, I sit back in wonderment. This seems so natural—this sitting down to a meal with a family. How I had yearned for this simple pleasure for years. This is what I had missed. But I mustn't fret, I have it now—a family and a true sense of belonging. So much has happened, so many heartaches, so much pain. But as Hugh said, it is all water under the bridge. I'm here now and I'm glad. Whatever can make me unhappy now?

"What's the secret?" Margaret asks. "Why are you smiling?"

"I can't tell you how happy you've made me."

"Come on, eat-*lah*! We're family, right?"

Her hand reaches out to grasp mine, squeezing affection. The fact that people here rarely display such outward emotion makes it doubly special that she did. How much more lucky can I get?

The trouble with The Malay Village is it is too clean, too pristine to bring back the rough and tumble atmosphere of the old *kampongs*, where small alleys or *lorongs* run into one another, tight between attap houses, dust always flying up to meet your nose and face. Rough planks made up the walls, gaps in between which allowed the sounds, chatter, quarrels and love-making of your neighbours to slip through so that you were like one big extended family privy to each others' diurnal and nocturnal activities. You smelled the food your neighbour cooked or brought in so that your mouth watered even when you didn't have food to eat. But the stalls selling the old crafts are set out nicely and I come across an oil painting of a *kampong* scene with water buffalos in the fields and attap houses in the background. The village is probably somewhere in the rural areas of Malaysia or even

Indonesia.

"Veronica will like this," I say to Margaret.

I'm pleased that the memory of the old language has surfaced enough for me to bargain with the stall-holder in his language and after a bit of haggling agreed on the price. As the old man is wrapping up the painting, I see the *congkak*. It is a beautiful piece of wood with batik print pressed into the wood. The sixteen holes are well carved and lacquered. I point it out excitedly to the children.

"This is it, a *congkak*! Look at the cowrie shells, aren't they smooth? We'll take this as well," I say to the stall-holder.

"Let me pay for it," Margaret says.

"Please, let me have the pleasure. Why don't you choose something for yourself. How about that *tempat sireh*? You know, my mother used to chew betel nut leaves and she had a set like this, carved in wood. Pity I never kept it. It's quite a collector's item nowadays, you know. Let me give it to you as a small present. It's nothing after all you have done for me. Or perhaps there is something else you like?"

"Ahh, but you don't have to-*lah*!"

Eventually, Margaret allows herself to be persuaded and we go away from the Malay Village happy with our purchases. I sit beside Margaret as she efficiently manoeuvres the car across streams of traffic and think how lucky I am to have recovered not only a son but a wonderful daughter-in-law as well, not to say anything of my grandchildren. There is nothing ordinary about family—it is a special thing, an invaluable knitting of feelings and relationships that can be one's lifeboat. I let out a huge sigh as if all the bad years are finally slipping away, as if I can really believe that I can now breathe easy. The weight of the tortured years fell from me in that long release of breath and I feel a lightness I haven't felt for a long time. Despite the fact that the air-conditioning is turned on full blast, I can feel the heat of the afternoon sun pressing in through the glass of the windscreen and windows. It makes me drowsy, my eye-lids getting heavy and Margaret's and the children's voices slurring, then breaking up and drifting. Despite my bid for optimism, there are still some things in my past that won't let me be free.

They had fled the English cold and had sought the warmth of the

Spanish sun. Robert liked the effect of the sun on Emas skin which toasted it cinnamon brown. From the photos I saw around the house, it was obvious that he adored her, he caught her in every angle, in mini-skirts and cropped tops and elegant gowns, and some even semi-naked. The image of her must be indelibly printed on his mind so that she is always there and he sees only her. I knew the day I saw him at her deathbed that he was utterly and hopelessly in love with his wife. Yet I coveted that love, insinuated my way into his life, nursed him back into health, made myself useful, tried to make myself indispensable. What foolish dreams! How could I have known that his love was so strong that he saw her instead of me? I was just a body that he pretended held her spirit. Like a medium. When he spoke to me, he was talking to her; when he touched me, he was touching her. Of course, I didn't think this then. I believed that he truly loved me—his deception was so complete. The interesting thing was that he was not just deceiving me but himself most of all.

The first time I questioned my own certainty about his love was the day I came home unexpectedly. What a clichéd situation! So many people have come home unexpectedly resulting in life-changing proportions. But I was determined I wouldn't let the event change mine, so stubborn was I. I should have insisted we moved when Robert and I married for this was his and Emas' home—their love nest. I slipped in like a shadow into what was already established. Nothing had changed for Robert. He could still be living with Emas. Everything in the home reminded me of her, showed me her hand. I knew her taste from the décor, the colours she chose, the type of furnishings, the worn-leather books, hardbacks, paperbacks, the artistic knick-knacks she picked, even the type of food she ate from what was left in the freezers.

That fateful day, the house was in shadow—no lights, no sound. I never knew if Robert was in or out just by the presence of his everyday car in the drive because he also drove his vintage Jaguar which was kept in a garage in the fields. If he went out with it, I wouldn't be able to tell unless I chose to hike up to the fields to check. Like many men, he was not one to leave notes. I had a call-out duty at the hospital where I waited for medical calls; if it was a call that did not require a doctor and a sister like myself could cope, I'd go out with a drive in a medical vehicle. After the last call-out which was near my home, I decided that it would be pointless to get the driver to take me back to the hospital fifteen miles away to collect my car. It was time for me to be off-duty and it would make more sense for the driver to drop me home and I could get the train in to the hospital the next day or Robert could drop me there. So the driver dropped me off at the main road and I walked down the lane to our house. Of course, since I did not come back in a car, I did not create any sound which might have alerted Robert to my return.

I walked into the house which showed no living presence at first. Then I heard sounds coming from Robert's study, a combination of voices and moans. I did not know what to think. Was he ill or was he having it away with someone? My emotions was all a fluster. I rushed towards the study where the door was ajar and was about to push the door open when I recognised her voice. He had played other videos of them for me and I had learnt the lilt of her voice, the angle of her fine jaw. Robert never tires of telling me about her...loves the sound of her name on his lips. I braked hard. He was so preoccupied he did not hear me arrive.

"How do I look?" she asked.

"Look what you are doing to me."

She laughed.

I quietly pushed the door open and though I was hidden, I could see that Robert was watching a replay of their Spanish holiday on his multimedia computer which sat on his desk. From where I was, I saw images of Emas flashing across the computer screen, beautiful Emas, elegant Emas, sexy Emas in a see-through white blouse and a skirt that skimmed the tops of her legs. Robert watching Robert taking a video of her. I could see the back of the real Robert's head resting on his executive-type chair, his legs stretched out rigidly in front of him, and the chair was bobbing up and down in a jerky fashion on its metal stand.

"Now take off your pants."

"Like this?" She teased.

"Now bend over....Jesus!"

219

Robert lay back in his armchair and from the sounds he was making, I am certain he climaxed. But even this was not as disarming as when he called out in a sad, dispirited voice, as if there was no joy in his present life, without her. "Oh Emas, sayang!"
Something inside me tears.

28

Once, on my down days, I had declared to Veronica, "I don't think I'm the type people love."

"Don't be silly, Kim. Of course you are loved. Even Victor loved you. Even if it is for a short moment, he did love you when he met you. People fall out of love, that's the problem. It's not something that you can control. People think that if you do this and that, behave in a certain way, your loved one will continue to stay with you. That's not the way it works." Her voice sounded bitter.

"My father never loved me or he would have come in search of me."

How indulgent I was. I should have thought less of myself and more of others. Veronica, for instance. Had Veronica been scarred by love? Veronica, who on the last occasion before I married Robert, had moved with difficulty from kitchen range to farmhouse table. It had been a lovely kitchen, with lots of sunlight streaming in through the tall French windows which opened onto a flagstone patio. It was not often that Veronica suggested a meal at her place; most of the time, she did not care if she ate or not, so long as she could paint. I knew that Veronica made a point to invite me because I had told her once that I found it strange that English people seemed not to want to invite new friends into their homes for meals. The remark must have stayed in Veronica's mind. I was a little sad to notice the signs of aging in my friend. She had no family to go to if she needed looking after, facing the prospect of a nursing home. She had been on her own as long as I knew her. But Veronica had made it clear that her personal life was not something to be discussed. She had hinted of past loves. Hints. That was all I received. Even that was plenty according to the way Veronica thinks. The English guard their private lives; they do not spill their feelings and emotions like my people to anyone who would listen, especially not in dramatic fashion. I must call Veronica again; emails are all right but not quite the same—you can't gauge a person or how they truly are feeling from typed words on a computer screen.

I wonder if it's possible for me to call Singapore home now. After all, I have imbibed another country and another culture. It was once *home* before but that was a lifetime ago: three husbands ago. What a failure I am. Three husbands! Not one of my marriages could be considered even remotely successful. Each husband had left his imprint on me, made his mark, changed some part of me. What was it about me that attracted those kind of men? What was it about me which made me so dispensable? Still, each did teach me something—showed me something worthwhile, too. Victor, even with his utter possessiveness, did make me feel protected; Hugh, with his good looks and easy laughter, was so nice to be with; and of course, Robert. In a way, I was wounded most by Robert because with Robert, I had let down my guard and let myself love him fully without reservation. Still, without Hugh and Robert, I wouldn't have learnt how to love England, its culture and countryside; my senses becoming refined so that I learnt how to tune them to new forms, new textures, new music. Coping with living outside a city was at first inconvenient, stores being so far away and public transport not as frequent or as efficient of those in my native city but the magic of life in the countryside surmounted the inconveniences. I have come to love the sight of trees and open fields and lakes, the changing colours of the seasons each with its own unique atmosphere and sounds. I take enormous pleasure in the whisper of the wind and the smell of gorse or heather, the sun striking the trees at different angles, the ducks taking off or landing on the lake, the swans preening themselves, the geese flying in formation against a backdrop of sky. Now, here in Singapore, the towers of concrete and glass break up the sky; flowering plants, bushes and trees, though beautiful, are cut and pruned by the ever-vigilant park authorities and somehow do not provide the sense that they are allowed to grow freely. To be comfortable in this country means seeking and staying in air-conditioned rooms, offices, hotels and shopping centers. To open windows and doors is to invite the cloying heat and mosquitoes in, and to be assaulted by the sound of traffic racing along the expressway, tires screeching. Living in this city-nation is to be continually subjected to the multitude of sounds that a burgeoning city thrives on.

"But I have to, won't I? This is where my family lives now. My family has been an invaluable gift to me. They should make me not mind my loss."

I mumble into the pillow. And even to me, it sounds like a second choice. What do I want, for goodness sakes? But I am finding it increasingly difficult to get to sleep because of the sound of television next door; of children in the apartment above sliding heavy things across tiled floor or leaping up and down, even at this late hour; of toilets flushing elsewhere; and of doors opening and shutting, sometimes banging hard. The next morning I look into the mirror and see shadows forming under my eyes, shadows that my sleeplessness have etched into my face. Yet I have gained moisture from the air and the wrinkles acquired in the dry cold of the English climate have smoothed out slightly, the cracks on my heels healing.

"But I am so used to working. What will I do with myself all day?"

Siti does all the housework and cooking. The children are at school in the mornings, Peter and Margaret are at work all day. After all, I can only read so much. Perhaps I can help out at the nearest old people's home. Yes, that's what I'll do if I live here. I can propose the idea to Margaret. For some reason, my mind skipped to the nightlight in Harry's room shaped like Pluto's head. Had Harry asked for it or did Peter buy it for him out of his own sentiments? In our flat on the twenty-sixth floor, there had been a polystyrene cut-out of a full-sized Pluto which I had drawn and painted for Peter. Of course, this is what I can do to while away my time besides helping out at old people's homes—I can draw and paint for my grandchildren now.

"Siti," I ask, "where can I find a shop that sells art supplies?"

"Oh, Marm, I won't be able to tell you. I'll get you the yellow pages," she said, proceeding to bring me the directory. "Can you do me a favour, Marm? Can you buy me a phone card?"

"A phone card? Why can't you use the telephone here?"

"No Marm, it's not fair on Marm and Sir to put the bill to them when I want to speak to my children. I only call them once a month because it's so expensive to call Jakarta. With the phone card, I can call from the telephone here but it will be charged to my card, not to Marm and Sir. Please only buy the ten-dollar card, Marm. That's all I can afford."

My heart crunches. This is a woman who had to sacrifice seeing her own children so that she can work to pay for their schooling. Why couldn't I have been a mother like that—devoted, self-sacrificing? Isn't that the underlying implications of the word, *mother*? Does it mean I'm a fraud, owning to a name that is not mine to own? I'm filled with a sense of great dislike for myself. A guru once said, *Guilt is usually a sign of self-hatred.* Well, I've got a lot of that all right. Fortunately, I had set myself an errand so that the thought can be pushed away. I'm in my element, recalling an old hobby, looking, buying. I return, laden with the paints and brushes, easels and art paper. It had been harder to find the polystyrene sheets but the young man at the art shop was helpful and had phoned around for me and when he finally gave me an address, I took a taxi to the factory which supplies the polystyrene boards to exhibitors and got them to cut out the sizes I required. I would paint them exactly as I had done all those years ago for Peter, but this time for his children. The project puts me into a more optimistic mood. I had also bought the phone card that Siti needed and intend not to take any money from her. How can I when every cent she earns is for her children? When I return to the apartment, I give her the card. A few minutes later, Siti comes back with the ten dollars.

"Here, Marm. Thank you, Marm."

"No, no, save it. See it as a small present."

"You don't have to give me anything."

"Please. I want to."

"So wat's all this?" Margaret asks when she comes home from work to see newspaper spread out on the dining table, sheets of polystyrene on top of them, the children propped on the dining chairs, paintbrushes in hand. They are copying from books and posters of *Harry Potter* and all the various objects mentioned in the books.

"I thought I'd teach them to paint. Do you mind?"

"No. It's great. Better den dem watching TV all day or playing Gameboy!"

"Mummy! Look at my drawing of Harry Potter!"

"I have drawn the *Sorting Hat*!" Diana exclaims, her elbow covered in a multitude of colours. Thank goodness, I had the foresight to get Siti to bring out their old T-shirts. So the mess did not matter.

By the time Peter comes home and the table has been cleared for dinner, there are painted polystyrene cut-outs everywhere. I am excited, wondering if he would remember when the two of us had done the same years before, mother and son side by side at our dining table, drawing and painting Pluto, his favourite cartoon character, our private project to decorate his room; when our lives were not yet irrevocably changed by my going, when he could still believe in mothers – in me. I had a secret longing for him to be pleased by the project. But the moment, he comes in, I feel that he is different. His stoop is more pronounced as if the weight of his work is still sitting on his shoulders as though he had not left it behind in the office. His face is pale as if the vampirish city has sucked out his life energy. The air around him is a pall of weariness.

"Wat a mess this place is," he says, tossing his briefcase onto the settee as though it is burdensome. His forelock of hair fell over his forehead, irritating him further, and he pushes it back roughly.

"Daddy! Grandma taught us how to paint!"

"I have drawn the *Sorting Hat*!"

"Wy must you all talk so loudly-*huh*?" He puts his hands up to his temples.

"*Ah boy*," Margaret, as usual very perceptive and quick to react is by his side in an instant. She clutches his arm, one hand caressing it, whispering her form of endearment in a soft, cajoling voice. "Come and have a rest before dinner-*lah*."

"Polysterene is a fire hazard," Peter says to no one in particular. "I want them to be thrown out. This minute. Siti!"

I am stung by his vehemence.

"But Daddy! We worked all afternoon on it." The children protest, their eyes in confusion.

"Do you want this apartment to go up in flames?"

There is an unnatural brightness in his eyes. Gently, Margaret leads him away.

"Your father is so clever," I tell the children, trying to ease their disappointment. "He knows all about these things. Grandma didn't know. Never mind, that was just practice for the real thing. Tomorrow I will buy you proper boards for painting, okay? Since you have already practiced painting today, your painting will be better still tomorrow. When the paint is dry, I will have them framed like real artists do."

I try not to mind my own pounding heart and keep my voice even.

"Am I a good artist, Grandma?"

"Yes, Harry. The best."

"If he is best, then what about me?"

"Just as good. You two share First Place."

"That's all right then. I would hate it if he is better than me."

"Let's play *congkak,* shall we? You get the set out and I will clear all these."

Margaret comes down from the bedroom floor and we sit down to dinner. Her face, too, is now drawn. Something had pricked her bubbly spirit and she is unnaturally quiet. Perhaps they had had an argument. These things happen in a marriage, as I well know, but it doesn't have to spell disaster.

"Isn't Daddy eating?"

"He had a huge business lunch and is still full."

But I notice that her eyes are darting when she speaks; there is just a slight, noticeable throb at her temples.

"Everything all right?" I ask.

"Ya, ya, okay-*lah*."

But she isn't convincing. Something has occurred. Something has changed. A finger has poked the pie of homeliness. I am unsettled by this new electricity in the air. Yet, I feel I haven't the right to ferret for information. It may be that something has happened at work which has proved to be stressful for Peter. These things happen in the course of life, unpleasant but not earth-shattering. Yet, the unease keeps on niggling me till I go to bed. I hope it's not something to do with me. Of course sleep won't come and I try to read but the words run all over the page without cohesion. All the time, my ears are poised to hear—hear what? Then it happens—the distant rumble of Peter's and Margaret's voices behind closed doors which grew into thundering proportions. Then a door opens, then slams. The flight of footsteps, light but hasty, passing my room, suggests that they are Margaret's, not Peter's. I get out of bed and pull a dressing gown 'round me, not because I'm cold but because I don't like to be seen in my nightdress. It's an old-fashioned notion—underwear, bra straps and petticoat edges are not meant to be seen, it's Madonna who started the fad of wearing your underwear to be seen. I pause by my bedroom door, ears primed for Peter's footsteps to follow but none came and I slowly open the door and softly walk down the stairs where some of the lights have been turned on. Instead of the usual overhead chandelier lamps which normally lights up the room, a small table lamp has been turned on splashing Margaret's shadow across the wall. I stop at the base of the stairs and say quietly so as not to startle her, "Margaret?"

Margaret is startled, nonetheless, neck swinging 'round in fright.

"Oh, it's you."

It is not welcoming, and I reel with embarrassment. It is obvious that there is an emotional minefield here and I hesitate awkwardly, unsure whether to retreat or move forward.

"Since you must have heard, you might as well sit down."

This is a very different Margaret from the girlish woman who is all smiles, her voice light and feathery. A certain tiredness has crept into her voice and body. Something or someone had pegged her with sorrow. She blows her nose.

"If it's something private…"

"I'm just finding it harder and harder to cope."

"Can I help?"

"Huh?"

Margaret's tone seems derisive or am I being overtly sensitive? I ask myself. I have an urge to move myself away. It's not too late. It's perhaps better not to know. I feel as if I'm stepping too close to the edge. I intuite that all the sunny, lovely days leading to this are about to end—and I want to stay bubble-wrapped in my illusion, that I was truly welcomed, that I was really wanted as part of the family. Perhaps I should have returned to England before this day, before this revelation that surely is about to ensue from Margaret.

"Peter suffers from bipolar depression disorder. His mood can change rapidly, elevated and happy one minute and de next depressed and bad-tempered. You can't tell when it's going to happen."

"You mean schizophrenia?"

"Similar. You saw how he was when he came home. He's like a different man. Sometimes the children get frightened of him."

"What causes this?"

"You're asking me dat?"

"What? What do you mean?"

"Wat did you expect? He had no mother, for god's sakes! You can't even begin to imagine how great a loss dat was to him!" Her voice is shrill, followed by more tears, but after a while she calms down. "I'm sorry. I'm not in my right mind. Peter had a tough childhood, you must have guessed dat. Granny Mui Yoke said he suffered severe nightmares for years after you left. He was a difficult child, losing his temper easily and throwing things about. He couldn't get on with his classmates. Eventually Victor took him to a psychiatrist and he's been having treatment since. Only now his depression has a fancy name. Bipolar depression or something."

So finally it is out! The result of my one action, of *my* ultimate sin.

"Forgive me," I mutter, vaguely aware that the gash in my heart has reopened and has resumed bleeding again. What else is there to say that could right my wrongs? Old sins do cast long shadows, indeed.

"But he's such a lovely person at udder times, so kind and generous."

"It's all my fault."

"No, No, I did not mean dat. I'm sorry. I'm not myself. I was just telling you wen his manic episodes began. He flips between being a lighthearted person to one who tinks dat everyone is finding fault with him and gunning him. It might be in his genetic make-up weder you had stayed or not. In my opinion, Granny Mui Yoke was also to blame. She made him take sides, tried to make him deny you. She wouldn't let him speak of you nor ask questions about you. He does love his grandmother, but he is also aware of how she had usurped her power from you, especially now that he is grown-up and can work tings out for himself. Surely dat must have stressed him out too."

"You're kind. I'm sorry that you have to suffer this."

"I'm all right, really. Forgive me. I've not behaved properly. You see, except for dese moments, he's a wonderful husband and a good father. I'm sure we can see it through together. He is having treatment and is on medication. I'm sure it will get better with time. Perhaps your being here will help."

29

The trouble about raking up the past is that you cannot change anything about it. What you can hope to change is the present, and through that process, perhaps, the future. Resting on regrets simply makes things worse. A spiritual teacher once said that if the past is painful, recalling it and the hurts means that you are feeding your pain. It's important to let go of it, otherwise every time you remember the pain, you are feeding it and it will become stronger and stronger and never go away. I attend all these lectures by gurus and read their books, but I don't seem to have learnt very much. What does one do? It's easy to say in theory to let the past go but the reality is that as much as I try to flip past the pages of the years, my mind keeps on hooking on to that moment when I decided to leave Peter behind.

"But it wasn't a moment's decision. Remind yourself that it was Victor you were leaving. And both he and his mother wouldn't let you have Peter. It grew from that. Keep things in perspective, Kim," Veronica says.

I had not intended to call Veronica to talk about this; I had actually intended to ask Veronica how she was getting on, about her flu and her arthritis, about things I missed at this time in England, the crocuses and daffodils bravely pushing their heads out of the thawing ground, the day shaking off the mantle of cold from its shoulders, the sun smiling harder. Yet, my concern must have been lying on the surface of my mind so that as soon as I hear Veronica's trusted voice, I had blurt out, "Oh, Veronica, how can

I forgive myself? Margaret says that Peter is suffering from a kind of schizophrenia and it all started after I left him! How could I have made a moment's decision like that?"

"Think of your true circumstances. Remind yourself what Victor was like. Memory *is* selective. It can also be deceptive or adulterated. Your guilt at your separation with Peter may have changed your perception about the way things had really happened. Try to return to the memory of things the way they really were.

From what you told me of Victor's behaviour and utter possessiveness, it was likely that he may not have been entirely balanced himself. It is possible that Victor had suffered from a kind of schizophrenia himself that went undiagnosed. Perhaps his son had inherited *his* depression and illness."

"Oh, Veronica, you're so helpful. You know what? I should have run away with Peter. How I wish I had. Is there a fairy godmother who could whisk me back in time?"

"Whichever way you did it, he would have been deprived of one parent. Remember you had no choice in the matter. Victor and his mother took the choice away from you."

"I have done the unforgivable, haven't I? A better person, a better mother would have stayed."

"Kim, Kim. We have been through this so many times. You can't crucify yourself forever."

Then through my earpiece comes a fit of coughing.

"Are you all right? Veronica?"

"I'll be all right," the voice says when it returns, feeble now and scraggy, which makes me guilty that I had approached Veronica with my problem. "I need a drink of water, that's all."

"You're like a sister to me. What would I do without you?"

"I'm old enough to be your mother. Don't worry, there's life in this old dog yet," Veronica tries to laugh.

Disconnecting from my friend is a wrench. Some people's voice and presence provides you with a little comfort, a little strength. It's a rope that ties you to the mooring so that you are secure. But away from that voice, that presence, you are like a skiff abandoned to the tidal swell. If Veronica was my post, Robert was my safe wall. How could I have been so wrong about him?

*   *   *

"When I look at you, I see a beautiful woman," he says.

We are sitting at the table at a restaurant that looks over a small cove of sandy beach at Balcon Del Mar. Our own Spanish holiday— Robert's and mine. I made sure we go where he had not gone before with Emas so that his memory of her did not stray into ours and cloud mine. We are close to the seaside resort of Javea but far away enough from tourists to enjoy the peace and tranquility of cliffs and private beaches. He looks into my face with such concentration that I am moved to believe that he can actually see some beauty in me that was not apparent to me.

"But I don't think I'm beautiful," I say.

"I wasn't aware that I was asking for your opinion," he says, smiling, the corners of his eyes crinkling.

And it is that strange combination of blue eyes and signs of aging that makes me feel tender towards this man I love, as if he is mine to mother and care. But what is love? Did Robert love me at all or were his words like Janus, each of them with two faces?

"We all make mistakes. Wrong judgments. No one is exempt. Except that some mistakes are more serious than others, some wielding a greater influence than others," Veronica had said. "The irony of it is that when you finally know what *not* to do to make mistakes, you cannot undo or correct the mistakes you've made."

"I'd give my life now to undo what I have done to Peter," I had responded.

"It's not you that have done this to Peter; it's a set of circumstances, where you and Victor and his mother, and life itself, played a part. In your own system of belief in the idea of reincarnation and karma, surely it is as much Peter's karma as it is yours to be separated from one another? Didn't you tell me that he was separated from you even from the moment of birth? Perhaps that was a precursor, an indication of things to come?"

"Ah, how easy it is to philosophise when it is not things of the heart."

"Do maintain your perspective, Kim!"

Maintain your perspective. It's a mantra I must repeat to myself. Maintain my perspective. Maintain my perspective. Maintain my perspective.

"What are you mumbling, Grandma?"

Now that's a reason for living, for continuing to stay here, a child calling you *grandma.* A simple word, an everyday word. But really, it is a magic bean. Giant stalks grow from a small bean. It is easy to undervalue the preciousness of ordinary things in life.

"Diana, you are really my dearest!"

I pull my granddaughter to me and Diana starts to tickle me. I act as if I'm really ticklish. This amuses Diana and gives her a sense of power so she tickles me all the more and we fall backward into the settee laughing, my granddaughter's laughter like sparkles of fairy lights showering me with some moments of lightness. My nostrils breathe in the scent of a child, clean sweat mingled with talcum and that unique scent which belongs only to a child. Like a baby's delicious, heart-stirring scent that can never be replicated in any form, by any one.

Young Mothers, hold onto the fragrance of your baby! Adolescence and adulthood rubs off the scent of innocence from a child. I shall never forget that day when my son is finally able to suckle at my breast. He smells so special that my heart aches. Because of a tiny lung that failed to inflate properly, he was rushed from birth canal to incubator, hooked to machines that helped him breathe and feed. And though we were separated by glass walls so early in his life, I learnt one fundamental thing about being a mother—your child's welfare is your concern as long as you both shall live. Physical separation is not equal to a separation of the spirit.

When he sucks on my nipple, I feel the sensation right through to my womb. There's an old wife's tale that it is this very act of suckling that helps the womb to tighten and shrink back to its former shape. Pity the women who will not breast-feed their babies. Not just because they will deprive themselves of its physical benefits but because they will not know the utter joy of it. Breast-feeding provides you with a feeling close to the one you feel when a life beats as one with you, inside your body, growing, feeding on you—with you. However powerful or successful a man may be, he is denied the power to wield this special magic. So young mothers, remember—treasure this gift that has been given to womankind.

My baby's fragrance will forever live in my mind, the shape and weight of his head and body, his untested voice. Though ordinary to everyone else, to a new mother, it seems an extraordinary thing that your baby comes out of yourself with ten tiny fingers, ten tiny toes, ears, eyes, mouth, all perfectly formed. The moment you see your baby for the very first time, you are changed irrevocably; you lose something of what you were before. Because you will no longer be able to live unattached, unconcerned. You have become a mother. This new being will be your joy and your cross. A pyrographer has burned my newborn babe's picture in my mind and I can still see him as he was, his chubby limbs, his penis, an innocent curlicue. Then later, his round eyes which swelled my pride when he continually searched out for my image and my voice. I was his sun. Yet it was also I who cast the shadows across the sun. How much more cruel could I have been?

I have betrayed him. The thought is a sledgehammer that pounds. How is it possible for one person to make that many mistakes? Even Diana's laughter cannot fully revive my optimism and I know my own laughter is hollow. *Kosong.* Empty. Without substance. I am *kosong.* How apt the Malay word signifies my state of mind and heart. Maintain your perspective! Veronica's voice echoes through my emptiness, but I vaguely note that I'm sliding, sliding: Peter's morose behaviour in the last few days, Margaret's oblique reference to me abandoning the child, Peter; Hugh's betrayal, Robert's marriage of falsehood. They are all pick-axes that are chipping away at the rock of my confidence.

"I need some air, darling," I say to Diana. "I must go outdoors."

It is actually escape I need. We all try to escape sometime or another—when we go to another country, another climate, when we lay on the beach, we walk, we ski, we explore the wilderness, we lose ourselves in city pursuits or we drink ourselves senseless. Or we escape by buying things, spending money, and eating. We think we are escaping from our humdrum lives, our pressures at work, at home, but all the time we are actually trying to escape from ourselves. Our dissatisfaction about our life and ourselves is a hard nugget within our soul. Can I escape from myself? Unless you can put away your own thoughts, prise yourself away from your own emotions, you are imprisoned in your own mind. The yogis and Buddhists are right to attempt to transcend the mind because unless you do so, it's a gaoler who will not set you free.

I go downstairs and walk around the park-like grounds of the condominium. Everything is so pristine, clean and tidy, no spectre of throwaway cartons, cigarette boxes or butts, or empty cans. The walls and wooden benches are free of graffiti, the public telephone sits unworried on its shelf under the hard plastic canopy, phone directory intact. Elsewhere in the world in cities like London, New York, Chicago, etc., it would be difficult to find a decent telephone box, free from the smell of urine, rubbish on the floor, graffiti scrawled all over the place, phone directory missing or torn in parts. Tacked to the telephone box will be business cards of escorts, prostitutes and massage girls offering their services. There is no suggestion of seediness around here. This is a family condominium, safe for everyone. Not a single leaf is out of place; flowering shrubs are properly trimmed, fan palms standing to attention like soldiers. In the heat, the sprawling swimming pool looks blue and inviting, calling me to lose myself in its waters. Just on the other side of the expressway is the sea, not quite so blue but calling me in a different kind of way. An underpass leads from the condominium under the road to the opposite side where the sandy beach hugs the coast. It will be so easy to wade in water too deep for you to swim. But that's a cop-out, not the kind of thing I usually contemplate. But feeling the way I'm feeling, it's a temptation nonetheless. It's one form of escape. Unfortunately, as a Buddhist, I don't believe in oblivion. Even if I escape my mortal coil, I shall have to deal with eternity and every action of mine counts, so it's best to sort this life out as best as I can.

I walk the path to the sea, anyway—it will provide some kind of relief. It will be a while before it gets dark; and even then, the paths will be lighted and therefore isn't a problem, though I wouldn't like to go under the underpass late as it will be creepy. I need to feel the sea breeze on my cheeks, taste the salt in the air. Once I have crossed under the major expressway to reach the beach, I kick off my sandals, hold them in one hand and let the soles of my feet taste dry, fine sand. The sand dribbles through my wide-spaced toes. When there is so much concrete and glass around you, it seems a small miracle to touch something that is not man-made. Yet there is a contrived feel about the beach, everything arranged in an orderly way, barbeque pits, waste bins, bicycle-path, bicycle rental stations, toilet-block; even the palm trees look arranged, like the kind of full-grown trees they plant in Las Vegas, brought from nurseries to be hoist into the air by mechanical cranes and put into ready-prepared desert holes for the roots. Here, there is no long vista of sea, no unbroken stretch of water. Just a few hundred metres away, the huge freighters scour the international waters. How I long for a sandy beach in Spain, Italy or in the West Country, in Ireland or North America, with the waves lashing at the rocks, the gulls screeching, green-topped cliffs standing tall behind the arc of water.

"I love you," Robert says, as he grinds me into the Oregon sand, the waters of the Pacific Ocean washing our feet. The fantasy of many— this love-making on the beach, under the stars and moon. And it has come true for this woman who can no longer turn the head of any man, young or old. For a while, I am filled with utter gratitude to Robert for fulfilling a desire for what had long been an imaginary exercise in my mind. I was taken to the heights of pleasure and joy to think that this man is so truly in love with me that he cannot wait for us to get back to the hotel.

But I know now that he speaks and make love, not to me but to the ghost of his loved one. I am literally just a body that reminds him of the corporeal substance of her existence. It's like in that Patrick Swayze and Demi Moore film, Ghost. *The wife makes love to her husband through the medium's body. It's not as corny as it sounds. People have a capacity to dupe themselves. People have a capacity to believe in their own fiction. Much later, I discovered that Robert and Emas had been to Oregon together, long before he and I went there. He took me there to rebirth his moments with her! How blind I had been. For in their attic,*

I found a beach towel bought in haste at the tourist shop with the words,
Cannon Beach, painted across a blue sea, so that they can consummate
a moment of lust in the hot sunshine, amongst the dunes whilst families
with children frolic by the water's edge.
I am kosong, *empty. Even my body is not me.*

There are not many people on the beach. But I spy someone ahead of me. It's a man with his shoulders stooped in a familiar way. His T-shirt is fluttering about his body, exposing his belly, his legs in shorts that reached to his knees. He is walking in a distinctive way, feet splayed because of his fallen arches, his arms flapping back and forth at his sides, like a penguin. The manner, the stance and the body brings a flash of memory to my mind and for a moment, I see Victor, Victor with the Johnny Weissmuller body, broad-shouldered, nipped waist. But it turns out to be his son. My son. The one I had failed. I walk briskly to catch up with him and then slow down so that he does not notice that I had made an effort.

"Peter, I didn't know you were out here."

"Uh,' he grunts, not a spark of welcome in his face.

It is possible for children to emulate their parents' mannerisms, for sons to emulate their father. A noncommittal grunt as if words are too expensive to spend. The same sort of grunt. The kind that Victor used to make when he did not wish to respond to me, or when his attention was elsewhere. It was not too different from the short grunt when he had come. You'd think he had just relieved himself and nothing more. All that jerking and heavy breathing to end in one short grunt. Unsatisfying to say the least. But this is not Victor who is here now; it is my son. The one I had left behind when I ran away from his father. Ran away for a different love, a different life.

He does not stop walking nor slows his pace so that I can keep up. He seems intent on creating the distance between us. Struggling to lengthen my strides, my breath comes out in short spurts. I feel hurt—and hard to admit to myself, a little cross, too, that he seems to disregard me so completely. This is a different Peter to the one I have known the last few weeks. The aura around him was not pleasant. Then I tell myself that I have only myself to blame. I swallow that nugget of pain and move rapidly to his side again, eager to try to bridge the gap, to be of help in some way. Perhaps I can be a mother to him again, offer my love, my arms, my understanding.

"Peter," I call.

At the sound of his own name, he reacts naturally and turns his head.

"I can't tell you how much I appreciate your contacting me and bringing me back here. You and your family have been so wonderful to me since Robert's death. Is there some way I can repay you for all you've done? You look like you've got a mountain of problems on your shoulders. Can I be of help to you in any way? Even if I am just an ear to listen to your troubles. You know, you can talk to me about anything you like."

He stops so suddenly that the sand in front of his feet banks up.

"Talk to you?" he asks, his voice hard, his eyes wide with a look I dare not name. "You're de last person on earth I will confide in."

20

The telephone rings just as we are sitting down to dinner. In Singapore, activities have to be arranged around meal times; this is a way of life here. It is something I love. You can't change a habit of a lifetime whichever country you choose to live in. But it's all right here than in England, where you could go out to the food centers to get cooked food or get your maids to do the cooking. It's not as easy in England when you have to do three or four meals a day. Siti has not served the meal because we are waiting for Peter to come downstairs. He said he had to search for something. He must have a reason for choosing this particular time to search for something. It must be important to him. There is a kind of urgent shrillness about the telephone's incessant ringing, especially in the quiet of the air-conditioned apartment, all windows shut to the outside noise. Margaret gets up to answer the telephone.

"Mum, it's for you."

I still sparkle with pleasure when Margaret addresses me in this manner.

"For me?"

Except for Veronica, no one else knew that I was here. Perhaps it's Linda, trying to revive our friendship, but then I don't think I had left her an address or number. Or it could be that young lady, Clarice, who helped me when I had that short fainting spell. Which reminds me—she suggested that I give talks about England. If I live here, it might be something for me to do. Perhaps I'll contact the girl. But, in the last few weeks, there had been no call for me. One experiences a sense of being on holiday or not belonging when the phone calls that come through are all not for you. A place is not yet a home until you get calls that are for you. So this call must be significant. The moment I hear the voice of Veronica's house-help, I freeze.

"I know how close you are to Veronica, so I thought you might like to know. Your name and number was on a notepad. Perhaps she had intended to call you before she collapsed. Luckily, it was my day to do the house. Otherwise she might not have been found for days."

So it has happened. Oh, don't let me be too late to see Veronica one more time.

"It's so kind of you to call. Do they know what's wrong? Which hospital is she at? How is she now?"

"Royal Surrey. She's in Intensive Care. But she won't be able to talk on the telephone, not yet anyway."

"Thanks…thanks for telling me. I'll get the next flight back."

So much has gone wrong in the last few days. Can it get worse?

"You've gone pale. Bad news-*huh*?"

"It was Veronica's house-help. Veronica has suffered some kind of stroke. I have to go back. She has been so kind to me. I must go and take care of her. She has no one else."

"Yes, yes, of course. But it's too bad. It seems as if you only just got here."

"Grandma, can we come?" both children say.

"Not this time, darlings. I have to go to the hospital a lot to look after my friend and you will have to go to school. I'll send you tickets during your school holidays and you can come and visit me, or come with your parents. Or I'll come back here when Veronica is better."

"When will you be back, Grandma?" Diana wants to know.

"As soon as possible. I will miss all of you. But I have to go and take care of Veronica. It won't be long."

Much as I hate the thought of being parted from my grandchildren, in some ways, I'm glad that I have to leave. A shift has occurred here in my standing with my family, a revelation that shows hairline cracks. I have decided after the incident on the beach that even if I should continue to stay on in Singapore, I would be better off in my own space, in my own home, so that I will not prove to be invasive in Peter's and Margaret's. But one had to be tactful in handling the situation. Perhaps going back to England for a time will provide a natural break, and my return can be conducted in a more orderly fashion; and if I wish to live on in Singapore indefinitely, it would not seem churlish or untoward to want my own apartment.

"I guess I'd better start packing."

Just at that moment, Peter descends the stairs. You can tell straightaway that the dark cloud that has been hovering over him for the last few days has dissipated and he is standing tall, his shoulders less rounded. Whatever demon has been strangling his psyche has released its grip on him and he looks freer, lighter. It almost seems as if the other Peter has not been.

"Look what I found," he says to me in a delighted voice as if he had not uttered those hurtful words just the day before.

Though he did not address me, it is obvious from the angle of his glance that he was talking to me. In his hands, he is holding a book fashioned from jotting paper, now yellowed, its spine an ant-crawl of staples.

"What is it?" Margaret asks.

He gives the book to me. For a second, I catch a fleeting look on Margaret's face and feel her hurt at being excluded from a private recollection. She is, after all, a woman, wanting every bit of the man she loves, even his past, his memories, his thoughts, just as she would give him the gift of her past, her memories, her thoughts.

"Do you remember it?" Peter asks.

Victor came home from work with the corners of his mouth dragged low down. When he pouted, his double-chin was accentuated.

"What's wrong?" I had asked.

"Dat bloody Chew from Finance! He really tries to score points with de boss! At our staff meeting today, he tries to say dat my production costs are way too high. Like he knows how to produce motherboards! Real *Sar Kar*! And I told him so afterwards, dat he is sucking up to an *ang mo*. And guess wat I found wen I was going out for lunch? Someone has sprayed the word '*bastard*' on the bonnet of my car. Must be Chew, but I have to prove it before I can take any action. Dat really make me frusco-*wat*!"

We sat down to dinner.

"Have you no care for my blood pressure? Dis *Itek Tim* sauce is too salty. Are you trying to kill me? And wat kind of rice do you call this? Is it rice or mocy? Pcter, cat proporly! You've got curry trailing down your arm!"

"He's still learning to eat with his fingers."

"He's my son. He's Chinese. Why don't you teach him to eat with chopsticks instead of with fork and spoon? For goodness sakes, look at you! Why don't you do someting about your hair? Looks like de bristles of a broom!"

He took another mouthful of food, then pushed away his plate angrily and scraped his chair back roughly.

"I can't eat this rubbish. A man works hard all day and come home to this kind of food! Not fit for a servant. I'm going out to eat."

He got up and went to his room to shower and change. Peter's mouth had gone wobbly and I pulled him to me, reassuring him, saying soothing words. Victor came out of our room with a fresh shirt on, freshly ironed trousers, scent heavy in the air. He was all ready to hit the cabaret, drowning his sorrow in drink, having his ego massaged by the beautiful young girls who plied their trade there. He saw me hugging Peter, soothing him.

"Do you have to *manja* him all de time? You treat him like a girl!"

He tried to pull Peter out of my arms and I held my son back and for a few minutes, Peter became the rope in a tug of war and started to cry.

"Look at him! Like a girl. A little bit and he cries. It's all your fault, de way you bring him up. Have it your way!" Victor said, releasing his hold.

When he left, I cleared our uneaten dinner. I have learnt that it was therapeutic to do things slowly and deliberately to calm yourself down. Let the frizzling energy settle. But there was Peter to calm too, so I jabbered on, with words and sounds that will reestablish his equilibrium.

"There is a funfair at Geylang. Shall we go? Would you like to ride on a round-a-bout? I shall treat you to satay and then a sugar floss."

Peter nodded his head enthusiastically and the tears that he did not shed slipped down his cheeks. He wiped them away with the back of his hand in a rough manner as if ashamed that he had let them loose.

"Go and choose what you want to wear and Mummy will get changed too."

Peter chose a T-shirt with a giant face of Pluto and a pair of dark blue dungarees. He also picked his favourite socks, a pair that he insisted he had wanted when we had gone shopping, a pair of white socks with frills and lace at the top. I had given in to his desire, but Victor used that incident to say that I treated our son like a girl. He could not see that the choice was not an aspersion on his gender but was a reflection of Peter's artistic temperament and that he saw something beautiful in the lace. It was Victor's interpretation which made it wrong, not the choice. We showered together and I helped him into his clothes. He was smiling again. As we were leaving, Peter ran into his room and came back with my jotter pad that I had left by his bedside. He must have always seen me with it, sketching and drawing.

"Mummy," he said, handing me the pad.

"Thank you, *sayang.* You like to see me draw, do you?"

He nodded. We took a bus to the fairground at Geylang. We sat at the satay stall, watching the satay man roasting the satay over the naked flame. Peter clapped when the satay man dabbed more oil to the sticks of satay making the fire sizzle and whoosh upward in bright orange flames; my son the pyromaniac, fond of fires and fireworks. Sitting there on the low stools, I was suddenly reminded of Victor when he had taken me to Penang to help me look for my father. We had eaten at a similar kind of satay stall as if we were already a married couple, Victor putting sticks of satay on my plate. What a different man he was then. Or maybe he wasn't different; his grown-up self was already lurking inside him. It took success and a fear of loss of that success to unleash his true personality.

Later, I bought Peter his sugar floss and sat him down as I sketched him licking his sugar floss and underneath I wrote, "Peter and His Sugar Floss." We went on the round-a-bout; Peter chose a bright red horse. I sketched that, too, afterwards, with Peter on the horse, although I had been with him in case he fell off. So 'round the funfair we went. Each time we took a ride or played a game, I made a sketch of it and gave each item a title. Peter seemed happy, his earlier trauma forgotten. He traced his finger around the picture. When we got home, I put him to bed and told him a story until his little chest rose up and down with the rhythm of sleep. Victor was still not back, and the knowledge of where he was kept sleep from me. So I tore the pages from the pad and started to paint the pictures, giving them a bit more life with watercolour. I had wished then that I could find some watercolour that will bring the bright hues back to my life. The next day, checking that the paint had dried, I stapled the loose pages together to make it into a book for Peter. On the front cover, I pasted a photo of Peter in his frilly socks. He clapped his hands when he saw the book. He never tires of me reading the words out and he clapped his hands again and again as we remembered the evening together.

"It's a book I did for Peter years ago," I tell Margaret, wanting to include her.

Peter's gesture is a pleasing one, but it also confuses me. I'm astonished as to why Peter had chosen this moment to retrieve the book for me. Was he sorry for his harsh words on the beach? Or had he forgotten that he had even uttered them? Did Dr. Jekyll know what Mr. Hyde said and did? Or the other way 'round? Did one personality know the other?

Margaret smiles, feeling included now. She is, after all, a good woman. The title is faint now: "Peter And Mummy at the Funfair." But the homemade book is in fair condition, the corners of the pages crinkly.

"Let me look."

"I found it in a box together with my frilly socks. Dad must have rescued some stuff from Granny Mui Yoke after all—kept them for me in case she destroys everything. There's even a birthday card from you on my twelfth birthday."

"Frilly socks?" Margaret says, one eyebrow lifting.

"Yes, I had an obsession with frilly socks when I was a kid. Don't know why."

"So, are there things about my husband I should know?" she says with a twinkle in her eye. She, too, is much lighter, the stress of the last few days having disappeared from her face.

"Dat was really good of your father," I say, sending good wishes to Victor's spirit. He hadn't meant to be bad.

"It was he who told me ware you might be-*wat*. I think dat wen he tort he was going to die after he suffered dat stroke, he wanted to make amends."

"My God, isn't Harry so like his father at de same age?" Margaret exclaims.

"Let me see, let me see," Harry says, leaping forward to snatch the book from his mother. Diana is close on his heels.

"Careful! The book is nearly thirty years old!" Peter admonishes.

"You were quite an artist? Why didn't you make it a profession?"

"There are many things I wish I had done in my youth."

"Peter, your mother has to leave us soon. There was just a phone call. Veronica is in Intensive Care."

"Wat's wrong with her?"

"Some kind of stroke or something."

Okay-*lah*," he says. "Let me see if I can get a ticket for you."

He does not express regret at my imminent departure. Is his haste in getting a ticket just the way of a man, efficient, decisive, eager to cope with the practical rather than the emotional? Or is he glad that I am going?

"I'd better start packing."

"Why don't you eat first, then pack afterwards? We don't know if you can get a flight back yet."

"Yes, that sounds sensible."

"I'll help you to pack, Grandma," Diana volunteers.

Siti serves a delicious meal of *nasi lemak*, coconut rice. The hot rice is still steaming and the fragrance of the freshly squeezed coconut milk brings back a memory of Ang Huay. There will never be a fragrance like this in the air in England.

"My nasi lemak is the best in the village."

"Yes, its' true. Your mother makes the best nasi lemak," Nenek Bongkok says. "The way to a man's heart is through his stomach. Nonya, you could capture any man's heart."

Mak was so beautiful, so talented. Why didn't she remarry? Why did she choose to live in deprivation? Why did she die alone?

"Isn't it amazing how stupid one realises one is as one gets older?"

"Wow, Mum. That's really *cheam*."

"What's *cheam*, Mummy?"

"I tort I told you before. It is Teochew for *deep*. Intellectual. Profound. And don't ask what they mean. Eat your dinner first."

After Siti has served the meal and gone back to the kitchen, I say, "Margaret. I had thought if I stayed that I might occupy myself by teaching Siti some English. That is, if she wanted to learn. She has told me several times that she wished she had gone to school. But her parents were poor. Did you know that she can't even receive letters from her children because she can't read? So she has to rely on the telephone to keep in touch with them."

"Yes, dat would be a good idea. She would be able to answer de telephone properly and write down the messages. She could read recipe books. And she would be able to cope better with de children."

"Now that I'm not going to be here, can I pay for her to go to English classes? Or get her a tutor?"

"Hold on," Peter says, catching the tail end of the conversation. "Better tink about it seriously, girlie. De problem is dat once de maids can speak English, dey start to demand more pay. Den dey tink dey can be choosy and look for new employers."

"Peter is right too. It's such a problem," Margaret says wearily. "You want to help de maids progress, provide a little comfort for dem and deir families. But at de same time, you hear such bad reports. Some maids have proved to be difficult—dey stole from employers. Some maids have even accused deir employers of sexual harassment. Others have abused de children dey looked after. Dere have been reports of maids killing children, shaking babies till deir brain hemorrhaged or beating young children, throwing dem out of windows…"

"Mummy, Daddy, we like Siti. We don't want a new maid," the children echo. "Esperanza was not very good. She was always meeting her boy friends downstairs. Sometimes wen we come home from school, lunch was not ready."

"You see wat I mean? We had a Filipino maid, Esperanza. She spent half the day looking for a man. Do you know that if a maid falls pregnant whilst in Singapore, she has to be sent back to her home country straight away? And the employer will lose the bond."

"What bond?"

"We have to put up a bond wen we get a maid. It's like the government is penalising us for having an easy life. These people are not citizens and never will be. Dey are here on two-year contracts which are renewable and dey cannot marry while dey are here."

"It's tough on both sides then, the employer's and the maid's. Yes, I can see it's not a clear-cut situation. One tends to think that maids in this country are being exploited, treated like slaves."

"Some people probably do make dem work seven days a week, morning to night. Some make dem work in deir businesses, without extra pay, wash deir cars besides housework. But some of the maids exploit back. Work here for two years, meanwhile steal all de expensive things to send back to deir homes; some have sex with deir sirs so dat dey can get more money for housekeeping and be in control radder den deir Marms. Majority of dose we get here are in deir teens or early twenties, early tirties at de most. Some are very attractive."

"What's sex?" Harry asks.

"Perhaps we should change de conversation," Peter interjects. "De travel agents are all closed now. I'll see if I can find anything on the Internet or book your flight tomorrow. What would you like to do dat will make your last few days here nice? Ware would you like to go? Wat would you like to eat?"

He is all smiles and ebullient now. It is as if the other Peter has never been.

"We haven't taken your mother on board the *Stamford Raffles* yet. Shall we do dat? Or maybe we should take a trip to Malacca to eat good Peranakan food. How about going to Penang? You were born dere, weren't you?"

"Don't go to too much trouble. You've all been so kind to me. I don't mind where we go so long as it's with you. But not Penang. I have no wish to be reminded of Penang."

"It's a shame you're going back before my mother gets back from Australia."

"Yes, it's a shame. I had so wanted to meet her—and to tell her how well she has raised her daughter."

"She loves everytink about England. Dat's why she named me after de princess. It's for her dat I named de kids after de royals."

247

"She's staying with her sister in Perth and will be back next week."

"But I'll be back."

"Yippee!" The kids yell. "Grandma says she'll be back."

Later I go to my room to start folding my clothes and putting them neatly into my case. Siti volunteered to do it, but I had waved her away. She was already doing so much; the girl could do with some leisure time. When Peter had come for me, it was Veronica who had helped me pack my bags, especially because I had been drugged and weighted by Robert's accident. That day seems so far away now. I hope that Veronica will be all right. I cannot bear the thought of losing another loved one this same year. It is strange that now that I'm planning on leaving my family and Singapore, I know I really want to stay. There is a way of righting my wrongs after all. If I stayed, I would devote myself to my grandchildren, give them the love I could not have given before, love rusting within me. Perhaps my relationship with his children will make Peter less bitter towards me.

"Grandma?" Diana puts her head 'round the door.

"Yes, my angel?"

"I have a present for you, to take to England."

My granddaughter proffers her favourite fairy, Tinkerbell, the soft-clothed one that she takes to bed with her each night.

"Tinkerbell has always looked after me. I want her to look after you, Grandma. Also, if you have Tinkerbell, you won't forget me, right?"

21

For the hundredth time, I glance at the illumined clock on my bedside table. Two a.m. Time is shuffling ever too slowly. I shift to face the window. The next minute I shift back to face the wall, then onto my back as though I'm meat being barbecued. My mind leapfrogs about, unable to keep still. Images of the child Peter, the adult Peter, Ang Huay, Victor, Hugh, and Robert keep on moving past my mind-screen, sometimes their faces overlapping, leering at me like gargoyles, misshapen and ugly, frightening me. It seems as if these are all people I have wronged in some way and they are making their unhappiness apparent. They are familiar yet not familiar. And, of course, there is Mui Yoke, who never let Victor forget that he is her son and wouldn't let him be a devoted husband to me. Then there is the ghost of Emas, forever beautiful, capable Emas, her power undiminished, casting a shadow over *my* life with Robert. And my father? The father I never met. The father who didn't love me enough to come looking for me. I feel alienated from all of them. Of course, it must have something to do with my personality that caused them to reject me. It's all my fault. *Mea culpa, mea culpa.* Is there some Latin word that I can shout to the world with glee when I am forgiven these crimes?

"Oh, Kim Hiok," my mother had said with a tattered voice. *"You have something of your father in you."*

249

The remark had whipped my face in a painful lash. Now unable to sleep, my mother's words ring in my ears like recurring tinnitus, damning. But I never found out if I am like my father.

Three a.m. Still, sleep won't come. Now images of Veronica flashed through my mind's eye—Veronica painting, Veronica helping me, Veronica dying. I can't sleep. I get up to pace the floor, then climb back into bed, then get up to pace the floor again. I'm caged in my own living hell. A few weeks back when I had arrived, I was so exhausted, I just slept and slept. But now, it's as if I had spent all my sleep quota and have none left. I'm used to the bed now so I should be comfortable enough to sleep. I remembered how I had woken up that first time in this bed and searched for Robert. The knowledge that the sheets had never embraced his body nor the pillows his head had devastated me. I had felt marooned in that bed without him. Yet, could I now return to the home I had shared with him, aware now that he would never grace the doorstep any longer? How could I go through his belongings, his and Emas' belongings, with this knowledge that I had never been loved for myself? It's not Emas' fault that Robert could not let go of her. Robert had never belonged to me, I am convinced of it now. I can't lose someone I had not gained. I'll have to make decisions—about the house, about many other things. And Veronica, what will become of Veronica? What will become of *me* if Veronica goes?

Four a.m. I have family now. Loving grandchildren. Diana is an absolute delight, her inquiring mind, her *joie de vivre*. And Harry, oh, how heartbreakingly alike he is to his father at the same age. Perhaps Harry is my salvation. Loving him, being with him, is like being with my young son again in so many ways. Perhaps that will repair me—stitch close the gaping wound in my heart. I can pretend secretly that he is mine, nurture him in the way I had meant to if I had been allowed. I have lovely Margaret to thank for Harry. I couldn't wish for a better daughter-in-law, so generous that she would call me, *Mum,* an accolade my own son wouldn't. Is he always going to be angry with me? His face on the day we were walking on the beach, oh! His eyes. So accusing. They burned into my mind. Supplants the image of the baby I had pyrographed into my memory. I try to say to myself that the man on the beach was not Peter, but a mutant from somewhere else. But it was Peter, his dark side, his pain-body emerging. And he was attacking the one who had caused the pain. A new tininitus started in my ears: *"Talk to you? You're de last person on earth I will confide in. Talk to you? You're de last person on earth I will confide in. Talk to you? You're de last person on earth I will confide in."*

My body trembles. My heart drums. All these are signals from my mind that all is not well. Five a.m. and I finally slip into sleep with the heaviness of the drugged. Veronica comes to me in a candescent cocoon of white light, her grey hair frizzing from her face as though there is static all about.

Maintain your perspective! Maintain your perspective!

I wake up with a start. Is Veronica dead? Our people tend to be superstitious. If someone is ill and you dream of that person, it is usually a message from the spirit that it has left the body. My mouth is dry. *Please, let me see her alive.* She means so much to me—has been so wonderful to me. I am exhausted. I feel as if I had not slept at all. You know the kind of feeling. Sluggish, head weighing like a boulder, fragments of a bad dream still clutching but not quite clear. It requires superhuman effort for me to rise above myself and smile for the family. *I have a family,* I say to revive my flagging happiness, *I have a family.* How true it is that the pursuit of the self can mean loneliness. Family does mean adjustments and compromises, but the rewards are great. An ad from a long time ago in Singapore comes into my mind, a cosmetic advertisement for a compressed face powder. *Pat on a happy face, pat on a happy face,* the jingle went. Janus' face. Two faces, not side by side but one on top of the other. How many face masks do we wear when out in public? Hopefully, I have selected the right one as I walk into the living room.

"Grandma," Harry says, getting up from his place at the settee to run to me as though he is already missing me. He is obviously an older soul, one who understands my need. He worms his small hand into mine. "I love you."

I feel as if my heart could burst. My small Peter, the son I had abandoned, *is* in Harry. Of course I have to return to Singapore! I can relive my life, pretend the rift never took place.

"Oh, Harry!" I say, squatting beside him to bury my face in his neck. "I love you too. Ever so much. Tell me, what are you two doing?"

"Doing our Chinese homework, Grandma," Diana informs me as she bends over the coffee table.

"Let me look."

She is writing Chinese characters, each character going into one box of a page filled not with lines but with squares. It is like looking at hieroglyphics or hitties. Neither makes sense to me.

"Wow, you are so clever. It looks so difficult."

"It's only difficult if you can't see the pictures they come from."

"What do you mean?"

"In the old days, right? They draw pictures and then the pictures become Chinese characters."

"Oh, I see," I say, but I don't really.

"Look. I will show you," Diana says confidently, drawing a squiggle of three downward flowing short lines on a separate sheet of paper. "What does this look like?"

"Er...a road? Water flowing down?"

"Right! Very simple, right? At first this is a picture to show water flowing down, then it changes into a character and it becomes like this." She draws the character in its stages of transformation into a Chinese character. This word is *shui*, water. Makes sense, right?"

"Isn't that amazing, pictures becoming words. The word *shui* is in the words *feng shui*!"

"You got it, Grandma. *Feng* is wind. Water is *shui*."

"Did you know dat de English word *typhoon* actually originates from Chinese?" Margaret asks, descending the stairs. "It means *high wind*. Tai is *great* or *high,* and feng is *wind*. Of course it has been anglicized."

"No, I didn't know that. There is a logic to the language. How stupid of me not to know. It doesn't look so daunting when it has been explained. You must be proud of Diana; she's so intelligent."

"She was top in her school last year."

"Let me show you another one, Grandma," Diana volunteers. "What does this look like?"

"A woman?"

"Wow, Grandma, you learn quickly. See, then, it becomes like this. The word is *nu*. You see this sign on ladies toilet. It means *female*. And look at this, what does this look like?"

"A baby?" My head is beginning to swim from the lack of sleep and I would like to stop, but Diana is in her element, boasting a little.

"Correct! But it is a boy baby, *erzi,* son. Put the two of them together and the word becomes *hao,* good."

I am still struggling with the noise in my ears and my cotton wool head, so I didn't get it and must have looked perplexed because Margaret explains, "You know wat de Chinese is like. De male heir is important to carry on de family name and to carry out all de rituals at de parents' funeral. So it means dat de Chinese view it dat a female who is with her son is good for society. Derefor de compound created by de two characters become de word, *hao,* good."

I feel as if she has just slung a sledgehammer at me. So *hao* is a woman with her son! The two of them together is so fundamental to Chinese thought, to the good of society. What does it make me—a mother who deserts her child? What Chinese character will depict a traitor like me?

"Mum, are you all right? Come sit down, sit down. Siti, bring some ginger water!"

"I'm okay. Didn't get much sleep last night."

Exactly at that moment, Peter descends the stairs.

"You want to go out?" he asks, eyeing me so I know that he is directing the question at me. "We have to pick up your flight ticket. You can also do your last-minute shopping, buy some orchids for Veronica. Let's all go to Suntec City. Wonderful shops dere. At de basement, dere is a wonderful food court and several restaurants. We can lunch at de Indonesian restaurant. It's quite a unique one, it serves Sudanese food. Deir speciality is crispy fried fish in a Sudanese sauce. You'll enjoy it. Dere is also a Fountain of Fortune, constructed by *feng shui* experts. It's good luck to touch de water. Let's go touch it. Maybe we'll win TOTO. Dere is even a tourist booth dat sells bottles of de water. Dat will double our chances!"

He has reverted to being the Peter I love; the other dark self has vanished or perhaps is in slumber.

"Mum is not feeling so good. Maybe she shouldn't go out."

"No, no. The fresh air will be good for me. *Hao,*" I say to show I've learnt a bit of Chinese though I don't feel in the least lighthearted. "I will be *hao.*

Now I can even write the word, *shui*. Your clever daughter has been teaching me Chinese."

Diana giggles and Harry claps his hands.

Margaret smiles. She is also back to being the Margaret I know. There is a smell of accomplished sex between her and Peter, a web of intimacy still lingering between them, a looseness of limbs. So that is what the two of them were doing upstairs in mid-morning on a Sunday.

"Where is Suntec City?"

"It's ware de sea used to be, near Queen Elizabeth Walk, de old esplanade."

"The sea is gone?"

"It's been pushed out further."

Has he a gift of prescience, here to rescue me from the despair that threatens to engulf me? His aura has changed, all about his head is a warm, sunny glow. His face, too, is glowing and is wreathed in smiles. A mother's heart can ache from such a smile, especially when given so heartily. Yet, I cannot help but wonder if he does censure me behind closed doors. Foolish woman! Why can't I just revel in the here and now? Why must I torture myself so?

Suntec City is a city of shops. A maze of passageways connect you to the luxurious mall above ground and another maze leads to the underground shopping mall between Suntec City and Raffles City. But I am not deceived. It's a place for rats. It is a fluorescent bright burrow that lures people into the disguised dank earth with its foul air to persuade them to dispense with their hard-earned money. Consumerism is intelligent propaganda—you whet people's appetite and desire for material things, then you supply the goods to make them feel fulfilled. It's a much more achievable goal than trying to wrest with abstract ideas and values.

It is Sunday, the place jammed packed with people who are not working, people out with their families for a bit of togetherness, shopping, looking not into each other's eyes but into the windows of shops. It is the same kind of togetherness that you get watching television with each other, minds distant form each other though the bodies are close. As though people have rushed indoors to get relief from the inclement weather outside, in this case the scorching midday sun, there is a multitude of bodies pushing pass each other, into each other. It is far too noisy and far too bright. Not natural, healing sunlight but artificial strobes of fluorescent lights which blinds and de-energises. It is all too much for me, especially after a sleepless night, but Peter's intention had been good and I do not want to voice any dissent. But I feel a migraine coming on. I feel crushed by the crowd as if a million people, couples, families with children, teenage schoolchildren in uniforms, youngsters in trendy gear, tourists, are all out and about.

Hao. Good. Mother and son together. Is *not hao* a mother and son apart? The thought pounds at my mind like a pneumatic drill. I am definitely having a migraine.

Every now and again, amongst the throng of Asians, a Caucasian man catches my eye. There is one whose hair is graying at the temples, his jaw so like Robert's. The sight fills me with a yearning. But it is not Robert—it never can be now. The finality of that knowledge is not easy to bear. Besides, he was never mine. He never really loved me. I don't know which thought is more painful. I have to try not to think, especially when my thoughts are so muddled. Some people are walking fast to their destinations but the majority are strolling leisurely, sauntering, as if this was a country park and the shops are offering scenic views and priceless treasures. I would like to see a lake with swans preening themselves, ducks taking off, or, perhaps, several acres of field with bright yellow rape or blue flax rolling in like waves, a bluebell wood with bluebells nodding and waving in the wind. That is what I would like to see right now, not this mess of humanity and parade of shops selling things I don't need. But no one else seems perturbed by the noise, the crowd and the bright lights. There is a germ of panic sprouting in my belly. An image of scuttling rats sweeps past my inner eye. Rats with their bristly bodies and beady eyes. I still have a strong aversion to rats. I've not outgrown them. They unsettle me, remind me too much of my youth, of my mistakes. Squeak, squeak, squeak.

"This place is unbelievable, all these shops! Do you know that in the colonial days, High Street is the main shopping prescient? We had only one major department store there. Metro, I think." I have to say something which sounds like praise because it is what Peter and Margaret would expect, what

Singaporeans expect. I speak with the rapid shots of one who is nervous, uncertain, my breath shallow.

"Yes, dose were de days wen policemen wore shorts," Peter says, using his favourite expression. "Den Orchard Road became the in-place to shop, and now all dese kinds of malls."

"Wasn't Robinsons located in Raffles Square den? It burned down, didn't it?"

"That's right," I answer Margaret's query, and we make polite conversation, but all the time my heart is fluttering from unease. I really hate this crowd, this noise.

"I want to hold Grandma's hand!" Harry argues with Diana for the privilege.

"We can both take one hand."

"No," Margaret says firmly. "It's too crowded to walk that way. You'll bump into people. Diana, let Harry hold Grandma's hand and you walk by my side."

For once, I would be glad to be without either of the children hanging on to me. I don't feel capable of hanging on to myself. Panic is in every cell of my body. I don't know what it is, whether it's because I've not slept well or because I've been worrying about Veronica or because I was thinking of Robert or because a simple Chinese word had disarmed me. But I'm not my usual self, though I'm trying not to let it show. This is my last day with my family and I want to show the best of me. But it's certainly a struggle. Sometimes I feel like I'm floating, my feet not on the ground. The noise and my thoughts create a cacophony in my head. Vaguely, I feel Harry pulling at my hand, proud that he has being given the privilege.

"It's so unfair!" Diana complains.

"You can take turns," Peter says amiably.

"Where is this fountain you were talking about?" I ask, thinking that it would be cooler there for despite the indoor air conditioning, I'm feeling warm, the heat rising from my belly. It would probably be quieter there, too.

"I want to see the fountain! I want to see the fountain!" Diana hops about, her mood a chameleon.

"Okay, okay! No need to act like *monyet kena sambal belachan*," Peter admonishes.

"How did you remember that?" I ask astonished.

Peter looks nonplused at first, unaware of the idiom he had just uttered. Of course, I myself must have been the trigger since I said it to him so many times in our years together. Perhaps I'm putting too much on a single expression. After all, it's quite a common one used in the Malay and Peranakan community. Margaret's mother might have used it. Then a corner of his mouth lifts as he remembers and he says, "Isn't amazing? You don't even know wat is lying waiting inside your own mind. It's as if all we have learnt and remembered is stored dere, seeds dat wait for de right climate to sprout and blossom."

"Why, Peter, what a lovely metaphor. I didn't know you have such a way with words."

He grins. An easiness he had never displayed in all this time with me is now expressed in that expression. It is when Harry grins that he looks most like his father. In that grin, Peter has become mine once more, my own little boy that I thought I had lost. Of course, the boy is not lost; he is there inside Peter, waiting for the right door to open. For a few seconds, the two of us are locked in a cameo of intimacy as if after long last the emotional synapse between us has been bridged. But what are the seeds that are lying in wait in my own mind, waiting for the right climate for them to sprout?

"Daddy, what is *monyet kena sambal belachan*?"

"You know wat *sambal belachan* is, right?"

"It's that fresh chilli pound with *belachan*, shrimp paste, right?"

"Well, you know dat de chillies used are usually chilli padi, de really hot ones. In de old days, wen children use bad words, deir mothers *sumbat*, dat is, stuff deir mouths, with *sambal belachan* so dey will never say bad words again. So imagine a monkey getting de *sambal* in its mouth. It would be leaping and hopping from de heat. So wen you are hopping and jumping, you are like dat *monyet*."

"You know, boy, since your mother has come home, you are using more Peranakan words."

"Oh, am I?"

"Daddy, why don't you say, *th-e, th-at, th-ey, th-eir?*" Harry asks, spittle escaping from his mouth.

"Daddy, did Grandma ever have to *sumbat* your mouth with *sambal belachan*?"

"Don't ask silly questions. Here we are, see, de Fountain of Fortune."

We have walked away from the main thoroughfare of the shopping mall and so the noise has lessened. I am relieved. My stomach settles itself. There are smart restaurants arranged around the arena that surround the fountain. The spewing fountain sits under an atrium of glass skylight which brings in natural light. In the cool of the air conditioning and the refreshing spray of water, the sun is kinder and more welcoming, unlike the aggression it displays outdoors. A wooden platform circles the fountain so that people can walk around it, a moving ring of people seeking solace, hope and riches. The movement reminds me of the much larger moving ring of people out on Salisbury Plain, pilgrims walking slowly around the stones. Once I had driven to the rise of the hill opposite, parked in a lay-by to view Stonehenge from a distance. I saw the age-old ring of stones and the slow circling of people, and imagined that they were on some kind of quest, some old ritual. It is the same here, the same intensity of feeling, the same gnawing hunger for some manna. People are walking in orderly fashion around the fountain to put their hands out to touch the lucky water. They are not here to toss a coin in like at the Trevi Fountain to ask to return to Rome, but to ask for more important things like to cure a sickly relative, to get a good job, a condominium, a Mercedes or, win the lottery or TOTO.

I follow as my family walk carefully 'round the fountain. There is splashed water on the platform, making the wood floor slightly slippery. I petition mentally for true unity with my family and forgiveness from my son. Diana and Harry splash water about to the disapproval of other more serious pilgrims so Margaret ticks them off. In pursuit of new activities, the children run off the platform and Margaret follows suit. A caring, protective mother. No matter how ugly a woman is, how stupid, however shrewish she is to her husband or other people, if she displays this selfless attitude toward her children without thinking of gain to herself, she is, indeed, a very special person. Their abrupt departure arrests my walk and I stop short and Peter, inattentive and caught by this sudden halting, bumps into me. I stumble with an exclamation and could have fallen off the platform if Peter had not caught me to stop the collision from causing damage. It's only a brief moment, almost over as soon as it happened, but for me, it lasts a lifetime, the feel of my body as it is held up by his arms, as if I am the child and he, the parent, in a kind of reversed *Pieta*, he, the noble embodiment of Mary holding on to the broken body and spirit of, not a son, but a mother. In that instance, a ray of sunshine from the skylight above shines down on us. I imagine it like in a Holy picture, the kind that Christians carry around, two figures encapsulated in Light. Peace makes his face serene. He sets me upright, then as if he is suddenly conscious of what he has done walks away quickly. But I am still glowing from that short encounter and do not feel rejected. Perhaps my earlier discomfiture and panic were all for nothing. There is nothing wrong. Everything is okay. My confidence in my son and his family has returned. Yes, they do want me. We resume our walk 'round the fountain. After we've navigated 'round the whole circle, he goes to the kiosk selling the bottled water of the Fountain and buys one, giving it to me.

"Take dis for Veronica. It might help."

"That's so thoughtful. Thanks." I'm touched. "I'll come back."

"Of course. I expect dat."

"Daddy, Daddy, come on, we're hungry!" The children yell.

We go to the promised Indonesian restaurant serving cuisine from Sudan, a region of Indonesia. Once again, Margaret is in charge, ordering the fresh lime juice in a jug and the various dishes, the special crispy fish, *rendang, sambal olek, pegedil, assam prawn, chilli and onion omellette, kangkong in sambal belachan, squids in soya sauce.*

"Wow, this is a feast."

"Ya, your goodbye lunch."

"It's only farewell, not goodbye. I will be back."

"*It's only farewell, not goodbye,*" Diana imitates, enunciating with her rounded mouth that make us adults smile.

"Hurray!" Harry claps his hands as if he has not heard it before. He even has his father's mannerism when he does that. "Grandma will be back. Grandma will be back!"

"You all right?" Margaret asks Peter. "You look spaced out."

"Dreaming again. Dat's all."

"Daddy, can I buy the *Harry Potter* mirror? So when Grandma is in England, I can talk to the mirror and see Grandma in it."

"Dere's no such ting-*lah*. It's only fiction."

"Let him believe in magic, boy."

"Is it all right if I buy it for him?" I ask Margaret, who nods with approval. "When we finish lunch, we can go and look for it. Where can we find it?"

"I'm sure one of de shops here will sell it."

"I wanted to get a farewell present for each of you, anyway. Diana, what would you like? What about you, Margaret? And Peter?"

"You don't have to get us anything. Anyway, you'll be back soon, right?"

"I would like *Artemis Fowl*…"

"Please…"

"Please…" Diana complies.

The reintroduction to the surging waves of people, noise and bright light seems a travesty after the lull of peace I had enjoyed. The threat they inflict on me is like that of a pack of unruly rats. Squeaking, squeaking. Lips draw back, exposing teeth—sharp teeth. Rats masked as people? Or people masquerading as rats? Wasn't it Chuang Sze who said, *"Am I a butterfly dreaming that I am a man or am I a man dreaming that I am a butterfly?"*

There's a great deal of posturing in the way people swagger, in the way mobile phones hang round necks like oversized necklaces, hands-free sets stuck into ears with microphones of all types protruding from 'round the ears or head, as though they are working at a switchboard. Every now and again, one can see an individual gesturing and talking loudly as if to the air, someone who would have been termed a lunatic in the old days but is now a modern, technologically advanced person. The days of the simple T-shirt and jeans are gone; it's all designer wear now and I wonder how many of these people who pay exorbitant sums of money for designer jeans realise that jeans made out of durable, lasting material to withstand the harshness of outdoor weather and labour abuse were once the work clothes for Canadian and American lumberjacks? Loud music blares from not only the PA system but also from individual shops so that the resulting mix is a cacophony of strident sounds. The bubble of panic that had rose earlier and then settled rises again in me once more. I'm truly a country girl now, not a city slicker. More images of rats run through my mind screen, their squeaking filling my ears.

As though something has been renewed between them, Margaret and Peter walk together with arms linked, Margaret obviously forgetting her earlier admonishment for the children to stay close to her and not walk holding hands. I try to maintain my distance from them so that I do not intrude on their revived amour. I pretend to look into windows and keep half an eye on the children who are skipping along ahead, sometimes pressing their noses into glass walls and pointing out things with glee, chattering to each other. I could not match their pace. Then a wall of teenagers come toward us, gesturing, talking in slang in broad *Singlish*. They move as one huge body, uncaring of the people around them. As they move toward us, the sea of people before them part, scattering families. When they pass, Margaret scans her family rapidly.

"Diana, ware is Harry?" Not managing to locate him, her voice rises several decibels. "Ware is he? My God, ware is he?"

"He was here a moment ago. He said he was going to Toys 'R' Us to get the *Harry Potter* mirror…" Diana says.

"Why didn't you stay with him? Is dere a Toys 'R' Us here?"

"I don't tink so. He might mean dat store on de 2nd floor."

"He could be anyware." Margaret voice comes out in a cry.

"Diana, you stay with Mummy. Girlie, you look on dis floor. I'll run up to de next. Call me on de handphone wen you find him. I'll do de same. Udderwise, we'll meet back at de Information counter in twenty minutes."

"He can't be far, Margaret. I'm sure he'll be all right. Why don't you look down this row of shops and I'll look in the opposite direction?" I offer, my voice not betraying the panic I feel. I want to help in locating my grandson, but I'm not confident to go into the lair of rats alone, all those big rats, brown rats, black rats, with their bristly bodies and beady eyes, teeth as sharp as razors, squeaking, squeaking, squeaking. My brow is already slick with sweat, my armpits damp. The thumping begins in the region of my chest. The thought that he may be kidnapped or injured makes me ill.

"Thank you, Mum. Come on, Diana, don't you move from my side!"

The fear for Harry's safety is so potent that it pulls back another memory from long ago. Let him be all right. Let it just be a simple case of an excited child looking for his toy. People in front of me are moving too rapidly, their movements becoming a haze. In my haste, I push into people and hear their curses. But I don't care. I need to keep my wits about me, keep my consciousness intact. But the bright lights, loud music and loud voices are magnified in my head. I'm getting muddled, fast losing control. My sight begins to blur.

How can it have happened? One minute he is by my side and the next he is gone. It is not easy to see a five-year-old child amongst the trees of adult legs. Young mothers everywhere: you must know what it is like to discover that your small child has strayed from your side. You must understand my anguish.

"Peter!" I cry out. "Peter! Where are you? Please don't play hide-and-seek here. Come out. Please!"

I run around like a crazed woman in the crowded department store, weaving amongst shoppers, pushing people aside. I don't care if people are angry with me, scolding, staring. I want my baby. How could I have not noticed that his hand had slipped from me? What a careless, careless mother I am. Please, please, let him be all right.

The toy department. He must have gone to the toy department. We were there only a few minutes ago and he wanted to look at the fire engine. I said we will look at it later after we have bought his Chinese New Year clothes. Did his hand slipped from me or did I let him go when I was taking my wallet out from my handbag to pay for the clothes? What does it matter; I have lost him however it happened.

"Peter! Peter!"

I hope he has not gone out of the store. There is traffic outside on the High Street. My breath comes out in spurts, my chest hurts from the constriction. If only Victor was here, he could have helped search for my baby. I shouldn't have come here today. Everyone is shopping for Chinese New Year. There are too many people, too much noise, he can't hear me. Oh, God! Oh, God! Kwan Yin, Mother of Mercy, help me. Where is Victor when I need him?

"Peter! Peter!"

"Oi! Look ware you're going!"

"Siau char bor! Crazy woman!"

"Eh! Gila-kah? Mad or wat?"

The jubilant cries of children greet me as I rush into the toy department. A man dressed as a jolly clown is blowing up long balloons and twisting them into shapes. The moment he finishes one, he tosses it into the circle of children standing around him. As one animal-shaped balloon floats into the air, the children cry out and several arms shoot out to try and catch it creating a milieu like net-ball players on a field going for a ball.

"Peter!" I call, trying to sift him from the others. "Peter!"

When you know your child so well, all it takes is the shape of his head, his height, the sound of his cough, his cry or his gurgle of laughter for you to identify him. And there he is, my son, thumb in his mouth, eyes round, all agog at the animals that are birthing before his very eyes. Relief makes me want to sink into the ground. I kneel down beside him.

"Sayang," I say softly to him, though my heart is still thudding, so as not to alarm him. "You shouldn't run away from Mummy."

He turns to look at me and he takes his thumb out of his mouth and grins—a delightful grin that makes me melt, makes me forgive him his misdemeanor.

*   *   *

Peter is frantic with worry. He uses his bulk to push against the crowd at the toy department. His height is in some ways a hindrance when it comes to looking for a small boy less than a metre tall. He had to bend and look around the thicket of legs to find his son. A clown in a bright yellow suit with a giant smile painted across a powder white face is entertaining the children, blowing up balloons and twisting them into shapes. When he finished one, he tosses the balloon into the air into the circle of children around him. The older children screech with joy and leap about trying to catch the balloon. And then he sees them—Harry first, standing there enthralled, and then his mother squatting beside Harry.

"Have you found him?" Margaret asks, her voice in shreds. She has Diana in tow and has turned up suddenly by his side as if she was a heat-seeking missile guided towards her son. This is a miracle of motherhood, directed by maternal instinct for the safety of her young.

"It's okay, girlie. Look!"

But Margaret is not calm. Cannot be calmed. She had been worried out of her mind, had searched high and low for her son, thinking the worse and expecting the worse, crying inside as she played out the drama of his injury and death. All mothers know this gamut of emotions that passed through one in moments of panic for a beloved child. She had told him a million times not to run away from her and here he is nonchalantly watching a clown blowing up balloons and twisting them into shapes. Relief shoots through her at the sight of him, but the moment she knows he is safe, something else replaces it. She is furious with him for making her worry so. She advances toward him, wanting him in her arms, but also ready to berate him. Peter reads her mood promptly, suspects her overwrought anxiety and puts out a hand to stop her, but she rushes forward, ignoring Kim Hiok, and pulls her son roughly to her in a mixture of joy and anger. Unprepared for this brusque action, Harry screams.

Just as I am about to fold Peter into my arm, she turns up. Mui Yoke. Victor's mother. Peter's grandmother. That woman has never wanted me to marry her son and now she won't even let me have mine. She yanks Peter from me, and my son screams in fright. I won't let her separate my son from me. I won't! So I fight her for Peter, there in the crowded store, two women pulling at one small child. I think the shock of my retaliation surprised her, for Mui Yoke lets go. Then I saw him, Victor, rushing toward us to help his mother to snatch Peter from me. Before he could reach me and before she could muster her strength, I sweep Peter up in my arms and make for the doorway.

"Mummy! Mummy!" Peter cries.

"It's all right, sayang. I've got you now. I'm not going to let them take you away from me. I'm never ever going to let you go."

My heart is pumping with vigour, the blood pounding in my ears. I did not realise I'm so unfit. But still I run; as fast as I can, with my son in my arms, his arms flailing, away from Victor and his mother, along the crowded passageway, pushing people aside, out onto High Street.

I will hail a taxi, take us to safety, find a hotel for the night then move out of the country where they will never find us. I will build a life for us, just my son and myself. It is all I really want. But Mui Yoke must have jump-started to action for I can see her coming out of the building, Victor with her, both of them making their way toward me, full of threat.

"Come back!" Victor shouts.

No, this time I must make sure that he does not force me home. I am never going to return to him. I am never going to allow him and his mother to take my son away from me. I shall not let them deprive me of my son's childhood and upbringing. The cars are racing along High Street. If I can find a gap, I can run across the road and lose Victor and his mother. Finally, a gap appears, the Mercedes in front speeding, the lorry behind, with its full load of home furniture slowing down. I shift Peter to the front of my body, put his legs around my waist, his arms around my neck; this way he is secure and I can hold him whilst protecting him. I pause only for a moment, seeing that Victor and his mother are about to act, to wrest my child from me. Then I dash out onto the road and run in between the two vehicles.

When Margaret pulls Harry to him and he starts to scream, Peter sees a change come over his mother. Her eyes are filled with horror. It appears that she is thinking that Margaret is about to harm him. Kim Hiok snatches Harry back from Margaret, lifts him, and runs out of the department store even before Peter can reach their sides. Margaret, in her surprise, had simply let go.

"My God, wat's happening? Why is your mother behaving like dis? Why is she taking my son away from me?"

"Something's wrong. Very wrong."

Peter is already out of the store and Margaret recovers from her stupor and dashes out too. Diana, not understanding it all runs after them, shouting, "Mummy! Daddy! Wait for me!"

The three of them are running hard, offending people by taking no heed of them; Peter is ahead, Margaret huffing and puffing to keep up. Because he is tall, Peter can see over the heads of others so he can see his mother scurrying along, Harry in her arms. She looks frenzied, searching for a way out. With all the network of passageways splitting to a multitude of shops in the two different towers in the massive building, he has to make sure that he doesn't lose sight of them. It is quite obvious that she is following the glare of natural sunlight coming in through the glass doors so that she can get outside. What is his mother thinking? It is impossible to know, but all he wants is to catch up with them before they come to any harm.

He is there at the doorway when he sees her standing poised by the curbside, right by Nichol Highway with its nonstop flow of traffic coming across the bridge over Kallang River. He stops abruptly, suddenly aware that she is running away from him, from Margaret. But why? He does not know—*cannot* know. All he knows is that if he continues to give chase, it will prompt her to dash across the busy highway with Harry in her arms. Still standing there watching her, unsure of the best action to take, Margaret appears by his side.

"My God, wat is she doing? Peter, stop her!"

"Mummy! Mummy!" Harry shouts when he sees his mother.

Margaret leaps forward but Peter pulls her back.

"No don't," he says with urgency.

"Wat are you doing? Let me go!"

Margaret shakes herself free and leaps forward. Kim Hiok must have heard Margaret's voice; she looks 'round swiftly and Peter knows that she has seen them. She hesitates only for a few seconds. Then, with Harry still in her arms, she dashes across the road between the Mecerdes that had just passed and the lorry with its load of home furniture. The lorry driver doesn't have time to slow down. As if Kim Hiok anticipates the collision, she turns her shoulder 'round so that her back can take the impact, protecting the child in her arms. Margaret comes to an abrupt stop and screams. The wheels of the lorry screeches in the driver's attempt to brake but he is unsuccessful and the lorry hits the woman head on and she tumbles and falls. The child is flung out of her arms and fortunately he lands where the Mercedes had been. The left front wheel of the lorry goes over the woman and her bulk halts the motion of the vehicle. His load of home-furniture, poorly rigged, shift and fall. As items of furniture rain from the lorry to land on the tarmac; all the other traffic on the road is brought to a standstill. It is probably fortuitous that this has happened to halt the traffic which might have run into Harry. The smell of burning rubber is strong in the heat.

Both Margaret and Peter rush out onto the road, automatically going to their son first. Harry is sobbing as Peter sweeps him up, examining him. Harry is sobbing with fright and there is a swelling on his forehead. His arms and knees are grazed, but nothing seems broken. Margaret reaches his side and he hands their son to her. Tears streaming down her face, Margaret smothers him with kisses as she clings to her son, checking his fingers and his toes, his limbs, every single part of him.

"Oh, Harry, my darling, my darling!"

Then Peter turns his attention to his mother, lying prone in an awkward angle, pinned under the wheel of the lorry, her face turned on one side. The twenty-something lorry driver in his singlet and shorts, is kneeling by her side calling out respectfully in Cantonese, "*Ah Poh! Ah Poh!* Grandmother! Grandmother!"

"Back up, you idiot! Back up your lorry off her body!"

The young man hastily went back into the cab of his lorry. Peter gives him the signal and the lorry driver roll the wheel off and in the process the bone of her arm cracks.

There is just a soft groan from Kim Hiok.

"You bloody nincompoop!"

"Sorry, sir, sorry, sir," the driver says when he got out of his vehicle. "But it's not my fault, sir, it's not my fault! She just ran out from the pavement. I didn't even see her until I hit her."

"Get out of the way. You should have been more alert. Let me attend to her," Peter says to the man, also in Cantonese, the language of his own grandmother. "She's my mother."

"Aiiyah!! " The man gesticulates in despair. "So bad-lah!!"

Peter kneels beside his mother. Someone is already on the mobile phone calling for the Emergency services. Peter notices that blood is seeping from under her head. Her eyes are closed. He reaches out to touch her shoulder.

"Peter…" she says in a fractured and diminished voice, eyes struggling to open. "Peter."

"I'm here," he says to her in English.

"Peter…Is he all right? Is my son all right?"

Peter hesitates only a fraction of a second as if it suddenly dawned on him what the debacle has been about. So she had thought that Harry was him. If she was stealing him away, it could only be that she thought he was Victor. That was why she reacted so violently when Margaret tried to pull Harry away from her. But why now? What had caused her mind to unhinge in that moment? Peter has to summon his voice to respond to his mother.

"Yes…yes, he's all right. He's safe now. We'll take care of him until you are well. He'll be with you soon. Are you in much pain?"

There is a short silence before she speaks again.

"Tell him…tell him I love him," she says, and stops as she spits blood. He takes out his handkerchief and wipes her mouth. Her words are slow and low so he puts his ear closer to her so that he can hear her clearly. "Tell him I never meant to leave him. Tell him I never stop loving him."

"I know. I will tell him."

Around them the crowd is gathering.

"Can help or not?"

"Shall we carry her off the road?"

"No, we better leave her where she is. Her back might be fractured. To move her would be dangerous."

Peter wishes the crowd would go away so that he can be alone with Kim Hiok. People are offering advice, making small talk around them. Peter can hear the sirens of the ambulance and police car, their sounds louder as they approach the location of the accident. He is aware that Margaret has walked up behind him. He hears her gulp in shock, then resting her hand on the back of his neck, can hear Harry's muffled sobs.

"Grandma!" Diana screams as she finally catches up with all of them.

"Take her away. Take them away," Peter says to Margaret. "I'll go in the ambulance and call you from the hospital."

"No! No! I want to be with Grandma! Grandma, wake up. Wake up, Grandma!"

Holding Harry with one arm, with the other, Margaret drags her screaming daughter away from the scene. An onlooker, a middle-aged woman, comes forward to help her and they reenter the building.

"The ambulance is coming, the ambulance is coming," the driver announces.

Peter hears that dreaded gurgle in his mother's throat and the bubble comes up and more blood spews. He wipes the blood off. Unwise as it may be, he has the insane longing to cradle her head in his lap and he tries to shift her shoulder so that he can put her head onto his lap. His shifting of her body roused her and her eyelids flutter open, and, for a while, Peter is looking directly into her eyes and she is returning his gaze, but is she seeing him?

"At last, Papa, you've come for me," she says.

Her eyelids flutter again, this time weaker.

"Mum," Peter says suddenly, vehement so that she does not slip into unconsciousness. "It's me, Peter. Your son. I'm here. I'll take care of you, Mum."

"What sweet, sweet words. Everythings's going to be all right now."

Then she smiles.

Printed in the United Kingdom
by Lightning Source UK Ltd.
105290UKS00001B/1-54